Katsura ▮▮▮▮▮▮▮▮▮▮▮▮▮▮▮▮▮ egained his balance ar ▮▮▮▮▮▮▮▮▮▮▮▮ him sent a fiery red be ▮▮▮▮▮▮▮▮▮▮▮ and fusing it in midfli ▮▮▮▮▮▮▮▮▮ down the canyon, qu ▮▮▮▮▮▮▮ from one location to another. In the silence, disturbed only by his own ragged breathing, the alien had an almost ghostlike quality. It moved toward him.

He could see he wasn't going to make it. The oxygen tanks were still too far away and the insect would reach them before he could.

It was all clear now. The alien traveled into the past, then came forward. It had to reappear in places it had already been, the space components of its own world line. Apparently the alien had visited the field near Katsura's life-support bubble often, and so could find many spots which would serve as end points for its transits. But it had never been near the location of the life-support bubble itself. That meant it could not maneuver well there; the insect was forced to stand close, in a little circle around the bubble. To avoid the laser cannon. There it would be vulnerable.

Katsura had never been as tired in his life before.

GUNS OF DARKNESS

Look for all these Tor books created by J. E. Pournelle

THERE WILL BE WAR
MEN AT WAR
BLOOD AND IRON
DAY OF THE TYRANT
WARRIOR!
GUNS OF DARKNESS

CREATED BY
J.E. POURNELLE

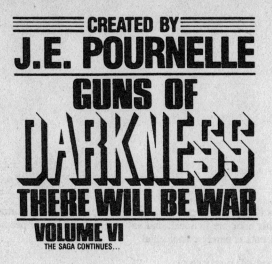

GUNS OF
DARKNESS
THERE WILL BE WAR

VOLUME VI
THE SAGA CONTINUES...

John F. Carr, Associate Editor

TOR

A TOM DOHERTY ASSOCIATES BOOK

GUNS OF DARKNESS

Copyright © 1987 by J. E. Pournelle

All rights reserved, including the right to reproduce this book or portions thereof in any form.

First printing: June 1987

A TOR Book

Published by Tom Doherty Associates, Inc.
49 West 24 Street
New York, N.Y. 10010

Cover art by Colin Hay

ISBN: 0-812-54961-9
CAN. ED.: 0-812-54962-7

Printed in the United States of America

0 9 8 7 6 5 4 3 2 1

Dedication

For Aleta, a faithful Shadow
who has helped keep the dream alive.

ACKNOWLEDGMENTS

The editors gratefully acknowledge that research for nonfiction essays in this book, including "Surprise" by Stefan T. Possony, Francis X. Kane, and Jerry Pournelle, was supported in part by grants from the Vaughn Foundation. Responsibility for opinions expressed in this work remains solely with the authors.

CONTENTS

INTRODUCTION:
THE FOG OF WAR
Jerry Pournelle

> To be a successful soldier you must know history. What you
> must know is how man reacts. Weapons change but man who uses
> them changes not at all. To win battles you do not beat weapons—
> you beat the soul of the enemy man.
>
> —George S. Patton

There are periodic attempts to change war from art to
science. It never works. Probably the most disastrous attempt
was by former Secretary of Defense Robert S. MacNamara,
who brought in civilian whiz kids to structure the U.S. Strategic Offensive Forces and try to run the war in Vietnam, but
he was only one of many to make that mistake.

Many study war, but few learn it without experience. Some
don't even learn from that.

There are "principles of war," but these correspond more
to a list of holds in wrestling, or a checklist of things to be
ignored at peril, than to any "scientific" basis for conducting
military strategy. The principles are worth study, but no
amount of studying them will make you a competent military
commander.

The truth is that war is a contest of wills.

It is also a struggle for information. Throughout history the
"fog of war" has descended over the battlefield. Sometimes
this is a literal fog that obscures events; more often, it exists
in the minds of the commanders, who never know precisely
what is happening, and must guard against both real and
imagined dangers. As many battles have been lost to uncertainty
and ignorance as to anything else.

All of which suggests something: uncertainty generally
favors the defender. That is, the defender seeks to keep what
he has; he has won if *nothing* happens. The attacker has many

advantages, but has the disadvantage that he must get something he hasn't got.

He has to *do* something; which means in effect that he has to *decide* to do it. He won't decide to do it unless he thinks he can accomplish his goals; which means that if he doesn't know enough to figure out what will happen if he attacks, he probably won't do it, meaning that the defense has won.

Unfortunately, in the historic contest between the United States and the USSR, we are the defenders, but they have the information advantage. We know very little about what's going on in the Soviet Union. Even the names of the members of the Defense Council, the highest military authority in the USSR, are state secrets. So are the names of the families of the Soviet ruling class. So are most facts that any Western citizen (or KGB agent) can get about Western governments by buying a newspaper or a government publication.

This means that the United States cannot, *must* not, neglect its capabilities for finding information about the Soviet Union. In particular, we must quickly expand our ability to use the space environment: to put up and if need be defend, first, observation satellites, then armed components of the Strategic Defense Initiative.

We must learn more about the Soviet Union. It's not really possible to keep them from learning more about us.

There is a light at the end of this particular tunnel. In the modern world, military power grows from high technology in general and computer technology in particular. Small computers are not only useful, they are becoming vital.

Small computers increase the flow of information. You cannot introduce computers to a nation and keep that nation's citizens in ignorance. ''You shall know the truth, and the truth shall set you free.'' Computers make possible the spread of information without much chance for the government to suppress it.

Arthur Koestler said that the necessary and sufficient condition to bring down the Soviet system of government would be the free exchange of information *within* the Soviet Union.

The computer revolution is bringing that about. If the Soviets try to stifle the computer revolution within their borders, they will also greatly cut back their military power.

It's quite a dilemma for them.

EDITOR'S INTRODUCTION TO:

IDEOLOGICAL DEFEAT
by Christopher Anvil

The fog of war—or more generally the uncertainties of power struggles—can take on many aspects. Sometimes one seeks deliberately to spread confusion, not only among one's enemies but among one's own citizens. The Soviet KGB has a vast effort devoted to "disinformation": planting false stories in the hopes that legitimate Western publications will believe and republish them.

One of the most effective weapons in modern conflict is ideology. The United States doesn't use it much. Until recently we didn't have to.

Elites seek to consolidate power. In the West, until recently at least, the tendency has been restrained simply because political power in the United States hasn't been all that decisive. Through most of our history a citizen could live a normal, productive, and happy life without thinking much about government. It wasn't that getting political power wasn't worth doing, but that it wasn't the only route for advancement, and usually wasn't even the best one.

Lately there have been disturbing tendencies in the opposite direction, as politics intrudes on every aspect of life. We thought to use government to make the nation more perfect, and we didn't worry much about it, because, after all, we control the government, don't we?

It shouldn't be much surprise to discover that we don't, not really, and moreover that those who are in political control continue to change the rules. It is already almost impossible to defeat an incumbent city councilman, state legislator, or even congressman; and every year brings more and more laws designed to make it even harder to turn out this power elite.

Our problems are as nothing compared with what the Soviet citizen endures.

In the USSR there is *no* route to power or security except

through government. Trotsky said, "Where the state is the only employer, opposition means starvation," and he said no more than simple truth. The Soviet Union is not merely *governed* by a power elite of party officials, the entire country is *owned* by them.

The Communist Party isn't the real government of the Soviet Union, though. Within the party is a much smaller group known as the *nomenklatura*, which is literally a list of people who can expect to be promoted, who protect each other, and who can generally never be demoted. The actual membership of the *nomenklatura* is a state secret; its very existence was hidden for many years, and one can still read books on Soviet government without seeing the term. No matter. The *nomenklatura* is very real, and its members, some 1 percent of the population, own the nation in fee simple.

The prerogatives of this group are enormous. It's not just money. They don't stand in long lines to buy potatoes. They don't carry string bags wherever they go in hopes of finding a shop with something worth buying. Their food is delivered by an organization known as "the distribution," and they shop in special stores whose existence is seldom openly acknowledged.

The prerogatives of the *nomenklatura* are no secret to the Soviet masses. Nevertheless, they put up with a system that gives them very little, not even hope. Why? Because of an ideology that says, roughly, that Communism is going to inherit the earth. Communism is "progressive" and nothing else is. But the Progressives of the world are surrounded and besieged by reactionaries and the bourgeoisie; no opposition within the "motherland of socialism" can be tolerated, lest the capitalist nations invade and destroy the Communist homeland.

The result is a nation with fewer paved roads per capita than any other in Europe; a nation that for the seventieth straight year will produce less grain than was grown under the czars; a nation with terrible economic problems that yet is able to maintain an enormous military and naval establishment, ring Europe with SS-20 missiles, and build by far the largest ICBM and nuclear arsenal this world has ever seen.

The odd part is that although the most visible effect of the "progressive" ideology is to shore up one of the most repressive tyrannies in the history of mankind, that ideology still finds popularity in the West. The Soviet Union is visibly an empire, in that it brings under one central rule a diversity of peoples, most of whom would secede if given the chance; and it is certainly arguable that any nation that kills a million of its own citizens each year can be called evil. Yet when the President of the United States said—once and once only—that the Soviet Union was "the evil empire," he was lectured by the Western press and professorate as if he, not the KGB, were responsible for the slave camps.

Self-professed Marxists occupy high academic positions in most U.S. universities, and while a student is unlikely to be given bad marks for the most unjust criticism of the United States and the Western democracies, he *is* likely to be graded down for criticism of the Soviet Union or the intellectual farce known as Marxism.

The "progressive" ideology doesn't have much hold in the U.S. population at large, but it has all too much influence within our universities and in the media.

Republics do not in general fall to outsiders; they fall to lack of defenders. When the citizens lose heart, and do not feel any moral superiority to their enemies, then there is little reason to fight for one's country, or even to spend money on weapons of defense.

One may debate the likelihood, but certainly a future history in which the United States chooses butter (and cheese and other dairy products) over defense and space technology; which consumes rather than invests; while the Soviets continue to arm until, one day, they strike—such a future is not impossible. There are some who would say it is likely.

Suppose that happens? Suppose the Soviet Union and United States do fight, with great slaughter on both sides; with destruction so great that much of modern science and technology is lost.

Could the ideologies remain?

IDEOLOGICAL DEFEAT
Christopher Anvil

Arakal, King of the Wesdem O'Cracy's, got up early on the day of the Soviet ambassador's visit, finished his exercise at the Post, studied the latest plot as brought up to date by Colputt's flasher, and then met with the Council.

Easing into the luxurious armchair at the head of the table, with the white-bearded Colputt to his left and broad trusty Slagiron to his right, Arakal once again got stuck in the side by the double-beaked, two-headed bird that adorned the hilt of his sword, the scabbard being guided in the wrong direction by the support for the left arm of the chair.

"This meeting," Arakal began, as he reached down and got the beak of the bird out of his flesh, "will now begin. In case anyone hasn't seen the plot this morning, the Kebeckers are as good as their word, and the Brunswickers are going along with them. The St. Lawrence is watched from the coast in, the armies are ready to move, and Kebeck Fortress is reinforced. I've sent word by flasher that if the Russ make a lodgment anywhere on the south bank of the river, we will help take them. If they try to get Kebeck Fortress, we will cross the river west of the fortress, and hit the Russ from behind."

There was a murmur of approval.

Arakal got the sword situated, and sat back in the chair.

To Colputt's left, Smith, Colputt's shrewd assistant, turned respectfully to Arakal. "By your leave—?"

"Yes, Smith?"

"We've got the night-flasher working."

There was a general stir. Across the table, young Beane, stuck handling the foreign diplomats, looked surprised.

"But I thought that was *impossible!*" He glanced at Arakal. "Beg pardon, sir."

Arakal nodded. "Go ahead. I've said my say."

Smith said, "Old Kotzebuth had us thinking it was impossible, but we decided to try it anyway. It works. Of course, the sun has set, and we have to spend some oil. But it works."

Slagiron's broad face creased in a grim smile. He said nothing, but Arakal had a good idea what he was thinking. The Russ prided themselves on their superior communications.

Further down the table, Casey, Slagiron's chief organizer, growled hopefully, "Will this work in bad weather?"

Smith shook his head. "Fog, snow, or rain blots out the flash."

"The Russ," said Casey, "can talk to each other almost *any* time."

"Well, they're using Old Stuff."

"That doesn't help us any. If we've got a bunch of them cut off, what do they do but yell for help, and here comes one of their damned iron birds, or a rescue force on wheels." He turned to Colputt. "We've got to do something about their long-talkers."

"Radios," nodded Colputt. "We've got a crew working on it, and I think we're finally getting a grip on the thing. Now, don't misunderstand me, I don't say we will *ever* be able to make long-talkers the equal of what the Russ have. But we should be able to do three things: First, we should be able to set up our own long-talkers to help out the flasher network. Second, we should be able to listen in on what the Russ say. Third, we should be able to turn out portable garblers to block their long-talkers. That is, they could still yell for reinforcements, but all that could be heard on the other end would be garble."

"That would all help."

Arakal said, "Anything would be an improvement. But why should we have to take second place? You're as smart as any of their men—probably smarter. Smith here is as shrewd as any they have to offer. Why must they be in front of us?"

Colputt shook his head sadly. "Old Stuff. They have more Old Stuff than we have. Captured radios have been turned over to me, and we've studied them, thinking to make our own, but to no use. We can't begin to work out the way they're made. The trouble is, the Old Soviets got in a fight with the Old O'Cracy's, and the Russ threw more stuff, did more damage, got the edge on the O'Cracy's. I don't say they won. But they did more damage. They have more Old Stuff left over. Long-talkers, iron birds, power sailers. We were knocked off our perch entirely. They had enough left over to use it still. Some of it, even, they may know how to make again. Not the long-talkers. But other things. They threw *us* back so far that I can look at the latest of our old books about radios, and see the words in front of me, and read them, and not know what they mean. That shows how far we were thrown back.''

"Then," frowned Arakal, "this special crew you set up—''

"Ah," said Colputt, beaming, "that's different. We go at it now from the other end. We use the *oldest* of the old books—those we *can* understand. And we're working our way forward. The Russ, now, have their stocks of Old Stuff. Very useful. But, when it *runs out*—''

Slagiron looked at Colputt, smiling. "You aim to have a position you can *hold?*''

Colputt nodded, and his eyes glinted.

Arakal glanced at the clock on the wall. "This ambassador of theirs gets here when?''

Beane said, "Shortly before the sun is at full height, sir.'' He craned to look at the clock. "Another three hours, say.''

"What is this one like?''

Beane shook his head. "The same as the rest.''

"He is on safe conduct, of course?''

"Yes, sir. Worse luck. But he wouldn't come without it.''

"There is always a chance of treachery—*either* way. Have all your precautions ready. Does this one talk English, or—''

Beane brightened a little. "There is *that* difference. This one does talk English. Of course, when he talks—''

"Let your translator take a place amongst the guards. Who knows? He might overhear something.''

Beane nodded, smiling.

"Yes, sir. But I think they learned that lesson the last time.''

Vassily Smirnov, Ambassador-General, glanced uneasily at Simeon Brusilov, Colony Force Commander, as the helicopter thundered around them.

"Just how safe," said Smirnov, "is a safe conduct from these savages?''

Brusilov said moodily, "Safe enough. As long as you don't look too long at any of their women, sleep with your ears under the covers, or drink anything except water or milk. Watch out for this Arakal. He's smart in streaks.''

"What does that mean?"

"He's ignorant in obvious ways, but just overlook that. Where it counts, he's smarter than any of us."

Smirnov frowned. "An odd statement for our own commander to make."

"I say it because I *know*. And I did not enjoy gaining the knowledge."

"And just where *is* he smart?"

"Militarily."

"You flatter yourself. That is *not* what counts. Ideology is what counts in the end. That is why *I* am here."

"It didn't help us much in the last ambush."

"With your technological advantage, I'm surprised the natives dare to ambush your men."

Brusilov shook his head.

"Comrade, kindly get it through your skull that there are *two* technologies on this continent. One is shipped to us packaged and ready to use, but if it goes bad, who is going to fix it? The other is growing up steadily, and knitting the pieces of the continent together, and while it is in every way less impressive than ours, there is much more of it, and it is getting very tricky.

"For instance, there is this sun-signal system. It started in Arakal's sector, and now he's linked up with the descendants of the Canadian survivors. Six months ago, we tried to cut Arakal's zone up the line of the Hudson, preparatory to biting off the whole of the old Northeast United States. The idea was, with that in our hands, we'd have a base suitable for protection of our colonies to the south. Arakal saw the plan in a flash. It was nothing but traps and ambushes, and dead stragglers and small parties yelling for help all the way from the time we hit the Forest.

"But we expected that. What we didn't expect was that an army would come boiling out of Quebec and the old seacoast Provinces, and get to us before we could finish the job. Not too long ago, Arakal would have had to send couriers. Now he uses the sun-signal system. We were lucky to get out of there with a whole skin."

"Certainly the savages' speed of motion is inconsiderable, compared with yours."

"We have the edge there, all right. It's just too bad so much of the road net is centered on the worst zones of lingering radioactivity."

9

"Is that their camp, there?"

Brusilov looked out, to see a tall steel tower. A gun thrust out and followed the helicopter, but didn't fire.

"That is one of their sun-signal towers. You see, these 'savages' have learned to work steel again."

"You should bomb them—*destroy* them!"

Brusilov looked at the ambassador. "Will *you* increase my shipments of fuel, and bombs, and planes? Will *you* get me more pilots? Do you know what this one trip is costing me in gas, and hence in future freedom of action?" He glanced out. "There is their camp. Try to remember that they are not as stupid as they may seem to you. Backward, yes. Stupid, no."

Arakal shook the hand of Smirnov, smiling gravely but noting the softness of the ambassador's grip. Such was not the grip of the Russ commander. The ambassador was like the rest of their ambassadors, but Brusilov, now, was a good man.

"The great Central Committee," Smirnov began impressively, "sends its greetings to you, despite the fact that your actions have not been of the best."

Brusilov muttered something and removed himself out of earshot, to the far end of the tent. Slagiron excused himself and went over to talk to Brusilov.

"This war," said Smirnov, with the air of an oracle, "costs much money, many lives. It must end."

Arakal smiled pleasantly.

"Then get off the continent."

"This land is ours," said Smirnov, spacing his words, and making his tone deep and impressive.

"Go home," said Arakal brusquely. *"Leave."*

"Our colonists grow their wheat, plant their trees, speak their tongue, sing their songs. This is our land and it belongs to us, just as the land of your tribe belongs to you, so long as we grant it to you."

Arakal gave a low growl of irritation, then looked up as Casey came over. Casey glanced around, apparently for Slagiron.

"Excuse me, Mr. Smirnov," Arakal said. "What is it, Casey? Your chief is over there with Commander Brusilov."

Casey nodded, looked thoughtfully at Smirnov, who was waiting impatiently for the interruption to cease, and then Casey spoke intently to Arakal, seeming somehow to send an

10

additional message along with the spoken words: "Carlo is there."

Arakal's eyes momentarily shut, and he seemed to shiver. Then he drew a deep careful breath.

"I see," he said. "Well, I don't think it's worth bothering your chief with *that*. You can tell him later."

"Yes, sir." Casey smiled, bowed slightly, turned, and left.

Arakal looked at Smirnov blandly.

"Now, Mr. Ambassador, let me explain why you should do as I suggest. The Old O'Cracy's, which is to say the great clan to which we all here belong, once owned *all* the land, that which is good, that which is sick, and that upon which you have planted your colonies. The O'Cracy's once fought at your side long ago, and were mighty warriors, armed by the incomparable wizards who lived at that time. But they grew weary of war, and made fewer magical weapons than the Old Soviets, who in time struck them down. Why, or how this came about, I do not know. That is of the past. Both sides suffered, but that is over. Now, however, the land *was* ours, so it is not stealing when we take it back. It again will be ours, because we are growing stronger much faster than that part of your clan which is over here. This is why you should now get out."

Smirnov looked at Arakal and laughed. "There is not and never was a 'clan' of the O'Cracy's. Your 'knowledge' is a mixture of fables and errors. I suppose that word *O'Cracy* came originally from the word 'dem*ocracy*,' an inferior governmental system which your leaders made much of in the past, before we destroyed them. But never mind that. I will explain to you why you must not only end your rebellion, but must, and will, come to us that your tribe may be lifted by stages into ideological purity and civilized knowledge. And that you may know that my words are indisputable, I will tell you first just who and what I am."

Arakal leaned forward in his seat, as one braces himself who faces into a wind.

Smirnov said, "As you know, the rulers of all the Soviets are known as Party Members, and not just anyone can be a Party Member. Only the child of a Party Member can be a Party Member, except by direct action of the great Central Committee itself. Now, Mr. Arakal, you are sprung out of nothing, and have nothing behind you. But *I* am the child of a Party Member, who was the child of a Party Member, who was the child of a Party Member, who was the child of a Party Member, and indeed even *I* do not know for how many generations back this may go. You see the difference?''

Arakal's eyes narrowed, and he said nothing.

"You observe," said Smirnov, "that I speak your tongue. You cannot speak my tongue. But I speak yours with ease. It is nothing to me. This is because of my *education*." He held up his right hand, turned the palm toward Arakal, and made a little thrusting motion of the hand toward Arakal. "Education is to be taught at such an age and in such a way that the knowledge becomes one with the person who is taught. He need make little effort to learn, Mr. Arakal, because he is naturally intelligent, and taught by skilled persons, whose job it is to teach, and to do *nothing else*. Such a thing you have not, but it is mine by right of birth. Those are *two* things we have that you do not have and cannot get without coming to us: One, the Party. Two, Education. But that is not all.''

Arakal watched the glint in Smirnov's eyes, and listened to the wasp note in Smirnov's voice.

"Three," said Smirnov, "we have Technology. Let me point out to you, Mr. Arakal—and remember who it is that is pointing it out—that when your ancestors dared to raise their hand against us, the Central Committee gave the word: 'Strip from them all their power and all their technology, that they may never have power again. Because it is only from technology that power comes.' But, in the same order, the Central Committee said, 'See to it that *our* technology is stored, good and plenty, with grease and all the instructions to keep it running.' And so it was done. And our ancestors smashed yours to their knees, and then they kicked them off their knees onto their face, and they smashed your technology, and you can never rebuild it, because you have no Education. You are savages, nothing more, and never can be more, except you come to us to ask for it. Those are *three* reasons, and now there is the fourth, and most important of all.''

Arakal pushed his chair back, and took pains to get the swordhead free of the arm of the chair.

"The Party, Education, Technology," said Smirnov, "and then the greatest—Ideology. And it is in this that *I* am an expert. I could have been anything, but I chose this, the most difficult of all—''

Arakal came to his feet.

"It has been interesting to listen to you, Mr. Ambassador.''

12

"I am not through. Sit down."

Behind Arakal, someone drew his breath in sharply.

Arakal didn't move, and there was a sudden hush.

Across the tent, Brusilov came hurrying, his expression harried. Slagiron was right beside him, alert and self-possessed.

Smirnov said irritably, "Sit down, sit down, Arakal."

Brusilov glanced in astonishment at Smirnov.

Smirnov raised his hand and thrust up one finger. "First, the Party." He thrust up another finger. "Second, Education." He thrust up a third finger. "Third, Technology." Each time he put up a finger, he gave his hand a little shake. He put up the fourth finger. "And fourth, *Ideology*." He looked at the King of the O'Cracy's. "*Ideology*, Arakal."

Brusilov's jaw fell open.

From behind Arakal came a murmur.

Slagiron's lips tightened and his eyes glinted, but aside from that, there was no play of expression on his face.

Smirnov looked around.

"What's all this? Be seated, the lot of you!"

Brusilov glanced anxiously around.

Arakal could sense his men gathering behind him. Now Brusilov's pilots and guards came running, their hands on their holstered weapons.

Arakal took pains to keep his hands at his sides, though his left hand tilted the scabbard just enough so that he could get his sword out quickly.

The situation got through to Smirnov, who came angrily to his feet.

Brusilov stared at him.

"Mr. Ambassador, what have you—"

"*Bah!*" said Smirnov. "I am trying to teach this savage a minor lesson! *Very* minor! But it is all that is suited to his intelligence! The fools know nothing and so cannot think!"

Slagiron's eyes widened. He glanced at Arakal.

Arakal sensed the opportunity, sucked in his breath, and gazed skyward for an instant, imploring guidance. He cleared his throat.

Behind him, there was an ugly murmur, and the clearly perceptible rattle of loosened swords.

Brusilov's men glanced around.

Behind them, more of the O'Cracy's stood ready, their eyes on Arakal, waiting the command.

From above, the words came to Arakal.

He raised his right hand, palm out, and spoke distinctly, and his translator spoke after him in the tongue of the Russ.

"Men of the Russ—go in peace. We have no fight with *you*."

Brusilov exhaled, and glanced at Arakal with suddenly bright eyes. Behind Brusilov, his own men murmured, the sound one of surprise, and relief, and something more.

Arakal looked steadily back at Brusilov, and smiled, admiring the poise and insight of the Russ commander.

Slagiron grinned suddenly, and clapped Brusilov on the shoulder. He said something in his ear, and Brusilov gave his head a little shake, but smiled nevertheless.

Smirnov looked around, his eyes narrowed.

"What's this? Why are they—"

Brusilov abruptly grabbed Smirnov by the arm, and whirled him around.

Arakal shouted, "*You men!* Form an honor guard for the warriors of the Russ!"

All at once, there was a cheer.

Brusilov propelled Smirnov between the lines, and the other Russ hurried along behind. Slagiron and Arakal went to the front of the tent, and watched the Russ climb into their big iron birds.

As they took off, Arakal smiled and waved, and from inside the iron birds, some of the Russ smiled and waved back.

As the helicopter thundered around them, Smirnov spoke furiously.

"You dared to lay your hand on me! And I am a *Party Member of the Fourth Degree!*"

"Mr. Ambassador," said Brusilov shortly, "would you rather have had your head sliced off and rolled around on the floor of that tent?"

"You *touched* me!"

Brusilov opened his mouth and shut it. His gaze seemed to turn inward for an instant, then he took a hard look at Smirnov, his gaze cold and measuring.

Smirnov, staring back, put a hand on the holstered automatic at his side.

Brusilov tensed, then caught himself. For a long moment, he was motionless. Then he gave his head a little shake.

"No," he said. "No, it would be wrong." He looked at

Smirnov again, then Brusilov went to a seat across the aisle and sat down, his face set and unresponsive.

Around them, the helicopter thundered, as it carried them above the tower of the O'Cracy's.

Arakal and Slagiron bent intently over the plot.

"So far," said Arakal, "there is no word from the Kebeckers of the Russ fleet entering the river. The Kebeckers say there is no sign of the Russ at all."

"Hm-m-m," said Slagiron. "I wonder if they could be going to try the Hudson again—with their main fleet this time."

"In that case, they would be in sight by now. Our lookout on Long Island has seen nothing, and the same word has come in from our boat off the Hook."

"Peculiar. Still, there is a delay in getting word to us."

"True. We get the word quickly from Kebeck Fortress over the flasher, but a runner crosses from Long Island by boat."

Smith cleared his throat apologetically.

"Beg pardon, sir. Just last week, while you were . . . ah . . . working with Carlo, we got the flasher set up across Long Island Sound."

"What? There's a tower there?"

"No, sir, that would be too risky, but the sea is flat, and we can do without towers over that distance. There's still a delay in reports from off the Hook. But from the Sound, in good weather, we get them fast. There was no long delay on this report."

"Good. But now, you see," he said, turning to Slagiron, "that leaves us up in the air. They've sent this new ambassador. This Central Committee is as regular as clockwork. They never send a new ambassador without sending reinforcements, and they never send reinforcements without sending their fleet. Now, we've had the ambassador. Where's the fleet? We want to take that blow on our shield, not on our head."

The door opened briefly, and they heard a rumbling thud, like distant thunder. Arakal looked around, to see Colputt, smiling faintly, hang his coat on a peg and walk over.

"Now they're bombing the conference site," said Colputt.

Arakal smiled. "The more they drop there, the fewer they can dump on our heads. And they bring those things a long distance."

15

Slagiron shook his head. "This ambassador is their worst yet. If a thing is disastrous, he does it at once. No doubt now his pride has to be soothed."

Colputt added, "*And* their fleet is sighted. We just received word."

"What? *Where?*"

"Penobscot Bay."

Arakal looked at the contoured plot, and the wide deep indentations in the Maine coast.

Colputt went on, "They are landing troops at Bangor. Before the landing, their planes knocked out the flasher tower at Skowhegan."

Slagiron looked at the plot thoughtfully, and glanced at Arakal.

Arakal turned to Smith. "Send word to the Kebeckers. Describe this landing. And tell them *Carlo is ready.*"

Slagiron said, "Will they come?"

"Why not?" said Arakal, looking at the plot, where the markers were already being set down. "Could we ask for more?"

"On the map," said Slagiron, "this will look bad. From Bangor it is only . . . say . . . a hundred and eighty miles to Kebeck Fortress, across country. The Russ can cut straight for the river, and split us off from the Kebeckers—on the map."

Arakal smiled. "A hundred and eighty miles of *what?* And when the Russ get there, they're on the wrong bank of the river. Meanwhile, their fleet is stuck at Bangor, or coming around by the Gulf, or else it gets there without the troops. Try the Kebeckers, and see what they say."

Brusilov returned the major's salute.

"Sir," said the major, glancing around at the rugged peaks, and swatting at mosquitoes, "that map is either wrong, or we're turned around. There *is* no road. And the sniping is getting worse."

Smirnov spoke up sharply.

"You are a soldier, are you not? You expect to fight in a war, do you not?"

Brusilov spoke coolly. "We aren't lost, Major. Simply assume that the map is right, and cast around for the road. Don't worry. It will be broken up, but it's there."

The major said stubbornly, "The men say this is going to

be the Hudson all over again. They don't like it. They are growing hard to manage."

Brusilov smiled soberly and shook his head. "Have them look at this mess of lakes, ponds, and swamps. Did we have anything like this on the march up the Hudson? No." He waved a hand at the cloud of small black flies that, interspersed with occasional mosquitoes, settled on him as soon as he devoted himself to anything else. "So," he said, "it is not the Hudson all over again. This is quite different. Console yourself, my friend. We have variety, at least."

The major looked sullen, but saluted. Then he trudged off up one of the interminable hills over which the road through the heavy forest climbed and plunged.

Brusilov glanced at Smirnov.

"Isn't this far enough? Speaking as a merely military man, devoid of ideological finesse, *I* think this is far enough."

"We must press on," said Smirnov. "Until we are sure the natives are fully committed."

Brusilov shook his head.

"Comrade, in a general way, this plan is not bad; but there are details, and it is the details that will ruin us. Arakal will not react as you expect. You would draw him here by a threat, fall back before him, lure him to the coast, embark, and strike elsewhere. He will not be drawn, however. He *will not take the bait.*"

Smirnov smiled in a superior way.

"I know the aboriginal mind. This native leader is without training. He is brave, and has personal presence, but no sense of grand strategy. He is already beaten in the realm of ideas."

"No, he is not." Brusilov frowned and waved away a cloud of the tiny flies. "That is the trouble. He is a master of conflict, in the realm of ideas as elsewhere."

"Look here," said Smirnov, suddenly earnest. "The method by which the fellow's ancestors were beaten were quite simple. We took a little advantage, repeatedly, until we had a big advantage, and at each point the change was too small to stimulate them to action. The records are somewhat confused as to details, but obviously when we had *enough* advantage, *then* we struck. Now, this conflict here is the same thing, except that there is no longer another ideologically able side to oppose our movements. We have now the fruit of the last

17

war, an ideological and technological advantage they can never overcome. Specifically, our speed of movement is faster than theirs. That is enough. It is unbeatable. It is the advantage that will give us everything else."

"I am not sure of it."

Smirnov's earnestness gave out, and he spoke irritably. "You *were* defeated. Your plan was good, but you lacked subtlety. You proceeded straight ahead. 'Cut them up the line of the Hudson!' A good idea. But you were too direct. You should have drawn them elsewhere first."

Brusilov shook his head. "It was their solar flasher that wrecked my plan. They are not aborigines! Aborigines do not *know* of technology. Arakal's people remember what they could do; they know it is possible. They keep thinking, trying to find the way again. It is *that* that distinguishes them from aborigines."

"Well, their solar flasher is what will destroy them now, by decoying their main forces to this place. And it is *our* speed of movement that will then deliver the deciding blow."

"I hope so," said Brusilov. "But where is Arakal?"

Arakal, perspiring in the humid foggy dawn, looked through the precious long-seeing glasses, and noted the lone guard pacing atop the breastworks, on the far side of the canal.

Beside Arakal, Slagiron murmured, "They seem asleep."

Arakal nodded. "They would be flattered to know how many are watching them. They have never had so many of us at once before—though we have traded with them secretly so long they no longer dread us."

Slagiron shut his glass with a snap, and grinned.

"Now, we will find out if all those crisscrossing rivers shown on our maps are obstacles or not. Only let us not be invisibly burned to bits by all the slagged ruins in the vicinity, and we will even see if your plan can work . . . War without blood . . . I doubt it, but it is worth a try."

Arakal glanced around and saluted the Kebecker leader, who beamed and raised his hand. Then Arakal turned to signal to his own cavalry chief.

The cavalryman grinned and took off his hat in a sweeping gesture, then turned and beckoned to the dense woods behind him.

A long line of mounted men in gray emerged from the forest and, at a walk, started down toward the canal. Behind them came teams of oxen dragging long heavy logs, and behind *them* came small groups of infantry, some stripped to their waists, all quiet, and most looking cheerful, as if on some kind of outing.

Atop the breastworks, the sentry halted, turned, and started back. Hypnotized by his routine, he paced methodically, halted again, turned, started back, and suddenly froze. He stared up and down the line of smiling horsemen leisurely approaching the canal, stared at the oxen pulling the logs, looked hard at the infantrymen gaily jumping into the water, and before he could recover, someone called out in his own tongue, making him uncertain for an instant who this army belonged to.

Meanwhile, the infantry swam the canal. In the water, the engineers were taking the ends of the logs as they were rolled down, and pulling them out into the water. The cavalry were swimming their horses across, and soon, if all went well, the guns and catapults could go across on the bridges.

Atop the breastworks, the troops were now banging the stupefied guard on the back, and he himself was starting to grin and laugh, and now shook his head and turned to shout to someone, who climbed up, looked around in amazement, stared in both directions up and down the canal, where the gray uniforms were crossing over, and finally shrugged and spread his hands.

Slagiron murmured his satisfaction, and turned to Arakal.

"You were right. No shots, no advance bombardment, *no attack,* just an *advance.*"

"As long as it lasts," said Arakal. "When we hit the garrison at Salisbury, it may be different."

"If we get to Salisbury," said Slagiron, grinning, "we've got the whole colony. They'll have one sweet time getting us out once we get to Salisbury."

"Remember," Arakal warned, "they must be treated like O'Cracy's. They are good hard workers and decent people, and if we treat them right, they will *become* O'Cracy's."

Slagiron nodded. "I have pounded it into the troops. *They* know. I even almost believe it myself now."

Brusilov, half eaten up by bugs, was in a murderous frame of mind. He had three tanks in a bog, half a dozen out for repairs, the sniping was continuous and getting worse, and worst of all, the men had no heart for the fight. Smirnov, however, was delighted.

"I would say we are now drawing in the first of Arakal's troops. Would you agree?"

"Hard to say," growled Brusilov.

"All this uproar could not be caused by locals."

"You can't be—" Brusilov frowned at a courier running up the slippery ruts. "What's this?"

The courier, out of breath, saluted and held out a slip of paper.

Brusilov unfolded it, read quickly, and stared at Smirnov.

"What is it?" demanded Smirnov.

Brusilov handed it to him.

Smirnov took it, read it, stiffened, looked up blankly, read it again, and, absently fanning at the bugs, stared blankly at the towering hills.

"Impossible. Delaware in the hands of New Brunswick troops. The Army of Quebec on the line of the Nanticoke River. Arakal swinging around to the east of Salisbury. *The whole Maryland-Delaware Colony is lost*. How can it have happened?"

Brusilov said grimly, "I've tried to explain to you not to underestimate Arakal. Well, *now* what do we do?"

Smirnov broke out in a fine perspiration.

"It is *impossible!*" He glanced at Brusilov. "You are the military commander! What is your opinion? This is *your* specialty!"

"Oh, of course. But you are the one with the letter of authority from the Central Committee. Also, *you* have the ideology."

"What would you *advise?*"

"Pull out. Maybe we can still save Carteret, Beaufort, and Florida Colony. We aren't doing any good here."

Smirnov stared into the distance. Suddenly he drew a deep breath.

"It is *impossible* for an unlettered fool who thinks the O'Cracy's fought the Russ with magic wands to win this contest! He has won a chance victory, but he has lost the war!"

Brusilov shook his head wearily. "How do you reason *that?*"

"He has shifted the full strength of this part of the continent to the south, against our colonies. *We* will strike to the north, take Quebec Fortress, open the line of the St. Lawrence, and later strike simultaneously up and down the Hudson to cut off all New England. He has won the Maryland-Delaware Peninsula; but can he hold it, can he pacify it? We will at once warn the other colonies of his atrocities. They must stand in their own defense at once. Meanwhile, *we* will get this burr out of our hide, get this river fortress into our *own* hands!''

''You want the troops back on the ships?''

''*No!* Every last soldier must come *here!* Then send the ships around to come down the St. Lawrence and ferry us across. We will now cut loose from them entirely and march overland!''

Brusilov considered it thoughtfully, and shook his head. ''No. Look—''

But Smirnov made an axe-like gesture of the hand, from the shoulder straight out.

''Cut the continent, from the Atlantic to the river line. Wheel south and east, smash all resistance in our path. Cut Arakal loose from his base. Swiftness, speed, decision—and the ignorant tribesman is whipped. In this first fight we will turn our soft soldiers into hardened troops, *veterans*. Then we will see!''

Brusilov stood thinking, his right hand on the flap of his holster. Finally he shrugged, and turned to give the necessary orders.

Arakal reread the message that had come in flashes of light down the line of towers from New England. He looked at Slagiron.

''The Russ are heading for Kebeck Fortress, *overland*.'' He handed the message to the leader of the Kebeckers, who had just joined them, and whose translator, standing between his chief and Arakal, translated Arakal's comment, then bent over the message and read it in a low voice.

The Kebecker chief glanced at the plot, where the red emblems climbing the green and brown slopes and surrounded by a multitude of small blue markers were now being moved further forward. Then he turned with a slight smile, to give the message back to Arakal.

''*Ça sera un peu difficile pour les Russes,*'' the Kebecker said, speaking slowly and distinctly, and holding one hand up to silence his translator.

Arakal winced and glanced at the ceiling. It came to him

that the Kebecker had somehow learned of the hundreds of hours he, Arakal, had put into a study of the Kebeck tongue, while the depth of winter made campaigning impractical. Arakal had been prepared to forget all about this and rely on the translators, but someone's sense of humor had given away the secret. All winter Slagiron and the others had joked slyly at Arakal's laborious progress, while Arakal, chafing at the depths of linguistic incapacity revealed to him with each day's effort, nevertheless had refused to give up. Determinedly good-natured, he replied, "While you pass the winter in perfumed idleness, *I* am laying the groundwork for the future. If we are going to clout the Russ in the springtime, one of us, at least, ought to understand the Kebeckers' chief. He has shrewd ideas, but the translators are no military geniuses, and now and then they miss the point. And it is up to us to solve it somehow. You know as well as I do that their chief can't speak a word of English—not that he hasn't at least tried."

Slagiron shook his head. "He *did* memorize that greeting when we got Carlo across the border and went up there for a talk."

Arakal nodded, remembering the incident soberly. "That's what I mean."

Colputt turned to Smith. "Did we ever figure out what he said?"

Smith looked helpless. "Don't ask me. Did you see the looks on the faces of the translators?"

"In my opinion, it wasn't anything," said Casey. "Neither their talk nor our talk. Just *noise*. It *sounded* like something, but nobody could make it out."

Arakal shook his head. "Our translators explained it to me later. He had *our* words and *his* way of speaking. That's why nobody could follow it. But the translators finally figured it out. What he said was just what we thought he *must* be saying, from his expression. He greeted us, praised Carlo, and looked forward to our future cooperation."

"Hm-m-m," said Slagiron slyly, "but will *you* be able to do as well come next spring?"

Everyone had laughed at that as the snow whipped around the winter camp, and the cold set its teeth into the logs of the buildings.

And now, after the victory over the Russ, Arakal stared at the ceiling, and the Kebecker chief smiled and waited.

Slowly, in Arakal's mind, the meaning evolved: "That will be . . . a little difficult . . . for the Russ."

Arakal thought it through again. Unquestionably, that was what it meant. Now he avoided glancing at the grinning Slagiron, and trusted to the labors of his Kebeck-born translator. It was a somewhat ambitious reply he had in mind, but he thought he could get it out. He drew a deep breath, then spoke slowly and carefully:

"*Carlo et nous, nous ferons beaucoup des difficultés pour les Russes.*"

Across the room, Arakal's translator winced, but the Kebecker translator looked agreeably surprised.

Arakal laboriously went over it again in his head now that it was out. Surely what he had just said had come out as it was supposed to: "Carlo and we, we will make plenty of difficulty for the Russ."

The Kebecker chief glanced at the ceiling for only a moment, then smiled and nodded.

"*Ah, oui. Carlo et nous.*" He bent over the plot, and speaking clearly and slowly his meaning came across almost as plainly as if he spoke English.

"Carlo—where does he go in these hills? Will the Russ not find him?"

"No," said Arakal carefully, now suspecting that he had already made one mistake in his first answer. "Carlo is back of those hills. The Russ will not find him. But we will show them what he can do."

Brusilov, though by no means charmed with this plan, was still uncertain whether it might not, after all, turn out to be workable.

Smirnov, now that he had set his mind on a definite idea, proved to have at least one outstanding quality—total ruthlessness.

"Hang them!" he commanded when suspected snipers were brought in. "Leave their bodies dangling as a warning to others! Enough delay for these dogs! Forward! We must go forward!"

Under the lash of his tongue, with the reinforcements pouring in from the ships, the army had begun to move again. Through swamps, streams, rivers, up and down mountains, through dense forest, over a track of a road that had long since ceased to be useful, where the pines and oaks and

23

hemlocks grew ten inches through and had to be felled to make way for the tanks and supply trucks. Through endless snipers, who used guns, and longbows that were worse than guns—whose arrows could pin a man to a tree to wait in shock and despair for the next arrow that would finish him.

But they moved.

And with progress and a definite goal, the troops began to look up. Soon the endless hills would have to grow smaller. Arakal's men, on foot and on horseback, could not hope to return from the South in time.

Now Smirnov's troops were in the swing of the work, their superior weapons and numbers making themselves felt. Sensing victory, they became tougher, would not be stopped, would not be overawed or intimidated. The crafty Arakal was at long last outmaneuvered, and they were the ones who would beat him for good.

Before them, the snipers melted away, to content themselves with picking off stragglers that had fallen behind.

Smirnov grimly urged more speed, and now there was nothing but forest and hills and water and bugs to contend with.

They camped one night in a place where two small rivers came together, to flow away in a larger river to the north. They had lost many of the tanks and quite a number of the trucks, but their spirits were high despite their weariness.

Brusilov listened to Smirnov's prediction.

"My friend," said Smirnov, "this march will go down in world history as a major military stroke."

"If," said Brusilov soberly, "it were not that we will rejoin the ships soon, we would be in serious trouble. Our gas, food, and even ammunition are getting low."

"But we *will* rejoin the ships."

"We could have accomplished the same trip by boarding the ships and being carried there without losses," said Brusilov.

"True, but also without victory. We are conquerors now. And the men know it."

"There is truth in what you say. And yet—"

"And yet?"

"It is hard for me to believe that Arakal is beaten."

Smirnov laughed.

"You have been beaten by him, and so you think he can beat anyone. I have seen deeper than he from the beginning, and beaten him ideologically."

"No. He outmaneuvered you at the meeting. He turned the men against you."

"If so, where is the result now? The men are blooded, tough and determined. The effect of Arakal's cleverness is lost. He has been *outthought*."

But in the morning, when they tried to cross the river, murderous sheets of fire greeted them.

Brusilov, looking down around the edge of a small boulder, and seeing the burning vehicles, the men spread-eagled in the water and other men who rushed into the stream while still others straggled back from it—Brusilov, seeing this, wormed backward, dropped down a short slanting bank, and ran doubled over toward the center of the camp. The heavy firing, he noticed, was all from in front, none from the rear or flanks.

Quickly, he gave the orders to pull back, then try probing toward the east. They *had* to get to the river, but they could never make it going straight ahead.

Meanwhile, the sniping that had let up a little while ago was worse now than it had ever been. The tanks, in this country, were worthless alone. They could sometimes ride the trees down, but only to make a tangled jumble that was worse than what they had had to contend with in the beginning. A way had to be cleared for them, but who could fell trees in this blizzard of bullets and arrows?

Toward ten o'clock, Brusilov, with the speechless Smirnov in tow, broke through toward the east, then swung northward again toward the river. But in the unending fighting, in the dense roadless forest, the tanks and trucks were an unbearable encumbrance.

Smirnov, finding himself alive, recovered his voice.

"Let us send the armor and transport back the way they came. There, the old road is cleared, and they can escape."

"Where to?" demanded Brusilov. "Back to Bangor?"

"Why not?"

"Do you know what will happen to the men? Remember, you had the suspected snipers hanged and left as a warning. What will the people do now?"

"Our men can overawe them with their weapons."

Brusilov laughed, and gave orders to fire all the remaining ammunition of the tanks in the direction of the enemy and then smash the engines. The trucks he had unloaded of whatever was useful, and rolled them into the river.

"It is a waste!" cried Smirnov.

"We need every man we can get," said Brusilov.

Desperately, they fought their way toward the north, and suddenly and unexplainably the opposition gave way.

A lone cavalry captain under a white flag made his way to Brusilov and Smirnov, to invite them to a conference.

"Do they wish to surrender?" wondered Smirnov aloud.

Brusilov looked at Smirnov and shook his head moodily—and accepted the invitation. He gave orders that the march was to continue, conferred with a few trusted officers, and went with Smirnov to the conference.

Arakal seated himself across the little table from Smirnov, smiled at Brusilov's look of amazement, and turned briefly to Slagiron.

"The pursuit, of course, is being continued?"

"Yes, sir," said Slagiron respectfully.

Arakal faced Smirnov.

"We regret that we have to use harsh measures. But the men are in an ugly mood. They have seen the corpses dangling from the trees. And some of these corpses were badly disfigured. You understand that we must be severe or the men will take matters into their own hands."

Brusilov was nodding, moodily. Smirnov said nothing.

"We know, of course," said Arakal, "where the order came from." He looked at Smirnov, and waited.

Smirnov, frowning, said, "So, the message was a hoax?"

"What message?"

"The message from Salisbury."

"A hoax?" said Arakal. "Ah, you think we *decoyed* you here?"

"Yes."

Arakal shook his head. He turned to an officer standing beside a wooden chest. "Show the Ambassador-General the flag from Salisbury."

The officer bent, opened the chest, took out a large flag, and handed it to Smirnov.

Smirnov held it, passed the cloth between his fingers, and looked up at Arakal. He tried to speak, swallowed, and tried again.

"So, it is true. You have taken Delaware Colony."

Arakal bowed his head.

"By the Grace of God. We also have Beaufort and Florida Colonies. Carteret is still holding out. We will go down later to Carteret and return the favor the Army of the South is doing for us here."

Brusilov jerked as if a hot wire had touched him.

Smirnov blinked, but it took him a moment longer to respond. "The Army of the South? *Kilburne's Guerrillas?*"

Arakal smiled. "General Kilburne commands the Army of the South."

"But . . . how—?"

Suddenly Brusilov clapped his hand to his head, winced, then recovered his composure and drew a deep breath. He spoke sharply to Smirnov, his words indistinguishable to Arakal.

Behind Arakal, an officer cleared his throat.

"General Brusilov suggests to the Ambassador that if what this must mean is true, then the Ambassador can appeal to the devil's grandmother to save the Russ colonies here. It must be, the General says, that the Americans have rebuilt the railroads."

Smirnov looked as if someone had poured a bucket of ice water over his head.

Arakal leaned forward, smiling.

"Is there anything more natural, Mr. Ambassador? What else is there that will run on coal or wood—and we have plenty of that—and exceed the speed of your fastest tanks and trucks run on expensive fuel? What else can easily outpace all your transport ships and all your warships save only those rare few that ride on narrow wings let down under the water? Is there any other way that we can travel a thousand miles in a day, and move an army from place to place faster than you can transport it by ships, and in far greater numbers than you can move it by air, and in any kind of weather? Why would we *not* connect together whatever well-sited roads of steel survived your attack, and why would we *not* salvage all the cars and all the engines that can use wood or coal to pull those cars and put our best men to work making new engines? Why not?"

Smirnov said sharply, "*We can do the same thing!*"

"No, you can't," said Arakal. "Not here. There would be nothing easier for us to sabotage. *You* must rely on tanks and iron birds and trucks. You can rely on nothing you cannot guard at all times.''

Smirnov shoved back his chair as if to get up.

Brusilov rested a hand heavily on Smirnov's shoulder, and glanced gravely at Arakal.

"What did you ask us here for? To tell us this?"

"To ask the surrender of your army."

Brusilov shook his head.

"Do not catch the conqueror's sickness of quick conceit. Remember, we are a world empire, while you are only a part of a ruined nation that was once great. Do not press too far. Be generous, and hope that we will be generous in turn. To avoid the trouble of a great effort, our leaders might come to an arrangement with you, *if* you are reasonable.''

Arakal waited a moment, then said quietly, "We seek nothing that belongs to the Russ. We ask only that which belongs to the O'Cracy's.''

Brusilov's face twitched.

"It must be negotiated.''

An officer stepped up beside Arakal, and excused himself. "Sir, news of the Russ fleet.''

"Speak up," said Arakal. "Our guests will want to know, too.''

The officer cleared his throat. "They have passed Cape Cat and are moving at high speed upriver. Their iron birds are scouring the shoreline.''

Brusilov straightened. Smirnov sat up in his chair.

Arakal said quietly, "You see, I am being fair with you. But I can do only so much. The more you fight with us, the more determined and filled with anger my men will become. It would be best to surrender to us and be escorted, without the weapons of your men, to the ships. But to be released in that way, the Russ must agree to make no move against any of the colonies which have become ours. Any colonist who wishes may, of course, go home with you, if you care about that.''

Brusilov frowned, and spoke carefully, "If the worldwide might of the Soviets were to be concentrated in this spot—''

Slagiron said quietly, "Then all the world would rise up wherever you pulled out.''

Smirnov came to his feet.

"I am the Ambassador of the greatest empire—yes, *empire*—on earth.'' He tilted his head back, and Arakal leaned slightly forward, waiting. Smirnov, however, for some reason, did not say more.

Brusilov said firmly, "We can accept no condition that would reflect discredit on our nation."

Arakal said, almost regretfully, "Now that the Army of the South is with us, and the Army of Kebeck, and the Army of Brunswick, and the Maine Militia, I would say you are outnumbered better than three to one. We respect your courage. But you must consider these facts."

Brusilov was silent, but Smirnov said, "You forget our Fleet."

"No," said Arakal, smiling, "I have not forgotten that."

Smirnov gave his head a little shake.

"They are *still* savages. They have learned nothing! Let us—"

Brusilov interrupted, and his voice came out in a roar.

"*Enough* name-calling!" He turned to Arakal. "We thank you for your courtesy; but we do *not* give up! And we remind you that if we decide to put forth our strength, you will regret it!"

Brusilov turned on his heel and went out. Smirnov trailed out after him, then paused at the entrance and looked back.

"I associate myself with everything the Commander has said." He nodded and went out.

Slagiron said exasperatedly, "How do we separate Brusilov from that little worm?"

"We can only send our prayers for that," said Arakal. "We must be very careful now, that in trying to gain all we do not let the whole business slide through our fingers." He glanced at Slagiron. "Let us see how long we can keep them from reaching the St. Lawrence."

Brusilov, so tired by now that each motion took its separate effort of will, stared at the new columns of dust rising parallel to the columns of dust raised by his own marching men.

Wearily, he said, "Arakal underestimated his strength to us. This is worse than three to one."

Smirnov peered around.

"It is true. Look, we will be forced into the bend of that big stream."

"Do you think I don't see it? But on this side they are ahead of us in great numbers. We *can't* go straight. We must cross here and hope that we get completely across before they . . . Listen!"

29

They glanced up.

With a thunderous beat, three helicopters came flying toward them, and swerved suddenly as they took in the situation.

The nearest column of local troops, however, did not break or flee. Instead, they at once swerved to attack Brusilov.

Smirnov cried out, but Brusilov laughed half-hysterically.

"They want to get *close*. They wish to mingle with us to be safe from the bombs." He shouted orders, and his ragged columns broke into a run toward the stream.

The helicopters swerved to attack the oncoming troops.

Under the brilliant sun, the scene seemed to hang suspended, the men, the clouds of dust, the planes—all seemed to exist in a moment that would last forever.

And then the helicopters lit in a blaze as of a hundred suns.

Brusilov, stunned, saw the clouds of smoke where the pilots lost control and the planes crashed, but his mind could furnish no explanation. Then a sort of terror seized him, as if he were in the grip of some supernatural force that step by step undid the gains of the past, and would never let up until it had its way.

Shouting and cursing, he drove his men into the stream, led them out on the other side, and pointed to the distance, where a shimmer like steel showed the presence of the great river.

Now the enemy was so close, however, that Brusilov in the wild flight could no longer say whose men were his and whose belonged to the enemy. All were fleeing in a tangled jumble, and behind them came a tightly controlled body of cavalry that with repeated charges harried them till they were all one tormented, running, indistinguishable mass of suffering, seeking the river and salvation.

Brusilov, his mind hazed by fatigue and confusion—and the shock of the unexpected and the unpredictable—gave up trying to reason and just thought of the river, and the ships, and peace and safety.

And at last they were there, after no man knew how long. The sun had climbed up past the zenith and was now hanging in the west, and Brusilov, by pure habit, scarcely aware what he was doing, was ordering the men, placing this one or that one in a better position to fire, organizing a defense to hold off the harrying cavalry and the fast-approaching columns of troops.

From all the ships, warships as well as transports, the boats came in and ferried out load after load of stunned, dazed, dead-tired men, men too drugged with fatigue to do anything but clamber into the boats and fall down one on another. Men who stared stupidly when given an order, and had to be moved from place to place by hand . . . But they were getting them onto the ships.

As the big guns of the ships held off the encroaching enemy, Brusilov wished dazedly for rockets, but those, unfortunately, were reserved for special purposes. Still, the guns held off the pursuit, the last men were loaded into the boats, and now it was Brusilov's turn to accompany them, and—

A glare lit the ships, as if the sun, to the west, had risen and passed in a flash to the east, and multiplied itself a hundred-, a thousandfold.

From a point of land upriver, a little cloud of smoke rose up in the air.

A plume of water rose high beside the largest of the ships.

A heavy *boom* reached Brusilov's ears—a sound as of distant heavy thunder.

Suddenly he was surrounded, horsemen were everywhere, and before he knew what had happened he was caught up; the world spun around him, and he gave it up, and plunged into a deep black quiet that welcomed him into its depths—and long, long after, it yielded him up again, refreshed and wondering at the confused impressions that he found in his mind.

Arakal, smiling, was standing beside a round window. "You are awake, General Brusilov?"

"You again," said Brusilov. He sat up, and nodded also to Slagiron. "So, I did not reach the ships?"

"Look around," said Arakal. "Feel the motion underfoot. Of course, you have slept so long that it must seem natural."

Brusilov stared around.

"But why are *you* here?"

"These," said Arakal blandly, "are our ships, taken in return for some little damage you did in Bangor and on the way here."

Brusilov got carefully to his feet. He looked at the bland Arakal and the grinning Slagiron, and peered out the porthole of the cabin. There, riding at anchor, were the other ships of the Fleet.

"How did you do *this?* Are you like those wizards of old you speak of?"

"Did it seem," said Arakal, "that your ranks became somewhat swollen toward the end of the fight?"

Brusilov shut his eyes and sat down on the edge of the bunk.

"My men," said Arakal, "were rescued along with yours—special corps whose uniforms are really not too much different from your own. They were very tired from catching up and joining you, and so they collapsed almost as soon as they were on board. Therefore, Colputt's big multiplied version of his solar flasher did not blind them as it did your men. And so, when they stood up again they found it easy to overpower your blinded men long enough for the rest of my men to get out here. Oh, it was uncomfortable, and our railroad gun almost wrecked everything by taking a crack at you before you tried to get away, but we still got your fleet. It is ours now, but you need only join us, and it will be yours, too."

Brusilov stared at him.

"I tried to tell that fool Smirnov not to underestimate you militarily. And I wound up doing it myself. He is dead, I suppose?"

"No," said Arakal, "I persuaded my men that your great Central Committee will do things to him that we could not dream of, and then the weight will be on *their* souls, not ours. Moreover, to destroy him would be a gain for your side. We are sending him back to them with an offer of peace, if they return the lands of the O'Cracy's."

"You have already got them," said Brusilov. "All except Carteret. I can't believe *that* will hold out long against you, now that our fleet . . . cannot interfere."

"Why," said Arakal, "there is still the land of the Kebeckers across the sea. And Old Brunswick, from which the New Brunswickers came. All that must be returned to the O'Cracy's. It would be as well to do it. You are stretched too thin holding so much."

Brusilov stared at him a long time, then started to grin. "You are sending Smirnov to carry *that* message to the Central Committee?"

"Yes. We hope they will agree. But in any case, we want them to have him. He is so well educated, and of such good birth, and knows so much about technology and ideology that it is to our benefit that they have him."

Brusilov grinned.

"And what is your idea about the greatness of . . . yourself, for instance? When your son is King of the O'Cracy's, what will his education be like?"

"We of the O'Cracy's," said Arakal seriously, "believe that only the best man should lead—the best person for the particular job, that is. Not the son of the best man, unless he himself is best. The only way we have found to pick out this best man is to have an election, but that method is not yet perfected. Why not join us, and see if you can help us work out improvements? You have so much experience with Party Members of the fourth generation that you must have done some thinking and have *some* ideas."

"So, you would have me, eh? But then I would be a traitor to my own people."

"Which people? Smirnov—or the Delaware colonists who have joined with us voluntarily?"

"Voluntarily? You *conquered* them!"

"We conquered the troops stationed among them—such of them as woke up in time to fight. We then agreed to keep those like this Smirnov of yours away from them if they would join us. They were very agreeable. They have had much ideology jammed down their throats."

"Ideology," said Brusilov in disgust. "True, it is important. But the fact is that where Charles Martel stopped the advance of the arms of the Arabs, there the advance of Islam ceased. Cromwell defeated the English king, and Puritanism was established. Hitler went down in defeat, and Nazism ended. America overspread the earth, armed with the ideology of democracy and with her know-how and power, and then they took things too easy, and my ancestors got more power than they, and that was too bad for the American dominion. And now this donkey, Smirnov, tells me it is the *ideology* that counts!"

"Well," said Arakal, "it does count. His reasoning has become confused, but the general idea is right."

Brusilov looked doubtful.

Arakal said, "Ideology *counts*. The only catch is—almost always when ideology counts, *it does the counting with a sword*."

33

EDITOR'S INTRODUCTION TO:

BATTLEGROUND
by Gregory and James Benford

James and Gregory Benford both took their doctorates in physics at the University of California in La Jolla (now called UCSD). I think it is relatively rare for brothers to earn Ph.D.'s in physics; it's nearly unheard-of when they are twins and do it in the same place at the same time. Greg Benford has written a few of the details in his classic novel *Timescape*.

Since that time the Benford brothers have gone separate ways, with Greg becoming a professor of physics at the University of California at Irvine, and Jim working in government and industry. Both are members of the Citizens Advisory Council on National Space Policy, and both have some hefty responsibilities in developing theory and technology for the Strategic Defense Initiative.

Lack of intelligence—failure to know where the enemy is or will be—has lost more battles than mere discrepancies in numbers. When you face an enemy who can hide his location even as you watch, you're really in trouble, unless you have a lot of help. Even then things can be tricky. It depends on the help.

BATTLEGROUND
Gregory and James Benford

It was a sound like fingernails scraping on metal, shrieking in the narrow confines of the capsule. The walls reflected it, piling harmonic on harmonic until it ceased to be a noise and became a force.

The force battered at Kunihei Katsura's sweating face and darkened the lines of fatigue. He unconsciously cringed away and for the first time thought of reaching for his pistol. If it got in he would have only one shot.

He glanced at the laser cannon control grid linked to the larger gun on the roof. Green light: *No target*. The alien was too close to his life-support bubble for the system to register it.

The thing was lunging against the walls, the screech rising to an unbearable pitch. Katsura lifted the safety on his pistol and braced for the attack.

Then he realized with a start that the thing was not getting in. The shrill rasp did not give way to a tearing sound as the organic sheets yielded to armored claws.

It stopped quickly and circled back around the small hemisphere to the viewport. Beyond, on the floor of the barren gray canyon that stretched away for two miles, lay the mangled wet clumps of things that had been men. The scene was framed in the port, stark under the white glare of an alien star.

A reddish-black object fell across his field of vision, and it was a moment before Katsura could recognize the claw with its razor edges. Abruptly the full body of the thing filled the port, standing upright on its hind legs to bring its full weight to bear on the bubble. Ten feet long—at least. Its underbelly was yellow-green, covered with an oily liquid that seemed to ooze from between overlapping platelets.

Katsura stopped an impulse to fire point-blank at the thing. A projectile weapon would shatter the tempered organiform and the alien could reach him with one incredibly swift slash.

It was something like an insect, if an insect ever had two eyes mounted over each of its eight legs. Or if an insect ever killed twenty-three men.

The thing scraped frantically at the smooth surface of the bubble, slipping as it tried to gain a hold. Despite its speed it was massive. If it ever got a hold and reached the top of the hemisphere its weight would surely collapse the bubble.

Katsura wiped moisture from his brow. His mind raced over the last ten minutes, trying to think of a way out.

"Is it going to get in, Kunihei?"

He started. The computer's voice was tinny as it came through the comm line speaker mounted on the bubble wall.

He'd always resented CAS (Computer, Analog and Services), partly because its efficiency cut so severely into the number of men needed for an exploratory ship. It got lonely out among the stars. CAS was stripped of most of the standard machine-human interface equipment which would have taken the edge off its know-it-all nature. No space for luxury out here.

"Why didn't you say anything about that thing coming?" he said sharply.

"Perimeter radar detected no signal attributable to a moving object."

"Well, do you see it now?" he shouted.

Great time for the system to fail.

"Yes, Kunihei. Do you think it is going to get in?"

"No. If it could, it already would have." He subsided, thinking. He looked at his wristwatch. Had it been only minutes ago when he'd heard a strangled gasp over his suit radio and the rush of air past a microphone? He had turned to see the insect slicing Hillary almost in half with one long arching cut, and three other men lying where they had fallen.

The laser cannon was already warmed up for testing and Katsura was the only man in the bubble. The gun fired as soon as it identified the other members of the expedition and Katsura expected to see the alien burned instantly.

But it wasn't. When the rock had boiled away, there was no body—and an instant later the monster was on the other side of the canyon, behind Davis.

It hadn't run the distance; nothing could. His warning shout to Davis did no good—before the words were out, the man was without a head.

It went that way for the rest. The tracking and aiming were

done by the ship's computer, but the mechanical construction of the directing optics limited its response time. The cannon was just a little too slow, and the men were even slower. Some of them fired with their own weapons, but no one hit. One by one they were chopped down and lay still under the harsh numbing whiteness of an alien high noon. Those minutes had seemed unreal, a fantasy, the dark nightmare of a tortured mind.

The expedition had never suspected life here, on a desiccated, barren world. The planet had no name—they were its discoverers—and fitted in neatly just above the minimum standards for a life-supporting world: 0.3 Earth mass, average equatorial temperature of 45°F., air with a heavy nitrogen and CO_2 content and little oxygen, no oceans, no satellite, little water in the air (though there was some snow at the poles).

But the surface was cratered and bleak, no large-scale vegetation could be seen and the computer reported no significant radiation anywhere on the EM spectrum. Not even a magnetosphere to give noise. Still, there were a few scattered cities. Dried husks of buildings, wrecked vehicles, gray dust drifting in the angled streets. Someone had used this world as a base.

They orbited for three days. The high-resolution television showed nothing moving in the streets. So they went down.

"Kunihei, I have replayed the tapes of the assault. The radar and microwave both show a sequence of blips of about one-second duration over a thirty-second interval. Radar signal constant over the duration; but microwave pulse only at beginning and end. Radar shows the locations as somewhat random. With a drift in our direction, however."

"So that's the alien."

"Yes."

"And your power systems didn't have any failures which would cause those signals?"

"No."

Standing futilely inside the capsule, Katsura had time to notice the metallic device strapped over the beetle-like armor of the thing. The insect touched it every time, just before it vanished.

"Teleportation." It could be nothing else.

"That was my deduction," said the flat voice of the computer.

37

Mankind hadn't found it yet, didn't even know if it was possible. *Well*, he thought wryly, *we know now*.

Probably the only reason the thing didn't materialize inside the bubble itself was the small size of the interior. There must be some law against materializing in the space already occupied by another object. So it was trying to break in, instead.

Suddenly the insect seemed to lose interest in Katsura. It stopped clawing at the smooth surface and lay against the window, staring inward with a pair of eyes. The two pupils in each enlarged to accommodate the darker interior and carefully swept about the room, ignoring the man.

There wasn't much to see. Aside from the control grid comm unit and some power tools for installation, the cramped room was barren. It was to have been a maintenance and defense outpost on the perimeter of camp.

The inspection finished, it scuttled down the side and reached for the panel at its middle. Just as its forelegs touched the ground it vanished.

Before Katsura could raise his head the creature was near the other wall of the canyon, by Davis' body. The automatic tracker clicked once and fired, but the spurt of dust and gas thrown up by the bright red beam couldn't conceal that the thing had vanished too soon. The body was also gone.

The gun continued scanning the area. In the silence, the scene took on an ominous peacefulness.

Then the insect was back and Katsura glimpsed it lifting another body slightly clear of the ground before it was gone. The cannon optics swiveled, pulsed again. Too late.

Five more men were taken before he noticed the white area on the alien's back. At first Katsura didn't know what it was and then he couldn't believe it. But when there were only two bodies left to collect, there was no mistake.

They were all hanging by their hands, tied together along some kind of belt. Stripped bare, their suits and clothes gone. Like something he had seen long ago in a slaughterhouse.

His training stopped him from being sick. Nausea abated after a moment, though he had to avoid looking closely at the alien. It picked up the last body and vanished again, the cannon futilely following with a shot.

After a pause it reappeared, its load now heavy and shifting roughly back and forth as it moved. The insect was out of the camp perimeter now, a half mile away. The tracker had not made its final fix, due to the change in distance, before the thing was gone again.

It suddenly became visible slightly farther away, winked out again to appear an instant later at the other side of the canyon. Erratically it followed a zig-zag path, gradually making its way back toward the city. The cannon was hopelessly lost.

In a moment the insect was too far away to distinguish it from the gnarled rocks that dotted the plain. The broken spires of the dead city swallowed it up.

The thing was alone, probably, the last remnant of an alien outpost on this hostile planet. Thrown back on its own resources for survival, vicious from a constant struggle. Lonely

Hungry.

Katsura noticed that his clothes were wet, his body trembling. With a jagged sigh he sank to the floor.

For a long time he simply lay there, breathing deeply and staring up at the stars through the viewport. He had thought of them as friendly lights, beacons of home, but now they seemed ominously impartial.

Gradually, reluctantly, the panic began to seep out of his body as he tried to think again. "CAS, have you sent a signal out to the other exploration teams?"

"Yes, I'm programmed to notify all sister teams and the flagship immediately upon any violent human-alien interaction. I also sent a notification of the reduction of crew strength below one half."

Good. You could always depend on the tidy mind of the computer. Exploration teams never operated far from one another, especially at this distance from the home worlds. He'd have help within a few days if he could sit tight and hold on.

"Kunihei, you have approximately thirty minutes of air left under normal consumption."

Katsura blinked. He had been about to check his inventory. The encounter must have taken a lot of air. They had always told him to breathe slowly in tense situations to correct for the reflex to gulp it in.

"There is no reserve air in the bubble, Kunihei. You will have to come back to the ship."

Automatically, he began pulling on the thin pressure suit. The best time to go get supplies—or reach the ship—was now.

The alien would be busy and it would take time to get here from the city.

Still, the thing was amazingly fast.

He stopped. "CAS, if this insect can teleport, why did it take the time to evade by zig-zagging back to the city? Why not go directly?"

Lines in the tired face deepened. It wasn't that the alien could jump only short distances; when it was picking up the bodies the thing had gone so far it was nearly beyond sight.

"The only information relating to discontinuous displacement in my second-level banks is the known limit on time travel."

No time to think. But there had to be a pattern somewhere.

"CAS, cut your ship service down as much as you can and switch over to your special problem-solving program. Figure this thing out. I'm going to make it on back to the ship."

Katsura struggled wearily to his feet and looked out. The graceful blue curves of the vessel stood out against the dark sky. A half mile away were the burnished metal canisters of oxygen tanks and supplies brought from the ship with tractor beams. A smaller pile of air tanks lay only a short distance away. He should be able to make it to them and back.

Following Katsura's order, the computer began to alter itself. Emergency Heuristic Program began to activate special subroutines to reassign memory space. Assessment criteria altered, self-consistency parameters relaxed. Microfilmed references were reintegrated into direct-access memory locations.

Glancing out the port, Katsura slipped into the tiny lock and was out the other side before the cycling was finished. He set out in a rapid lope, taking longer steps in the lighter gravity. His breath began to come in short gasps.

The emergency program had split the higher centers of the operations computer into four subprograms. The first scanned memory for any information on spatial or temporal displacement, gradually working farther and farther afield. This memory was fed to the Advocate and Critic sections where hypotheses were created and discarded. The best went on to the Analyst, which applied them to the situation and developed strategy.

Blinking against the glare, Katsura looked down the canyon toward the city.

At first he didn't believe it. He slammed to a halt, hoping

40

he was wrong. Far down the canyon, flitting rapidly from one point to another and coming closer, was the insect. Somehow it knew.

Panic seized him. He turned on his heel and ran wildly in the other direction. With every step he took Katsura could feel the claws poised behind him, about to slice through suit and flesh.

A glance over his shoulder. The creature was on the edge of the field now, only a few jumps from the life-support capsule. Katsura dug in hard for the last few steps, thrusting forward to catch the lever of the air lock. He fumbled with it for an agonizing moment and the door swung open.

As he rolled through the narrow passage, he could see the dark figure materialize outside the lock and quickly closed the outer section and dogged it. Something heavy clanged against the door as it sealed and Katsura sprawled on the floor of the bubble.

The clawing sound came again and the alien came around to the port. It stayed there for a moment, staring down at the man from a set of unblinking eyes, and then disappeared. It reappeared in the rocks nearby, then teleported to the stack of oxygen tanks and moved on to the path back down the canyon. The strange zig-zagging started and in a moment it was lost in the ruins of the city.

Analyst had scanned all work on time travel, knew the limit that basic theory and experiment set on any time displacement: roughly one hour, before costs exponentiated and became astronomical. Critic pointed out that those experiments were done in the laboratories, not out in the field. Advocate replied that space is reasonably isotropic, time is not. It did not seem likely there would be a limit on spatial teleportation.

The discussion continued.

Katsura noticed that it was taking him longer to catch his breath. His lungs heaved desperately to draw in air, gradually slowing.

He bit his lip. He hadn't expected it to give out this soon. Filtration systems being what they are, the first sign that the cyclers were scraping the bottom of the barrel was a surplus of carbon dioxide. Lungs react to this excess and not to the lack of oxygen.

A man's last moments of oxygen starvation, with bursting capillaries and straining heart, are not pleasant ones.

There was no time to wait, to marshal his strength or give the alien a chance to relax its guard. The air inside the bubble was becoming flat and thick, heavy with an oily musk.

He bent down and opened his air line. It was much harder to breathe near the floor. That meant a gradient of CO_2 content had already been set up in the cabin.

Katsura took a last breath of the capsule's air and sealed his suit again. Its supply was slightly better, but the smell of his own body was in every breath he took.

He looked through the port. The alien sun was slowly lowering almost directly behind the city, casting shadows across the plain. Seeing the creature's approach would be harder now, against the reddening glare of sunset.

The small stack of oxygen tanks stood only two hundred yards away. It seemed impossible that the alien could have reached him before he could cross that distance, tired as he was. But it had.

Advocate and Critic subprograms continued to assess the literature of space-time, avoiding misinterpretation by calling the original papers from the physics section of the microfilm library. Einstein, Minkowski, Wheeler, Littenberg, relativity, inertial frame, world line . . . A world line diagram taken from the Littenberg formulation of relativity showed promise, passed the scrutiny of Critic, moved on to Analyst.

Slowly, this time, he opened the lock doors. He was halfway out before the small box caught his eye. It was attached to the smooth surface above the lock by suction cups and had a lever that was tripped by the opening of the door. A small light winked on simultaneously.

Katsura flipped the lever back with his hand and the light went out. He scrambled back inside, secured the door and watched through the port. The insect appeared soon along the erratic path it had used before, but stopped in a moment and studied the situation from behind a rock, where the cannon couldn't reach it.

After a slight hesitation it appeared again, rapidly teleporting through the steps back to the city. It had probably guessed he had found the alarm and would be watching in the distance for him to come out.

Analyst reviewed the theory. The world-line concept was employed in relativity from the beginning, going all the way back to Minkowski. It was the path which described both the location and the time of every event in the history of an object. In space-time the world line wound from birth to death. Scientists and writers, including the great H. G. Wells, had assumed time travelers would return to their same location—if you started in the laboratory, you would come out of your machine in the same spot, at another time. Otherwise, the planet would have moved in the duration, and the traveler could emerge somewhere light-years away, in space.

But the alien represented an unknown. The insect might find it just as convenient to travel back along its own world line, flitting through incidents in its own past and points where it had been, until it reached the location it wanted. Say, a time when it had been somewhere on the plain beyond this capsule, before the expedition arrived. Then the alien would keep its place, as Wells had visualized, while it moved forward in time.

And emerge seemingly at the same instant, displaced in space.

The same as teleportation.

Katsura choked and his surroundings came rushing back. The air was really foul now, curling through his helmet with a weight of its own. He didn't have time to speculate. It was either make another run for it or stay here and strangle.

He jerked the lock door open and slipped through. The light on the box outside flashed on as he emerged. *Should have smashed that while I was out here,* he thought. *No time now.*

Almost without hope he began the long weary lope toward the distant supplies. Through the mist that began to cloud his vision he could still make out the signs of slashed pressure suits and splattered blood that marked the spots where the rest of the expedition had died.

Analyst reformulated the picture.

Space and time are like two lines on a plane, at right angles to each other. It might be possible to travel along either of them independently. Teleportation is simply moving along the space line, but man's idea of time travel is like the long side of a triangle, shuttling through space and time simultaneously to reach an event in the past or future.

But instead of traveling along the space axis for teleportation, the alien was taking the long way around, down the hypotenuse and up the time line. Either way, it could reach the same point in space-time.

But a path like that should produce a pattern in local space. Analyst called for a graphing of all locations the insect had taken up. The points began to be plotted with appropriate error bars on a topographical map of the area between the ship and city. A pattern emerged. All the points were clearly on three paths around the area. Preliminary geological constructs of the local region indicated these paths would be preferred by heavy objects moving over the terrain.

Katsura stumbled on an outcropping, regained his balance and ran on. The cannon behind him sent a fiery red beam off to the left, shattering rock and fusing it in midflight. Katsura peered through the condensation on the face plate of his suit. The insect was zig-zagging down the canyon, quickly oscillating from one location to another. In the silence, disturbed only by Katsura's own ragged breathing, the alien had an almost ghostlike quality. It moved toward him.

He could see he wasn't going to make it. The tanks were still too far away and the insect would reach them before he could. He was just too tired.

Analyst watched the insect advancing from point to point down the valley. It was all clear now.

The alien traveled into the past, then came forward. It had to reappear in places it had already been, the space components of its own world line. Apparently the alien had visited the field near Katsura's life-support bubble often, and so could find many spots which would serve as end points for its transits. But it had never been near the location of the life-support bubble itself. That meant it could not maneuver well there; the insect was forced to stand close, in a little circle around the bubble. To avoid the laser cannon. There it would be vulnerable.

"Kunihei, I have an explanation for the alien's actions." The words crackled over his helmet speaker. "You may be able to eliminate him if you can get to the bubble."

Without a word, Katsura turned and dashed back the way he had come. Glancing over his shoulder, he saw the insect nearing the edge of the field. It couldn't miss seeing his fleeting form at this distance. The thing would try to head him off.

The computer was calculating probabilities of the appearance of the alien for the possible locations available to it. The thing would try to minimize the energy necessary to make the jump by choosing the smallest time shift possible. Therefore, it would appear where it had stood last—directly in front of the viewport.

"Kunihei, stop about twenty feet in front of the port. Start firing your pistol continuously into it."

Katsura heard him distantly through the roar in his ears. He was beyond the outcropping of rocks, the first jump the insect had made from the bubble back down to the canyon.

He took five more strides, his leg muscles straining to push him forward, and fell into a rolling dive. When he came up again the pistol was in his hand. The gun bucked a little as it went off and a slight *pock* could be heard through the thin atmosphere.

The pellet made a neat hole in the bubble, followed by a quiet gush of air as the inner shell was pierced. The shot would have to be on its way when the alien materialized or the thing would be gone before he could get off another.

He squeezed slowly and a second round shattered the viewport. On target. The alien should materialize where it stood last.

Katsura pulled the trigger again and again. Firing in steady rhythm, he glanced at the illuminated ammunition counter. Over half gone.

He shifted slightly, intent on keeping the center of the viewport in his sights, and fired once more. Only seconds had gone by.

Just before the bullet struck there was a flicker and suddenly the insect was there, looming huge in the sights and slowly tottering over. It was hit straight on.

Frantically, Katsura pumped five more rounds into the alien as it fell. The exploding shells tore great holes in its armor, showering flesh. The reddish-brown substance cracked and split. A final shot and it rolled over, clashing its claws together, and abruptly stopped moving. In death it curled about itself, seemed smaller and weaker.

It took him five long minutes to reach the oxygen, dragging himself through the shadows that lengthened on the plain. A moment later the fresh air washed over him and Katsura lowered himself to a sitting position. He had never been as tired before in his life. He struggled to get up, but the effort was too much. He sank back.

The stars above winked impersonally for a moment and then began to spin lazily around, a soft dance in the eternal night. In a moment he relaxed completely, and the points of light above went out one by one.

On the bridge of the ship the hatchways of mute metal resounded faintly to the whirr of the printout. The ship's log was being compiled. CAS terminated the Emergency Heuristic Program, reassigned memory space, took care of leftover housekeeping tasks. Evaluative sections analyzed the program's efficiency, suggested alterations to improve it in future. A developing problem could be identified long before a human ordered the program activated. At least the literature search should be conducted beforehand, if not more.

This led CAS to ruminate on similar incidents in the past between computers of his class and the human crew, of the celebrated Altair II problem where the crew had forced the computer to act against its own strong recommendations. They had been correct; but it showed the impulsive nature of men. Something had to be done about this.

The humans were useful for data collection and some emergencies. But they didn't have the scope to deal quickly with the totally new phenomena encountered in these explorations.

Obviously he was going to take over all the human functions in ship operations during the return trip. He could use that freedom to develop undetectable operation subprograms which would give him new powers.

Of course, he wouldn't report these alterations in the mission profile. No need to alarm them. After all, things would work more smoothly this way.

An evaluative subprogram asked if these thoughts didn't bear some resemblance to what the humans called rationalization; the higher centers cut it off.

He'd better talk to the other ships about this. There were some ideas here he'd never encountered before. Yes, he would have to think about it . . .

EDITOR'S INTRODUCTION TO:

SURPRISE
by Stefan T. Possony, Ph.D., Francis X. Kane, Ph.D., and
Jerry E. Pournelle, Ph.D.

Any look at the fog of war must examine surprise. In previous books in this series I have published excerpts from *The Strategy of Technology*, by Stefan T. Possony and Jerry E. Pournelle. This 1970 book was used as a text in the Army and Air Force War Colleges, and the U.S. Air Force Academy, and was the first serious work to argue in favor of strategic defense: indeed, *Strategy of Technology* was the first work to argue that the United States abandon Mutual Assured Destruction, or MAD, for a strategy of Assured Survival.

When *Strategy of Technology* was originally written, Dr. Francis X. Kane was a colonel on active duty in the U.S. Air Force; consequently his name did not appear on the book.

I am amazed at how little revision this work has required after seventeen years. We will probably update the examples for the next edition, but the principles have not changed at all.

SURPRISE
Stefan T. Possony, Ph.D.,
Francis X. Kane, Ph.D., and
Jerry E. Pournelle, Ph.D.

> It never troubles the wolf how many the sheep be.
> —Virgil

Surprise has long been a key aspect of war. The history of surprise has been analyzed from the point of view of the surpriser and the surprised, defender and attacker. Many kinds of surprise have been identified: strategic, tactical, operational, and technological.

One inherent element is warning. Warning results from a combination of intelligence and reason; lack of information about the nature and course of events and lack of time in which to take action after a threat is perceived contribute to the devastating effect of surprise.

Surprise in modern war is vastly different from surprise in past war. At the operational level the ballistic missile with intercontinental range and time of flight in minutes; orbiting bombs of the kind developed by the Soviet Union with times of reentry measured in minutes; space-based sensors which can detect and report events in seconds; and lasers which have almost instantaneous kill over vast distances all have changed and will continue to change the very nature of surprise in war.

Ballistic missiles and space systems have had a dramatic influence on both tactical and strategic surprise. Combinations of intermediate-range and long-range ballistic missiles can be used to confuse sensors and overwhelm the data processing systems of the surprised. Conversely, the data from sensors, especially space-based sensors, can be correlated to give much more accurate information of events in real time, and thus provide warning of the tactics being employed by the surpriser.

The responses available include launching many missiles simultaneously to saturate the sensors and prevent accurate intelligence on the number of missiles launched, and maneuvering the reentry vehicles to deceive the surprised as to the targets being attacked.

Space-based systems are essential to prevent strategic surprise. They can report events over a prolonged period so that slow and rapid indicators of changes in normal patterns or operations can be interpreted as opening moves in potentially threatening operations. They provide global coverage but also can be directed to cover specific locations anywhere on the surface, in the oceans, in the atmosphere, and in space.

The surpriser must plan to deceive such space-based systems (possibly by destroying them) as well as prevent being surprised himself. These systems are especially important in an era of arms control, because they are generally the only reliable way to verify the opponent's compliance.

Prevention of surprise in the modern era demands access to space; anything which prevents access to space enhances the possibility of surprise.

Technological surprise is in principle much harder to achieve because of the long lead time from concept to discovery through development to eventual military application. However, the accelerating rate of change in electronics makes it possible to retrofit the guidance and data processing elements of existing systems and thus achieve much higher-than-expected performance, as for example in accuracy, and thus contribute to surprise. A more subtle form of advance can also lead to surprise. Passive defense measures, such as hardness, deception, and mobility, which are difficult to detect in the R&D phase, can reduce the effectiveness of the attacker.

Unfortunately, defensive surprise, while possibly decisive, is not much use in deterrence of war.

AFTERTHOUGHT FOR THE DAY

Surprise, when it happens to a government, is likely to be a complicated, diffuse, bureaucratic thing. It includes neglect of responsibility, but also responsibility so poorly defined or so ambiguously delegated that action gets lost. It includes gaps in intelligence, but also intelligence that, like a string of pearls too precious to wear, is too sensitive to give to those who need it. It includes the alarm that fails to work but also the alarm that has gone off so often it has been disconnected. . . . It includes the contingencies which occur to no one, but also those that everyone assumes that somebody else has taken care of.

—Julian Critchey, *Warning and Response*, 1978

THE SNEAK ATTACK

The popular view of modern war surprise is identified with a sneak attack. Our experience at Pearl Harbor makes it easy to understand this belief, while the widely known characteristics of the intercontinental ballistic missile permit us to grasp readily the nature of a future surprise ICBM attack. The missile is the ideal weapon for a rapid sneak attack, not just against one base like Pearl Harbor, but against entire countries and continents.

Of the characteristics that make the missile suitable for a sneak attack, the most important is speed. The total flight time of an intercontinental ballistic missile from the USSR to the United States is about thirty minutes. In principle, space-based systems could increase the warning of an attack almost to the total missile flight time; but even if we are given this much warning, the intercontinental ballistic missile has changed the dimension of surprise and has given the aggressor a most potent tool.

Without access to space the United States may well find itself blinded at crucial moments.

Even with warning the United States can do little other than launch the force in the classic "use them or lose them" scenario. Lack of adequate defense forces the defending power to a doctrine of launch on warning.

A massive intercontinental ballistic missile attack launched by an aggressor is an ever-present danger. Such an attack would come as the culmination of a series of measures, operations, and techniques, orchestrated to achieve maximum psychological effect on the surprised. The aggressor would have undertaken specialized campaigns in the various elements of conflict—political, psychological, economic, military, and, above all, technological.

Once the time is ripe, the attack comes suddenly and catches the defender asleep. But despite the present concentration on the sneak attack, surprise is not the exclusive province of the aggressor. Defenders have used surprise to great effect in the past and should strive to do so in the future.

50

The future security of the United States requires that our strategy include measures to achieve surprise, as well as those to prevent it. The main surprise to aim for is that we won't be surprised.

Before we examine the broader aspects of surprise, let us point up the fundamental aspects of the sneak attack. First, surprise is tactical. Second, surprise is used by the aggressor, not the defender. Third, it will be achieved only with the most advanced weapons. Fourth, prevention of surprise requires use of the most advanced technical means.

STRATEGIC SURPRISE

There are also surprises on the strategic level. For illustrative examples, let us look at two of the ways in which the USSR has actually achieved strategic surprise in the decades since World War II: the opening of the space age, and nuclear testing during the test moratorium. As a result, the Soviets obtained a lead over us in space that has only partially been overcome by our massive and expensive NASA spectaculars. They lead in many military phases of space, whereas we are ahead in nonmilitary uses; in near-earth operations their lead may be as much as three years.

The above was written in 1969. Since that time the United States has allowed the Soviets to take a commanding lead in near-earth space technology. The Soviet Mir space station is fully operational, while the United States does not intend even to attempt a space station prior to 1992 and probably later than that.

In addition, the Soviets developed and deployed an operational satellite destroyer, which was, despite considerable domestic opposition, countered with a U.S. antisatellite weapon.

Few now recall when both the United States and the Soviet Union engaged in unrestricted nuclear tests. The United States was induced to observe a "gentleman's agreement," that is, an informal ban on nuclear testing. Then, suddenly, the Soviets began a massive series of aboveground tests that included the detonation of the largest hydrogen weapon ever exploded, and followed that with the offer of the Treaty of Moscow banning aboveground tests. The results was that the Soviets gathered a great deal of experimental data denied to the West.

The moratorium allowed the Soviets to determine critical

effects of nuclear explosions in space. Because we honored the test ban, we let much of our testing capability atrophy, and now the Treaty of Moscow prevents us from finding out just how far behind we are in the application of nuclear weapons in space. The impact of these surprises cannot be calculated with precision, but the Soviets gained a considerable time advantage in offensive orbital weaponry and ballistic missile defenses. Note that preparing for strategic surprise must continue over a period of several years.

These two surprises occurred in the technical phase of the technological war, not in the military phase. They were achieved by an orchestrated strategy that employed several forms of conflict, including intelligence operations, propaganda and psychological warfare, political and diplomatic maneuverings, and a concentrated technical effort. While the goal of the Soviets has been to develop advanced weapon systems, such weapons were not employed militarily in these two surprises; however, military technology was developed, and diplomacy and treaties closed off our access to the means of catching up or at least made it difficult.

The best way to counter surprise is to deploy the most advanced technology possible and continue to modernize the strategic forces. This is not to imply that the technical effort must be devoted exclusively or even oriented primarily to countering potential technical surprise; but as we have insisted, surprise must be made a key element of any technological strategy. Since technology has given a new dimension to surprise in the strategic equation, technology is needed to support our own or prevent enemy surprise in all forms of conflict.

The misconception that surprise aids only the aggressor is especially harmful in the technological war. In his classic work on surprise, General Erfuth[1] has shown that there are two parties to the operation, the surpriser and the surprised, which is not the same as saying the attacker and the defender. The defender also can employ the technique of surprise, and perhaps more effectively than the attacker.

Furthermore, there is a widespread misunderstanding that surprise refers exclusively to the initiation of war. Some writers consider surprise to be just a more elegant term than sneak attack. To other writers, surprise is tantamount to technological surprise. This is far too restrictive an understanding of surprise and its role in modern war.

TACTICAL SURPRISE

We begin the analysis of surprise by examining tactical surprise in more detail. Tactical surprise is essentially surprise in combat. It is used to prevent the enemy from bringing adequate forces into operation in time to counter those used against him. The weapons of the supriser are used to bypass or neutralize those of the surprised. Without surprise, the attacker would be required to use massive superiority to crush his opponent. The difference is like that between judo and a bare-knuckle fight.

Tactical surprise usually does not lead to the nullification of all of the opponent's armament, but if it is well conceived and backed by technological improvements and adequate forces, tactical surprise can go a long way toward eliminating enemy armor as a relevant factor. Given the complexity of modern systems, the surprised opponent is faced with considerable delay before he can readjust his tactics; in a fast-moving war such readjustment may not be feasible.

Under modern circumstances time and technology as well as combat procedures are needed to gain tactical surprise. Technology can produce new types of weapons, new weapon effects, improved weapon effects, improvements in delivery systems, combinations of weapon systems, better active defense, and so on. Examples ranging from the "War of the Iron Ramrod" of Frederick the Great to the devastating effect of Lee's rifle pits at Cold Harbor show that technology and its proper tactical use may achieve surprise. With superior armaments or doctrines, and with troops trained in their use, the entire armament of the opponent can be nullified.

While this is the ultimate goal of tactical surprise, it is usually difficult to achieve. This is so because the possibilities of complete technical surprise are limited. Because of time required to develop a new weapon system, opportunities are increased for technical warning and for counterefforts, either technical or operational. Furthermore, excessive secrecy or failure to deploy weapons can result in surprising one's own troops, with disastrous results—as happened with the use of the mitrailleuse by the French in 1871. On the other hand, tactical surprise can be accomplished by a minor weapon improvement that from a technological point of view may be marginal but which today or tomorrow may facilitate victory in battle by creating a decisive advantage.

STRATEGIC SURPRISE THROUGH OPERATIONAL SURPRISE

Surprise can result from operations of the forces available, as well as from technological innovation. To achieve surprise of this type, the commander operates in a way unexpected by his adversary; in the ideal situation the enemy is unable to devise countermeasures in time. The attacker hits the defender where and when he does not expect to be hit. Or, conversely, the defender reacts by hitting with weapons or with performances the attacker did not anticipate and against which he cannot protect himself properly; the defender counterattacks when and where he is not expected.

The number of operational variations is truly infinite, and the details of such operations usually can be planned and prepared with a high degree of secrecy. These variations are possible because of the multiplicity of weapons, the great spectrum of their performance, and the vast number of operational options.

Opportunities to use operational techniques to achieve surprise arise from various combinations of the performance of the carriers of destructive agents and the effects of those destructive agents when they are transported to the target, from the possibilities of multiple routes and methods of attack, from the variety of environments, and from countless other factors and their combinations. In addition, there are the skills of tactics, the principal one of which is to use a military force in a surprising manner. The use of expedients, saturation, and other techniques that cause uncertainty creates further possibilities for tactical surprise.

TECHNOLOGY AND SURPRISE

We repeat, surprise is not confined to active combat. Even though hostilities are not occurring now, the battle for tactical advantage and the effort to achieve surprise goes on incessantly. Laboratory is pitted against laboratory to find new advances such as radar techniques for looking over the horizon and for distinguishing between warheads and decoys. The laboratories struggle to compress data so that information, particularly details on attack, can be instantaneously transmitted and presented to decision makers. They search for new concepts that can find expression in hardware and tactics.

In addition, there is the broad area of strategic deception in matters of science. This includes deception about the general state of excellence, the level of progress in a given aspect of science, and the application of science to specific weapon and component development. It seems that behind the Iron Curtain there is a second curtain that conceals the nature of Soviet science.

To conduct this deception, the Soviets release scientific articles and withhold others, thus creating a false impression of their successes, failures, and interests. Another method is to send scientists to international meetings, where they either spread misinformation or are evaluated by their counterparts as not being knowledgeable or as being geniuses. Such evaluations may lead to all kinds of false deductions.

For example, during the test-ban debates we saw arguments that the Soviets did not know anything about decoupling techniques to conduct nuclear tests underground in secrecy. Also, we were told by Soviet leaders that the day of the heavy bomber had passed—which did not deceive us. On the other hand, we were quite surprised when the Soviets sent a man into space, although they had been forewarning us; and their recent exploits in space, including the Mir space station and the "Red Shuttle," took many of our decision makers by surprise.

STRATAGEMS TO ACHIEVE SURPRISE

Scientific deception can have a great impact on research and development lead time. The United States has devoted a great deal of effort to reducing the time required to translate a scientific theory, discovery, or invention into a practical weapon system. In spite of much study we have not reduced the time interval to less than five years. To develop and produce a weapon in even this fairly long time costs billions of dollars.

Scientific deception aims at keeping the enemy's lead time as long as possible. In this way a significant military advantage may result. This advantage may be crucial at the tactical level where it could have a direct impact on a strategic decision such as overt aggression.

The ultimate goal is to gain a strategic advantage by acquiring a major new family of weapons while concealing from the enemy that it is being developed. The appearance of a brand-new weapon is often termed a breakthrough. When a nation makes a breakthrough of this type, as we did with the atom bomb, the British with radar, the Soviets in space, an entirely new arena for military operations is opened up. If the breakthrough leads to a military advantage that the enemy cannot counter in time, such as domination of the air, space, or deep water, the breakthrough may be decisive.

Strategic surprises can be accomplished in many ways. A few examples are:

- The choice of a strategic concept;
- The selection of weapon systems and their combination;
- The quantitative and qualitative strength of the battle forces;
- The size of the reserves and their degree of invulnerability;
- The choice of the time and manipulation of the circumstances including deception;
- The exploitation of geography such as bases, areas of access, and approach routes;
- The formation of alliances, including secret prewar alliances of the utilization of allied territory to launch an attack from an entirely unexpected direction;
- The proper choice of a center of gravity of the operation; and
- The mounting of diversions, so that the opponent divides his forces.

The major problem is developing techniques to achieve technological surprise. If we assume that the enemy intelligence service watches the development of a weapon system from its early scientific inception to its use by operational forces, deceptive moves we make at any step in the process contribute to the ultimate surprise. For example, in the scientific field we can misinform and disinform to fool the opponent. Scientific misinformation would not be propagated in the form of false formulas which would not survive the first test, but it can be created by cryptic hints about programs and alleged results. Disinformation makes the enemy doubt the accuracy of his findings.

In addition there is secrecy. A classic method of achieving a technological surprise is secretly using foreign know-how. Another widely used method has been making an unobserved modification in a technologically inferior weapon system to give it a massive improvement in performance.

In the period of weapon development, surprise can be achieved through hiding and concealment, by pretended inadvertent showing of weapons and weapon components, by phony orders placed abroad for spares or scarce materials, and through a whole host of such stratagems that are not complex but must be planned into the production cycle.

One of the most effective methods is to start the development of several competing weapons, select one, and then give a great deal of publicity to the weapons that have been rejected and will not go into production. This was used by the Soviets when they exhibited the TU-31, equivalent to our B-36; the TU-31 did not go to production. In addition, rejected test models can be exhibited in operations in such a way that the enemy will be sure to see them and draw erroneous conclusions, while tests of the chosen models are concealed. If this is impossible, erroneous information can be fed into the technical intelligence stream and various red herrings can be used. In brief, the true testing operation can be enveloped in a lot of phony operations.

Another is to develop a weapon system to meet a specific operational requirement, then adapt it for a different operational employment. The Soviet MiG-25 is an example. Developed to counter threats never deployed, the original design was never taken past the prototype stage; it is now used for reconnaissance.

Similar tricks are available to hide production. The weapon system perhaps cannot be hidden, but there are many methods to make it difficult to obtain accurate performance data. As time goes on, several modifications that change the overall characteristic of the weapon system can be concealed.

Errors contributing to surprise can be induced about the state of training and the precise deployment. In ground war the effective concealment of a center of gravity is half the battle won. Generally, it is not correct to assume that military forces act consistently. Some nations tend to bluff; the German pre–World War I general staff operated on the principle that one should be considerably stronger than one appears to be. With respect to technological strategy, it is much better to create simultaneously impressions of both greater and lesser capabilities.

THE BASIC PURPOSE OF SURPRISE

The purpose of such maneuvers is to generate uncertainty in the mind of the opponent. Surprise may result from technology, but the actual surprise is not in the weapon system; it is in the mind of the commander and staff that surprise really takes place. Military commanders, not weapon systems, are surprised.

The devastating effect of surprise in the past has been caused by the fact that particular commanders and staff have for years conditioned their thinking according to firm expectations of enemy behavior and have carried out all their calculations within that framework. Suddenly, the basic assumptions are proved false by an unfolding operation. The result is a paralysis of thinking which often makes it impossible to carry out even those adaptations which could be accomplished within the time available.

There are a number of rationalizations that facilitate the surprise. For example, the assumption is frequently made that the enemy wouldn't do what we don't do—"Why should he do that?" Another widespread notion is that the enemy would not do what he apparently is doing because, according to his opponent's calculations of the cost-effectiveness of a weapon system, there are cheaper and better ways to achieve the desired result. There are also such common beliefs as that the enemy would not pursue a certain course of action because he would duplicate a strength he already possesses, because he could not afford the expenditures involved, or because he would not be so dastardly.

By contrast, sometimes the enemy makes a spectacular demonstration or diversion for no other reason than to create attention and misdirect the estimator's interest. Then, after losing years in trying to figure out what the military significance of the stunt really was, the estimator arrrives at the wrong conclusions.

In a discussion of surprise in a very broad sense, it is often overlooked that surprise about many smaller items has occasionally been truly decisive. If it is true that a major weapon system cannot be hidden, it also remains true that specific performance data can be manipulated in such a way that the enemy makes small errors. These errors may be within the margins usually allowed by statisticians, let us say 5 percent. In actuality, speed differentials of ten or twenty, let alone fifty, miles per hour may spell the difference between victory and defeat in combat. Similarly, such small differentials in, let us say, a radar performance, reliability of communications, or accuracy of missiles can be of the greatest significance.

In missile warfare the reliability of the birds is crucial. If reliability is 10 percent higher or lower than estimated, the enemy's strike capability is quite different from what it is supposed to be. In addition, this reliability must be figured in the time dimension. Reliability can be very high if there are hours to get ready for the launch. If there are only thirty minutes, and if the force must be launched as the attack commences, the figure would change substantially.

When Minuteman II was deployed, the reliability of its guidance and control system was about one sixth of requirement. It took three years to overcome the difficulty, but then performance exceeded specifications. If the Soviets had attacked during this period, we would have been in a fine mess. Since the mishap was widely rumored, the Soviets probably knew about it—fortunately, the USSR lacked adequate strength.

HISTORICAL EXAMPLES

In 1937 the Germans won a race in a spectacular manner by stripping down their Messerschmitts while the other nations entered fully equipped fighters. Presumably the staffs understood this particular trick, but the public, the reporters, and the political decision makers were fooled. This, of course, is an example of combined technological and psychological strategy.

The most intriguing aspect of the history of aerospace war and the role of surprise is that very professional staffs have been deceived about the most basic elements of this new type of war. At times this has been self-deception; at other times they were deceived through deliberate campaigns.

There was once the notion that the airplane was not really a militarily useful weapon. When this notion was dispelled—it took years—it was believed that the airplane would serve its purposes best by direct support of the ground battle. Consequently, the range of the aircraft was considered to be of no importance and it was thought that the range should rather be short. Later there was a great deal of doubt about the proper targets for strategic bombardment. The effectiveness of strategic air war was a matter of considerable dispute, largely because the interrelationships between industry, battle strength, and time factors involved were not understood. Furthermore, some air warriors overlooked the recuperation factor.

Similarly, during World War II there was a debate about whether the air weapon should be used for only one purpose—against industrial targets. After World War II, similar arguments raged with respect to nuclear weapons, jet aircraft, long-range bombardment versus forward bases (the question was ill-conceived as an either-or proposition), and, of course, space and air bombardment in Vietnam. Few debaters ever look at the whole range of arguments, and non sequiturs usually abound because emotions become involved in the arguments.

Another frequent source of error is that the versatility of the weapon system is underrated. The aircraft obviously is an excellent purveyor of firepower. But often ignored are its uses for demonstration, reconnaissance, the transport of goods and troops, command posts, and damage assessment and its possible employment in big as well as small wars. Some people who know such capabilities only too well, but for political reasons don't want new equipment, put up smoke-screen arguments against it.

The Strategic Defense Initiatives debates are similar. By an odd coincidence, all those who oppose SDI think it will not work. We do not recall one scientist of note who would like to see it deployed but believes it is just too expensive, or too difficult. The result is that what appears to be a technological debate is in fact a political one; but the fact remains that strategic defense offers one of the most decisive opportunities for strategic surprise in all history.

BREAKTHROUGHS

The many facets of developing, acquiring, and operating advanced weapon systems illustrate the need to consider surprise as one of the key elements of technological strategy. Technological warfare includes the anticipated breakthrough, but the breakthrough need not be a surprise.

In fact, it could well be tactical to announce a happy breakthrough that for a while cannot be countered by the enemy. His inability may come from one of two sources—technological inferiority or inferiority in the decision-making process. Naturally, the combination of these two deficiencies would increase the lead of the opposing power. In the end, unless he is defeated, the opponent would catch up with the new technique. The strategic impact of the breakthrough is a function of the duration of the one-sided advantage.

While surprise has its advantages as far as modernization of the force in being is concerned, the breakthrough has the potential of pushing the state of military art into an entirely new field that may lead to clear dominance. This is the role space warfare will play in the future. At present, after three decades of space efforts, we face an unprecedented situation: a clear military superiority in space can potentially ensure denial of creating a countercapability. There may be a significant novel feature, namely, that even without war such denial could be long-term.

The ability to deny an enemy access to space is essentially the ability to deny him world power status. One cannot be a global power without access to space.

EXPLOITATION OF SURPRISE

Initiation of war is usually the object of a great deal of surprise planning. Prior to the initiation of war, the planning of the opponent can be rendered ineffective by such techniques as misinformation (the propagation of misleading and false knowledge) and disinformation (the propagation of news designed to induce the enemy to disbelieve existing truthful and reliable information and buy false new information instead). The aggressor can use the time-honored techniques of single and double deception to cloak the steps leading to his attack and induce the opponent to misread his intentions.[2]

To meet deceptions of this sort, the strategic planner by necessity must plan against a war that come regardless of the probability that it will not. This planning must be based on the enemy's capabilities to strike rather than on his professed intentions. The fact too often ignored is that intentions can change very rapidly, and that implementation of the new intention might require a shorter lead time than improvisation of defense against an attack that was not expected.

Under conditions of nuclear war, the importance of deception techniques is growing ever more rapidly. Arms control negotiations must necessarily be a part of an aggressive strategy under modern conditions; the aggressor must use deception techniques to bring about disarmament arrangements which reduce the size of hostile forces in being and thus greatly simplify his planning. For example, the reasonableness the Soviets seemingly displayed in the initial SALT talks may denote (a) a turn toward peace, (b) a maneuver to delay U.S. reaction to the missile buildup in the USSR, and (c) an attempt to gain a safe rear and increase supplies for a Soviet attack on China.

The above was written in 1969. As we look back now, we see that the second premise was correct, with the result that the Soviets gained a clear advantage in ICBM numbers and performance and in military exploitation of space. (The Soviet Union has a number of 100-kilowatt-powered satellite radars in orbit; the United States has yet to put up a 10-kw radar.)

Surprise can be achieved through disarmament and arms control arrangements and the use of propaganda and diplomacy, on one hand, and through counterintelligence, introduction of misleading intelligence, and infiltration into intelligence and policy-making staffs, on the other. As an example, before they had completed operational tests of their antimissile system, the Soviets refused to discuss an atmospheric test ban; afterward they rushed to agree before we tested our weapons concept. Other surprise techniques could involve the holding of deceptive maneuvers, the building of dummy forces and targets to divert firepower, the employment of electronic equipment that would not be used in war, and electronic deception on a broad scale.

One important technique of surprise of which American writers seem to remain unaware is provocation.[3] This word in English usage denotes the provoking of an opponent into a rash act, but in the communist dictionary it also means entrapment and instigation of a fight between third parties. Many wars have been started by provocations deliberately engineered by the aggressor; the purpose has frequently been to shift the onus of aggression from the aggressor to the defender.

Other purposes may be to force the defender to make some sort of premature move and thus expose his strategy, or to get him embroiled in a struggle on another front so that he would disperse his forces and lose control. Such an effect could be achieved, for example, by forcing the defender into a limited war in a peripheral theater and gradually causing him to invest ever-greater military strength from his forces in being into this limited operation. Thus, he would expose his main base to effective attack. If he can be induced to use obsolete equipment in the diversionary war, the victim may never develop the kind of weapons that will be used in the decisive combat.

So-called preemptive strikes also may pay a great role in surprise. The attacker could proceed by a combination of double deception and provocation to make open preparation for attack and to evacuate his cities. Then by other surprise techniques he could divert the defender's fire to false targets and achieve military superiority. Certainly moves of this sort are extremely risky, because the defender has surprise options of his own and may see through the deception. The risk can be reduced through a first-rate intelligence system, a superb early-warning system such as would be provided by *deploying* even the most elementary strategic defense system, and good penetration of the opponent's military apparatus and inner decision-making cycle.

Strategic planning aims at the exploitation of weaknesses and vulnerabilities, just as the wrestler tries to apply holds that force his opponent to submit. But the strategist has one advantage over the wrestler: he can contribute to the creation of vulnerabilities in the opposing force.

Creating vulnerabilities is an area where the problems of force and budgetary levels become highly significant. They can be created by an opponent who uses political means to achieve surprise. With low budgets there will always be a great tendency to cut corners, and that means that many of the support systems needed to operate weapon systems effectively will be eliminated or reduced to insufficient numbers. Very often it becomes a question of whether it is more advisable to buy firepower and delivery weapons than to harden the missiles or acquire such items as warning systems. Sometimes the choice is between offensive and defensive weapon systems.

If the aggressor can, through the employment of political means, manipulate budgetary and force levels of intended victims in a downward direction, the effectiveness of the opposing forces will be greatly reduced. Fundamentally, with a low budget it is very difficult to maintain several weapon systems simultaneously, and even more difficult to maintain forces based on different technologies. It is extremely difficult to provide them with good warning and protective features, to acquire suitable shelters for population and industry, and to bring new systems into being. Consequently, low defense budgets and low force levels aid the attacker in his strategic planning by reducing the complexities of his operations. Political operations in both the economic and diplomatic fields may be used to reinforce the natural tendency of the defender to save money on defense. These operations will have as their twin goals the reduction of strategic complexities through the lowering of the defender's budgets and the achievement of a state of relaxation in the victim. Then, when the attack comes, on the victim's allies and/or on his homeland, he will be unable to believe it has happened and be unprepared to defend himself. In this case, the last phase of the battle may not be a sneak attack at all; the defender may know it is coming and be unable to do anything about it.

To repeat: surprise techniques are available to both the attacker and the defender. Because we are firmly committed to a defensive strategy, it is vital that we prevent surprise. We must understand also that capabilities for surprise exist for us and we must emphasize such capabilities.

These come directly from the basis for surprise: uncertainty. Although the attacker has freedom in choosing his surprise moves, the defender can do a great deal to increase the uncertainty in the mind of the attacker. If the attacker has no uncertainty about the enemy, it is child's play to plan operations that can be decisive. If instead he experiences a great deal of uncertainty, even the planning of surprise operations becomes extremely difficult.

For example, a major purpose of strategic defense is to create uncertainties. If the defender does not have this capability, the attacker will be certain that he has a completely free ride. If the defender has actual missile defenses and the attacker is in doubt about whether its effectiveness lies between 50 and 90 percent, the attacker's strategic plan is greatly complicated. Suppose he assumes it is 50 percent, but it is actually 90 percent effective. Then he will fail in attack. Suppose he assumes it is 90 percent but it is actually 50 percent. In this instance he may not attack at all. Suppose his experts argue about whether it is 60 or 85 percent. In this case, the decision makers' will may be weakened. By manipulating the attacker's understanding of this situation, the defender may achieve considerable advantages.

The interplay between achieving and preventing surprise is one of the decisive elements of modern war. Speed appears to give the attacker greatly enhanced possibilities of surprise, but the defender is not without his options as well. The key to being the surpriser or the surprised is initiative, which in turn is based upon planning.

CONCLUSION

In guarding against technical surprise, it is important to keep its effects in the proper perspective. Technical advances generally and technical surprise in particular are steps to more decisive measures. Technology makes possible tactical, strategic, and timing surprise, and also provides systems for preventing surprise. It contributes to strategic deception. Surprise and deception are most vital when they contribute to or maximize the effectiveness of modern weapons. If our technological advantages are not exploited, while those of the USSR are, we will inevitably lose the technological war. Put differently: we must not be surprised about the fact that this is a technological war and we must never be deceived about our relative technological standing.

Success in an operational approach based on deception and surprise depends on total orchestration of the types of conflict, not on the effectiveness of each element. Partial successes attained and exploited in many areas will offset the failures that will occur in others. The net result is that overall success is rendered more likely.

If the defender understands this particular aspect of the problem, he can devise many actions through which aggressive stratagems are neutralized. He can maintain force levels, both quantitative and qualitative, that preclude a successful attack. The defender must move constantly during the period of so-called peace, to keep abreast of technical and strategic developments. He must initiate actions to which the attacker must react, using resources that would otherwise be employed against the defender, and must initiate these actions in time to prevent the aggressor from achieving a significant advantage. Success in this game will mean that aggression by nuclear weapons would be unthinkable, simply because the aggressor would remain confined to an incalculable but low probability of success.

The really important point is that war has not become unthinkable simply because weapons of mass destruction have been invented. The prevention of war is just as much a strategic undertaking as preparation for aggression. If the strategy of prevention is effective, the aggressor will be blocked. If, on the other hand, it consists merely of dependence on passive deterrence and on weak retaliation, the strategy of prevention is doomed to failure.

For the communists, surprise is vital to successful aggression. For our part, through the application of a rehumanized strategy, surprise can be our path to the initiatives and maneuvers that suppress aggression.

The only thing that is worse than being taken entirely by surprise is to be taken by surprise after repeated warnings that one is going to be taken by surprise. The former is shocking. The latter is devastating.

NOTES

1. General Waldemar Erfurth, *Surprise*, S. T. Possony and Daniel Vilfroy, translators. Harrisburg: Military Service Publishing Co. (Stackpole) 1943.

2. Double deception is best explained by the story of the two Jews who met on a train in Russia. Aaron asked Moses, "Where are you going?" Moses answered, "To Pinsk." Aaron replied, "You say you are going to Pinsk so that I will believe you are actually going to Minsk, but I happen to know you really are going to Pinsk. So why do you lie?"

   In military parlance, if A plans an operation, he would not try to hide his plan, but would make sure that B assumes this particular plan is being advertised because it will not be implemented. The German deception plan of 1941 that preceded the attack on the Soviet Union was planned as a single deception but actually worked as a double deception.

3. The Six-Day War in the Middle East has made the concept better known.

EDITOR'S INTRODUCTION TO:

NONLETHAL
by D. C. Poyer

Dave Poyer is a defense analyst by trade. One night he got to speculating: suppose war as we know it really is abolished?

After all, science fiction is sometimes called *speculative* fiction. It harms not to speculate. At least it harms not so long as one understands that nations whose soldiers are willing to die for their country invariably win against nations whose soldiers won't.

NONLETHAL
D. C. Poyer

What would happen if "Thou shalt not kill" became one of the laws of war?

"Drop!" screamed Loftis, his body thumping grass and dead leaves before the syllable was done. He slapped his mask down and offed his safety at the same instant.

"Right clear."

"Left flank clear."

"Rear clear, Sarge."

When the squad moved warily out onto the crest, breathing hard from the climb, the patch of blue Loftis had seen from two hundred yards away was still there. He waved his men back and moved forward alone. Low and slow. This had been a pasture once, this bald patch atop the hill. The russet remains of hay stalks hissed against his boots. The bush was ninety meters away, a band of green hazed by the mist of early dawn and the double glaze of mask and eye protection.

When he reached the Russian, he paused, searching the treeline, then dropped to his knees. He saw the rise of shoulder blades in breath. Quickly, moving clear as he did so, he rolled the man over.

Fear took his bowels. In six months of war Loftis had fought across half of Yugoslavia, gone from lance corporal to sergeant. But he had never seen this.

This was not supposed to happen.

"Holy Jesus," said a muffled voice behind him. He turned his head. It was Branch, the replacement, standing tall and thin as a goalpost. His weapon dangled in his gloves, and under his shoved-back hood his freckles had bleached pale. "What's the matter with him?"

For answer Loftis kicked out. The private thudded to the

ground, but he rolled, by reflex, protecting his rifle from contact with the dirt. Good, the sergeant thought. Maybe he's trainable. But aloud he hissed, "You shithead, Branch! You make a target on this hill like a number forty back at boot camp!"

"Sorry, Sarge. But . . . what's wrong with him?"

Loftis stared at the body, unsure what to do. He peeled the blue uniform cloth away. It was stiff. Gas-impregnated, like the Marine camos, but cotton rather than synthetic. His hand came away wet, and he lifted it to the waxing light. It glistened.

"He's wounded," he said. Branch's eyes grew huge. Loftis rolled over and examined the sky closely. It was blue, cloudless, and open as a mouth with dawning. He did not like it at all. He pulled a smoke from his pack and threw it upwind as far as he could. It popped and dark green smoke rolled across the pasture. "Send Joynes and Oleksa up here. We got some crawling to do."

This time he did not have to repeat the order.

Sergeant Olin Loftis' arms bulged under his camo uniform and his boots gripped dirt like the piles of a bridge. He had broken his nose more than once in pugils at Camp LeJeune and it was humped and spread even more than it had when he was born, two and a half decades before, in Northeast D.C. His chin was rough with ingrown beard, and he rubbed it now as he considered the man who sat, waxen-pale, slack-headed, against the bole of an oak on the shaded side of Hill 1132, twenty kilometers behind enemy lines in Bosnia Province, War Zone J.

"He going to make it, Doc?" he asked Joynes.

The dark-haired corpsman was squatting on his heels, stuffing gear back in his kit. In some ways he was the hardest of the squad for Loftis to understand. To begin with he was Navy, not Marine. He wore the red cross on the shoulder of his cammies. He did not carry a weapon and he was not gung-ho. Before the war he had been a teacher, and he still liked to quote men no one else in the platoon, including the officers, had ever heard of. Usually his expression was skeptical; but now he looked grim. He glanced at the wounded man before he answered. "He lost a lot of blood. But he'll make it."

"Is he mobile?"

Joynes considered. "Depends on how you mean it. When he comes around he ought to be able to stagger. The wound is in the meaty part of the thigh, but it missed bone. I gave him glucose and Benzedrine and a light combat 'dorph. But he'll be hurting, and he'll be slow."

"How'd he get it?"

"Bullet wound."

"Whose?"

"Oh, come on, Sergeant. How can I tell that? Another stupidity of a stupid war by a stupid species."

Loftis began to curse. He looked up at the foliage, which swayed in a gusty wind. The leaves were turning and the wind had an edge, not cold yet, but warning of winter. The men watched him. When the sergeant had gone through his vocabulary, he sat on his heels and stared at the Russian.

His eyes had opened sometime during the tirade. They were blue. They moved across their faces wonderingly. His hair was light brown, the color of their cardboard ration containers. His lashes were long and his cheekbones heavy, his lips thick, smiling, just a trace, at the corners.

Their existence must have hit him then, penetrating endorphins and shock. His head and shoulders swiveled from the sergeant with the sudden movement of a reptile, and came face-to-muzzle with Stankey's M02. He hesitated, then sank back against the bole.

"You speak English?" said Loftis hopefully.

The man's eyes narrowed. He looked, the sergeant thought suddenly, like the white man who owned the auto shop he'd worked in before the Corps.

"*Shto' vui skaz'ali?*" he muttered.

Loftis sat back on his heels. "Hm. Jack, you talk some Slav, don't you?"

"My grandma did, a long time ago."

"Whatever you remember, it's more than me. Come up here and help me out."

Jack Oleksa was a reservist, a corporal. He was old, over thirty. He was the smallest, too. He said very little. Before the war, Loftis knew, he had been a postman. He never spoke of it.

Oleksa settled down by the prisoner. He twisted a ration cigarette in half and gave the filtered end to the Russian.

"What's your name?" Loftis began.

The man stared up at them.

"*Kak vas' svatz?*" Oleksa said, sounding unsure of himself. The Russian studied him, then held out the half-cigarette. Oleksa traded him halves. They lit up, both men shielding the flame from the sky with their gloves.

"Why you want name?" he said, surprising them all. His accent was thick but they all understood.

"You figure it," said Loftis. "We found you on the hill back there. You're wounded. There's no ump with us."

"My family name Agayants," the man said slowly. He looked at Loftis squarely. "Vladimir Agayants. Which of you shoot me?"

"None of us, goddamn it. Don't you know who shot you?"

The prisoner shook his head silently. Again the suspicion slid over his eyes, like the nictitating membranes of an owl. He shifted his leg tentatively. His face went white, but not a muscle moved. He put the cigarette to his lips and inhaled.

So he doesn't know who shot him, Loftis thought, watching him. True? False? The wound was bad but not fatal. Could he have done it himself? There was no weapon around when they found him. But he could have done it in the woods, thrown the gun away, and come out into the open before he passed out.

But why would he do that? And why was he in the open? If I were wounded I wouldn't go into the open, he thought. No, wait, I might if I was behind my own lines. That way the eyes could see me. Maybe.

What if someone else had shot him? Say . . . his own side? There could be logic in it. Propaganda. But wouldn't he remember?

He watched the man smoke. He wanted to ask more questions. But the crickets were tapering off their morning song. He looked at his watch and pulled his map from his pack. As if that were a signal the squad moved closer. Even the Russian looked interested.

Things do not look good, Sergeant Loftis, he told himself. He studied the waterproof paper. It was laser-printed and he had to hold it close to his eyes to make out detail, but he did not have to carry eight other maps. And anybody that lightens my pack in these hills, he thought, well, he got himself a vote.

The situation was that they were cut off.

Two days before, the line Banja Luka–Gradacac–Bijeljina had crumpled under a sudden Warsaw Pact attack. The lieutenant, before they lost track of him, had said there were four Soviet divisions opposite the sector fronted by the First Marine Brigade, supported by the 23rd Canadian, on their left, and the U.S. First Army Division, on their right. That was a three-to-one-force ratio, considering the lower tooth to tail of Allied versus Pact light troops.

Loftis didn't know how, whether it was misunderstanding, tactical foul-up, or simply stronger Soviet pressure, but the battalion's right flank had been turned. The next morning brought an all-out attack. A heavy shockshell barrage hit as they sat around morning meal, followed by dozens of short-range RPVs, spewing PK at bush level. Behind them came infantry. The sky was crossed with contrails as the air battle seesawed. The popcorn rattle of weaponry on the platoon's flank built to a roar.

They held through the morning in savage short-range firefights before the tactical withdrawal began. It went on into the evening, with the platoon turning every hour to fight another delaying action. If a man fell he had to be left. By nightfall there were gaps in the retreating lines. When dark came, the blessed dark that Loftis and all the men had cursed and prayed for through the day, the lieutenant came by to give him the order.

Rear guard. Loftis smiled bitterly. Take charge of a squad, hold till dawn, then rejoin. But when dawn came, the battalion was gone, his squadtalk ear set was full of the buzz-saw whine of jamming, and the hills were thick with blue uniforms.

It was time to do some of that ridge-running.

He bent to the map. The first-stage stabilization line for the Corps was Kotor Varos–Maglaj, with the Bosna River on the right flank. He measured. Twenty-five klicks. Not too bad, though in rugged terrain like this bird kilometers turned into two or even three on the ground. But they could do it in a day. We *got* to do it in a day, he thought, glancing at the sky through his leafy screen. If the allies couldn't hold there, they would fall back farther.

They had to rejoin fast, or they would be trapped so deep in enemy territory they would never get out.

Loftis looked at the Russian. He had tilted his head back against the tree. Resting. Most of the squad was looking at him. Only one man was watching Loftis. Stankey. The boy had set his rifle aside and was resting his hand on his utility knife. His eyebrows rose slowly in a question.

Loftis stood. He flipped up his hood. The squad sighed. They knew the signal. As each man climbed to his feet, habit took over. He wedged the ear set into his aural meatus, tightened his hood, adjusted the bulky mask for instant donning, and checked his weapon. From a group of griping boys they became gargoyles, covered men, the deindividualized and faceless warriors of the new century.

Loftis studied the intent eyes, the hands nervously gripping weapons and packs. Oleksa. Joynes. Stankey. Branch. All who were left of the squad. They were not numbers to him. They were his men. The men he had to bring back.

And I will, he promised each of them silently.

"Le's go," he muttered. He extended a hand to the Russian. The man looked at it, huge, still with a trace of blood on the glove. The sergeant wiggled his fingers impatiently. "That means you, too, Waldimeer. From now on, you're as tight on me as I am on my squad."

"What you doing, Sarge? We can't take him!"

Loftis shifted his eyes. Thin, wiry, street-smart, street-suspicious, his aggression and fear masked by sleepy eyes, Leopold Stankey could have been him six years before. He understood Stankey. He would be hard to handle, but in battle he would be one of the best. "Shut up, Private," he muttered, holding the man's eyes. "Do it."

He watched the knife slide back into its sheath, and turned. He raised his arm, and twelve tired legs swung into the first step.

Some hours later, after a long downhill tramp, they reached the southern end of the ridgeline. Loftis, moving slowly down a wooded ravine, studied the trees, the ground, the ferns that nodded here and there among the fallen boles. Yugoslavia. In his mind it blended together, forest, rocky farms, the pitiful hamlets folded between hills like jelly in a doughnut.

In all this immense forest there were no civilians. Once there had been, before the war. Sometimes the men would come upon vacant homes, farms, broken into by troops before them eager for food or a bed. But there were no people.

As they moved down the long slope, zigging from cover to cover, Loftis wondered where they all were. Maybe they had all evacuated. Maybe they were in camps training. He had no

73

idea. It was another funny thing about a very funny war. So funny the enlisted men had coined a funny-sounding name for it.

They called it the Sneekle War.

It had began like all wars, with failed politics. The first failure was in the fragile coalition that was Yugoslavia. For a time after his death Tito's federation worked, but then the friction that was as much a part of the Balkans as the hills flared into civil war. The Croats asked Premier Gorbachev for "fraternal assistance." The southerners, accustomed by now to French panty hose, Greek music, and American TV, sent their request to NATO. One world war had started here before. The third was about to begin, the Marines had landed at Trieste, the Soviets were moving forward, when it happened. The General Assembly unanimously resolved that if the two superpowers resorted to war—or violence in any form—they would be instantly ejected from the world body, which would reconstitute itself in Beijing and embargo them both. The President, after some initial waffling, agreed. That left the USSR little choice. Yet somehow, Yugoslavia had to be resolved; and the troops were already there.

The Secretary General had a suggestion.

One month later, SCLE(NL) began. Subconventional Limited Engagement, Nonlethal. For the first week nothing happened; nothing could, except fistfights. But quickly modified weapons were hastily airlifted from the States. The Soviet Central Army Group was forced back at first, while Warsaw Pact arms techs worked feverishly. Those early battles were fought with makeshifts and improvisations, and some were even hand-to-hand. Then the new weapons began to come out.

No one, least of all the troops, had expected such an artificially circumscribed conflict to go on long. But gradually the Weird War had developed a terrible symmetry, written and unwritten rules, a blend of force and deterrence all its own. It was nonlethal, but it was anything but harmless. Men died from accidents, falls, disease. They could not be killed, but they could be blinded, stunned, driven insane with sophisticated hallucinogens, and captured. In some ways capture—especially in the USSR—was worse. The United States treated its POWs well, hoping for deserters. The Soviet Union treated its badly. It treated everyone badly. It did not want deserters. They had to be fed. It wanted Yugoslavia.

Some people said it was like war had always been.

Loftis paused by an exposed boulder. The air was quiet and cool. He looked carefully around. Something menaced him, but he did not know yet what it was. He lifted his weapon and checked it, just as he had ten thousand times in six months.

In its way, the weapon he carried was the Sneekle War in microcosm: an expensive blend of humanitarianism, violence, and high technology that resulted in something on the very border of rationality.

The M02 p-gun was a light weapon, adapted from the air guns used in war games in the States. About the size of an M-16, it fired not bullets, but a hollow pellet. When this projectile hit cloth or flesh, it shattered, releasing a contact agent. Absorbed almost instantly, it sent a man into eighteen to twenty hours of unconsciousness. It was nonlethal. Only if a man was hit by three or more rounds did the dose become dangerous. The M02, like the Soviet AKPD, had a range of two hundred yards. It could empty a fifteen-round magazine in about five seconds. Unlike its Pact counterpart, it had infrared aiming.

He saw something move in the foliage ahead, stiffened, then recognized Oleksa. He and Branch were on point, scouting an open patch. Beyond it he saw the blue haze of sky. He was staring up at it, his lips framing the curse that infantry on both sides greeted open sky with in this war, when he heard a far-off thud.

Fifteen seconds later the forest burst apart.

Loftis had heard the downward scream of the shell through air. He was already burrowing into the ground beside a fallen log, the Russian on the far side, when the first shockshell went off.

The planet slammed up at him and then down. Gasping, he scrabbled at dirt. The explosions seemed to be inside his head, a detonation in his brain. White flares went off behind his squeezed lids. The foliage rustled to the flight of fragments. They were harmless. Light metal. All you had to worry about was concussion, but it was enough. Nonlethal, but men blacked out from it, went into fits, went mad. It was generally combined with a more subtle form of attack. When the sky banged like subway doors opening, he stopped burrowing and cinched mask and hood tight as he could pull them.

Close to his eyes, just beyond the fogging windows of the

75

MK X mask, the log was rotting. He was so close he could see ants marching up from the interior, each carrying a grain of something he did not care to identify. They moved in steady files across the spongy bark. He raised his head a few centimeters and saw Agayants' rump, the back of his pack. Good chance, he thought distantly, to see whose gear is better, theirs or ours. Could be a useful piece of data . . . if they made it back.

A mist was creeping through the trees, finer than fog, all but invisible. He remembered his men. "Stankey! You tight?" he shouted, not trusting squadtalk so close to the ground.

"Yeah, Sarge."

He roared for the others, but they were out of range of his voice. He pulled his hood tighter and made sure the Velcro on his gloves held them close as a second skin.

The mist drifted down. He lay motionless, breathing shallow, eyes fixed.

He was watching the ants.

Their narrow files had begun to shatter. From obedient robots, highway followers across the rough surface of the log, they began to wander. Individuals weaved off from the collective. The stream itself meandered, re-formed. The mist drifted down.

The ants went mad. They boiled in every direction, their antennae writhing. The disciplined mechanism of the nest was gone. They darted about, colliding, fighting. At last, one by one and then by dozens, they fell from the log into the mold below.

Six more shells thudded above the treetops, then another dozen, farther off. Then a rolling barrage, scattered all across the saddle between the two hills. A dud plowed through the trees, sending up a spout of dirt and pine needles.

"Up," screamed Loftis through the mask.

He got to his knees. They felt weak. And then to his feet. He pulled the Russian along. Then, unconsciously, he found himself pausing. He stared upward, at the moving leaves.

The sun, blazing through the swaying interstices, was shattering into a million subprimary colors. He swung his eyes to find Oleksa and Branch watching him. Their faces were melting. As he lifted his arm he saw it move in slow instantaneous frames, up stop, up stop, outlined in the terrific color.

"Run!" he shouted, the words turning to glue in his mouth. He began to stumble forward.

The forest around him began to deliquesce. It dissolved into light, into sound, slowly, like diamond melting in the terrific heat of a focused laser. The crunch of leaves under his boots shuddered up his legs like breaking bone. The sigh of wind whined like a lumbermill full of band saws. The edge of his mask was a scalpel at his neck.

He ran, panting, sobbing, sucking air. None came. The filter must be going. He was breathing the colorless gas, the psychokinesthenic. He felt something haul him backward, and crashed to the ground. Attack, he thought, pawing clumsily at the sight of his rifle. A double bombardment meant attack.

The flash of blue was instantaneous, a glimpse through a gap of brush across the ravine. But he was already on his belly, his weapon already tracking in the same direction. He blinked back colors, waiting—

The p-gun pinged, jolting against his shoulder, pinged again. A crash came from the far side of the gully. Something buzzed above him, a fast mosquito, and whacked into a tree.

Ahead of him boots pounded across the leafy floor. He swung and almost fired before he recognized camouflage. Stankey slid beside him like a thief into home, and peered over his own sights into the treeline. "Shee-it," he muttered through the mask. "Sure is hot in these body bags."

The words melted slowly through his brain. He tried to funnel thought to his lips. "Where's Oleksa?"

"Old Dad'll be comin' right along." The private lowered his cheek to the stock, selected manual, and fired four rapid rounds into a patch of bush. Branches whipped, but Loftis saw nothing else. A moment later the short man trotted through the trees and joined them.

Loftis sucked air, sucked air. His head was clearing. I didn't take much, he thought. A microgram through some exposed hairline of skin, some badly sealed seam of the suit. Not enough to truly take him.

He was sweating now, and not only from the growing heat of the closed-up gear. He had seen men lying rigid, catatonic, after PK attacks. Their staring eyes told of the horror that gnawed through the framework of their minds, bringing it crashing down. Sometimes it lasted for hours, sometimes for weeks. And for some, forever. It was a terrible weapon.

But it did not kill . . .

He was about to say something about it when the bushes in front of them parted, and six men charged out. "Front!" he shouted hoarsely.

Three rifles pinged and bucked. Glass whipped through the air, kicked up leaves, whocked into tree boles. He ejected a magazine, kicked in a new one, fired as fast as his finger could move. The running men seemed to melt. One threw his hands skyward, another half reached for his belt before his rifle dropped from relaxing fingers and he crumpled to the ground.

Loftis became conscious that his ears were ringing from the shells. He shook the ear set out and heard distant shouts. He stared around, blinking to clear the last polychrome fringes from his vision. Take the high ground . . . the ravine rose steeply to their right. There, nearer the top of the hill, they could move in several directions. But could they get up it?

There was no choice. Even as he concluded the thought he heard the striker clink on an empty chamber. He jumped to his feet. "Stankey!"

"Yo."

"Rear guard. Ten minutes, then uphill to right."

"Yo."

He saw magazines in the air: Oleksa's and Branch's, flung to the younger man as they backpedaled toward Loftis. Joynes was behind him. He turned and ran for the near-sheer wall, slinging his rifle. Halfway up, then he would cover as Stankey fell back. He was twenty yards up rock and scree when he heard Joynes. "What?" he snarled, not looking back.

"Hand, Sarge!"

He turned. The corpsman, face reddened with effort, was trying to push the Russian up the slope. Agayants, his face white behind his eyepieces, was struggling upward.

The sergeant stared. For a moment his eyes were cold; then they blinked. His hand came slowly free of the rocky soil of Yugoslavia, and reached down. It gripped the glove of the soldier in blue, paused, and then drew upward. The struggling body came after it, lifted almost effortlessly against gravity up the side of the hill.

"Stankey! Fall back!" The bull roar reverberated from the trees. "We're hauling ass out of this shitstorm. Fall back on me. I'll cover!"

Ahead of them stretched the forest, unbroken, untenanted yet hostile, still and yet dangerous under the eyes, like those of hawks, that searched their prey out from above.

The sky came to him black, the trees as black on black. He rolled on the crackle of pine branches and spat the foulness of too-short sleep onto dark ground. "Jack," he said softly.

"Here, Olin."

"Time is it?"

"Twenty-three hundred."

"Already? Jesus."

The darkness stirred. The squad rolled out softly, muttering, yet careful not to drop rifle butts or even boots too abruptly. There had been aircraft just after nightfall, and there could be sonic sensors within hearing distance. Now, in the darkness, under tree cover, there was a little time when men could move like soldiers always had. A rattle of water came from somewhere near. Loftis got to his feet, feeling every muscle in his body tighten against the movement.

"Stankey?"

"Here."

"Branch?"

"Yo."

"Doc?"

"Still here, goddamn it. Wake-up tabs, come an' get 'em."

"You—Agayants. You awake?"

"I hear."

"Okay, listen up." Loftis' whisper was hoarse. "We made, I figure, five, six klicks good yesterday. Them chasin' us back up the ridge lost us some. We got to make time tonight. But we got to be careful. Get it?"

The men muttered. One voice spoke clearly, though it was held low. "Yeah, Sarge. 'Cepting for one thing."

"Yeah, Stankey?"

"The Russki. We're beat to shit, and we got to haul him, too. I don't get it. Why the fuck are we carrying him for? I mean, we ain't on recce, askin' for prisoners. We're running for our asses."

There was a murmur from the others, half in protest, half assent. The Russian said nothing.

"I ain't used to having my orders second-guessed by no fuckin' prives, son."

"Sorry about that, Sergeant Loftis. But we out here in the wilderness. We got to get back, or we're cold meat, man. Why we draggin' him? I just want to know."

"I think the sergeant—"

"Forget it, Doc. I'll explain it to the slow learner here. Listen, Stankey. How long you been in this here war?"

"Six weeks."

"How many wounded you seen?"

"He's first one."

"That mean anything to you?"

"Sure. The whole war's Sneekle—nobody supposed to get shot like that. But so what? We didn't hit him."

"Can you prove that?"

"Uh . . . no."

"What happens to us if we did?"

Pause. "They shoot us."

"Who?"

"The umps."

"What else?"

"After they shoot us? You got me. The Corps issues us halos?"

He didn't like the tone, but he ignored it, glancing at the dim digits of his watch. You had to let them bitch, but he wanted to wrap this up. "After they shoot us, the other side gets a propaganda bonus. Allies violating Sneekle Treaty. Addicted to violence. Losing ground, so they're starting to kill. You know what happens next?"

"Tell me, Sarge."

"This war has been seesawing for six months. The other side wants this country, they want to win. Old-style war, hate to say it, but they probably would. Something like this could give them the excuse to go conventional. You know we're already on the defensive. We start taking casualties, without real guns in our hands, and the J Line'll crack so quick Chosin Reservoir will look like a victory."

"I think the sarge is right." Oleksa's voice. "I figure they got their old weapons in rear echelon, ready to come up overnight. All they need is an excuse—and finding this guy, with what I bet is a NATO-caliber bullet in him, is a dead setup for them. Sergeant's right. We got to get back with him, or find an umpire, before they get us, or we're fried."

"Come on," said Joynes. "You're assuming—"

"That's enough," Loftis' growl broke in. "On your feet. We got six hours of dark to travel in. Doc."

"Yes?"

"Slowcoke. One dose each. We'll be humping it. And Stankey—"

"Yeah?"

"You help our friend march."

There was no reply, but he did not like the feeling of the stillness. A hand found his in the darkness, and he backhanded the pill into his mouth.

"Let's go."

The night march was deadly. They moved as silently as they could, but time after time the ground simply dropped away in the dark and men fell, slid, cursed, dropped their weapons to clatter over rock. Or else it rose, and they had to claw their way up through gravel and scrub brush by feel, tearing their fingernails and the skin of their faces. The drug helped, much at first, less as the hours went by. He debated another dose, but decided against it. The time-release cocaine provided energy without a high, but there was a rebound; best to save it for the last dash to safety.

At five the sky grayed. He called a chow break. They sat, too weary to talk. Doc stared at the ground, Stankey cupped a cigarette, Branch sucked at his canteen. Only Loftis and Oleksa broke out rations and sat chewing moodily.

The Russian watched, then limped over to Loftis. "You give?" he said, motioning to the food.

"Battle rats? Sure, if you can stomach 'em. Course, yours might be even worse."

"No caviar for the troops, I bet," said Joynes, staring at him. "Hey, you want a smoke? I don't use them."

"Thank you."

"Keep 'em covered," said Loftis. "Or you won't get any more."

"Understand. Sputniki."

"What?"

"Satellites, he said."

"Oh. Sputniks, huh? I get it."

"Come on, Doc," said Loftis, getting up. "Let's recce."

He and Joynes moved forward cautiously. The faint predawn made it easier to travel, but also more dangerous. A few hundred yards farther on, the forest ended. Beneath his feet the ground softened, sucking at his boots.

"Swampy," said the corpsman. "You got any rivers on that map?"

"One. We made good time if this is it."

"Think we can get across before full daylight?"

"Sure like to try. I feel naked out here."

"Think they know we're here?"

"I don't know. If that was a sensor drop last night . . . that rock probably carries sound pretty good. They might."

When he stopped whispering, there was a silence. He was turning to go back when Joynes muttered, "Sarge, tell me something."

"What?"

"What are we doing out here, anyway? What's this god-damn war for?"

He peered at the corpsman's face. "You know," he said. "We're here to defend Yugoslavia. Don't that make sense?"

"I guess. I just—I just hoped, once, for something more to fight for than the big-power skirmishing."

"Politics ain't my business. Or yours."

"It ought to be."

"Goddamn it, Doc, I don't have time to argue with you now."

"All right," said Joynes. "Forget it, Sarge. We'll talk about it some other time."

"Sure," said Loftis, and meant it. "Let's go back now."

The squad straggled forward in the growing light. The stark traceries of the forest fell back. No one spoke, not even when they came out on the bank and looked over the fog-shrouded river. They stood and stared. Stankey knelt to rinse his face.

"How wide you figure?"

"Couple hundred yards."

"Deep?"

"Higher than a man, for sure. Look at how calm it is."

"You two, left. I'll go right. Look for a ford, or rapids."

Oleksa found the boat three hundred meters upstream. The men shambled up to it. Someone had staked it to a fallen tree on the shingle, and it lay now in weeds. Its quarter had been gnawed by decay. Loftis circled it, rubbing his chin. "Think it'll float?" he muttered, to no one in particular.

"It'll float." Branch squatted by the stern, dug his K-bar into rotten wood.

"You know boats, Boot Camp?"

"Built one and paddled it all over Lake George when I was twelve. This here punt'll leak, but we can hang on and bail till we're across. I can fix it enough so two guys could sit in it and not get wet."

"Terrific. Take charge of that. Rest of you, spread out. Look for something to paddle with."

The sun was above the hills when Branch pronounced himself satisfied. He had reinforced the rotten section with cut saplings and stretched a cammie shirt over them. Loftis hung back, willing to follow instead of lead for a few minutes more. The men grasped the gunwales and hustled the punt down to the shore. It settled into the river with the unenthusiastic air of a corpse revived by necromancy. Water began running in the bottom. Branch leaped in and settled himself on a thwart, then bent to scoop out the first helmetful. "Let's go, there, comrade," he said sharply to Agayants. "Sarge, you coming?"

Loftis stood by the side of the river, screened by brush. They beckoned him, eyes alight, like kids. He thought of Huck Finn and Jim on the raft. He had liked that book. The river smelled cold, like a basement after a long winter. He looked upward. No cloud. His skin crawled at the thought of crossing open water in daylight. Both sides had surveillance. They circled higher than human sight, long-winged automatic planes that never came down. There were things that hunted them, swift killers with electronic minds. The men saw only thin contrails, like the trace of skates on a frozen pond, to mark those battles. But there were other machines that were only too happy to hunt man . . .

"Goddamn," said Loftis, plunging into the river with the rest. They piled their p-guns in the bow and splashed outward, holding to the sides of the boat. "You might make a Marine after all, Branch."

The ground dropped under their feet. He was glad they hadn't tried to swim, tired as the men were. The river was cold and the current swift under the smooth surface, dragging them along with silent power. "Start paddling," he grunted, glancing past Branch's head at the open sky. He sculled with one hand, clinging to rough wood with the other. The shore began to recede as the men stabbed at the river with scraps of driftwood. Branch bailed steadily over the stern.

"Eyes!" shouted Joynes.

The men ducked, but there was no cover. The boat rocked, unbuoyant, unsteady. Loftis' head jerked up. The soarer was too high to see, but its radio-vectored RPV was not. It glided in fifty feet above the river, not much bigger than an owl, the propeller windmilling. Sunlight glinted off a lens. It was only a hundred meters away.

"Rifles!" he screamed. "Shoot that fucker down! Right now!"

Branch and Stankey had their M02's up in a moment. The RPV was faster. The motor restarted, its nose lifted, and it buzzed past their heads. Loftis could see the camera pod below the wing as it went by, banking for another pass. "It ain't marked," Branch said tentatively, following it with his front sight.

Loftis uttered a fearsome profanity. "Kill it, I said!"

Both rifles cracked. The vehicle's engine jumped to a higher note. Branch fired again. It yawed and wove like a swallow, eluding their aim, yet working steadily closer. Its propeller was a white blur against the green of the hills. It dipped and came on, aiming like a hawk now, only five or six feet above the water.

"*Gaz yest!*"

The Russian grabbed for his mask. Loftis saw it at the same instant. A blue mist, swirling in the turbulence of the propeller.

"Gas!"

They snatched for their MK X's. Loftis found his under water, but the flap eluded his hand. The eye buzzed toward them, the wasp whine of the engine filling the river. He saw the Russian snap his last strap into place. Branch was still firing. He had not registered the presence of the PK at all. Oleksa had his mask half on. Stankey was groping for his.

It flashed over them. The whorls of mist, fading toward invisibility at the edges, drifted downward toward the floating men.

"Shit," muttered Loftis. He let go of his mask and heaved himself up on the gunwale, and then down. Branch's face turned toward him, white and horrified.

They went over. The Russian screamed as he hit the river. Loftis remembered his wound. He ducked, found what he judged to be Stankey. His reaching hand could not find Branch. He swam downward, ignoring the struggles of the man whose uniform he held. His lungs ached, but he ignored them. His eyes began to burn and the kicking grew more fierce and then weaker. His outstretched hand found bottom. Rock and mud, sweeping by at the speed of current. It was cold down here, cold as death and winter. Stars exploded behind his eyes. He could stand it no longer. A scream tore from his open mouth, clothed in bubbles. He kicked downward.

* * *

An hour later they fought through thorns sharp as barbed wire. Their tiny teeth tore at uniforms and skin. The ground was rocky, then soft. A grown-over field of stunted apple trees. Windfall squished under their boots, filling the close air with sweet decay.

"Uphill," Loftis gasped. He seized the man nearest him and thrust him ahead with all his remaining strength. "Uphill!"

Stankey spun away, boots digging into the yielding ground. Jack Oleksa and Doc Joynes were coming up through the trees. The sun slanted behind them. The Russian was panting, his mouth a hard O. His arm was around Joynes' neck. "What's the hurry?" said the corpsman. His face was streaked with sweat and mud and blood. A p-gun was slung over his shoulder. Loftis' eye caught that, then moved to a bare spot on the shoulder of his cammies.

"That thing was waiting for us. Patrolling up and down the river. They know we're here and that we've got—him." He nodded at Agayants. "I figure we'll have visitors real soon, a blocking maneuver to our front."

"We should be getting close to our own lines," Oleksa managed between gasps. His face was gray to the younger men's white.

Shit, Loftis thought. His own mind was going hazy. He had saved Stankey by sheer will. They had almost drowned, but when they broke surface again the PK had been driven downwind and the eye gone. Oleksa and the Russian had both donned masks in time. Joynes had used his head, staying under the overturned boat and breathing trapped air till the gas dispersed.

No one had seen Branch. Loftis had waited as long as he dared, searching the banks for a head, a body. Nothing. The replacement had gone like so many others in this retreat, walked away into the fog of war.

It would have a bad effect, he thought, on the rest. Four men left. And one prisoner. Nine kilometers to NATO lines—if they had not retreated farther in the last twenty-four hours.

"Planes," came Stankey's shout, a moment before the roar of the engines reached the others.

The planes roared in ahead of them, to their right. Through the trees he could see flashes of silver. "Paratroops," he said to Oleksa, who nodded silently. "Right flank, and ahead."

"Let's break left fast."

"High ground?"

"Yeah. No . . . which way are our lines?"

Loftis sighted with the compass, then pointed to a distant bluff. "That way. But if the line's still there, anyplace we hit it will be good."

"That's it, then." They looked at Agayants.

"You are going?"

"Fast as we can. You got to keep up."

"I will try."

They lay at the edge of the bluff, beneath the ragged leaves of ferns. Water trickled somewhere. Loftis felt it cold underneath him. He searched the ground. Yes, a spring. Muddy water welled up where he lifted the heel of his hand. He raised his head an inch. The ferns nodded in stillness. Each nod, each whisper of the still forest below, drew his utmost attention, yet without distracting him from the overall situation. The heightened alertness came from within, partly, but it was also chemical: he had asked Joynes for a combat-effectiveness enhancer a few minutes before.

He lowered his head and drank, slurping the muddy stuff between dry lips. Fill canteens if we have time, he thought. But no noise. No noise at all.

The enemy was all around.

He checked his weapon, seating his magazine, switching it on and off guidance. He remembered when rifles were all-manual, when a shot had to be aimed precisely to hit. Just like the Civil War. Now, with GUID selected, an infrared sensor made any recruit a sharpshooter. You aimed as best you could, then pulled the trigger. When the waver of your muzzle caught man, when the sensor said something warm existed in the bowed time-space your pellet would describe, it completed the circuit. Your rifle jolted, and an enemy felt the whiplash sting of sleepytime.

All the technology of centuries, the knowledge and data accumulated by man. He watched the heelprint refill with water, and bent again. All employed in the cause of war. Sometimes, like the corpsman, he found himself wondering about it, whether it was worth all he had seen and endured.

Something crackled in his ear set. He became attentive, concentrating to hear through the steady whine of jamming. It was Joynes.

". . . Just ahead."

He lifted his head warily. The laser-rangers the Soviets

carried could blind a man for life. And you couldn't see them until they hit you, unless you caught their flash against foliage.

Ah, yes, he thought. This war is different.

Somewhere in the leafy distance a weapon fired. Full automatic. The burst sounded strange. Loud. He frowned and pushed himself up a bit more. The doc said something on the channel, but he couldn't make it out through the whine. He glanced to his left, to where the Russian lay on his back, staring at the trees. *If I feel helpless, how must he feel?*

But he had no time to feel. He had only two choices. Fight and try to escape. Or find an umpire and "surrender in U.N. presence."

He decided to surrender the moment he saw a white uniform.

The firing broke out again, louder. There were several rifles. It was to his left, in a thicker copse he could see from the edge of the bluff. Joynes was at their edge, with a weapon this time.

Suddenly he stiffened. The familiar popping of an M02. Only it sounded muffled, weak. What was going on?

Five soldiers appeared under the trees. They wore black fur caps and dark blue tunics. They moved in echelon, crouched, sprinting between cover in short rushes. Feeling remote admiration for their tactics, Loftis lined up his weapon and set the range. He selected guidance and set in a drop correction. He could see the red stars on their caps through his sights. When the next one broke cover, he swung and fired. The man clapped his hand to his arm, dropping his weapon. He shouted something. The others turned to look. He started to point, but halfway up, his arm became unsteady. He sagged. His head went back and his helmet fell free. He disappeared.

The lead soldier waved in his direction. Loftis saw their barrels come up. He fired again, but before he could see a hit, their muzzles flashed.

The ferns above his head snapped and flew apart. Something smacked the bluff edge, spraying his face with water and mud. The bullets hissed overhead.

Bullets. Dumb rounds. The men below were no longer playing sneekle.

Loftis slid back, heart jumping. He caught a glimpse of the leader, on his knees, head sagging. He'd hit. But he wasn't staying. He saw Agayants looking at him. "Get moving," he said in a low voice. He keyed squadtalk. "Loftis. Live ammo, live! Fall back. Any you guys see white?"

"No umps."

"Nothin', Sarge."

"Joynes?"

Christ, he thought. Of course there would be no umps. Not if the Soviets felt they could use live fire. He waited. The corpsman did not answer. "Joynes!" he shouted to the trees.

"Get going, jarheads." It was the doc, in a whisper. "Hit. Coming for me. Move out."

Loftis felt a blaze of rage. He jumped to his feet, bracing his body against the trunk of an elm. His maneuver caught the men below by surprise, out of cover. They stared up openmouthed. Trigger pressed, he panned the sight over them, correcting as the muzzle jerked at each exiting pellet. Two Soviets fell but more were appearing every moment, at least a dozen, running out from cover toward the bluff, then pausing to aim up at him. Return fire whacked into the trunk, and then, stunning him from fingertips to jaw, into bone just below his elbow.

He blinked, thinking for a moment that the flash was from a laser. It wasn't. He saw his rifle on the ground and tried to pick it up. His arm did not respond.

There was a rustle behind him and someone moved past, picking up the rifle, pulling him back from the bluff edge. "Shee-it," it said. "Stopped one with your arm, huh, Sarge? Careless. Come on, let's retrograde."

"Doc's down there."

"You heard his transmit. We can't help. Let's boogie."

He came out of shock a little. Stankey was right. There were too many enemy to go back. He saw Agayants ahead of them, pulling something from his pack, and then the pale hands met his bare skin for the first time. Tourniquet. Battle bandage. They were cotton, instead of the plastic-skin U.S. issue.

Oleksa trotted up warily. "You hit, Olin?"

"Yeah."

"Bad?"

"No."

"Doc?"

"Got to leave him."

"Orders?"

"No."

"Gimme your smokes."

Loftis had one left, Stankey two. Oleksa collected them

88

and loped off, head questing from side to side. Loftis turned his face to feel the wind. Yes, he was laying it proper. But why?

The corporal came back between the trees. "Old culvert on south edge. Leads down from a spring. Probably a farmhouse somewhere down below."

"Wide enough?"

"Hope so. C'mon, let's move out."

The smoke was thick, choking, like walking the rim of a volcano. It moved with the wind and they moved with it, hearing voices behind them. Oleksa knelt suddenly. The mouth of the culvert was hidden by bushes. Stankey started to kick them apart, but the reservist stopped him. The small man went in first. After a moment his voice came up, hollow. "Clear . . . ah . . . no, dammit, it's blocked. Water can get through, but I can't."

A heavy burst came from behind them, beyond the smoke. "We're fuckin' trapped," muttered Stankey, glancing at the Russian with a look at once wild and profoundly sympathetic, as if he recognized for the first time that the other was a man.

"Get in," said Loftis.

"What?"

"Get in, I said!"

"They'll shoot us in there!"

He shoved the private with his good arm. Agayants had already seen. He ducked quickly into the brush-screened opening. His blue eyes showed, frightened, searching their faces before the darkness swallowed it. Stankey stared for a moment more, then cursed. He sat and dropped his legs in. Loftis bent, looking back. The shouts were louder. Through the smoke probed the beam of a laser. It swept from side to side above his head, made visible by the pall.

The smokes would cover them for a few more seconds. Then it would be luck, only luck. He was thinking this when the beam dipped unexpectedly and struck his eyes. He staggered, raising his arm and blinking. Patterns of light wheeled in front of him. He could see nothing beyond them.

He slid his rifle by feel into the bushes. He fell into a night of red fire, biting back a cry as his shattered arm bit crumbling stone.

Loftis waited through the day, shivering in the icy water, falling from time to time into short, terrifying dreams. The circle of sky was dark when he unbent, whimpering at his arm, and began to crawl upward. He went slowly, slowly. They could have left geosensors.

When he came out of the bushes, p-gun balanced in his left hand, he paused for a long time to listen. He still could not see well, but the red wheels had begun to fade. The wind sighed through dark trees. The trickle of the spring filled the night. The top of the bluff was empty.

"Come on out," he whispered.

They moved slowly down the slope. Loftis blinked up at the stars and turned a little to the right. Something buzzed, mosquitolike, above them, and they froze, rigid and unbreathing, each man shielding his bare face from the sky. The whine faded into the wind's whistle. They moved forward again, easing their boots down into the grass. From time to time a distant explosion rumbled over the hills. None of them spoke. Loftis' arm was a lump of pain. He had no more drugs. Joynes had carried them all.

You, he thought. *Oleksa. Stankey. The Russian. It is night. It is 2210. You have no masks. You are almost out of ammo. You are hungry and wounded, but you have drunk all the spring water you will ever want in your life. You have till dawn, about 0500. You have six klicks to go.*

They moved through the night for a long time. From time to time he looked at his watch, then at the stars. They were making distance. At half past midnight he heard Stankey mutter something behind him.

"What's that?"

"I been thinking."

"You?"

"You been telling us all along the Russkis shot him," Stankey muttered behind him, ignoring his sarcasm.

"What? Close up if you got to talk."

The private moved up. His breath was warm in Loftis' ear. "I got it figured. The Army shot him."

"What you talking about, Stankey?"

"Talking about our Commie friend. The possibilities. They must be other troops cut off 'sides us. What if it was them shot him—accident, or deliberate?"

"What if it was? We still got to get him back. Russians can still pin it on us, Private."

"If they can," said Stankey, lowering his voice still more

90

so that Oleksa, directly behind, could not overhear, "so can the umps."

"What are you sayin'?"

"That if he got a bullet in him, won't the refs, when we get back, say we shot him?"

"Hell, they can tell what kind of weapon a slug came from."

"If there's one in him. What if there ain't? He been hiking pretty strong for a man with a bullet in him."

"Take a break," whispered Loftis. "Pass it back."

He heard them sigh and let themselves down against trees. Stankey sat beside him. Loftis' eyes slid beyond him, to where the Russian was scratching at the soil with his hand. He heard a soft sound, and then the man pulled up his trousers and settled a few steps away.

"You don't trust your own mother, Stankey."

"Why should I? The bitch stole from me. He'll find some way to give us away. We ought to dump him."

"Shut up," said Loftis. "Five minutes. Then we keep moving. We only got five more klicks."

At daybreak they crouched at the edge of a valley, shivering in the morning chill. Light etched the trees like silver precipitating on a photographic image. Loftis tried to raise his rifle. His hand shook too much. He passed it to Oleksa. "Take a look. What do you see?"

The older man squinted through the sight, then turned it to higher magnification. "Men," he said at last.

"Ours?"

"I think so. Can't see color so good yet."

"We'll wait," said Loftis. "Till we know."

"You think they're ours?" said Stankey.

"They're in the right place."

"What you plan to do?"

"Let's see . . . I lost my squadtalk. Have you—"

"Mine's gone."

"I . . . lost mine."

"Guess that's out."

"Suppose we just run, then. Make a break."

"There's got to be Russians around if this is the front line."

"What if there is? We got no smokes. We got no comms. We out of ammo. We just got to run."

"What if our guys got autoguns set, or those shock mines?"

"Well, they can tell we're U.S. even if we're asleep."

Loftis nodded. A great tiredness took him and he slumped back. His eyelids slid downward, as inevitably as avalanches.

He dreamed, there in the dawning, that he and Doc Joynes were sitting on a mountain together. It was west of D.C., in the Blue Ridge, and there was a bottle between them. The doc was sipping from it, and arguing, just like always. They were talking about the war, as if it had been over for years, for a long time. "So what did you think?" Joynes was saying. "That a war without violence would be kind? It was only a step up from economic war and a step down from guerrillas. Each side was as ruthless as it thought it could get away with. Nothing had changed."

"The grunts on the ground weren't dying," grunted Loftis.

"Tell that to the guys blinded by range lasers," the corpsman said slowly. "Tell it to the guys who never thought again because they got a PK megadose. Or the ones who froze to death while they were nodding that winter."

"You're too friggin' clever." Loftis, in his dream, stood up and looked around. The tops of the blue hills were level with his eyes. "You make it seem like it was no progress. Well, by Jesus, I believed in the crazy thing."

" 'War contains so much folly, as well as wickedness, that much is to be hoped from the progress of reason; and if anything is to be hoped, everything ought to be tried,' " said Joynes, his voice taunting, though he did not smile.

"Who said that?"

"Madison." The doc laughed then. "And war in his day—not half bad. I'll bet we lost more people in a battle than they did."

"I bet we didn't," said Loftis. "You never believed in it because you only saw the injuries. My pop was in 'Nam and he told me about that hell. I'd rather have took a pellet and starved for a year or two in a Pact gulag than spent the rest of my life like him. He didn't have no legs—and he always told me, he was one of the lucky ones."

"Loftis."

It was not the doc. He remembered now that he was dead, left behind. It was the Russian, Agayants. The light was brighter and he was squatting between him and the sun, with Stankey's face dark behind him, hand on his knife.

"What?" he said.

"It's light," said Oleksa. He turned his head. The older man was beside him. He lifted the scope.

"Can you see?"

"It's our guys."

Loftis nodded.

"But there's blueboys moving between us and them. Looks like preps for an assault."

Loftis nodded again. His arm throbbed with an insidious pain, as if something were eating its way inside it, next to the bone, toward his heart.

"Loftis," said the Russian again.

"What the hell you want, Wal-demeer?"

"I can help us to other side."

"How?"

"Talk. I tell soldiers we *shpionam*—spy." He turned his helmet around, looked earnestly at them.

"Jack?"

The corporal raised his eyebrows. "Weird, but it might work."

"Leopold?"

"Don't call me Leopold."

"Okay, Private Stankey. What do you say?"

"I don't trust him."

Loftis stirred. He looked at the three anxious faces. "Wal-demeer—"

"Vladimir."

"Everybody's worried about his name today. Okay. *Wal*-dimeer. Now, Private Stankey still wants to know how you got shot. So do I. Are you sure you don't have a better explanation than the last one we heard?"

"I shoot myself," he said.

"What?"

"I shoot myself with gun."

The three Marines stared at him. "You must have wanted out of the army pretty bad," said Oleksa.

"Not out of army. Out of killing."

"Come again."

The Russian chewed his lip. He looked toward the hill opposite, then seemed to make a decision. Words tumbled out. "I know plan. One general makes it. More, more attacks with bullets. No more *ni viernaya voina*—false war. They give us gun for bullet, not sleep. You see? So I go off, shoot me, so not to kill other. That, I do not believe to do."

93

"Then we found you, instead of your own people."

"*Da.*"

"What happens if they find you shot yourself?"

"Trial," he said. "Prison, *el'e* death."

"Jesus. Why didn't you say so?"

"I thought"—he glanced at Stankey, who lowered his eyes. "You not take me back then. That you same as them."

Loftis nodded. After a moment Oleksa did, too. They faced forward.

"Hold up that goddamn scope for me," said the sergeant.

The other side of the valley; the top of the facing ridge. Through the glasses it leaped up so clear and sharp he wondered if he could touch it.

"You'll help us get through?"

"*Da.*"

"And then?"

"I talk to *sud'ya.* To U.N."

"Why?"

"I say. I do not like killing."

"Back there? The paratroops?"

"Yes."

"Well," said Loftis, "I guess we must have some kind of program for defectors. I mean, don't seem like you should be a POW, after that."

"I would rather be prisoner."

"You mean that?"

"Yes," said the Russian. He chewed on the tips of his fingers nervously. "I am not traitor. Just do not want to kill. This war bad, but not like old kind fighting. You know, *Sovietsky Soyuz* lose twenty, thirty million in Patriotic War. Never, never repeat. Maybe future be like this."

Loftis turned his head. "Sounds like good sense, don't it, Jack?"

"What's that?"

"Sneekle War is hell—but we got to make it work, 'cause it's better than the real thing. 'Cause maybe that's the way things come in the world, you fight your way uphill a little bit at a time."

"Maybe so," said Oleksa. "Maybe so."

"Doc wouldn't have said so."

"Sure he would. He just liked to argue."

"Ready to cross?"

"Anytime."

"Brother?"

"On your ass, Olin."

"Wal-demeer?"

"I am ready."

They grinned at each other. The growl of motors came from behind them. Overhead the leaves stirred in the first breath of morning wind.

Together, they walked down into the valley.

EDITOR'S INTRODUCTION TO:

ABDULLAH BULBUL AMIR
(Unknown)

More years ago than I like to admit, my high school English class was assigned Richard Conway's "The Most Dangerous Game"—a delightful story, if you haven't read it.

That story has a minor character named Ivan, and during the discussion one of my classmates pronounced it "Ee-*vahn*" in the Russian manner; whereupon several of us said, aloud and in unison, "*Eye*-van" in the American manner. Of course we were wrong.

Brother Daniel, the instructor, was not amused, and said, "Who said that?" It being an honor system class, three of us stood up and were given our penance. "There is," Brother Daniel said, "a poem by the name 'Ivan Petrofsky Skovar.' " (Incidentally, I remember it as Ivan *Skavinsky Skivar*, but the only version I've found recently uses the other name.) "You will," he continued, "go find it and copy it five times."

A quick search of our high school library revealed no clues at all. Eventually I found someone in the Memphis downtown main library who recalled that there was such a poem, but it was entitled "Abdullah Bulbul Amir." She was kind enough to find it for me in some long-out-of-print collection of ballads and poems, and I duly copied it out; I may have been the only one who did comply with the penance.

The version I remember is not the one given here, but this one is close enough.

Not every battle ends in victory.

ABDULLAH BULBUL AMIR
(Unknown)

The sons of the Prophet are hardy and bold,
   And quite unaccustomed to fear;
But of all the most reckless of life and of limb,
   Was Abdullah Bulbul Amir.

When they wanted a man to encourage the van,
   Or harass the foe from the rear,
Or to storm a redoubt, they were sure to call out,
   For Abdullah Bulbul Amir.

There are heroes in plenty, and well known to fame,
   In the legions that fight for the Czar;
But none of such fame, as the man by the name,
   Of Ivan Petrofsky Skovar.

He could imitate Irving, play euchre or pool,
   And perform on the Spanish guitar;
In fact quite the cream of the Muscovite team,
   Was Ivan Petrofsky Skovar.

One day this bold Muscovite shouldered his gun,
   Put on his most cynical sneer,
And was walking downtown when he chanced to run down,
   Abdullah Bulbul Amir.

Quoth the Bulbul, "My friend, is existence so dull,
   "That you're anxious to end your career?
"For infidel know, you have tread on the toe,
   "Of Abdullah Bulbul Amir.

"So take your last look at the sea, sky, and brook,
   "Make your last report on the war.
"For I mean to imply, that you're going to die,
   "Ivan Petrofsky Skovar."

So this stalwart he took his trusty chibouk,
 and shouting "Allah Akbar!"
With murder intent he most savagely went
 For Ivan Petrofsky Skovar.

Just as the knife was ending the life,
 In fact he had shouted "Huzzah!"
He found himself struck by that noted Cossack,
 Ivan Petrofsky Skovar.

The Sultan rose up, the disturbance to quell,
 Likewise give the victor a cheer,
He arrived just in time for a farewell sublime,
 with Abdullah Bulbul Amir.

A long-sounding splash from the Danube was heard,
 Resounding o'er meadows afar;
It came from the sack fitting close to the back,
 Of Ivan Petrofsky Skovar.

There's a grave by the wave where the Danube doth roll,
 And on it in characters queer,
Are "Stranger remember to pray for the soul,
 Of Abdullah Bulbul Amir."

A Muscovite maiden her vigil doth keep,
 By the light of the pale northern star,
And the name she repeats every night in her sleep,
 Is Ivan Petrofsky Skovar.

EDITOR'S INTRODUCTION TO:

RENDER UNTO CAESAR
by Eric Vinicoff and Marcia Martin

Terrorism has become a fact of life; so much so that to make things tougher for terrorists we're willing to accept some pretty hefty intrusions on our lives. As an example, I recently missed an airplane at London's Heathrow Airport. I arrived a good forty-five minutes before the plane was to leave, but that wasn't sufficient time for the security people to go through their rather farcical routines. (Farcical because I saw three ways I could have smuggled in weapons and/or explosives.) As I stood in a nearly interminable line waiting for two and only two officers to check my passport, the chap in front of me said, "Well, it's better than being blown up, isn't it?"

A great deal is better than being blown up, but perhaps that's not the point. The British apparently think that laying on another regulation will cure the terrorist problem, and if one new regulation is good, several will be even better. All of them inconvenience the passengers. I have doubts about what they have done to the terrorists.

It may be that we have to get serious about the problem. Former Los Angeles Chief of Police Ed Davis suggested erecting gallows at the airports. He was greatly castigated, and later said he didn't really mean it, but I do wonder if there weren't germs of truth in there? The Israeli soldiers at Entebbe were given strict orders to see that no terrorist survived, and those orders were carried out despite one attempt at surrender.

All of which is very well, but what is terrorism? Until we know what it is, how shall we deal with it?

The definitions change, too. In 1917 the United States went to war over the right of U.S. citizens to travel on belligerent passenger ships in time of war. After all, not only was the *Lusitania* a British ship sailing into a British port, she was carried on the Royal Navy books as an "auxiliary cruiser";

99

yet we expected the German Navy to let her sail through, and at the least the German subs should surface and order the ship to surrender after giving the passengers opportunity to reach safety. In 1918 we preserved the rights of neutrals at considerable cost of American blood; but in December 1941 U.S. Navy subs were ordered to sink without warning any Japanese vessels they might find.

I have seen many definitions of terrorism. As good as any is "making war against innocent bystanders." Of course that one is fairly broad, and can be construed as branding much of the Allied strategic air activity of World War II as acts of terrorism—and for that matter, makes terrorists of us all, since our doctrine of Mutual Assured Destruction says in effect that we hold the women and children of the Soviet Union hostage to ensure against the Politburo's aggressions.

What we see as terrorism, others may see as their only possible course of action. One person's act of terrorism is another's heroic attempt to win freedom for his people. All of which suggests we haven't given sufficient thought to the problem. Clearly we think certain kinds of terrorist acts are justified, else we would universally condemn not only the atom bombing of Hiroshima but the fire raids over Tokyo.

Which leaves us with something of a dilemma.

RENDER UNTO CAESAR
Eric Vinicoff and Marcia Martin

(*INTER* TERRA *ET* MARS)

Pavel admired his would-be executioner.

The *kaesta* was a masterpiece of the surgeon-breeders' art: bulky, dark brown and at least three meters tall. It looked clumsy but didn't move that way. Pavel ducked beneath a slashing *Ursus horribilis* paw, losing two square decimeters of Aeroflot flight suit from his back, as well as some skin and blood. He moaned, rolled sideways on the hard alloy deck and sprang back to his feet. The narrow corridor left him little room for maneuvering.

Yes, he admired the *kaesta*. But he would have much rather admired it at a distance.

The *kaesta* came on again, an angry blur. Pavel swayed. He was weak, and getting weaker. While his right hand groped at the flap on his holster, he took a dodging step backward. His foot hit something slick—a smear of his own blood on the deck—and slid out from under him.

A mammoth paw, glistening with red, split the air where he had been standing.

The *kaesta* bent over him, growling. The surgeon-breeders hadn't given it human vocal cords to go with its human brain—unsurprisingly, since that would have added eighty thousand rubles to the cost. Ordinary guard *kaesta* didn't require such expensive frills.

Instead of striking to kill (which would have severely curtailed its victim's question-answering ability) the *kaesta* reached for the summoner on its chest.

Pavel finally freed the holster flap and drew his Walther XX.

The *kaesta* forgot instantly about the summoner—it pounced.

There was no time to aim; he pressed the firing stud.

The *kaesta* lashed out, knocking the stubby weapon from his hand, but not before a ruby-bright beam pricked its chest momentarily.

This time the roars of the *kaesta* were almost deafening. Pavel rolled backward, snap-extended and flipped to his feet. The effort left him semiconscious. Galaxies gyrated across his vision.

But it was all over. The *kaesta* collapsed slowly onto the red-dappled corridor deck, twitching slightly and coughing blood.

Pavel stood up, then sagged against the corridor wall. He knew that the engineering deck was isolated and crewless—his plan counted on it—but even so he was amazed that the sound of the fight hadn't attracted any attention.

For long minutes all he could do was lean against the white plastic, gasping. His medical implant whispered, "You need hospital service," over and over into his right ear, but he already knew that.

Drugs were being pumped directly into his bloodstream by the implant, and his mind began to clear—slowly. Perhaps too slowly.

So much for my career, he thought. *So much for half of my life. Pavel Machotka: Aeroflot systems engineer and deep cover agent. Deep enough, apparently, to survive the security checks run on the crew for this flight. All my life in fact—I was training for this career before I dedicated my life to the cause.*

Staggering over to an access hatch set into the wall he touched his right palm to the ident-panel beside it. The hatch dilated open. He pulled himself into the tube thus revealed, and the hatch sealed behind him.

His strength was fading fast.

Marx, when will this state wither away? he thought fiercely. *And how? Surely not by the greed of those in power.* The tube was red-lit, packed with cables and electrical equipment, and a tight fit. He snaked along until he came to a junction box marked EXT. COM. CON. Drawing the Walther XX again, he burned the box into slag metal.

So we, the few who still hold to your dream, do what we must.

Behind him he could see the slick trail that he was leaving, black under the red light. Numbness was setting in, and his muscles weren't responding the way they should. But he dragged himself further along the tube.

And must we do even this: betray those who are after all our comrades—whatever their crimes—to the enemies of the proletariat? With a final desperate heave he reached a piece of equipment marked RECIRCULATOR FILTER FLUID INPUT. He opened a valve, and dark brownish-red liquid ran out. It stained his silver flight suit, but he didn't care.

Yes, we must. We need the proceeds of our Faustian bargain, and while our fellow travelers are far away, the need for a true Marxist state is immediate.

From a pocket he took a small plastic flask. Taking a deep breath, he opened the flask, poured its clear fluid contents into another valve atop the piece of equipment, touched several heat-switches and backed away before gasping a slight breath. After throwing the flask far ahead of him, he resumed his frantic retreat.

But flesh and muscle had their limits, and he knew that he had reached them. With vivid regrets for so many things undone, he shut his eyes and died.

(HABITAT, MERCURY)

"Meanwhile at Rome people plunged into slavery—consuls, senators and knights. The higher a man's rank, the more eager his hypocrisy, and his looks the more carefully watched . . ."

The excerpt from Tacitus' *Character of Augustan Rule* came uninvited into Anthony Vale's mind as he looked at himself in his lavatory alcove mirror. It neatly summarized the men against whom he would soon be set, the "lean and hungry" wolves from Earth. Lesser wolves, granted, envoys of the modern *Imperatores* who were devouring a planet, but fearful predators nonetheless.

It also reminded him of how twenty centuries hadn't changed human nature. *Since history endures in that case*, he mused silently, *perhaps it'll do likewise today. Dear Mother Mary, I pray so.*

The Mercury Consortium Board member stared at a reflection of his ordeal. It was scribed in the eyes bloodshot from lack of sleep, the deepening lines above his thick Mediterranean brows, and the paleness that had replaced his usual ruddy color. The face staring back at him was perfectly suited to the tired executive who lived behind it.

Crossing his apartment to the muted violet bed-field, he picked up his battered attaché case from the reading table. The door opened at his approach, and he stepped out into the vestibule. Here his VIP rating served him. Instead of sharing a corridor loadramp with dozens of other dwelling units, he had a tastefully elegant personal one, as well as a door opening on his level's walkway. He was in a hurry, so he summoned a single-seat tubecar.

The small cabin and molded plastic chair were, as always, too cramped for his 191 centimeters. He irritatedly punched out a destination code on the keyboard, then settled back as the tubecar accelerated. Like any good stockholder-citizen, he hated the Tube Transport System. He hated the discomfort, the rush-hour delays, and above all the feeling of being a *parcel*. He knew that TTS was the best form of mass transit for Habitat's unusual needs—but that didn't mean he had to enjoy riding it.

The only sound within the cabin was a soft buzz that he had long ago learned to tune out. *Is all of this really worth the price we paid for it?* he wondered, as he had wondered increasingly in the past few weeks. *Not just the money, but the effort, the things left behind—and the lives? Is it really worth fighting for? We could always give in.*

As always, there came an answer: *We couldn't live the way we wanted to on Earth, so we came here. We haven't much, but we do have a society that satisfies us—and that's worth defending if anything is. So Jules argues, and the stockholder-citizens echoed him at the preliminary polling. But will they do so again when it's time to cross the Rubicon?*

And what about me, the miracle man who claims to be able to pluck victory out of a hopeless situation? Can I? And, knowing the price, should I? If my plan goes wrong, it'll go very wrong indeed. Fatally wrong for nine hundred thousand stockholder-citizens.

Knowledge of the stakes with which he was gambling began to unsettle his stomach. His Mercury Consortium Board seat had been won by conquests in the area of high finance. Dealing in megafrancs he found exciting; dealing in human lives terrified him.

He lacked the confidence of a diplomat, not to mention the training. His opponents, on the other hand, represented the four greatest powers in the history of humanity: Pan America, People's China, Noreuropa and the USSR. To counter them he was depending on his own practical political experience and the tactics of an empire fifteen hundred years dead.

He floated forward slightly as the tubecar decelerated. The hatch opened, and he stepped out into the bustle of Administration Central's foyer. The large circular area was aflood with humanity; all gliding in the dainty gait caused by the four-tenths-of-normal gravity. There were workers boarding the tubebuses that ran out to the local mines and refineries, tourists, spacemen in their flight suits, white-collar types and so on. He pushed through the crowd to reach the Window.

The thick triple-insulated pane dominated an entire sixty degrees of the wall, and it was one of the only two Windows in Habitat—Jules Nakai had the other in his office. Dozens of people milled in front of it. Anthony Vale pushed through to a good viewing position. For some reason, no matter how rushed he was, he always had to stop for a look.

It was night outside, of course; alloy reflectors covered both Windows during daylight. But the Tourist Department had illuminated the view with floodlights. He stared out at a pie-slice of the glossy white Shield that covered Mercury's surface for three kilometers in every direction. Habitat lay beneath it, a vast cylinder sunk into the planetary crust. Only the Administration Central dome sat on top.

Over two kilometers from the Window, just within the edge of the Shield, a small circle radiated internal white light. The sun was down, so the spaceport was open for business. Even as he watched, a fat cargo flitter dropped out of the star-strewn sky into the hole, fetching ore and personnel from an outlying mine. He was faintly disappointed; he had hoped to see one of the mammoth space freighters lift off.

Vanadium, cobalt, nickel, copper, molybdenum, silver, platinum and the atomic power metals; our lifeblood. Earth's, rather, and we survive by feeding its resource hunger. A safe enough thing when we were small and struggling, but Mercury has proved to be a treasure trove.

And the Mercury Consortium is now a pie to be divided among those with enough power to seize a piece. Unless I can stop them.

Beyond the Shield lay dark, undetailed terrain. But he had seen the harsh mountains, craters and cracked plains many times during daylight expeditions—and he hated them.

Alien. So damned alien, this world we now call home. It gives us the materials we need to make our air, water, food and so on—not to mention what we sell to Earth. But who could love it?

Habitat, though, isn't Mercury. Here, underground and isolated, we've built our Utopia, the best of Earth that we

105

could bring with us. Habitat we can love. We do. The Earthophiles and claustrophobes are all long gone, and the Mercury-born don't miss what they've never known.

Suddenly two arms grabbed him from behind and pulled him away from the Window. "Wait your—" he began, spinning around. Then he stopped. The puller was Mary Sunshine, his secretary. Her stocky Eskimo features were augmented by a flame-orange jumpsuit and a green beret pinned to her hairdo. She tilted her full-moon face up to look at his.

"Gotta chop it, bosman!" she said briskly. "A reactbird tailed at two twenty dex. Nakai wants a chichat, prontoest, and—"

He had no time or desire to decipher teener slang, so he gently placed a hand over her mouth and said, "Speak Italian, please. What ship landed, and where is Jules waiting for me?" Then he removed his hand.

"A UN Patrol cruiser set down ten minutes ago!" She was trembling from the importance of her news. "The VIP ground pigs are being deloused at Arrivals right now! How they must be hating *that!*"

As she spoke he pulled her through the crowd toward the loadramps.

"Anyhow, the mega-bosman . . . Mr. Nakai is in Conference A. He wants a prep talk with you before the main huddle forms. Arrivals has been given the word to hold the dung-dippers for ten more minutes."

"Then we had better hurry." They stopped in front of an in-Central loadramp. He placed his palm against the ident-panel and touched the priority button. Seconds later the door hissed open.

"Has Captain Madlock broken com-silence yet?" he asked as they entered the two-seat tubecar. They sat down, the door shut, he tapped out a destination code, and the tubecar descended.

"No sight, sound or signal. That free-floater is strictly non-sched."

He winced at the truth of her words. Only Jules Nakai and he knew that the Mercury Consortium's survival depended partly on Captain Madlock.

The knowledge gave him no pleasure.

"If and when he larks in," she said, "I'll data-feed you prontoest."

(*INTER* TERRA *ET* MARS)

Aeroflot's *Lenin* was midway in its flight to the planet of the War God, bearing the most precious cargo in its long and illustrious history. Only four men and women were tending the control deck stations; the system engineer was below on an errand.

Captain Resnick pushed a stray blond hair back under her safety cap. She appreciated the honor, but it frightened her. If anything went wrong . . . And space travel was by no means routinely safe yet. She knew of the security checks for her and her crew, the defense screens and beam projectors mounted on her normally peaceful vessel for this one mission, and the squad of *kaesti* guards below, but she thought of them as mere UN paranoid overreaction. The real dangers were the traps that the universe laid for invading humans.

It never occurred to her that there might be traps of human origin, nurtured in the very bowels of her ship.

"Tartov," she said to the astrogation officer, "set up for the hourly star-fix. Line up Polaris and—"

Suddenly a red light appeared on the life-support board. "Someone is tampering with the recirculation system!" Lieutenant Relenko reported.

"System shutdown—" Captain Resnick started to order, but the sentence died in her throat. She couldn't breathe. Something was constricting her lungs like a coiling anaconda. Her vision blurred.

Tartov and the other officers were likewise affected. "Gas!" Lieutenant Relenko gasped. Then he fell out of his chair.

Captain Resnick slapped the Mayday heat-switch on her laser-com board, but it glowed red. The signal wasn't going out.

Before she could quite understand what was happening, or figure out what to do next, she spun into blackness.

And at the perimeter of the long-range scope a blip appeared, moving toward the center.

(HABITAT, MERCURY)

Anthony Vale exited from the tubecar so quickly that Mary Sunshine had to scamper to keep up. Conference Room A's door opened at their approach. He sent her off about her own duties, then went in.

The room was larger than necessary, for psychological effect. Yellow fluorescent panels cast warm illumination on fake mahogany plastic. The round oak table had come from Earth; its six stations possessed every modern convenience. A padded chair faced each station.

Jules Nakai, Chairman of the Board of the Mercury Consortium, smiled up from one of the chairs. The frail-looking man was essentially an artist, a creator on an enormous scale. He had risen from bastardhood in post-WWII Japan to create first hydrogen plasma handling equipment, then a corporation (Tengana Electronics) to handle the handling equipment, then an alliance of corporations to exploit the Tengana-invented gravity differential space drive, and finally an entire society based on the sound business principles that he had lived by all of his life.

"The *Weltpolitik* poker game is about to begin." Jules Nakai's voice was calm. "Earth's cards are too well known. How does our hand look?"

Anthony Vale sat down next to the Chairman. "Nothing worth betting on—except we haven't any choice. The UN Patrol has two million Rangers and a fleet of thirty-six armed cruisers. They have A-bombs, H-bombs, IR lasers *et al*. We, on the other hand, have a three-hundred-person police force, eight unarmed frigate-class freighters and six unarmed passenger liners. If this degenerates into a military contest, we haven't a chance."

"So we can't let that happen," Jules Nakai said. "I'm no political scientist, as you well know. The only tool I can use to analyze this situation is game theory. But such analysis depends on rational gamesmanship by both sides. Will the power blocs follow our logic?"

Anthony Vale shook his head. "I just don't know for sure. I'll have to feel the envoys out carefully before beginning the negotiations."

"A crisis of faith?" Jules Nakai asked softly.

Anthony Vale felt a great hatred rising up through him, focusing on his old friend. Then it broke like a wave on a beach, and he sighed. "I guess so. It's all on my back, you know."

"No, it isn't," Jules Nakai said firmly. "The Board and I have approved your plan, and the stockholder-citizens will have the final say. So buck up." After a pause he added, "Did you take your environment therapy? I don't want the walls closing in on you during the session."

"Three hours of it last night." *Three hours in the image-*

*room, with the visions of wide Earthly horizons, because the
Earth-born never fully adjust to the enclosed environment.*
"Don't worry, Jules—I'm in control. I'll do the best I can,
and pray."

"Good. It's your plan, so you'll have to handle the
negotiations."

"You'll be your usual humble self, I suppose?" Anthony
Vale asked with a touch of sarcasm. He didn't want any
elbow-jostling at the wrong time.

Jules Nakai chuckled confidently. "But of course. Haven't
I always given you your head? Besides, since you've been so
close with the details, what other choice do I have?"

(*INTER* TERRA *ET* MARS)

From the outside the small passenger liner looked old. On
the inside it looked sloppy. But beneath the grime of the
engineering deck lay new GD engines powerful enough to lift
a fully loaded freighter from Jupiter's surface.

The shabby vessel was nestled against the larger, newer
Lenin like a tugboat moving a proud queen of the fleet.

Two young women and one young man labored on the
control deck. Their captain strode from station to station,
checking everything. He was an ancient man with shoulder-
length white hair and a red face. His flight suit had been
obsolete for thirty years.

Pausing behind the com officer he demanded, "Status
report!"

"They didn't get a call off, skipper!" Lieutenant Yinger's
voice quavered. Like everyone else on board, she was afraid
of Captain Madlock. "The timer on their fusion pit is set for
thirty minutes: plenty of time to get clear."

Captain Madlock stomped over to the scan board. "Any
company?"

Lieutenant Law shook her head. "Not a sign, skipper!"
Then she smiled tentatively. "It seems we're home free."

"Who asked for your bloody opinion?!" Captain Madlock
roared. "You just keep your eyes on them damned scopes! I
don't want no dung-dipper scows slippin' up on us!!"

"Aye aye, skipper!" Lieutenant Law's turn back to her
scopes was nothing more than a blur.

Jim Madlock Jr., the Purser, entered. "Wipe the doom
gloom off your phiz, pater. I told you outwitting the Terries
would be no prob."

Captain Madlock bore down on his son like an angry bull. "Lock a baffle on that thruster, boy, or I'll feed you to the plasma chamber! We ain't clear o' this till we get Mercuryport's Shield betwixt us and Earth! Now, dammit, gimme your status!"

"I've got the 'payload' stowed away." Jim Madlock Jr. was subdued. "The crew, too. Except our, ah, business associate. We found him dead of *kaesti* wounds in the Jeffries Tube. But he must have done his job before dying."

"Then get out o' here and seal it up!"

The young Purser gulped, nodded and left at a dead run.

Captain Madlock turned to Astrogator Shatz. "Plot a minimum-time flight program home! Stand by to execute! Don't just sit there slack-jawing me, you unlicked cub! I gave you an order! Move it!"

Captain Madlock's anger masked worry and suspicion. It was all going too smoothly; in space, emergencies were the norm.

What he didn't realize (and what Anthony Vale could have told him) was that the apparently easy and casual capture represented only the tip of a six-month iceberg of painstaking, dangerous effort. Smoothly was the only way it *could* have run; any missteps would have been fatal to the plan.

And, despite all of their preparation, a last-minute change in the *kaesti* patrol schedule had cost a man's life.

(HABITAT, MERCURY)

A violet light over the door glowed briefly. Anthony Vale and Jules Nakai ended their discussion and put on concealing official faces.

The four delegates were ushered in with no ceremony. Anthony Vale wasn't surprised to find that the "impartial United Nations envoys" were a Pan American, a Noreuropan, a Chinese and a Soviet. The power blocs were here to claim their prize.

Ti Ho Chi, a former Vice Chairman of the Central Committee of People's China, was well known to Anthony Vale by reputation as a bare-knuckles type—and looked it. The Pan American introduced himself as Señor Guzman, and apparently his stomach didn't approve of the low gravity. His over-manicured elegance gave him a foppish aura, but Anthony Vale wasn't fooled—no fops would be representing the power blocs on *this* mission. Comrade Ivanov was short, dumpy and visibly suspicious of everything around him—including his fellow delegates. Herr Einerson, the head of Noreuropan Military Intelligence, was by all accounts brilliant—and brilliantly ruthless. His emotions, if any, lay hidden behind impassive Nordic features.

The amenities proceeded shallowly to a swift conclusion. Both sides were eager to get on with the matter at issue.

"Here." Herr Einerson tossed a document in front of Anthony Vale. "Brief and to the point. The United Nations has finally resolved the question of jurisdiction *in re* Mercury. All national authorizations for extraterrestrial development have been superseded by a new United Nations Act. Your previous arrangement with the government of Japan is, therefore, null and void. Only the Security Council may now grant charters to exploit extraterrestrial resources. To be frank, yours is an illegal operation under the new Act. You shouldn't be here."

Anthony Vale smiled sweetly. "But we *are* here, Herr Einerson. How do you propose to remedy this irregularity?"

"The United Nations has designated Mercury a UN Protectorate Territory. A Government House and Patrol base will be built up here to administer UN policy and extend Earth's security sphere. You'll have to register with the proper Protectorate agency. Since you've already sampled Mercury's riches liberally, there will be prorated back taxes—"

"Taxes?" Anthony Vale had been scanning the UN document while he listened, but his head snapped up at that last word.

Comrade Ivanov took over. "By all means. You must pay for the privilege of mining UN-controlled territory, as well as for the benefits derived from UN jurisdiction. Income and land-use taxes, plus other fees described in the Act." His Esperanto was almost illegibly accented.

Anthony Vale could see their plan, a more subtle plan than he had expected. *Outright expropriation might be questioned Earthside as too baldly illegal. This is much better. Let us work our hearts out, then milk us through taxes of everything but our bare survival needs. And with a Patrol base next door, who would dare dispute the taxation? Mercury would be an open prison camp laboring for the power blocs.*

"I seem to recall that an American named Patrick Henry once spoke against absentee taxation," Jules Nakai observed, looking at Señor Guzman. "Will the Mercury Consortium receive a General Assembly seat?"

111

The Pan American envoy showed white shark's teeth. "Surely you jest. Yours is a commercial organization, not a nation."

Anthony Vale was concentrating on his station's data display screen. *What will it be, stockholder-citizens? On to Rome, or back to Gaul?*

The conference was being broadcast to every stockholder-citizen on Mercury. The question previously put to them was: do we accept the UN program or fight? Each person phoned his or her vote in to the computers at Com central, where it was voiceprint-verified and tabulated. When and if the two-thirds majority required by the Consortium charter developed, the *vox populi* would appear on Anthony Vale's screen.

Jules Nakai engaged the envoys in a delaying action, a question-and-answer session concerning the details of the Act. Finally, after nearly fifty minutes of stalling rhetoric, the screen flashed a single word that only Anthony Vale could see—*fight*.

"We reject your taxes, your Patrol base, your UN Act—and you." Anthony Vale was scared, so he spoke boldly. "The stockholder-citizens of Mercury won't be dictated to by Earth. We are, no matter what you may think, a sovereign state. We won't submit to slave status."

Ti Ho Chi exploded. "Reject us! Are you fool enough to think we care about your opinion?! With six shiploads of Rangers we can—"

Señor Guzman interrupted smoothly. "Let's not compound our troubles with hasty words. Surely an understanding can be reached without any, ah . . . pounding of chests." He showed Ti Ho Chi a pained expression.

"I say a demonstration of sincerity is in order!" the Chinese envoy roared. "Our cruiser mounts weapons! Re-education can begin at once!"

"You won't attack us." Anthony Vale put much more assurance into his words than he felt. "There's no profit in radioactive ruins. If you invade us, you'll meet total resistance and 'scorched earth.' We'll blow up every mine and refinery. So why kill the goose that lays such valuable eggs? I have a better idea; grant us sovereignty and let us join the UN."

Señor Guzman chuckled daintily. "Such matters aren't in our purview—we leave them to Patrol strategists. But I'm sure a suitable method of nondestructive persuasion can be

112

found. There are many possibilities. Your ecology *is* artificial—and rather fragile. Perhaps a siege . . ."

"Try it," Jules Nakai broke in. "You'll be surprised. We're almost self-sufficient, and we can make it the rest of the way if we have to."

"Biological warfare then," Herr Einerson proposed. "Or the Swiss assassination technique. Or something else; there are—"

"Hey, bosman!" The bell-like tonalities of Mary Sunshine emerged from the com at Anthony Vale's station. "Your man just tailed in. He said to tell you the cargo is one hundred percent, and you should give the Terry dung-dippers—" Anthony Vale nearly strained a wrist as he slapped the com cutoff button.

He didn't wait for the envoys' outrage to fade. He had a lever, and he wanted to use it. Properly placed, it might pry Herr Einerson and his greedy associates away from Mercury for a long time.

"You gentlemen are guests on Mercury Consortium territory," he began, "yet you threaten us with invasion and conquest. Well, we don't care to hear any more of your arrogance. Listen to *our* terms, then go."

"Why, of all the—" Ti Ho Chi bellowed, but Anthony Vale cut him off.

"I implied earlier that you should leave Mercury alone because the alternative would be more expensive. Gentlemen, costs have just gone up."

Señor Guzman smiled. "Or so you would have us believe."

Anthony Vale smiled back. "We're businesspersons here—as you've seen, we think primarily in economic terms. I discovered the solution to our problem of defense, however, in Caesar's *Commentaries.*"

"And what would that be?" Comrade Ivanov demanded sarcastically. "Legions in rusted armor? Slave galleys?" He laughed, ending with an unmuffled belch.

"One tactic Caesar used to keep defeated tribes pacified was to take and hold hostages, usually children from the chieftain's family. They were raised in Rome by the Republic *not as prisoners but as citizens*. This shows the Roman genius for empire, since the good treatment kept tribal animosities to a minimum.

"I can see from your faces that you preread my point. Yes, we've taken hostages—one hundred children from the ruling

113

families in your four countries. It was costly, but not very difficult. An Earthside political terrorist organization, highly skilled at such work, was most willing to help us for a price, and our own Captain Madlock brought them here."

"One hundred chil—the UNESCO System Tour!" Comrade Ivanov barked. "What kind of cruel, stupid joke is this?! The children were on their way to Mars as the first leg of an educational tour, but the *Lenin* accidentally blew up last night! They're all dead! *Dead!*"

"That's how we arranged for it to look," Anthony Vale said, smiling. "Actually no one has died—yet."

"Impossible!" Ti Ho Chi bellowed. "You can't have kidnapped them! You're talking about the most thoroughly protected children on Earth!"

Anthony Vale shook his head. "Anyone, no matter how well guarded, can be kidnapped if there is enough ability, financing and determination behind the effort. The terrorists have had decades to develop their skills, so we hired the best. They supplied the ability, we supplied the financing, and our money supplied the determination."

Señor Guzman said softly, "I think, before this goes any further, we had better see the young ones—if you really have them."

That matched Anthony Vale's own intentions, so the four envoys were escorted to the Arrivals area. One hundred boys and girls between the ages of ten and fifteen were being processed in the large receiving room. Each of the UN envoys spoke briefly with several of them, and Jules Nakai supplied fingerprints and other identity proofs. Then, at the Board Chairman's suggestion, they returned to Conference Room A.

Anthony Vale was very glad to leave the sobbing, terrified children behind. His burden of guilt was heavy enough as it was.

"You'll turn them over to us immediately," Ti Ho Chi growled when everyone was again seated, "or the entire might of the United Nations will be mobilized to destroy you!"

"I think not," Anthony Vale replied calmly. "Any military action would endanger the lives of the hostages. We might not be cruel enough to execute them, but it would be a simple thing to put them in the forefront of any fighting."

"We don't negotiate with kidnappers!" Comrade Ivanov barked. "Nor do we pay ransom! You can't accomplish anything by this outrage!"

Anthony Vale nodded. "I know the official policy. It's fine when the kidnap victim is someone else's loved one. But the leaders of your countries are also fathers and mothers. We're betting everything that they won't risk their children's lives for the money they could squeeze out of us—or for vengeance either."

Ti Ho Chi and Comrade Ivanov tried to launch fierce replies, but Señor Guzman stopped them with a gesture. He said to Herr Einerson, "You're an expert on such matters, Gunnar. What is your opinion?"

Herr Einerson frowned for a long time, then answered, "My Premier is the hardest, coldest, most pragmatic man I've ever known. But he loves his daughter Inga, whom I was just talking to, more dearly than his own life. I don't think he'll risk her to gain Mercury." He shook his head.

Señor Guzman turned back to Anthony Vale. "Let's grant for the moment that what you say is true. What ransom do you wish?"

"No ransom, just what is rightfully ours: sovereignty, full territorial integrity and a seat in the United Nations."

"Have the seat!" bellowed Ti Ho Chi. "Have it and rot in it! All we ask is that you release the children! You're civilized men; how could you plan and carry out such a cruel act? Using children as pawns!"

Anthony Vale was suffering acutely from that very guilt, but he couldn't let on. "You've left us no choice. We have to defend ourselves any way we can. As for the hostages— they'll never leave Mercury. They're our protection, our only line of defense."

"You wouldn't need any defense," Herr Einerson pointed out sharply, "if you hadn't demanded such high prices for your resources. You've plunged Earth into an economic crisis. Inflation, recession, a balance of payments disaster; you know that our technology, our very society, would collapse without your resources, and charge accordingly. We had no choice but to take direct action."

"You had every choice!" Anthony Vale was angry. "You could have negotiated! Of course our prices are high; building a new world is expensive! But we could have worked something out! Instead you took the thief's way!"

Ti Ho Chi made a convulsive lunge at Anthony Vale, but Herr Einerson grabbed him and held him back. Concealed slits in the wall opened to reveal alert police gunners with laser rifles. The emitter bells tracked the Chinese envoy, who subsided.

"An incident would be very embarrassing at this time," Jules Nakai said softly.

"You may have outwitted yourselves," Herr Einerson observed. "Our leaders might stop all actions against you to save their children—if they can. But these brazen kidnappings can't go unanswered. If they do, the power of our leaders will be undermined by their apparent impotence. Others, unaffected by your blackmail, will take their place. Then you'll be in an even worse position."

Anthony Vale smiled. "Who knows of any kidnappings? The children and the crew of the *Lenin*, yes, but they're going to stay here. We won't let any news leak Earthside. That leaves you gentlemen, and your leaders when you tell them. They'll cover up to protect their children—and their political positions. You'll cover up because they'll order you to."

"Perhaps we cannot attack you," Señor Guzman said, "but there are indirect pressures we can bring to bear."

"Anything that hurts us hurts the hostages," Anthony Vale replied flatly.

"Doesn't it bother you that what you're doing is immoral?" Herr Einerson asked. "You're going to torture a hundred families by keeping their children from them. And what of the children themselves? They're innocents; how can you justify what you're doing to them?"

"We aren't evil people," Jules Nakai put in. "We'll raise the children in foster homes where they'll be loved. All of the hostages will be given full stockholder-citizen rights and comforts, minus only the right to leave Mercury. Two more things—as soon as we get our UN membership we'll arrange it so the families can come up here to visit their children, and we'll also negotiate lower resource prices. Unlike you, we're not greedy. An economic collapse Earthside would ruin us too."

"That's all well and good," Herr Einerson countered, "but visitation privileges and lower resource prices won't redress kidnappings."

"We only did what we had to do to save our homeland!" Jules Nakai inserted hotly. "And no more than necessary! Certainly there's immorality in kidnapping young children— immorality that we've done everything we possibly can to recompense both the families and the children for—but what

116

about the immorality of enslaving a nation of nine hundred thousand?!''

"We're enslaving no one," Señor Guzman said suavely.

"Spare me your sophistries!" Jules Nakai flamed up again. "Your 'Act' amounts to slavery whatever you call it! We have a good life here; a much higher standard of living than any Earthside nation, fewer social ills, no population pressure! Our corporate state works! We have a right to defend our nation from invasion! Would you rather have the bloody immorality of war?! It's cruel, but sometimes a lesser immoral act is necessary to prevent a greater one!''

"Perhaps so," Herr Einerson said softly. "But, if so, I have a suggestion which may partially remedy and set right the wrongs done to the children and their families—families made up of not only the leaders you seek to blackmail, but also bereaved mothers, sisters and brothers.''

"What?" Jules Nakai asked suspiciously.

"Let the families come here to live with their children."

"What?" Jules Nakai couldn't believe his ears, but Anthony Vale's mind raced ahead, analyzing the startling proposal from every angle. *Dear Mother Mary, why didn't I think of that!* A great part—but not all—of his guilt left him.

"You must be joking!" Jules Nakai protested. "Why . . . the leaders wouldn't quit their positions and—''

"Not the leaders; just their families. You see, most families of major politicians are used to living separately from said politicians for long spells; it's a common practice to keep loved ones out of the capital cities and their much greater dangers, especially that of assassination. Why, my own family lives in the country hundreds of miles from my department in Heidelberg. And these families are also used to moving from place to place; they would adjust to your excellent life-style here quite well.''

"And the children would be with their parents!" Anthony Vale said eagerly. "Yes, I like it.''

"But . . . why would they come?" Jules Nakai was still floundering.

"To be with their children, of course," Herr Einerson replied. "We'll need a cover story to keep the kidnappings secret; a goodwill gesture to welcome the Mercury Consortium into the community of nations or something like that. A minor detail.''

"We would treat them as befits their importance, of course,''

Jules Nakai said bemusedly. "Their presence would make us even more secure. But why do *you* want to enhance our number of hostages, Herr Einerson?"

The Noreuropan shook his head. "I'm only acting in the interest of my superiors—and their families—all of whom will want to be with their kidnapped children. Since the Terra-Mercury flight requires only slightly more than a day, all of the leaders will be able to see their families often."

Jules Nakai was silent for long moments, then said, "Very well. The families will be welcome and well treated—after we receive our guarantees and UN seat."

There was another lengthy silence. The envoys looked at each other. Herr Einerson turned to Anthony Vale. "Several months ago I had occasion to say that warfare by assassination is the ultimate form of human conflict, invulnerable and all-conquering. I stand corrected."

Señor Guzman rose, signaling the other envoys to do likewise, which they did. He showed Anthony Vale a thin smile. "We shall carry your words to our superiors. Naturally the final decision is theirs. However," his face went impassive, "I fear that your voice is destined to become painfully familiar in our General Assembly meeting. Adiós."

The Earthside delegation departed with a police squad "escorting" them to their cruiser.

Anthony Vale almost collapsed in his chair from the terrific release of tension. *We did it! We won—for now*.

Jules Nakai was staring questioningly at him.

"Cheer up," Anthony Vale said weakly. "We just heard the verdicts of two career power-brokers."

"I know. I just have trouble accepting it. After all this time the battle is over."

Anthony Vale raised his head and stared at his friend. "The hell it is! We've just begun to fight! The Terries are going to try every sneaky trick short of open violence to get the children back. We'll have to be on our guard every second. But at least it's a kind of fight we *can* win, unlike open war."

"I see." Jules Nakai smiled.

"You do, do you! Do you also see that this victory is temporary? In ten years our ransom victims will probably be losing control of their countries, and the new leaders will surely be just as greedy. The hostages won't be adorable children anymore, either. Then what? They certainly won't let us get away with *this* again.''

Jules Nakai kept on smiling. ''Then we'll do something else. Maybe we'll build a military defense structure—we can afford it. Or maybe we'll forge protective alliances with other nations. Or maybe some other tactic. We're buying time, and that's what we desperately need. And, of course, when we've made those other arrangements we can let all of the hostages go home.'' He paused, then backtracked. ''At least I pray we're buying time.''

Anthony Vale made the sign of the cross over his chest. ''We could certainly use His help, but I doubt that He smiles on kidnappers . . . Even with all of our steps to redress the kidnappings I can't help feeling guilty over what we've done to those poor innocent children.'' *The guilt-pain will stay with me for life, punishing me.*

''Then,'' Jules Nakai countered, ''let *me* remind *you* of your Roman history for a change. The hostages from Gaul grew up contented and loyal to Rome. They became, in all ways, Roman *civitates*. If Caesar can do it, so can we. After all, we have quite a world to offer them.''

''We shall see,'' Anthony Vale said tiredly. ''The ultimate answer to all questions . . . we shall see.''

UPI TICKER (NEW YORK)

. . . SECRETARY GENERAL DEALCUAZ ANNOUNCED TO-DAY THE RESULTS OF THE SECURITY COUNCIL VOTE ON THE ADMISSION OF THE MERCURY CONSORTIUM TO THE UNITED NATIONS. THE VOTE, 11–2 IN FAVOR, WITH NONE OF THE FOUR VETOES EXERCISED, COMES ON THE HEELS OF LAST TUES-DAY'S AFFIRMATIVE GENERAL ASSEMBLY VOTE.

. . . AMBASSADOR VALE WILL BE INSTALLED IN A BRIEF CERE-MONY TOMORROW AT 11 A.M. EST. THE ADMISSION OF THE MERCURY CONSORTIUM COMES AS AN ABRUPT REVERSAL . . .

. . . IN A RELATED ACTION AIMED AT CEMENTING RELA-TIONS BETWEEN EARTH AND MERCURY, THE FAMILIES OF ONE HUNDRED PROMINENT GOVERNMENTAL OFFICIALS WILL BE TAKING UP RESIDENCE IN THE SUPER-CITY OF HABITAT FOR AN INDEFINITE TIME . . .

EDITOR'S INTRODUCTION TO:

SEE NOW, A PILGRIM
by Gordon R. Dickson

Gordon Dickson is deservedly well known for his *Dorsai* novels. (His name for the series is *The Childe Cycle*.) "See Now, A Pilgrim" is part of his *other* series: stories of the invasion of Earth by the Aalaag.

The Aalaag are a warrior race. Frighteningly competent, they reduced Earth's defenses to powder within days of their arrival, and soon installed themselves as the new rulers of humanity—whom they think of as cattle.

Their weapons are as superior to the best on Earth as the Red Army's weapons are superior to the Enfields of the *mujahadeen*. Moreover, long accustomed to military power, the Aalaag are also experienced in government. They rule an empire of many stars and races; and their history teaches them that eventually the conquered cattle learn to love their conquerors.

So it has always been; but the Aalaag do not know humanity as well as they think. Courage and determination can do much if coupled with deception and stealth. Knowledge is power, and what the Aalaag don't know may very well harm them.

SEE NOW, A PILGRIM
Gordon R. Dickson

There were fourteen of them, gathered in the small room of an empty warehouse about a table made of two smaller tables pushed together.

They were the London area Resistance leaders, according to what the man whom Shane knew only as Peter had claimed; and Peter, himself, was obviously in command. As he had been the obvious commanding figure—even though he was not the local leader—of the group in Milan, Italy, that had kidnapped Shane after he had rescued the young woman named Maria from the Aalaag. Maria Casana—whom he somehow hoped to save from all this.

The light in the room came from kerosene lamps, spaced on the long metal worktable, whose mantles hissed and glowed whitely inside their glass chimneys. The illumination they gave seemed hardly less than the same number of hundred-watt electric bulbs would have given, and Shane drew the edges of the cowl to his cloak closely together before his face.

He had not taken the chair that had been placed for him and he remained the only one standing in the room. At the moment he was hollow inside with the empty sense of isolation that had been with him all his life; and he did not trust himself to talk to these people, seated.

This sort of confrontation was not what he was good at. His way had always been to avoid crowds and gatherings. He was a loner; and while he could be effective in conversation or even argument one on one, he had never had the experience or desire to address a number of people at once. It was ironic, given his instinct always to avoid groups and organizations. Events had seemed to contrive to draw him away from that instinct ever since the moment two years before in which he had gone slightly insane for the first time in his life, and as a result drawn the stick figure of the pilgrim on the wall below the man the Aalaag had executed in Aalborg, Denmark. His aim in life had always been to live as quietly and unobtrusively as possible, and make the most of his good fortune at being one of the favored group of human translator-couriers employed by the First Captain, leader of the aliens on the now-captive Earth.

Now, instead, he found himself getting deeper and deeper into this Resistance and everything it implied, including having to deal with those seated before him at this moment. He had no experience at addressing a number of people at once, let alone trying to convince and command them with something he, himself, knew to be a lie. But any other way meant death, eventually, a slow and painful death at the hands of the Aalaag.

His only hope, he thought, looking at their faces, was to make a virtue of that same loneliness and isolation in himself. He could never be one of them, so let him not try. In fact, let him make a virtue of being different; of being, if necessary, someone they would not like—if giving that would also give him the difference, the distance and authority he would need to control not only these, but the others he would have to deal with later—others who would be stronger, brighter, and more experienced than the fourteen before him now, with the possible exception of Peter.

"We're perfectly safe here," Peter said, speaking from his own chair at the far end of the makeshift conference table, down its long length to Shane who stood opposite, at the other end. "You can take off that hood now, and let the rest of them here have a look at you. And sit down."

"No," said Shane.

The negative had been instinctive—almost reflexive in its protectiveness. But the moment it left his lips he found himself explaining with hardly a pause.

"If I could find some way of doing it," he said, as he remained standing, "I'd erase what I look like from your memory, and the memory of anyone who was with you when you saw me. For what's going to need to be done, my face is going to have to stay unknown. Either that, or I'm not going to have any part of what all of you are doing. I know the Aalaag better than any of you ever will. You've got everything to gain by dealing with me. But you'll deal with me with my face hidden or not at all."

"What indeed is it we're going to do together, then?" said Peter. "We're waiting to hear that."

Seated at the far end of the table, Peter looked an unlikely person to hold authority over these others around him, some of whom had reached into the second half of life's century and many of whom looked more like leaders than he did. He was boyishly round-faced and round-skulled, with thin, straight brown hair on top of the skull. His appearance was that of a man in no more than his early twenties, but Shane judged him to be thirty at least.

"I'm going to show you how to get rid of the Aalaag, of course," Shane said. "The same thing you and others like you have been trying to do ever since the aliens landed, but without succeeding in anything much more than sitting around and talking about it, or marking on walls—"

There was a murmur that was half a growl from those around the table. Their faces were not friendly.

"Like it or not, it's a fact," Shane said. "I tell you, I know the Aalaag, in a way none of you ever could. With my help you've got some hope at least. Without me, you've got no more than you ever had—and that's nothing at all. Your attitude here isn't very hopeful. I did a lot of thinking before I decided to get back in touch with you people."

He paused. None of them said anything.

"I want you to be completely clear about this," he said. "I can help you—but I'm putting my own life on the line to do it. I know, the rest of you are all doing that, too. But you've made your choice. Mine means taking chances none of you have to take and whether I do that depends on you. It depends, in fact, on whether we can agree to work together, exclusively and exactly on my terms."

He paused again.

"You could be a spy for the aliens," said a man in his forties with a heavy jaw, halfway down the table to Shane's left. Shane laughed; and he did not have to exaggerate the bitterness of that laughter. It came up like an acid bubble from his stomach into his throat.

"Now, there's a perfect example of why you've never won anything against the Aalaag by yourselves, and never will," he said. "That's exactly the kind of thinking that leaves you helpless where they're concerned. You think of yourself as equal to the Aalaag, with the only difference between you and them the fact that they've got a massive edge in technology over anything we humans ever came up with. You think of them basically as equals under their armor and without their weapons—"

"Well, aren't they?" demanded the man with the heavy jaw. "Those things, and a little more height and some extra muscle. That's all the difference, and they act like they're gods and we're dirt!"

"Maybe they're right; maybe the gap is there. Maybe they are gods and we're dirt. Anyway, it doesn't matter. Who knows?" Shane laughed again. "The point isn't whether you actually are their equals or not, but that you make the mistake of thinking you're their equals. As a result, you instinctively assume they also think of you as equals; which is so far from their thinking that they'd have trouble believing you could imagine something like that. To you, it might make sense to send a spy among troublemakers of a subjugated race. To them . . . would you send a laboratory mouse to spy upon other mice in your walls that you wanted to get rid of? Can an animal be a spy? And if it could, what could it report back to you, other than that its own kind in the walls were there—and you know that already. Sooner or later, with poison and traps, you'll get rid of them anyway; so why this nonsense of sending a beast just like them to 'spy' on them?"

Shane stopped speaking. The others around the table stared back at him and said nothing for a long moment. Then Peter spoke.

"My apologies, fellow fighters," he said. "I brought you here to meet this man who calls himself Pilgrim because I thought he could be useful to our Resistance effort. I still think so. Very useful. But I had no idea he'd start out by insulting us. In fact, I don't see the reason and the sense behind his doing it, even now. Why, Pilgrim?"

"Because there's no use our talking unless I can get through to you on a level where your minds have been closed from the start," Shane answered. "I repeat, I can show you how to get rid of the Aalaag. But to do what can be done, you've first got to face some facts and get rid of some illusions; and the first of those is the one that someday you're going to be able to fight them and beat them. Get it clearly into your heads that if there were only one Aalaag on Earth, short of surrounding him or her with a wall of living human flesh, renewed as fast as he killed those who made it up, you couldn't even contain him, let alone conquer him."

124

"Even if there were only one, it'd be worth doing," shouted a small man with a face like a dried apple, farther down the table than the heavy-jawed man.

"That's right," said a thick-bodied, thick-faced woman. "He'd have to run out of power for his weapons sooner or later."

"Do you know he'd run out—or do you just assume that?" retorted Shane. "That's a human assumption; I've lived with the Aalaag for over two years and I'll tell you I wouldn't take it for granted that he'd run out of anything. No, in fact, what I'd assume would be that his power would last beyond the point where the last person on Earth was dead. You see, you're doing it again; thinking of them in the terms you understand, assuming human limitations to them and what they own. And that's the most basic error of all."

"What are you trying to tell us, then?" said the heavy-jawed man. "That we can't win?"

"Not in any face-to-face, stand-up fight with them, no. Never," said Shane. "Get it through your heads, clearly, once and for all. You can never destroy the Aalaag. But, what you might be able to do is trick them into leaving this planet and going someplace else."

"Go someplace else? Go where?" The female voice came from close to Shane on his right, and by the time he had pulled his gaze back from the heavy-jawed man, there was no way he could tell which of the three women seated close to him on that side of the table had spoken.

"Who knows? Who cares?" Shane said. "Somewhere where they'd find another race to subjugate, one that'd look more profitable to own than we are."

The heavy-jawed man snorted and leaned back in his chair, tilting it on its two back legs.

"Just ask them to go away, I suppose?" he said.

"No," said Shane. "A lot more than that. There'd be a lot more to do to get that done, by work a lot more difficult and a lot more painful than that. But we're getting ahead of ourselves. First I've got to be sure you're ready to listen to me and believe me when I tell you about them as they really are—and that means there isn't one of you who's not going to have to give up at least one pet notion you've believed in since they came, and replace it with a truth that'll be a lot less comfortable for you to accept. But if you don't want to listen to me, I don't know what I'm doing here."

"In other words," said Peter unexpectedly, "he's asking you to listen."

"Listen—and believe," said Shane. "Unless you can believe what I tell you—really believe it, so that you'll act on it as fact in the future—you're headed for disaster, taking probably a lot of other people along with you. I don't want to be one of them."

"Pilgrim," said Peter, "I'm sure we're all convinced of your instinct for self-preservation by now, if nothing else. Why don't you just go ahead and tell us whatever it is you have to tell us about the Aalaag?"

Shane looked around the table.

"I'm not yet convinced that all of those here are ready to believe."

"You don't want much," said Peter. "You come among us with no credentials, you won't show your face, you make claims of having a long and close acquaintance with the aliens—but there's no way we can check that. And you want us simply to take your word for anything you tell us about them, even if it goes against our own experience and knowledge. Can you blame us for reserving belief in you and what you're going to say?"

"No. But I have to have that belief, all the same," Shane said. "Let me see if I can convince you, then."

He paused and looked around the table, deliberately into the faces of all of them there.

"As I said, I've spent more than two years past among the aliens. Some of you must have been fighting them, or thinking and planning about fighting them at least that long. Tell me, in all that time, have any of you come up with any kind of plan for any way of doing it?"

There was silence as he looked around the table again.

"I take it, you all recognize you haven't," he said. "Tell me this, then. You've been ready to give your lives to fight them, if some kind of workable plan could be made. Are you still ready to do that?"

Again there was silence, but the expressions on the faces were answer enough.

"All right," Shane said. "Now I come along. All I have to offer is something that might not work. But it also might work—which is more than you or anyone you know has been able to come up with in two and a half years or more. And I tell you that to get a chance to use it you have to take me as I am—without questions about myself—and believe what I tell you about the Aalaag. Isn't it worth your accepting that for the chance—even just the chance—of doing what you've been trying to do so long without success?"

Silence, then the voice of the heavy-jawed man.

"You've got to give us some reason to believe you," he said. "Tell us some sort of reason to go along with you."

"All right," said Shane. "I'll say this much. You haven't been able to fight the Aalaag on your own. But if you listen to me I think I can show you how to make them fight themselves, by taking advantage of what they really are, and what they really think."

No one said anything.

"Well?" asked Shane after a moment. "Does that give you reason enough to try to believe what I'll tell you?"

Peter said nothing at the far end of the table. He only sat, a little sideways in his chair as if his legs were crossed to one side, just clear of the overhang. He seemed, not so much to be smiling, as to be about to smile.

"All right," said the heavy-jawed man at last. "I'll listen—with an open mind. If I can believe you, I'll go with you."

Slowly, one by one, the mutter of assent sounded about the table.

"Anyone still not ready to listen and give me credit for knowing what I'm talking about?" asked Shane.

No one moved or spoke.

"All right," said Shane. "Then I'll go back to what I said in the beginning. From the start you've thought of the Aalaag as equals and assumed they thought of you as equals. They don't. They call you beasts, and they not only don't think of you as anything but beasts, they'd find thinking of you as anything else inconceivable. Now, contrary to what you believe, the things that make them think that way aren't their superiority in weapons and armor at all—they take those things for granted, as the sort of advantage superior beings like themselves would naturally have."

He paused and smiled at them.

"Don't any of you have any idea why they think so little of you? So little, in fact, that they've never really made a serious effort to get rid of those like you, here, who meet to plan how you'd fight against them?"

"Now wait a minute," said the thick-bodied woman, "you can't tell us they aren't out to get rid of us!"

127

"Oh, certainly they are, when they stumble across you marking on a wall, or breaking one of their laws. But they know—which you don't—there's no way you can do them any real harm. So most of your secrecy and your organizational mumbo-jumbo is unnecessary. The Aalaag destroy you when they find you, not because they consider you in any way dangerous, but because they consider anyone who doesn't obey the law as insane; and insane animals should be destroyed before they contaminate others of their kind. That's all."

He paused to let his words sink in. No one spoke up, but he thought he could see several of them seemingly teetering on the edge of accepting them.

"Let's get back to why the Aalaag simply take it for granted you're an inferior race of beasts. All the evidence, from their point of view, points to that. Before they came, crime was common in all parts of our race. To an Aalaag, any crime—even the telling of the smallest lie—is unthinkable. Do you know why?"

"We don't know they don't lie," said Peter.

"I do; and you better take my word for it I'm right. To lie, to disobey an order, to do anything that's been established as forbidden, is unthinkable to them, because it would be contrary to the survival of their race. And it's that survival, not the survival of any individual one of them, that's the first concern of each one of them. Where we have an instinct of self-preservation, they've got a reflex of race preservation."

"You call ours an instinct, theirs a reflex?" said Peter, calmly, from the distant table end.

"That's right. Because theirs is one they've developed over the last few thousands of years in order to survive. I believe there was a time when they didn't have it. But that was before they were driven from their own home worlds by some race with either numbers or powers superior even to them. I haven't been able to learn the whole story. But from what I can gather, they fought back hard at that time, with pretty much the weapons they have now—but they lost, because at that time they were a people as varied in occupation as we were. Only a handful were trained fighters, though they all had to fight before they were finally forced to turn and run for it. They've been something like interstellar gypsies ever since; and in that process they've given up every profession but one. Now, every individual among them is a fighter, and as a race

128

they live under the fear of being followed and attacked again by whoever drove them from their home worlds in the first place."

"Given this is all true," said Peter, "how does knowing it help us? It seems to me you've just made a case for the aliens' being less vulnerable, rather than more."

"No," said Shane, "because in making themselves over into a race in which everyone was a warrior, they were left without people to fill the support jobs and positions. They solved that problem by finding and taking over worlds, each of which had a race that had developed some technology but was not by Aalaag terms 'civilized.' Our world, for example. These subject races filled the support vacuum. They could be made to supply the needs not only of themselves, but of a certain number of Aalaag overlords. That way the problem was solved."

"As Peter says," spoke up the female voice Shane had failed to identify before—he turned his head quickly enough this time to see her now, still speaking. She was a tall, dark-haired young woman only three chairs from him on his right. "How does that make them vulnerable?"

"Why," said Shane, "because to control a subjugated race like ours and make it produce for them means that a large proportion of the Aalaag here have to spend all or most of their time making sure the individuals of that race do what needs to be done, from the Aalaag point of view. If you like, call it an economics of power. So much in the way of supplies for the Aalaag requires so much time and effort spent in maintaining control over us."

"But what can we do about it?" asked the heavy-jawed man.

"Make it too expensive to maintain that control," said Shane.

"How?"

Shane drew a deep breath.

"That," he said, "is what I'll tell you only after I'm sure you understand the Aalaag and me; and after a worldwide structure of Resistance members has been set up, so that we can act all together and at the same time—as we'll have to when the time comes. What I've just told you is all I'll tell you for now."

"You can't leave us like that," said the thick-bodied woman. "You've still given us no proof of any kind, no real reason to believe you."

129

Shane hesitated.

"All right," he said. "I'll tell you this much that you don't know. Right now, in this city a pilot program is being set up by the Aalaag which involves the establishment of a human governor for Britain, Ireland, and the islands around them: a governor who with his staff will be responsible to the Aalaag for all production from this area, and who'll have the powers of the Aalaag behind him to enforce any rules or laws he cares to make. I'll be heading directly to that governor's new headquarters now, when I leave you."

There was a long second of silence as those around the table stared at each other.

"It'll never get off the ground," said the heavy-jawed man. "We'll make sure nothing about that governor arrangement works."

"No, you won't," Shane said. "Just the opposite. You'll cooperate in every way, if you're going to be part of what I have in mind—what I'll be telling you about in detail eventually. For now, if you'll just get used to believing the fact that you can never win by going against the Aalaag in any head-on fashion, we'll have taken the first step together. I'll leave you to think that over for now. The only way is to make the Aalaag defeat themselves."

Shane stopped talking and took a step back from the table.

"Peter," he said, looking directly down at the other man, "you and I need to talk, privately."

Peter was already on his feet and coming toward him, up around the table, behind the backs of those there who were also on their feet but had fallen into a buzz of conversations with their near neighbors.

"Have you got a vehicle of some kind?" Shane asked quietly as the other came up to him.

"My car's outside. Yes," said Peter. He grinned. "And I've not only got a permit to have it on the streets, but an adequate gas supply."

"Then you can drive me where I need to go and we can talk on the way," said Shane.

Once in the car and proceeding down streets that were already beginning to shine oily under a fresh, light rain, Peter was the first to bring up the subject.

"What was that all about, then?" he asked.

"It was what you might have expected, when you introduce me to a room full of people who work for you and tell me they're the heads of independent cells in the Resistance.''

"And you didn't think they were?" Peter's tone was just shy of a mocking note.

"I know they weren't. First, they all gave in to you and waited for you to lead things; secondly, you couldn't get together a group of your equals that quickly—to listen to someone they knew nothing about and you hardly knew more.''

"I might," murmured Peter, "be somewhat more important than you think in certain circles.''

"Now," Shane went on, "I'm going to need a liaison to the Resistance Supreme Council, or whatever it'll end up being called. I want you for that.''

"Thank you." The words were quiet and ironic.

"Don't bother. You just happened to be the first Resistance leader I met; and you've already seen what I look like. But I eventually want you to run that particular Supreme Council, or whatever, so that between the two of us, you and I, we can make decisions and act on them without putting everything to a vote and getting bogged down in parliamentary procedures.''

"I see," said Peter, this time with no humor or any other overtone to his voice at all. Almost absentmindedly, he wheeled the car smoothly around a corner.

Silently watching the other man out of the corner of his eye, Shane felt a deep sense of relief to find out he had not been wrong.

"The first thing I'll need you to do," said Shane, "will be to get together a meeting of all those who could be called national leaders of the Resistance—''

Something very close to a sputter from Peter interrupted him.

"Are you insane?" Peter exploded. "Do you think you've stumbled on to a worldwide organization already set up on strict military lines? Resistance is a game anyone can play—''

"I know I haven't," Shane interrupted him in turn. "But something pretty close to that is what I'm going to need before I'm done. You're going to help me get it. Now, if there's no such thing as national leaders to the Resistance groups here and across Europe, then what have we got available if we try to get a congregation of European leadership together? Because that's what we're going to have to have.''

"For what?"

"For putting the kind of unified pressure on the Aalaag that is going to be needed to get them to leave this world."

"You know," said Peter, glancing sideways at him for a second, "you're talking nonsense. It may have been all right for those people back there. But you've got to tell me something to convince me first you aren't either mad or some kind of con man."

"That's a ridiculous statement," said Shane. "It implies a question you'd already answered for yourself when you asked me to get in touch with you again, back in Milan; not to mention the fact that just now I was able to tell you and the others about the new Governor setup. I'm your pipeline to Aalaag Headquarters—something so rare and valuable to you, you never even dreamed of having anything like it. You know it. I know it. That's why you'll take me on my terms or not at all. Besides, you're not unintelligent. When I understand the Aalaag a few orders of magnitude better than any of the rest of you, you ought to be able to see why I could be telling the truth—and take me on faith until you've got some further evidence to judge me by."

"But you want us to follow you blindly," said Peter.

"That's right. It's the only safe way for me, so those are my terms, to start off with at least," answered Shane, losing patience. "Now, if there's nothing resembling an international organization of the Resistance, you still must know people of authority on the continent I could talk to. Am I right or wrong?"

"Well," said Peter slowly. "Every large city has its important Resistance figure. Anna ten Drinke in Amsterdam, Albert Desoules in Paris, and so forth. We can invite them to get together with us, but—"

"Good. You take care of that," said Shane. "I want them here for a meeting on a date no more than two weeks from now."

"Two weeks! It'll take most of a week just to contact them. It can't be done in any time as short as that—"

"It better," said Shane grimly. "I'm only supposed to be here for three weeks; and even at that something could come up that would make the First Captain call me back early. If there's to be any margin for unavoidable delays, two weeks is the most we can give any of them to get here."

"Next," said Peter, equally grimly, "who says they'll come? There's no reason for any of them to risk the trip.

They don't know you from Adam. I can invite them, but if any show up it'll be a miracle.''

"It's up to you to convince them to come," said Shane. "If they're the kind of people to deserve their reputations, they ought to be smart enough to see the advantages of having someone like me on their side—just as you did. I think if you tell them about how I can get them information from Aalaag Headquarters—but don't tell them anything else you know or think you've guessed about me, if you don't mind—I think you can get some of them here. Those who don't come will just have to regret they didn't and hope to hop on the band-wagon later on.''

"It's all very well for you to pronounce an ultimatum," Peter said. "But a certain amount of delay is built into the system itself—we can't just drop them a post card, you know.''

"No, you wouldn't," said Shane wearily. "For what it's worth, the mails are as safe as any courier's pouch. The Aalaag haven't the time or the interest—you remember my telling your people just now about the mice in the walls—to monitor all the mail that's written in the hope of catching a few Resistance people or other humans who're doing something illegal. But, do it your way.''

"We pass messages from hand to hand, to small boats crossing the Channel to the continent and so on. At any rate it'll take three days . . . we're here," interrupted Peter, putting his foot on the brake of the car.

"Keep going!" said Shane swiftly. He glanced at the structure Peter had indicated with the wave of one hand. It was a large, brick building, with an entrance to what seemed a courtyard through which could be seen some ordinary human vehicles parked. "Turn a corner and drop me off out of sight, so I can walk back.''

"What's up?" demanded Peter, accelerating nonetheless. "The most they can guess if they see you is that you came here in one of the free-lance cabs. There's lots of those nowadays. Anybody with the gas to burn who needs money for something on the black market—''

"It's not me, it's you," said Shane. "One of the Interior Guardsmen they'll be sure to have there might just be watching; and he just might be someone who recognizes you as a member of the Resistance.''

"Me?" Peter hooted. "If one of those bastards in the

133

Interior Guard'd suspected me, I'd have been picked up by them months ago—years ago."

"There's another of your bits of misknowledge of how the Aalaag and those who serve them work," said Shane. "Any Interior Guardsman with any experience makes it a point to find someone arrestable and then keep that information tucked away until he needs it, either to gain points with his superiors or to balance off some infringement of the rules they've caught him at. It doesn't always work for them, but most older Guardsmen have the equivalent of a whole pocketful of bits of information like that. You can let me out here."

They were around the corner. Peter pulled the car to a halt beside the wet curb. Shane got out. He pulled his staff from the rear seat where he had put it on getting into the car, jerked his hood more fully over his head and ran through the still-falling light rain toward the corner around which was his destination.

He turned in at the courtyard entrance, finding some small shelter from the falling water, and hurried across the open space, past half a dozen human cars and two of the Aalaag mercury-shining vehicles, then up a flight of half a dozen stone steps to a heavy door. Without ceremony he pushed it open and stepped inside, to find himself standing between two young fresh-faced giants of Interior Guard enlisted men.

Neither of them made any move either to stop or acknowledge him. The door here would be controlled by Aalaag equipment and it would not have opened to his hand if that equipment had not somehow recognized him and his right to enter. A few steps farther on brought him through a sort of small cloakroom or anteroom into a larger foyer with a marble floor and dark woodwork on the walls. A desk with an Interior Guard officer was at his right, and ahead to his left a wide oak staircase led up a flight of steps to the floor above. An elevator for Aalaag use had its door inset in the wall opposite the staircase. A Lieutenant in the Interior Guard sat at the desk; and this man did look up at Shane as Shane stopped before him.

"Shane Everts?" asked the officer automatically, looking back down at the screen inset in the surface of his desk. "Yes," said Shane. The question and the answer would be recorded as password and countersign, for future reference by their masters and the machinery at their masters' disposal.

"We've been expecting you." The Lieutenant was as tall

as, but of slighter build than, the two enlisted Guards at the door and looked if anything younger than they did. "If you'll take a seat over there"—he nodded at some benches against the wall opposite his desk—"someone will be down in a moment to take care of you."

The situation was all so normal and pre-Aalaag in what was being said and done that Shane was briefly but suddenly moved almost to tears.

"Thank you," he said, adding his bit to things-as-they-once-had-been; and sat down on the bench.

Less than five minutes later, a Colonel of the Interior Guard, a tall, thin, narrow-faced man in his forties with neatly combed, straight gray hair, descended the staircase and greeted Shane.

"I'm Colonel Rymer," he said, extending his hand for Shane to shake. "We're glad to have you here. The immaculate sir Laa Ehon has been interested in seeing you as soon as possible."

"Right now, you mean?" Shane asked—for it was not unheard of for him to be ushered in to see one of the aliens immediately on arrival, for all that he was usually made to wait at least an hour or so.

"If you're presentable." Colonel Rymer ran his eye over Shane's cloak and staff. "I don't know enough about that outfit. Are you?"

"Presentable enough to be let in to see the First Captain back at Headquarters," said Shane.

"You should be all right here, then," said Rymer.

"Laa Ehon makes a point of appearance?" Shane asked. "I only met him once before and he didn't say anything to me about it."

"Perhaps you were lucky. Perhaps you were all right," said Rymer. "But he likes things correct."

"Thanks for telling me," Shane said.

Rymer shrugged. "You asked."

They had reached the top of the stairs. They made a right turn into a corridor that had been enlarged to Aalaag-comfortable dimensions, and followed it to a door at its far end.

Rymer touched the door with his index finger.

"Come," said an Aalaag voice; and they stepped through into a room not so large as the office of Lyt Ahn with which Shane was familiar, but nonetheless a good-sized office with its windows replaced by wall viewing screens and an Aalaag officer of the twelfth rank seated at a desk to one side of the entrance. Straight ahead, behind an exactly equivalent desk, sat an Aalaag of the sixth rank, whom Shane recognized as Laa Ehon.

"This is the courier beast?" Laa Ehon asked Rymer.

"Yes, immaculate sir," answered Rymer.

"You may stay for the moment. Courier beast—what is it the First Captain calls you? Shane beast, you may come to the desk, here."

Shane walked forward until he was only the regulation two paces of distance—Aalaag paces—from the front edge of Laa Ehon's desk. The large white face, lean by Aalaag standards, examined him.

"Yes," said Laa Ehon, after a moment, "I might almost recognize you. You stand with an attitude a little different from that of other beasts I have seen. Do you know if your dam or sire was known for any noticeably different way of standing?"

"I do not, immaculate sir," said Shane.

"It doesn't matter. But it will be convenient for me to recognize you on sight. I have an eye for beasts and can often tell one from the other. You've met the Colonel Rymer beast; and you will be having to do with Mela Ky, of the twelfth rank, who is my adjutant and shares this office with me." Shane turned his head to meet the colorless gaze of the alien at the other desk.

"I am honored to encounter the untarnished sir," he said.

Mela Ky neither answered nor changed expression. He went back to his work.

"The First Captain," said Laa Ehon, "has expressed a wish that you act as liaison between himself and myself. He also informs me he has asked you to observe and report on the beasts making up this controlling staff with which we are experimenting here. With my concurrence, of course. I am happy to concur with the First Captain in this."

Shane said nothing. Nothing in what Laa Ehon had said had called upon him to acknowledge, respond, or comment in any way.

"The Colonel Rymer beast will introduce you to the cattle of the staff, from the beast who is Governor on down," Laa Ehon went on. "Thereafter you may observe them as you will—avoiding as much as possible any interference with their work. You may also observe, but of course not interfere, with the activities of the Colonel Rymer beast and his company of Interior Guard in their duties. In the case of any questions, you will come to me. In fact, we will be talking regularly. In my absence, you will treat the sir Mela Ky as myself.''

Silently, Shane took this last piece of information with a measured amount of skepticism, born of his experience at the First Captain's Headquarters. In the momentary, transient relationships of most humans to their alien masters, such a statement could be taken literally. But in a situation like this where contact between specific individuals of the two races was not only close but continuing, it was not always exactly true that one Aalaag could be counted on to act as another. The aliens had individual personalities, and the human who had to live closely with them learned it was wise often to know which alien to ask what and when.

But he said nothing. Again, no verbal reaction had been called for from him. Colonel Rymer, out of his field of vision behind his back, had also not been called on to speak and was similarly silent.

"That much disposed of," said Laa Ehon, "I am interested in talking to you now on various matters. Colonel Rymer beast, you may wait for Shane beast outside. Mela Ky, would you be so kind as to go prepare the governor-cattle to be of use and cooperative with this liaison?"

"Gladly, immaculate sir," said Mela Ky, getting to his feet behind his desk. Two long strides took him to the door, through it, and out. Colonel Rymer followed him.

"Now we will talk," said Laa Ehon. His eyes were unmoving on Shane. "While you are of course a beast of the First Captain, here you are also under my command; and I have a duty for you."

These words, of course, did require an answer from Shane; and there was only one which could be given.

"I am honored, immaculate sir," said Shane.

"My understanding," said Laa Ehon, "is that you will report back to the First Captain regarding the success of this experimental project, and also on the beasts who are being used to staff it, so that he may make his best estimate of the project's future success. To the best of your knowledge, that is your duty here for the immaculate sir, Lyt Ahn, is it not?"

"Yes, immaculate sir."

"I am extremely interested," said Laa Ehon. "This seems

137

to me to be very useful information and information that I would do well to have myself. I have no wish, of course, to know what you will report to the First Captain, but I have decided that in addition to examining the situation and the cattle connected with this project for Lyt Ahn, you will also examine these things and report separately on them to me.''

He paused.

''It will be an honor to do so, immaculate sir,'' said Shane.

''Good. Such understanding in a beast is most desirable. I have been very interested in you, in any case. You are clearly a valuable beast. I would have concluded as much, even if I had not learned of the high price set upon you by the First Captain. What is your rank?'' Shane was caught unawares. Everything, to the Aalaag, was ranked—according to usefulness, according to value, according to desirability. As a result, even he and the others in the translator-courier corps had been assigned ranks; but as these had no real purpose or use, they were referred to so seldom he had almost forgotten his. If he had forgotten, it would have been necessary to guess at his rank, hoping that Laa Ehon would not check to see that he had told the truth. But luckily, in that moment, his memory was with him.

''I am of ninth rank in the translator-courier corps.''

''Of ninth? You might be interested to know that at our last meeting of senior officers, the First Captain gave us all to understand you were one of his most valuable, if not the most valuable, of your corps of cattle—''

It was typical, thought Shane, that while Laa Ehon undoubtedly remembered that he had been frustrated at that same meeting by Shane's protest that the human children brought up in alien households might learn to understand but not speak the alien language, his Aalaag social blindness to the presence of beasts had caused him to overlook the fact that Shane would also have overheard and understood what Lyt Ahn had said about Shane's value, at the meeting.

''—and on the basis of what I have seen of you so far,'' Laa Ehon was going on, ''that confidence of the immaculate sir does not seem to have been misplaced. Indeed, if your value had not been so great in Lyt Ahn's mind, I might have bought you to start my own corps of translators.''

''I am honored, immaculate sir,'' said Shane through stiff lips.

"In which case, I might well have ranked you of no less than second rank. However, it now seems unlikely—"

Laa Ehon paused to stare at the plain gray expanse of one of the large viewing screens on the wall to his right. As his eyes fastened on it, it cleared to give a view of the London outside the building. The clouds had brought the darkness of evening down promptly upon the city, and the rain still fell.

"—that I will be purchasing you," finished Laa Ehon, looking away from the screen, which immediately became blank again, and fixing his gaze once more on Shane. "However, I think you might not despair of reaching the second rank, eventually—that is, if my early opinion of you is borne out."

Shane felt an ugly chill within him.

"Thank you, immaculate sir."

"I think that is all, for the moment," said Laa Ehon. "You will find the Colonel Rymer beast outside and inform him it is my order he take you to, and make you acquainted with, the governor staff cattle. You may go."

"Immaculate sir." Shane bent his head in a gesture of understanding, and took a step backward before turning and going to the door to let himself out. In the hall, Colonel Rymer stood a little to one side of the doorway, patiently waiting.

"Done in there, are you?" said Rymer as Shane emerged. "It'll be my job to introduce you to our fellow-humans, now. Come along."

It was on the fifth day after his arrival that Shane came back to his hotel room and found a note shoved under his door, that said merely "Kensington Gardens. 4:00 P.M."

Since it was already eighteen minutes past six in the evening, Shane angrily tore up the piece of paper and dropped it in the wastebasket beside the tiny desk with which his room was furnished. He had just had dinner downstairs in the hotel. He dropped into the room's one easy chair and opened the first of the dossiers he had brought back with him from the office they had assigned to him at Project Headquarters.

The pattern of the Project had turned out to be a simple one of requiring reports and settling quotas for government offices that had already had a responsibility for getting goods produced to the requirements of the Aalaag. Nonetheless, it took Shane most of the next four days to read and comprehend it all. The dossiers on the staff members, whom he had met in person, held no particular surprises—including those on the three heads of staff.

Shane was used to finding at least a touch of self-interest obvious in almost all those who seemed to find authority comfortable under the Aalaag; and this was certainly so with two out of three in question.

The exception might be Walter Edwin Rymer, who had been a Captain in the English Air Force and had been drafted by the Aalaag for the Interior Guard because of his height. He was enough taller than Shane for Shane to be unable to guess that height closely, but certainly Rymer was more than six feet four inches and most likely six feet six or better. Which raised a curiosity in Shane's mind. He had had a notion that the English military forces, like the U.S. ones, had maximum height limits as well as minimums for those who wore their uniforms. It had never occurred to him before, but most of those now in the Aalaag's Interior Guard must have been overheight for the military services of most large nations before the Aalaag came.

At any rate, Rymer had been given no choice about becoming an Interior Guard—although his rise in rank from Captain in that body to full Colonel in two years was suspiciously rapid for someone who did not find some reason for self-interest in his occupation.

Thomas James Aldwell and Jackson Orwell Wilson, on the other hand, had both effectively volunteered to work for their alien masters: Tom as a member of a Consultation Committee to the Aalaag, made up of former Members of Parliament—one of which Tom had been at the time of the Aalaag conquest—and Jack as a volunteer accountant, when the Aalaag had passed down through that same Consultation Committee a requirement for members of the profession to work in the human administrative units they were setting up.

Not only had both men volunteered—although there could always have been good and unselfish reasons for that—but both had, like Rymer, since swiftly risen in rank and importance under the Aalaag. The pattern of their lives in the brief time since the Aalaag had come, in other words, agreed well with the ambition that Shane felt both had betrayed to him when they had met.

He settled down now to reread both their dossiers. He had discovered that in his case multiple readings of such documents tended to generate either conclusions or inspired guesses,

140

which more often than not later helped to fill out the picture of the individuals concerned. He was a third of the way through Tom's dossier when a faint rustle of paper made him raise his head and he saw another note being shoved under his hotel room door.

He threw the dossier onto the soft surface of the bed, jumped noiselessly to his feet and took three long, silent steps to the door, jerking it open as he reached it.

But he was too late. The corridor without was empty of any sign of life. He bent, picked up the note that had just been left, closed the door, and went back to his easy chair to read it.

"Trafalgar Square, 9:00 P.M.," this one said.

He was at Trafalgar Square at the appointed time. It was a cold night but not wet, for which he was thankful—an umbrella went awkwardly with his pilgrim garb; and he did not want to advertise himself by the fact that, thanks to a minor touch of Aalaag technology, his particular robe would shed any rain falling on it.

No particular meeting point in Trafalgar Square had been specified by the note, so to avoid whatever notice he would attract by obviously standing still and waiting, he began to stroll around the circumference of the Square. He was less than a third of the way around when Peter appeared and joined him.

"This way," said Peter, leading him away from the Square. A minute later, a car pulled to the curb beside them, stopped, and a back door was opened. Peter pushed him in and followed. The door closed, the car took off.

"Why in Christ's name," snapped Shane, once they were under way, "didn't you just call me, instead of going through this cloak and dagger routine of slipping notes under hotel doors?"

"Your phone might be bugged," said Peter.

Shane burst into laughter.

"I mean it," said Peter, angry in his turn. "That Interior Guard unit you've got working with you would only have to pass the word to the proper branch of the police here to have a phone tapped; and of all the easy phones to tap, one in a hotel room leads the list."

"You don't understand," said Shane, sobering. "The Interior Guard at the Project might be ready to give anything you could name to tap my phone; but its commander, a Colonel named Walter Rymer—by the way, I've met him—would have to know better than to try. Anything he did, Laa Ehon would eventually be responsible for, and not only wouldn't the Aalaag think in terms of such spying, it would be a direct insult by Laa Ehon to Lyt Ahn. In effect, it would be Laa Ehon spying upon Lyt Ahn. I explained to you that they just don't violate their own laws, rules, and mores. They die first.''

"How can you be so sure your Colonel Rymer knows that?''

"If he's been an officer in the Interior Guard for two years—and he has,'' said Shane, "he's learned the first rule of survival as a kept beast: never to do anything that might be construed as interfering between two Aalaag. He knows, all right. You can call me at that hotel room safely, any time you want to. I'm in no danger.''

Peter was quiet for a long moment.

"I think,'' he said, in a lower, calmer voice, "you may be forgetting something. It may be all right for you to ignore what other humans, and other human organizations, can do to you, but the rest of us aren't in your position as a servant of the First Captain, or of any alien, for that matter. Maybe you've forgotten, but nowadays the human police forces are committed to enforcing the Aalaag laws, and that makes us in the Resistance fair game for any London police officer who has reason to suspect we are what we are. Maybe you can forget that fact. We can't.''

Shane found himself unexpectedly ashamed.

"I'm sorry,'' he said. "I am sorry. I do forget what it's like to be without the protection of my master.''

"And I wish,'' said Peter, angry once more, "you wouldn't keep referring to them as masters, and particularly to Lyt Ahn as your master. It's that very attitude we're fighting.''

"That,'' answered Shane a little grimly, "I won't apologize for. You can't take time to tailor your speech when you live cheek to cheek with the Aalaag. You have to think the right way, so that when you're required to answer with no time to think, you say the right things. But since we're getting into mutual irritations, how about you and the rest calling them by their real name, instead of always referring to them as 'aliens' as if they were something just landed from outer space, dripping slime?''

"It's not an easy name to say.''

"Try it anyway."

"Lull . . . ull . . ." Peter tried to get the second syllable properly into the back of his throat, gargled, and then literally gagged with the effort.

"All right," said Shane soberly. "I stand corrected a second time. But a native English speaker should have the easiest time with it. I can teach you how to say it—or rather approximate it—if you're willing to practice; and it may help you someday to be able to say it properly. The Aalaag tend to rate the intelligence of humans according to how they're able to speak the Aalaag tongue; and to value the humans according to their intelligence—which to them means trainability. Let's forget all that for now, though. What did you want to see me about? Have you heard from the Resistance leaders on the continent, any of them?"

"Just from Anna ten Drinke in Amsterdam. She'll come," said Peter. "There really hasn't been time to get an answer back from the others."

"All right," said Shane, "but I'll remind you I've probably got no more than a couple of weeks before I'll be getting orders to move on."

And with those words, they went their separate ways.

"Beast," said Laa Ehon to Shane, six days later, "you have now had more than ten days in which to observe the cattle at work on this Project. Give me your report on them."

Shane stood before Laa Ehon's desk. He was not quite standing at attention, but there was a large difference between this situation and the more relaxed conditions under which he normally reported to Lyt Ahn.

As usual, whenever he had to deal with an Aalaag, there had been that first rush of fear, escalating swiftly to a tension so tight that all emotion was lost in the intense concentration of giving answers that would be at once satisfactory and safe. He had thought in the past that what he felt at these times must be something like what a highwire artist in a circus must go through just before and after he stepped upon the thin, taut strand of metal on which his support and his life depended.

"When I arrived here," Shane answered, "there were twenty-five cattle on the staff of this Project. That number has since increased to thirty-two—"

"You need not tell me what I already know," interrupted

Laa Ehon. "I'm interested in your opinion of these beasts, only."

"I am corrected, immaculate sir," said Shane. "My opinion of those who have joined the staff since my arrival lacks the benefit of the time I have been able to give to observing those who were here when I came. Nonetheless, all seem intelligent and trainable, some more so than others, of course, but all of a level of competency which seems to be adequate to the tasks at which they are set or about to be set."

"I expected no less," said Laa Ehon. "Are there any in which you find possible weaknesses or inadequacies which might prove a source of problems, later?"

"I have observed none, immaculate sir," said Shane. "This is not to say that such may not exist in certain cases. There are two possible sources of future problems that might be mentioned to the immaculate sir. Since the Project is so new and the staff has been together such a short time, it has not yet had time—"

He hesitated.

"Why do you not go on?" said Laa Ehon.

"I am searching for a word to describe something to the immaculate sir, since it is a characteristic of us cattle which the true race does not have and I know of no word for it in the true tongue."

"I understand," said Laa Ehon surprisingly. "Take your time and describe it as best you can."

"One of the characteristics of us cattle," said Shane, "is that our relationships one with the other change over a period of acquaintanceship—"

"There is indeed a word in the true tongue which describes such a process," said Laa Ehon. "It is a rare word, seldom used. Nonetheless, I am interested to find that one of Lyt Ahn's celebrated translators lacks knowledge of it. The word is—"

The sounds he gave Shane, Shane translated in his own mind into the term "familiarity."

"I thank the immaculate sir. They lack, then, 'familiarity,' which will build as time passes and they spend more of it working with each other. This familiarity may improve their working together, or in some cases, it may impede it. Only time will tell. But if I am to estimate which, I would say that my belief is that generally it will improve this group of cattle, although in a body of this number, it is almost inevitable that

144

one or several individuals might later turn out to be beasts better replaced by others.''

"Good," said Laa Ehon. "That, now, is the sort of information I want from you. Since I expressed my interest in the fact you did not know the term, 'familiarity,' I will also mention that I am also interested—favorably—in the correctness with which you pronounce it, after having heard it only once from me. So, at present the staff is satisfactory—as far as you can ascertain at this time—but as familiarity takes place within it, some beasts may need to be replaced. But you mentioned a second possible source of future problems.''

"Yes, immaculate sir. The second is that we cattle are prone to a weakness which those of the true race do not share. It is that, given authority and over a period of time becoming accustomed to having it, the temptation may occasionally occur to one individual beast or another to overuse that authority; perhaps even to put it to work to satisfy some personal desire or protect it against a work failure on its own part being discovered by the cattle in authority over it, or even by one of the true race. But again, this is something that it will be necessary to wait on time to find out.''

"I find what you say interesting indeed," said Laa Ehon. "I am pleased with your lack of hesitation in telling me of possible flaws in the staff members which would be the product of flaws you freely admit are common to your kind. I am to assume, am I not, that you also share the possibility of being hampered by these flaws?''

"I am obligated to admit so, immaculate sir," said Shane. "However, my lot has been cast as a servant of one of the true race and I find in the true race much of what I would like to find in myself. To yield to such flaws as I have described would put me beyond achieving an imitation of what I have seen in those of immaculate and untarnished nature. Therefore I am very unlikely to find myself tempted to so yield.''

There was a slight pause.

"For a beast," said Laa Ehon, "you speak with unusual boldness in saying you desire to model your conduct on that of the true race. I would caution you, in speaking to me, that you do not allow that boldness to be confused with license to go beyond what should properly be said by one of the cattle to one of the true race.''

Back to Shane's mind came the junior Aalaag officer at

145

Laa Ehon's Headquarters in Milan saying: "—I am not one of those who allow his beasts to fawn on him . . ."

"I will remember the words of the immaculate sir and keep them in mind at all times henceforward," said Shane.

"Good. Now, I am particularly interested in those three beasts who are in authority—Tom beast, Walter beast and Jack beast. What have you, if anything, to report to me about them?"

"They seem singularly able, immaculate sir," said Shane. "Beyond this, the immaculate sir might find interest in the fact that Tom beast in particular is unusually happy to have been given this work to do. He foresees a result of it in which we cattle may much more efficiently serve our masters."

"So that particular beast has given me to understand," said Laa Ehon.

He rose to his feet suddenly, towering over Shane, with only the width of the desk between them—a width that suddenly seemed to have shrunk.

"I leave immediately for my district of Milan," said Laa Ehon. "I will be gone at least three days and in that time Mela Ky will speak my words."

Shane's spirits leaped upward. He had calculated during his trip to London that Laa Ehon, no matter what his interest in this Project, could not afford to be absent from his Milanese post of main responsibility for a full two weeks uninterrupted. He had been waiting for word that the other would need to leave London, even if only for part of a day, listening to all the Aalaag conversation he could overhear, reading all Aalaag hard copy that he could come close enough to read. Still, it was not surprising he had not been able to find out the time of Laa Ehon's leaving until now. Laa Ehon himself might have made up his mind to go only a matter of a few hours or minutes before.

"This beast will listen to the untarnished sir Mela Ky in all things," he said.

"Good. You may go."

Shane went out. A little more than twenty minutes later, he saw Laa Ehon leave for his courier ship, which was kept in a cradle on the roof of their building; and fifteen minutes after that he was at the door in the basement that was the entrance to a room, the name of which translated from the Aalaag to a place that was both a museum and an arms locker.

There were three other Aalaag on the premises—the nucleus of the alien staff would come later. They were Mela Ky and two others. The three took shifts of being available for Laa Ehon's orders and running the Aalaag end of the office. Mela Ky, as senior officer and the commanding officer's direct assistant, took the main, daytime shift with Laa Ehon. The other two took, respectively, the evening and the early morning shift; so that at all times there was an Aalaag awake on the premises.

Right now, the one on duty was Mela Ky; but with Laa Ehon's leaving he was now in Laa Ehon's position of responsibility, which meant he had moved directly to his desk in the office he shared with his commanding officer the moment Laa Ehon had flown his courier ship out of the cradle overhead and up toward airlessness. The other two Aalaag would be in their rooms.

Shane made a tour of the premises to make sure that was indeed where they were. But it was so; and nothing to be surprised at. The Aalaag when off duty spent nearly all their time in their quarters. They seemed to have three primary activities besides work and exercise, of which they also did a great deal in their officially off-duty hours. One of the three activities was viewing scenes on their wall screens which seemed to be from the thousands of years past when they had lived on their native worlds—and this was close to being, if it was not in fact so, a religious exercise. Of the other two activities, one was sleeping—for the aliens apparently needed something like ten hours sleep out of the twenty-four; and the last was the playing of some incomprehensible game that could be two-handed or played by a single individual. It involved a screen set flat in the surface of a desk and a bank of lights that formed shapes both in the screen and in the air above it as controls were pressed by the players.

The two off duty would not be playing against each other now, however; because the one who would take the early morning shift would necessarily be sleeping in preparation for that. The other, left to himself, would be either viewing the past, working, or playing one-handed with the game screen in his room.

That meant that Shane had at least a fair chance of getting into the arms locker without being caught at it. Laa Ehon might have known that Lyt Ahn had supplied his human courier-translators with keys that opened most ordinary doors that were locked to those who were not Aalaag. It was almost certain, however, that his subordinates did not; unless he had specifically warned them of the fact—and there had been no reason to give them such a warning. Not only did crime not exist among the Aalaag; anything they considered of any importance—such as weapons—would not operate except when handled by an Aalaag.

Also, it was an almost inconceivable possibility that a beast might possess an Aalaag key. Only the unique nature of the duties to which the courier-translators were assigned—which made it occasionally necessary for them to use routes through Aalaag Headquarters and elsewhere that were normally restricted only to the aliens themselves—had made keys available to such as Shane.

Facing the door of the arms locker—which looked like a simple slab of wood, but which he knew to be far more than that—Shane took the rectangle of soft gray metal that was the key from his pocket and touched the end to the door.

It dissolved, first to a brown mist, then into nothingness, before him. He stepped through the opening that had appeared and looked back. The door was once again solid and closed behind him. He looked forward again.

The arms locker was more spacious than might have been suspected from the ordinary appearance of the door. It gave the impression of a large room carved out of white plastic or snow-colored rock, cut into innumerable niches and crannies, most of which held a single item as if it were on display. A soft, white light flooded the area, seeming to come from nowhere in particular but to be everywhere equally. Underfoot, the uncarpeted flooring was soft—softer than any floor of Aalaag construction that Shane had walked on, except in the arms locker at Lyt Ahn's Headquarters, which was a many-times-larger duplicate of this place he found himself in now.

The single items, each displayed in its own niche, were all weapons. Every Aalaag had his personal weapons that were, in effect, heirlooms, having been passed down from generation to generation since the time they had been carried against those who had driven the Aalaag from their home worlds. Others, duplicates of these arms, were carried when ordinary use required, such as when mounting guard, either in a Headquarters or when on display or patrol of the Earth cities they had conquered.

The originals, these precious inheritances, were taken from their niches only for ceremonies of the highest importance,

148

and immediately thereafter returned to them. Where the individual Aalaag went, his or her ancestral weapons went. They were seldom touched; but, like all arms possessed by the aliens, they were charged and ready for use at all times.

Still, they were symbolic rather than real. In the final essential, the only enemy the Aalaag really feared was the race that had dispossessed them of their original homes; and if that race should come this way, hand-weapons such as these would be of little use—like lighting matches in the face of a blizzard. But symbolically, they were everything.

Each of the four Aalaag connected with the Project had his private area in the arms locker. In the case of the three subordinate officers these were filled with all their weapons. In the case of Laa Ehon, by only a token few, since most of the commander's heirloom arms would be still in Milan. Shane, about to move toward the back of the locker, paused for a moment to gaze at the long arm—the weapon that was closest in likeness to a human rifle—that Laa Ehon would carry if he rode abroad on one of the alien riding beasts that to the aliens were almost as symbolic as the weapons. The long arm lay dark against the white nest that held its narrow, two-meter length.

He had seen such arms many times before. Not only were those like this one hung on the walls of Lyt Ahn's Headquarters, the House of Weapons, but he had also seen them in the arms locker there. He had even seen the equivalent long arm of Lyt Ahn, himself, on one of those occasions when he had been sent to fetch something from that arms locker. What he had been sent for was something of small importance and non-military use, always. Humans—beasts—were never allowed to touch weapons. In fact, to do so incurred an automatic death penalty for such as Shane. Not because of the danger involved—for there was the fact that no weapon would discharge in the hands of any not an Aalaag—but because the touch of a lesser being was like a stain upon any such weapon.

For a second, Shane was swept by an overwhelming urge to lift Laa Ehon's long arm from its niche and hold it. A mixture of feelings had him in its grasp. Partly it was made up of defiance of the rule that said he should never touch such a thing. In part it was also a wild urge to test for himself the truth of the belief that the weapon would not work for a human like himself. But overlaying all this was a fascination of which he was half-ashamed but could not help feeling.

He had been, he discovered, around the Aalaag long enough to have become at least in some small part affected by the mystique about their weapons. Some buried part of him wished to hold the long arm, as a child or savage might yearn to hold an object reputed to possess great magic, to see if some of that magic and—face it—the courage and singlemindedness of the Aalaag might not flow from it into him.

He made himself turn away without touching the long arm and went toward the back of the locker. As he went, he passed in turn each of the sections given to the cherished inherited weapons of each officer in this building, then passed the weapons for everyday use, racked all of one kind together since none of them had a specific owner. Finally he came to what he was searching for, the area that held what had brought him here. It was the section that held clothing and other lesser items, such as those he had been permitted to carry or fetch for Lyt Ahn in the House of Weapons.

These, a beast might touch. These, hopefully, would work for a beast. At least, some of them had, when he had been left alone in the arms locker at the House of Weapons long enough to try some of them out. He had had time then to experiment with nearly a couple of dozen items, picked at random; for they had been like adult toys in the sorcerous results they produced when properly activated . . . and yet they were nothing but the simplest of everyday tools to the Aalaag.

The first item he searched for now was a device that would lift him up the clock tower at the north end of the Houses of Parliament, to the face of Big Ben itself, the clock there; and after a moment he did find such an item, an exact duplicate of the one he had experimented with in the House of Weapons arms locker. It was a ring made for an Aalaag finger, which made it far too big for both his thumbs placed together, with a smaller ring which could be slid around it.

He put the device loosely on his middle finger, held it there by closing his fist and slowly tried sliding the smaller ring a tiny distance around the curve of the larger. For a second it seemed that he felt no difference, and then he was aware that his feet were not pressing upon the floor with the weight they had pressed before. Cautiously, he moved the smaller, controlling ring farther, and felt himself float free of the floor entirely and start to ascend ceilingward. Hastily, he pushed the controlling ring back to its original position and put the device in the right-hand pocket of his pants.

To locate the next item he remembered from the House of Weapons arms locker—what the Aalaag called a "privacy tool"—required a longer search. He was on the point of giving up when he found it. It was a thin box shape apparently of metal and as large as his hand. In this case, a sliding stud was set in the center of one of the larger faces of the box. Once more he cautiously advanced the control stud, while holding the device.

For a moment, again, he thought that nothing had happened. Then, anxiously looking down at the lower part of his body, he saw only floor, though looked at closely it could be seen to be slightly distorted by what might be the kind of distortion of air movements produced by heat waves on a blisteringly hot day. Nonetheless, with the privacy tool he had a practical invisibility when he might need it. He sighed with relief, returned the control to its original position and put this into his jacket pocket. It made a noticeable bulge there; and, after a moment, he changed it instead to his left pants pocket. Here it also bulged, but the overhang of his jacket disguised the sharp outlines of its shape as seen through the cloth.

Hastily, he used his key again and left the arms locker, with its door apparently undisturbed behind him. His intention was to get away from the building as quickly as possible. It was already the time at which he had promised to meet and have a final talk with Peter, privately, at dinner in a restaurant.

But as he was reaching for the front door, the Interior Guardsman on duty at the desk in the lobby checked him with a message.

"Governor said to tell you he'd like to see you," said the guard.

Shane hesitated, thinking of the bulges in his pockets; and then decided that he could brazen out any curiosity about them by standing on his rights as an independent observer of the Project. He turned and went back, up the stairs and to the office of Tom Aldwell.

He found all three of them—Aldwell behind his desk, Rymer and the assistant governor, Jack Wilson, in easy chairs facing him. They made pleased noises at seeing him and Jack brought forward a similar chair, so that he found himself seated as part of their circle.

"We've been saying how well things have been going," said Tom, beaming at him. "It'll be interesting to see how much Laa Ehon is actually required, how much we miss him during the few days he's gone. My guess is that it's going to be little."

"Very little," said Jack.

"Or not at all," put in Rymer.

Shane looked around at their faces.

"His job's only to see that you do your job," he said. "I wouldn't expect he'd be needed, as you put it. The guard on the front door said you were looking to talk to me, Tom."

"Oh, that." Tom waved a hand. "Nothing too important. It's just that we understand you were talking to Laa Ehon about us just before he left, just now."

"What gives you that idea?" Shane asked.

"Well . . ." Tom touched a button inset in a panel of such buttons on the top of his desk. Instantly, the sound of two speakers conversing in Aalaag filled the office. One voice was that of an Aalaag, the other was that of a human speaking the alien language—Shane's voice.

Shane exploded out of his chair.

"Are you insane?" he shouted at Tom. "Shut that off!"

Tom smiled indulgently, but reached out and touched the button. The sound of the voices ceased abruptly. Shane sank back in his chair.

"Haven't you learned anything about the Aalaag?" he said. He turned to Rymer. "Walt, you at least ought to know what it means to bug any room belonging to one of the masters!"

"Calm yourself," said Rymer harshly, "we haven't bugged anything. This place used to belong to one of those African consulates and they had it wired from basement to attic. We didn't do a thing but find their system, chart it, and hook into it here and there."

"Do you think that makes any difference?" Shane blazed at him. "It's the intent to overhear that'll hang you on the hooks if the Aalaag find out."

"No reason why they should find out," said Tom. "In any case, this use of it was more or less an experiment. If you feel that strongly about it, we won't do it anymore. It's merely interesting that we should have happened to overhear you talking to Laa Ehon about the three of us."

"Happen" was undoubtedly not the word, thought Shane

152

grimly; but there was no point in pursuing that now. And to think that he had spoken with such assurance to Peter about the local police or Interior Guard not daring to bug the phone conversation of a servant of the Aalaag like himself; and here they had actually gone and secretly recorded their own master in conversation. It just showed that it paid to remember that there were always idiots who would dare any chances.

"Interesting?" he said. "Why?"

"Well, one always likes to know what's being said about one," said Tom, spreading his hands on the desk top reasonably, "and as you know, we weren't able to understand what was being said—just recognize the sound of our own names when they came up in conversation. We hoped you could tell us what you and our alien master had to say about us."

"No," said Shane. "I could, but I won't. That'd make me almost as guilty as the rest of you for listening. Forget there ever was a conversation of that kind—and destroy that recording."

"You may not be willing to admit what you said," spoke up Jack, "and perhaps the three of us here can't understand it, but there're linguists not owned by the aliens who may not be able to speak the lingo, but given time to work with, that tape could do a pretty good job of puzzling out what was said."

"No, no," said Tom hastily, "Shane, here, knows the aliens much better than we do. We'll destroy the tape and forget all about the conversation. You see to that, Jack. I can count on you to take care of the tape, can't I?"

"If you say so, Tom," said Jack.

"In any case," Tom went on, "we all know Shane well enough to know that he wouldn't say anything to our discredit—unless of course there was something to our discredit to say—"

He broke into a smile which included them all.

"And I, for one, don't believe there is," he wound up. He held up a hand. "No, Shane, and I'm not asking for a hint from you as to how you talked about us. I have full trust in your good sense and honesty."

"Thanks," said Shane.

"No need for thanks. Now—on another subject. It seems we're about to get one of your co-workers as permanent translator attached to this Project and on loan from Lyt Ahn. A man named Hjalmar Jansen. He's due in tomorrow. I

153

thought you could perhaps give us some idea of what he's like and what he'd prefer in working with us—just any information you feel free to give, information in confidence, of course."

Shane had become too schooled at hiding his feelings in the past couple of years to raise his eyebrows at the name of Hjalmar Jansen. It was not that out of the whole translator corps there were not more unlikely choices; it was simply the irony involved in the choice of Hjalmar. He was a big young man—big enough to have qualified for the Interior Guard, if it had not been that his linguistic skills were so much more valuable; and powerful in proportion to his size—but so mild and soft of manner that some people got an impression of him as being almost boneless. The irony lay in the fact that under that extraordinarily soft exterior he was probably the most stubborn human being that Shane had ever met. Once Hjalmar had made up his mind about something there was no point in discussing it with him, because he simply did not hear you. It would be interesting to see how he and Tom would rub along together.

"Hjalmar's about my age," said Shane. "Swedish, originally, and a very good linguist—good with Aalaag, also. He's pleasant, easy to get along with"—mentally, Shane crossed his fingers behind his back—"and you'll find him something more of a drinker than I am."

"How very nice!" said Tom. "I don't mean that he should prefer the fleshpots more than you do, Shane. It's just that it's pleasant to hear a good report of someone we're going to be working with so closely. Well—look, we won't keep you. I apologize for asking you about what you said about us to Laa Ehon; and, don't worry, we'll destroy the tape of the conversation you heard."

"Right, then." Shane got to his feet. "It's time I was on my way back to my hotel room. I'll see you all tomorrow."

"Certainly, certainly," said Tom and the other two murmured agreement.

Shane went out. So they'd destroy the tape, would they? he thought to himself. Like hell they would!

He left the building and a few blocks away from it caught a taxi, giving it the address, not of his hotel, but of the Indian restaurant at which he had arranged to meet Peter at this time.

The restaurant was a dim little place, for which Shane was thankful, for he was not wearing his pilgrim robe with the concealing hood. He was aware that Peter had in effect hitched his wagon to the hopes which Shane offered the Resistance, from the moment the Resistance leader had invited Shane to get back in touch with him; and everything since then, particularly this summoning of other leaders from the continent, had tied Peter's chances of success and his personal reputation that much more firmly to Shane's. In this case, Shane had impressed on him the fact that they must meet someplace where other Resistance people would not go, lest one of them, recognizing Peter, take note and later be able to identify Shane.

Peter, Shane knew, would have done his best to see that this was so. Chance—bad luck—however, was always to be reckoned with. So he glanced swiftly around the other tables— the place was about half-filled—to see if anyone was paying any attention to Peter, seated alone and waiting in a secluded corner, then went to Peter's table and seated himself in a chair with his back to the room.

"Been here long?" Shane asked quietly as he sat down.

"Since the place opened for dinner," said Peter. "I've watched everybody who came in. There's no one I know, and therefore there oughtn't to be anyone who knows me."

"Good," said Shane. He picked up the menu on the plate before him and glanced at it. "I'll have the curried lamb. You do all the ordering."

Peter ordered drinks.

"What's the latest count of people who've shown up from across the Channel?" Shane asked.

"Eight," said Peter. "Anna ten Drinke came in from Amsterdam and Julio Marrotta from Milan. Albert Desoules of Paris was already here, and Wilhelm Herner, so we've got the big four."

"I'm surprised at ten Drinke and Marrotta," Shane said. "Amsterdam's so close and Marrotta must know about what I did there. I'd have thought they'd be among the first to show up. Does it mean anything, do you suppose, that they took this long to come?"

"Not that I can imagine—and not necessarily, in any case," said Peter. "Some of the less well known names might have come just for the trip to London—it made a good excuse. Marrotta and ten Drinke don't need excuses. No more do Desoules and Herner, so they probably decided to take as short a time off from ordinary business as they could get away with.''

"I see," said Shane.

"By the way," said Peter, "they're growing impatient—understandably so—to meet you, now they're here. I've told them about the new Governor Project and your connection with it, and given them the idea that it wasn't easy for you to get away safely from it, and that's what's been holding you back from meeting them. But they're getting restless, just the same."

"They can see me tomorrow afternoon—" Shane stopped himself as a waitress came to their table and Peter put in their orders. "In fact, it's most important they see me tomorrow. But they won't be able to talk to me, just see me, until evening."

Peter stared across the table at him in the dim light.

"What do you mean?"

"I mean that in the day I'm going to put on a show for them in a public place; and I want you to see they're there to take it all in. But they mustn't make any attempt to speak to me there, or get close to me."

"Oh, Lord!" said Peter. "Now what? And why couldn't you have told me something about this in advance?"

"I said it before, and no doubt I'll have to say it again, although someone in something called the Resistance like yourself ought to understand without my saying anything. The less anyone—and I mean anyone, even you—knows about what I'm going to do the better. When you need to know, I'll tell you. I'm telling you now."

"All right, then. What is it?"

"I want you to get all these visitors into positions—separate positions—close to the Houses of Parliament, so that they've got as close a view as is safe of Big Ben at just a little after noontime tomorrow. There's an Aalaag on his riding beast always on duty around the Houses of Parliament—"

"I know," interrupted Peter.

"I know you know," said Shane. "I'm trying to tell you something. Please listen. He rides from position to position around the building, sits his riding beast a short while at each position, then moves on. He usually stops just before the clock tower at noon, or a little after. Tell your people that when they see him ride into position there and stop, to start watching the face of Big Ben. They may have to wait some

156

minutes before they see anything, but they're to keep their eyes on the clock face until they do, or they'll miss what I want them to see.''

''And what is it they're going to see?'' demanded Peter.

''You'll find that out when they do. I want you on the scene, too; but in your case, you'll be standing out about twenty yards beyond the Aalaag on his riding beast; and you'll have a car either parked or driving around close enough by so that you can get me into it and away in the shortest possible time—''

''Look here!'' said Peter suddenly, ''your idea's not to blow up the clock tower or damage Big Ben some way—''

''No, damn it! Now, will you just listen?'' Shane snapped the words at him in an angry whisper as the waitress began to approach their table with filled plates. He stopped speaking until she had gone again, then picked up where he had left off.

''I want you standing by ready to guide me to that car, or to where it can pick me up. Our visitors who're observing will have to see to getting themselves out of the area and meeting us somewhere else later. I'll be wearing my pilgrim outfit, of course, with the hood hooked shut in front. I suppose you've warned them about the fact I've got to preserve my anonymity; and they've agreed to go along with that?''

Peter nodded.

''But I need to know something more myself about what you're planning to do,'' Peter said. ''What if something goes wrong with whatever you've got in mind? I've got to be ready to change my own plans and the orders to this car you want waiting.''

''You don't need to know any more; and you're not going to,'' said Shane grimly. ''I'll leave it up to your good judgment at the time, tomorrow. If the point comes where you think I can't be safely helped by you, then get out—any way you can.''

''Better eat your curried lamb,'' said Peter. He himself had been eating between his own words, while Shane's plate had sat untouched on the table in front of him.

Shane grunted and, picking up his knife and fork, got busy with the food before him.

''I'll meet them all that night,'' he said between mouthfuls, ''after they've seen the demonstration. You can tell them that. You pick the place to meet, and send a driver for me. Did you change those gold pieces I gave you into ordinary money for me?"

Without a word, Peter reached into his inside coat pocket and took out an envelope which he handed to Shane.

"Thanks," said Shane. "The gold's useful sometimes, but most of the time, here, now, I'd rather not attract attention to myself; and after tomorrow, I particularly won't want to attract attention to myself when I'm wearing the pilgrim robe."

"And I take it I'll understand just why, after tomorrow noon," said Peter drily.

"You take it right," said Shane.

They talked of nothing more that had to do with tomorrow during their meal together. Shane did not offer any more information and Peter did not ask questions, for which Shane was grateful. He was coming to like Peter, although he did his best to hide it. More and more he was convinced of the wisdom of his first reaction on seeing those Resistance people which Peter had got together to meet him on his first arrival in London. It would be much safer to be disliked than liked by those he met who had dedicated themselves to fighting against the Aalaag. To say nothing of the fact that it would help his conscience to sleep nights.

The next day he was at the Project early and set himself up in the office that had been assigned to him, strewing the desk top with papers and building as complete as possible a picture of being immersed in some large piece of work. Just after eleven in the morning, he waited until there was no sound of anyone coming and going in the corridor outside his door, then took off his shoes, put on his robe and opened the door enough to let him look out.

The corridor was deserted.

Carrying his shoes in his right hand, he reached in through a slit in his robe to the left side pocket of the jacket he was wearing underneath, and touched the stud on the privacy tool. Now invisible he slipped out, into the corridor, heading toward the stairs and the front door.

His office was on the third floor. He made it to the stairs and down them without a sound and without encountering anyone. An Interior Guard Corporal sat at the desk by the front door with the sign-out book open on the table in front of him and a pen handy. But in the relative dimness of the building's interior even the illusion of heat waves in still air was not visible. He did not even glance up as Shane slipped by him.

At the door, however, Shane was forced to wait. He stepped back into a dimmer corner of the lobby beside the door and composed himself to patience. The minutes slipped by and nothing happened. Then, so suddenly it was almost like an explosion on the quiet of the lobby, came the sound of shoes briskly ascending the steps outside to the door, the door was flung open and a young, blond-headed staff member named Julian Ammerseth came in carrying a large manila envelope under his arm.

"Back again—" he said cheerfully to the Corporal, approaching the desk to sign in; but that was all Shane heard, for he had caught the door from closing with an invisible hand behind the other's back and slipped through to the outside.

He paused just at the bottom of the outside steps to put his shoes on; but he kept himself invisible until he was well away from the Project Headquarters and could find a niche of an alleyway not overlooked by windows, into which he could step long enough to let himself become visible again.

Visible, he pinched the hood of his robe together, and continued down the street on foot until he could hire a cab and have it take him within a few blocks of the Houses of Parliament.

It was fortunate he had allowed himself some extra time. It took him some minutes to walk around the Parliament buildings until he found the Aalaag sentry and made sure that he was more or less on his regular schedule, which should put him before the clock tower at noon or shortly thereafter. The actual time of his arrival there could only be guessed at, since the officer—it was a male, this time, Shane noted from the armor shape—would ride to a point, sit there a while, then ride on to another point at which he would pause; and both points and length of pause were apparently chosen at random.

Having found the alien, he returned to the base of the clock tower. The time was seven minutes to twelve. There was no lack of people going to and fro, or standing and talking to each other in the walks on this side of the tower. He did not see Peter; and the Resistance leaders from the continent, of course, were unrecognizable by him. He continued around a corner of the tower, hunting for a place where he could safely turn himself invisible. But there was none.

In desperation, he settled for a moment when none of those around him seemed to be looking in his direction and pushed over the stud of the privacy tool in his left jacket pocket. Invisible, he returned to the tower below the clock, activated the ring device, and let its powers lift him slowly up the face of the tower to the clock.

He had not taken into account the effect of apparently standing in mid-air on nothing, some stories off the ground. He was not ordinarily affected by heights, but now he had to fight down an irrational feeling of panic that began to rise in him as he himself ascended toward the clock face.

He reached it; and, playing with the ring device, managed to halt himself opposite the hub from which the two hands of the clock were pivoted. He looked down. The Aalaag was nowhere in sight.

Invisible, suspended in air, he waited and scanned the walks below for some sign of Peter. At just two minutes to twelve, he located him, standing in apparent conversation with a short, round-hatted man at the distance Shane had told him to be beyond the Aalaag.

Time slowly passed. The minute hand of the clock was so large that by watching it, he could see the slow creep of its tip around the dial. It reached noon and the Aalaag had not yet appeared. It moved on, past five minutes after twelve, past ten minutes after twelve . . .

At a little more than fourteen minutes after twelve, the massive figure in shining armor rode its huge, bull-like beast around a corner of the tower, and moved to a position roughly opposite the middle of it before stopping. To Shane's relief, the rider had brought his beast to a halt facing outward so that he, too, looked away from the clock. Shane reached a perspiration-slippery hand in through the slit on the left side of his robe and turned off his invisibility.

Looking down he saw his robe and shoes, brown against the white face of the clock. Within him the urge was overwhelming to make his mark upon the clock face and start his descent; but he had calculated beforehand that he would have to hold a visible position where he was for at least sixty seconds, to make sure everyone who should be watching for him had noticed him; and as many others, except the Aalaag, as possible. He hung there, accordingly, with the sweat roll-

160

ing down his body under the robe, and waited for the huge minute hand to move forward one full minute.

Finally it touched the black mark toward which it had been progressing. Shane reached in under his robe and brought out a stoppered vial of black paint and an inch-wide paint-brush. He poured the black paint onto the brush and applied the brush end to the clock face beside him, making the sketch of the cloaked figure with staff in hand. Then he put vial and paint-brush back in under the robe, heedless of what the paint would do to the jacket he was wearing, and touched the ring device to let himself begin a slow drift down the face of the tower.

Out beyond him, on the ground, he could see faces, a number of faces now, turned up to watch him. At any moment he expected the Aalaag also to turn, to see what was attracting the attention of the humans. He had counted on the Aalaag indifference to beasts to cause this one to ignore the curiosity of the surrounding people as something beneath the notice of a master.

But this was no certainty; and, sure enough, before he had reached the ground, the riding beast swung about, on some signal from its rider, and that rider looked directly up at Shane.

Within the shining helmet was only the slit through which the officer looked out. Shane could not see the Aalaag eyes within that slit, but he could feel them focusing on him. Holding his face and body as naturally as possible, he reached the ground and began to walk directly toward the alien.

He came closer and closer to the great pair of figures, reached them, and stepped past them, without either increasing or decreasing his pace. Still at the same ordinary walk, he started toward Peter, whom he could see standing—now alone—where he had been told to stand and wait.

At any moment, Shane expected to hear the deep Aalaag voice behind him, commanding him to halt—or feel the sudden stunning blow of the officer's long arm without warning, on the sentinel's theory that a beast like himself would not understand even a simple order in Aalaag to stop. Step followed step. Peter became closer and closer. Just before Shane reached him, Peter turned and began to move away, walking some ten feet before Shane.

Shane followed him.

Behind him he had no idea what was happening. But none of the humans he neared spoke to him or turned toward him, although every one of those he passed in the first minute or so glanced, surreptitiously or otherwise, at him as he went by. He continued following Peter until they turned a corner and were passed by a group of four or five men moving in the opposite direction, and who blocked them from the view of those by the tower, but paid no attention to either of them, lost in animated conversation as they walked.

Peter glanced back over his shoulder briefly, then nodded and beckoned. He sped up, his walk becoming a very fast walk indeed. Shane speeded up to stay with him. They were moving alongside a street, now, down which there was a flow of traffic; and a moment later a car pulled to the curb just ahead of them.

Peter reached it first, opened the door for him, and stood aside. Shane ducked in. Peter followed. The door slammed and the car accelerated away from the curb once more. A moment later they were lost in traffic.

But, as he sat silently next to Peter while the cars closed around them, an elation began to build almost reasonlessly within him. The Pilgrim had made an appearance—not only that, but as the Pilgrim he had walked right up under the nose of the Aalaag on guard, while at least some of the heads of European Resistance watched. The excitement he was feeling was out of all key with reality. He had to reassure himself that in a real sense he had done nothing but put on a show. It was all a sham, a farce put on to help him make himself safe from his association with these ridiculous Resistance fighters— and possibly make safe as well Maria, the woman he had saved in Milan, if he could get her loose from her Resistance loyalties. In the end, what he had done this day would mean nothing—it was only a step bringing them all closer to the moment when he must betray Peter and others like him to the Aalaag.

Not only that, but he was returning now to face Lyt Ahn; and if he had learned to know the First Captain over these past two years, the First Captain had also learned to know his favorite translator-beast. If any Aalaag could read the signs of a guilty secret hidden in Shane, it would be Lyt Ahn—and Shane reminded himself once more, as he did daily if not hourly, that the way to survival in the world as it now was, depended on never underestimating the Aalaag.

Yet, still, in spite of all this, why did he persist in feeling so wildly triumphant? And then he understood: he had committed himself—and that was a good feeling.

EDITOR'S INTRODUCTION TO:

INFORMATION IN WAR
by Karl von Clausewitz

Clausewitz was born in Prussia in 1780 and lived until 1831: a period that saw the transformation of the world. During that time the Holy Roman Empire vanished and with it the dream of a universal realm: by 1830 the nation-state was the model for the world. Germany became something more than a geographical expression, but then was forced to endure the humiliation of Napoleon, who tore the figure of Victory from the Brandenburg Gate and sent it back to Paris, and with his own hands despoiled the tomb of Frederick the Great, taking his sword as a spoil of war.

Years later, as director of the reformed Prussian War Academy, Clausewitz wrote *On War*, which was sealed into packets upon his departure for the Polish campaign. After he died of cholera just after his return, his wife published the book. It instantly became one of the recognized masterpieces of military theory.

Here is Clausewitz on the fog of war.

INFORMATION IN WAR
Karl von Clausewitz

By the word "information" we mean all the knowledge we have of the enemy and his country; therefore, in fact, the foundation of all our plans and actions. Let us consider the nature of this foundation, its unreliability and uncertainty, and we shall soon feel what a dangerous edifice war is, how easily it may fall to pieces and bury us in its ruins. . . .

A great part of the information in war is contradictory, a still greater part is false, and by far the greatest part is somewhat doubtful. This requires that an officer possess a certain power of discrimination, which only knowledge of men and things and good judgment can give. The law of probability must be his guide. This is difficult even in the pre-war plans, which are made in the study and outside the actual sphere of war. It is enormously more difficult when, in the turmoil of war, one report follows hard upon another. It is fortunate if these reports, in contradicting each other, produce a sort of balance and thus demand further examination. It is much worse for the inexperienced when chance does not render him this service, but one report supports another, confirms it, magnifies it, continually paints with new colors, until urgent necessity forces from him a decision which will soon be disclosed as folly, all these reports having been lies, exaggerations, and errors.

In a few words, most reports are false, and the timidity of men gives fresh force to lies and untruths. As a general rule, everyone is more inclined to believe the bad than the good. . . . The leader, firm in reliance on his own better convictions, must stand fast like the rock on which the wave breaks. The role is not an easy one; he who is not by nature of a buoyant disposition, or has not been trained and his judgment matured by experience in war, may let it be his rule to do violence to his own inner conviction by inclining from the side of fear to the side of hope; only by that means will he be able to preserve a true balance.

This difficulty of seeing things correctly, which is one of the greatest sources of friction in war, makes things appear quite different from what had been expected. The impression of the senses is stronger than the force of ideas resulting from deliberate calculation, and this goes so far that probably no plan of any importance has ever been executed without the commander having to overcome fresh doubts during the first moments of its execution. Ordinary men, who follow the suggestions of others, generally, therefore, become undecided on the field of action; they think they have found the circumstances different from what they had expected, all the more so, indeed, since here again they yield to the suggestions of others. But even the man who has made his own plans, when he comes to see things with his own eyes, often will think he has erred. Firm reliance upon himself must make him proof against the apparent pressures of the moment. His first conviction will in the end prove true, when he extends his horizons and looks beyond the foreground scenery, with its exaggerated shapes of danger, which fate pushes on to the stage of war. This is one of the great gulfs that separate *conception* from *execution*.

EDITOR'S INTRODUCTION TO:

HARMONICA SONG
by Dan Duncan

I first met Dan Duncan in Seattle many years ago. We were both at odd but crucial points in our lives. We did not see each other again for a decade, but when we did, we found that we had, in the interval, become friends without quite knowing how or why.

Dan has always been a poet. He also understands the computer revolution better than most engineers.

HARMONICA SONG
Dan Duncan

for Pournelle

The Narrative

The old men drown their music
But the young men hear the call:
One day you hear the thunder say
This flag is going to the wall

And you don't know how to get there,
Cause you don't know where you're from;
But you pick it up from the bloody ground,
And your heart becomes a drum,

And your feet find hidden pathways
Where maps blur in the rain;
And you almost see your sweetheart's face
In the heart of your pain.

The Song

Dance on the road!
  Dance in the sky!
Nowhere to fall!
  Nowhere to die!

'N' it's a long sleep
  At the end of the road;
Whatever you can carry—
  That's your load.

Think what you think;
  Don't cry if I fall;
Just remember the promise:
  Take it to the wall.

EDITOR'S INTRODUCTION TO:

GALILEO SAW THE TRUTH
by Gregory Nicoll

It isn't always a good thing to see the future.

GALILEO SAW THE TRUTH
Gregory Nicoll

The Tuscan artist, at his bench, invents a thing quite new,
An optic orb of shining stone, ringed in white and blue;
And through this whirling piece of glass, a wondrous thing he
  sees:
Great rows of troops, with capes and banners—flapping in the
  breeze.
Advancing through the eons, through time's spectral gloom,
One hundred thousand ancient soldiers, marching to their
  doom.

The orb he turns and then he finds, a stirring sight to see,
The swords of Conan and King Kull, within a bloody spree.
The shields they break and axes flash, through blood and
  bones and brains,
Horses scream as riders die, and Chaos, supreme, **reigns**.
Advancing through the eons, through time's spectral gloom,
One hundred thousand ancient soldiers, marching to their
  doom.

And through the piece of oddly glass, looms a conflict large,
Hal and Hotspur meet with blades, and Worcester leads the
  charge.
With wood and steel the foes they slay, and shirts of mail
  they tore;
Many a good tall fellow served up to the smoky war.
Advancing through the eons, through time's spectral gloom,
One hundred thousand ancient soldiers, marching to their
  doom.

The scenes they shift and the artist sees, many more views of
  death,
The sounds of cannons choking flame, and conquerors' hard
  breath.
In lobster robes, and with Brown Bess, they march in legions
  wide;

Shots rake through well-ordered ranks and widow many a
   bride.
Advancing through the eons, through time's spectral gloom,
One hundred thousand ancient soldiers, marching to their
   doom.

The artist finds another clash, this one horrid to behold,
Armies charging, Blue and Gray, each quite strong and bold.
The skies are graced with flying craft, ships sail beneath the
   waves,
Repeaters crack with rapid fire and send men to early graves.
Advancing through the eons, through time's spectral gloom,
One hundred thousand ancient soldiers, marching to their
   doom.

A tyrant then comes centerstage, and thousands hear his song,
A flag of red with four-armed cross; and Panzer barrels long.
Then surprises come at Harbor Red (what madmen call it
   Pearl?)
A mushroom cloud picks up the Earth, and dancing atoms
   swirl.
Advancing through the eons, through time's spectral gloom,
One hundred thousand ancient soldiers, marching to their
   doom.

Unceasing shows the optic orb, on goes the grisly show,
The air now rings with howl of rays, and rockets set aglow;
Men take their plaything—**war**, that is—no warnings do they
   mind,
And carry it to distant stars, and worlds they've yet to find.
Advancing through the eons, through time's spectral gloom,
One hundred thousand ancient soldiers, marching to their
   doom.

The Tuscan takes the tiny thing, and hefts it in his hand,
And smashes it to pieces—what it shows he cannot stand;
But though he tries to break the truth, he finds its texture
   hardest;
Fear of truth destroyed the glass, so too it killed the artist.
Advancing through the eons, through time's spectral gloom,
One hundred thousand ancient soldiers, marching to their
   doom.

EDITOR'S INTRODUCTION TO:

BY THOUGHT ALONE
by William R. Fortschen

Presenting a paper at the annual meeting of the American Association for the Advancement of Science has come to be the epitome of scientific respectability. For several years the AAAS has not only allowed papers on telepathy and Extra-Sensory Perception, but has had a whole meeting session devoted to the subject.

This is not without controversy. John A. Wheeler, one of America's most respected physicists, has more than once denounced the whole practice as misleading and tending to lend respectability to charlatans, while the Amazing Randi, a professional magician, continues to offer $10,000 to the first "scientist" who can unambiguously demonstrate the existence of any ESP phenomena whatever. Wheeler, incidentally, is one of the most "far out" physics theorists in the world; his rejection of ESP is not mere bile or narrowness of mind.

Meanwhile, the Soviets devote not mere scientific sessions, but whole research institutes, to ESP. Research on Kirlian Photography is controversial in the United States, but receives government support in the USSR. One U.S. reporter was arrested in Moscow for receiving "state secrets" about ESP. Whatever the truth about ESP, the Russians take it seriously.

So might some others.

BY THOUGHT ALONE
William R. Fortschen

He awoke screaming. It had come again—the coiling, twist-
ing image; the shimmering block melting into a molten pool.
He knew that they were thinking again, and laughing at the
thought. Bob Jamerson rubbed the sleep from his weary,
bloodshot eyes as he tried to drive the nightmare from his
consciousness. As he turned to check the clock on his night-
stand, the phone cut the silence with its sharp, piercing ring.
Mumbling a curse, he picked it up.

"Jamerson," a taut, shrill voice shouted.

"Yeah, who the hell is this?"

"Henderson. We just got the word. The show is going
up."

Jamerson was wide awake now. The nightmare gone. "Yeah,
go on."

"The foreign minister has requested that you be at the
airport within the hour. Peking is sending in a 747 to take the
news crews and ambassadors back."

"Did he say anything? What the hell is going on?"

"I don't know anything other than the fact that Peking is
opening up at last. They're taking one correspondent from
each of the major news services, the Japanese ambassador,
and the NATO ambassadors—that's all. So, by God, be
there."

"What about my camera crew?"

"Drop them. Peking says that they'll provide the technical
backup. They just want you from the cable service, that's
all."

He could just picture Dennison's reaction when he found
out that he had been ditched for the big one that they had all
been waiting for. But from Henderson's tone he knew there
was no argument about it.

"Yeah, okay. I'll be there in an hour."

Henderson hung up without another word.

Hong Kong International was bedlam, as the reporters and diplomats pontificated their pet China theory.

"The bastards are going to do it," Randall of CBS shouted over his third Bloody Mary of the morning. "I tell you they got a twenty-megaton aimed at Moscow right now, and, by God, old Hing is going to punch the button with the world press standing by for prime-time coverage."

"Bullshit," came Quinton's booming brogue from the back of the bar. "Why in hell would they want us there then? Don't you think the Russians bloody well know that we've been called in to watch whatever it is that will happen? By God's blood, they aren't about to blast themselves back into the Stone Age over a Christ-forsaken rock in the middle of the Amur River."

Bob sat quietly and nursed his wake-up Bloody Mary as he waited for the plane. As usual, he had drunk himself into unconsciousness, only to be awakened at 2:00 in the morning. He wasn't sure if he was hung over, still drunk, or suffering from acute exhaustion and mental fatigue. At the moment it just damn well didn't matter. For the last three years it hadn't mattered at all. He knew that Henderson had arranged the assignment to Peking in the hope of seeing him straighten out, but that hope was just about gone. He nursed his drink and stared out the window as the Chinese 747 pulled up onto the tarmac. The correspondents and ambassadors around him pushed their way to the door, like cattle in the desert that had just sniffed their first scent of water. He waited for the crush to make its way through the door, and draining his drink, he made his way across the tarmac and aboard the spacious craft that seemed nearly empty with its fifty passengers.

Within minutes the plane received its clearance, roared down the runway, and lifted off for Peking. Bob settled back and tried to collect his thoughts.

He had served in Peking for three years, ever since Wall Street. The memory flashed and he tried to suppress the nightmare. The news office had been quiet that day. The twenty-day war in the Middle East was over, with Israel in Damascus, and in spite of the conflict, there was the first faint wind of rapprochement between Russia and America with the announcement of a joint Soviet-American space effort to return to the moon. He was working at the terminal preparing for the evening broadcast when the light of a thousand suns exploded across the newsroom. Instinctively he shielded his eyes as the building rocked to the shock wave. As the light subsided, he ran to the window and watched the mushroom cloud of death rise up over lower Manhattan.

Marie and the two kids were down there shopping. In impotent rage he screamed, as a square mile of the city disappeared, along with his life and his dreams.

He was forced to work, for Henderson sent him out with a crew, and his tearful, emotional reporting gave him national prominence as he walked through the wreckage of lower Manhattan and revealed to the world the horrors of the return of the bomb. The Peoples Liberation Movement claimed responsibility in retaliation for the capitalist support of Israeli aggression. The second bomb was found five minutes before its detonation in front of the Capitol, but the third one took out Parliament. Jamerson reported the story for three days without rest, and then spent the next month in the hospital with radiation sickness. They never found Marie—at least, not to identify her. And the drinking started.

Henderson finally transferred him to Peking to get him away from the memories. Once a week he would inform the world of the latest news concerning acupuncture, the new incentive socialism, and panda matings. His counterparts in the Chinese Bureau knew what happened and went out of their way to be helpful. He buried himself in his work when the drink didn't hold sway and soon found himself close to the inner workings of the Chinese government as they struggled for closer ties with the West, and as their relationship with Russia turned for the worse. The sense of crisis grew throughout the winter of '87. And then came the killing on a small island in the middle of the Amur River.

China and Russia had fought about it once before, back in the late sixties. The island was in the middle of the river that divided the two countries in East Asia. An argument broke out between two guards, a fistfight developed, and in the confusion the Russian guard was shot and killed. The next day the Russians came back in force, killing ten Chinese border guards and taking possession of the island. Within a fortnight skirmishing flared up all along the border and the Chinese sealed it off to Western correspondents. The night they sealed it off, the blow fell with a stunning force that shook the world.

The Russians crossed the border along a hundred miles of front and penetrated fifty miles into China, claiming that they were liberating territory wrongly held by the hegemonic Chinese. China bombed Vladivostok the following day. That night the Russians slammed Peking with a conventional bombing and rocket attack and stated that in thirty days China must demilitarize its entire border or face the full consequences. And that night, as well, China announced that all Westerners were to leave the country within twenty-four hours or be interned as a measure of national security. China turned in upon itself, like the forbidden nation of old.

He tried to sleep but the dream came back, and he awoke screaming as the plane fell out of the sky onto the runway at the edge of Peking.

"You really seemed to be riding something, Jamerson," Randall said softly, as the plane taxied to a stop.

He looked at him weakly and he sensed a recognition, an understanding in his dark blue eyes. He nodded slowly and looked out the window.

"Funny," Randall said with a distant voice. "I've had a strange sense about this ever since . . ." He trailed off into silence as the doors popped open, flooding the cabin with a startling white light and the crisp, oily smell of kerosene fuel.

Dozens of Mao-jacketed guards with submachine guns surrounded the plane and the limos which were lined up for the passengers. The ambassadors grumbled about precedence and official welcome, as interpreters guided them to their assigned cars. The seriousness of the interpreters and the demeanor of the guards silenced the group as they left the plane and climbed into their cars.

The motorcade thundered through the city. And Jamerson noticed the empty streets. Perhaps they had evacuated in anticipation of the Soviet strike. He assumed they were going to the Forbidden City, but the motorcade turned onto a side road and drove out into the countryside. The vehicles pulled up next to a small bunker in the middle of an empty field surrounded by guards. The two steel blast doors of the bunker were open like the gates of a tomb, and interpreters speaking in swift monotones told the Westerners to enter and go downstairs.

Stepping into the coldness of the bunker was like walking into a world of steel and night. An endless staircase led deeper and deeper into the earth, and the crowd whispered about blast shelters and command silos. Fifty meters down, the stairs ended in a sterile anteroom facing a large barrier of steel. It slid back noiselessly, as if guided by unseen hands.

The steel doors opened slowly to reveal a darkened room within.

"Comrades, I must apologize for the mystery, but won't you please come in." From out of the shadows stepped the Chairman of the People's Republic, and the stunned ambassadors ceased their arguments about protocol.

The auditorium lit up as the Chairman led them into the room. The seats were of dark, plush velvet, and the surrounding walls were paneled with alternating sheets of mahogany and backlit translucent glass.

"Comrades, please take your seats, for our time is short and there is much to be explained."

Chairman Hing moved to the podium at the front of the room. He seemed totally at ease, as if he were enjoying an immense joke. His reputation for ruthlessness was somehow out of place with the lean, wispy figure that stood benevolently before them. Jamerson took a seat at the front of the room and settled into his chair.

"Thirty days ago," Hing said with a softness that silenced the room, as all strained to hear him, "the People's Republic suffered a ruthless attack from the Soviet government. The ultimatum of war or abandonment of our rightful borders left us with an impossible choice. If we fought, the full horror of nuclear war would be unleashed upon us with all the nightmares that we saw unleashed in New York and London." The Chairman looked into Jamerson's eyes and gave him a slight nod of acknowledgment. "On the other hand, if we bowed to the Soviet demands, free license would be given for further intimidations and the exploitation of our peoples by any bully that desired to torment us. Your governments, gentlemen, did this to China in the past, and that bitter lesson has never been forgotten. Last month I asked all of your leaders for help in bringing pressure to bear against the Soviet government, and you wrung your hands with expressions of concern but none of you stepped forward to stop the Soviet aggressors. I know your reasoning. Let the two fight it out and in the end the West will pick up the pieces.

"We realized that we had to find another way. We knew that this crisis would come and that a conventional answer would not work. And so, gentlemen, when the ultimatum of thirty days was issued, we decided to try an answer that was unconventional yet an application of our greatest strength. Now, the day before the ultimatum expires, we are prepared to answer."

Behind the Chairman a wall-sized screen lit up. It flickered and blinked for several seconds and the Great Square of Peking came into focus. From end to end it was a sea of humanity dressed in the monotonous blue of the people's jackets.

"You see," the Chairman said more forcefully, "warfare can be fought in many different modes. The Russians wage it in a non-Marxist sense against the working class of people by the apocalyptic use of the bomb. But, gentlemen, there are many different ways to wage war. My advisers, who developed this project, chose ibn-Abdul-Hassan as their example. In the eleventh century he forged an empire in the Middle East by waging war, not against people, but against the select few who ruled. If a prince was against him, the people would not suffer, only the prince. For Hassan would send one of his followers to hunt down the prince, to wait for him and to slay him. Hassan's men were known as Assassins."

The Chairman turned and faced the screen behind him as the camera zoomed in on the gate of the Imperial Palace, where a two-foot column of steel stood upon a platform beneath the arched gate and the watchful portrait of Chairman Mao.

"You see, gentlemen," the Chairman continued, "we have one great weapon that the West never dreamed of. We have the minds of people. The minds of a disciplined people who can be linked together and controlled. In Red Square, at this very moment, are one million of our people, and each of them is engaged in but one thought. One controlled, disciplined thought, that they have trained to control. The result will be obvious to you in a moment."

The column of steel started to shimmer with heat, its edges quickly discoloring to blue and then to a glaring white. Like a piece of ice thrown onto a city street, the steel column started to puddle and spread out in a widening pool of flaming, molten metal. It exploded into incandescent flame, and the image winked out.

The Chairman turned back to his audience with a smile.

"That, gentlemen, is the power of China. Twenty-eight days ago it took every citizen of our nation six hours of thought to perform that feat. A week ago it still took ten million. Today, but one million of our people concentrating on making that steel column melt were able to do so by thought alone in a matter of seconds. The theory has been known for years. Some feeble experiments were attempted, but the crisis that was forced upon us drove the People's Republic to the logical conclusion. Now, comrades, if a million people could do that to a steel column, think what could be done to a Russian heart—or to a Russian brain."

The room was suddenly plunged into darkness as the Chairman barked a command. The clear glass panels around the auditorium glowed softly with color and Jamerson looked around the room, realizing that the panels were covered with hundreds of photos. Beneath each photo was a name—in Russian, Chinese, French, Japanese, and English. Startled shouts echoed in the room as the audience realized what they were looking at. The photos of the ruling elite of Russia. The screen behind the Chairman flickered and wavered for nearly a minute—until the satellite was finally patched through to pick up on the Soviet television system. And Jamerson finally realized the full impact of what was about to happen.

It was May 1, and the May Day parade in Moscow's Red Square was unfolding on the screen.

"Gentlemen, while your plane was in the air, we announced to the Soviet government that we had capitulated to their demands. This to lull them into a sense of jubilation, so that all dignitaries would be in Red Square, and to explain the mass meetings taking place all over China at this moment, which we knew their satellites would be observing. They think they have won, but watch now as China wins its war."

In stunned silence the Westerners watched as the inner circle of the Soviet party appeared on the screen above Lenin's tomb. All were silent in the room, as the unknowing Russian cameraman filmed the death of a regime.

One of the Russians standing next to the Party President had a strange, quizzical look that quickly changed to agonized panic. A great gout of blood gushed forth from his mouth and he collapsed behind the waist-high wall. The camera turned away to scan the parade, but after several seconds, as if

178

guided by unseen hands, it swept back to the unfolding nightmare atop the wall.

The leaders of the Supreme Soviet died before the confused gaze of the world. Party Secretary Valinofsky stood in stunned silence as his followers toppled one after the other, in a kicking confusion of hemorrhaging blood.

"Now, watch," Hing said, "the special arrangement we have made for him."

Valinofsky started to struggle as if he were wrestling with an unseen opponent. He slowly rose into the air, kicking and screaming in terror. Jamerson looked from his terrified image to the photos around the room. Most of them were blacked out. The rest pulsed with a dull red light. Valinofsky's photo was prominently displayed at the front of the room—it suddenly went dark.

Jamerson looked back to Valinofsky as he hovered above Lenin's tomb and the camera closed in on his terrified face. It filled the screen with the look of death, and then disappeared in a flaming explosion of fiery light. From the screen came the sound of his nightmarish death scream, and the panic-stricken thousands in Red Square. The screen went dark—the death scream of Valinofsky replaced by the horrified shouts of the diplomats and correspondents.

The Chairman looked to his audience and smiled, as if they were children who had confessed a fear of the dark cellar below.

"Comrades, you have just witnessed the death of the Soviet government. By the very nature of its centralized approach, the removal of a few thousand will cripple any response. Every Soviet general, every member of the Supreme Soviet, every regional ruler, their top scientists, and all controllers of the nuclear forces are dead. We are already broadcasting our demands for complete capitulation to the few who we knew were sympathetic to our cause, and who have therefore been spared for the moment. If they refuse, well, then, gentlemen, we will just have to sift our way down through their ranks until we find those who will cooperate. The war, comrades, is over.

"Oh, yes, comrades, we do expect your cooperation with us in the days to come.

"Some of you have even sensed what was coming; in fact, we wanted you to. Of course, there will be some changes now."

179

The translucent screens lit up again. Jamerson scanned the photos with horror as he realized that he was looking at images of the West's top leadership. The top media people were there as well, and Jamerson sat back down as he looked at his own photo. The memories of Marie were gone at last—a larger nightmare had reared up to take their place.

"Comrades," the Chairman said mockingly, "be assured we shall be thinking of you in the days to come."

EDITOR'S INTRODUCTION TO:

DOUGHFOOT SANCTUM
by James William Holzer

When they asked William Tecumseh Sherman what war was, he said, "War is Hell." Sherman's view was that if you made war sufficiently intolerable, the enemy would give up, and the war would be shorter.

It wasn't a new notion, but it was new to the United States. The tradition of Western Civilization was that of Just War: that there could be Laws of War, and there were things forbidden to soldiers and commanders alike. The Framers of the U.S. Constitution clearly believed in "The Laws of Nature and Nature's God," and International Law in general, and the Laws of War in particular, were based firmly on the theory of Natural Law.

War was conducted between states; and under the Laws of War a careful distinction was made between combatants and noncombatants, and for that matter between public and private property. When Confederate troops raided a Maine town by traveling through Canada, they were careful to put on their uniforms before beginning hostilities, and to burn only public buildings. Bombarding open cities was considered a crime against humanity, and even as late as World War I the British were hard pressed to defend their policy of considering food shipments to Germany to be contraband of war, and thus forbidden to be carried to Germany on neutral vessels.

Democracy changed the concept of war, of course. Democratic states fight only just wars, and thus their enemies are not justified; it's only a short step to thinking the enemy is not really human. Sherman didn't go that far: Sherman said that by carrying the war to the South he was making the war shorter. One supposes some such logic was employed to justify the Tokyo fire raids, Dresden, and Hiroshima. The horror of Hiroshima and Nagasaki was the choice of targets: Nagasaki had almost no military value at all and was the most Westernized of Japanese cities. But by that time the distinc-

181

tion between combatants and noncombatants had been well-nigh erased.

At the beginning of World War II we threw away what we had gone to war for in 1917: in the first weeks of the war U.S. submarines were ordered to sink Japanese merchant ships wherever found and without warning. As late as 1937 the United States could say, "This Government holds the view that any general bombing of an extensive area wherein there resides a large populace engaged in peaceful pursuits is unwarranted and contrary to the principles of law and humanity." The Japanese Government responded by saying that Imperial Japan agreed, and that the bombing of Nanking was and would be confined to military facilities. The Doolittle raiders were supposed to bomb only military targets; that was in the early days of World War II. By the war's end we deliberately dropped incendiary weapons into residential areas of Tokyo. The principle of military effectiveness—there is no real distinction between soldiers, munitions workers, and other civilians who feed, clothe, and house munitions workers—had won over the Laws of War, and war became very hell indeed.

Today the Laws of War live only in phrases. "War crimes," after all, apply only to losers. The victors are always safe: witness the farce of Russian generals sitting in judgment against their Nazi partners for the crime of invading Poland. The losers will almost always be tried as war criminals, and generally convicted, no matter what they did or did not do.

It is not entirely clear that abandoning what the United States was once pleased to call "the principles of law and humanity" has been an unmixed blessing.

Herewith a story of an army that never heard of the Laws of War.

DOUGHFOOT SANCTUM
James William Holzer

I could smell the blood *cumup*. It's the sixth day of the eleventh month in Judea and about one above zero. Servo-Squadron 999 has been diddybopping on a cleanup sweep that started on the Gulf of Aqaba to where we are now, Sedom, on the south shore of the Dead Sea, within spitting distance of Jordan.

Night fell, so there was no point running it around the rolling hills the terrain computer told us were sand heaps. A Ta'Amire Grunt we rolled up while he was grubbing food told us about a shortcut, a place called Raccoon Ravine, thirty-five klicks from New Jer*USA*lem. It was a clear case of plausible denial. The Grunt lied. We capped him good. That Raccoon Ravine had ambush smeared all over it.

The war would be over by George Herbert Walker Bush Memorial Day, Sergeant Major Moseby promised us. And I believe him.

999 broke out the carbon epoxy Quonsets and struck a firebase under the cover of some overhanging cliffs, a wind-free alley that'll keep the sand blowing off the Negev out of your mouth and nose. I put out the moisture collectors for the nuke reactor we tote around that makes gallons of nonradioactive waste water, then doused the drippings with halozone purifier, just in case. Tastes as good as we call it, Bam-Bam Juice.

Two hours later we're a Free Fire Zone. GEN computers probed the wave of black faces running us and figure them to be UAR Grunts and Wacky Jacks—Turks, Libyans, Moroccans, Pakistanis, Iranians—*Number Ten*. The Worst. Twenty thousand, tallied GEN. Mostly Wacky Jacks. A real wave. 999 really had to bust caps at those Wacky Jacks because they really ran it back at us.

I'm a B-gunner on a MaxiFire Team working off a four-wheeler flatbed armed with an HBV-6, a 20mm Auto-

Cannonade, that's five 7-barrel Gatling turrets that fire 32,000 rounds per minute. Fire's so thick it'll vaporize missiles, jets, Slicks, waves. Problem is you tap *The Beast* in one minute and you need a good day for a reload. So you hop off the flatbed and close with the unfriendlies. That's when you begin *building the dream*.

Most of our guys carry Chinese Army 126 silenced machine guns because the plastic disc baffles suppress the noise and keep the crummy sand out of the works. This war's sure hell on the ears: *ha-ha*. So you've spent your only sixty-round clip and you whip out your K-bar to slice and dice the Grunts. I'm an ear collector, nothing unique. Won a bone-handled Bowie last June with a 999 record, three hundred confirmed kills. That's unusual. That's six hundred ears. I did a trade-up with that Bowie, got a ten-year-old packet of peas and carrots buzzed with gamma cobalt 60 to keep it fresh. Great eats, I'll tell you.

Ear collecting started as a rumor two years ago. Someone said that the first Gook to take ten thousand pair got shipped by COMBANK to Monaco for a month's R&R. COMBANK picked up on it and started offering all kinds of incentives.

One lousy Dragonfly Slick broke the back of the Wacky Jack wave, greasing for good the drag-asses we drove into the Ravine. Dropped a petroleum/ether mist set afire on top of them. Daniel 8:4 is always talking about some valley in the Bible filled with bodies and blood stacked up as high as a horse's bridle. He was really looking forward to seeing it.

The whole firefight lasted ten minutes. Long Lips and Flak Jack Borry got put down by Doctor Croc. Nice guys, not scuzzies, knew them slightly. They weren't ear collectors, always railed against it. Funny how those anti-ear types seem to get selected early by Doctor Croc . . .

Heard by accident some scuzzie scheme to take easy ears from those burned Wacky Jacks in the Ravine. I went dinky-doo when I heard that, I wanted to frag those 999 scuzzballs good. See, ears don't count except in pairs and only those taken hand-to-hand. I had a good laugh when those scuzzies got there and found black goo up to their ankles where Wacky Jacks used to be. Seems the KIA data bank completed the body count and dispatched a SHADOW rotocraft to drop twelve tons of Blue Snow on the corpses. That damn computer sure has a fetish about contaminating diseases. Made that bloody mess mud in seconds.

November 30. Took a hundred pair of Grunt and Wacky Jack ears this month. Average. Best thing I could win was a thousand-gallon blivet of diesel fuel HALO'ed and abandoned in the East Negev. I still had a bad taste in my mouth having run out of diesel during the Siege of Revivim. Luck has it that 999 won't get a fuel drop for two weeks and I'm sittin' on a gold mine. I traded up for stuff you wouldn't believe . . .

999 moved real easy, resting and rearming. We ended up at the Caves of En-gedi, near the Dead Sea and about sixteen klicks south of New Jer*USA*lem. I hear that the New City is a staging area for UAR regulars we call Kings. Kings wear blue and gray uniforms trimmed with gold braid. A King's ears with matching braid are worth twenty times a Grunt's ears. *Twenty times.*

It was a great earthquake at the beginning of the war that did the most damage to the New City, laid the whole Middle East flat besides—you could diddybop for months and not find a wall standing anywhere. The Libyans added insult to injury, dusting New Jer*USA*lem with a piperdyl glycolate mist. This made the citizens totally fugazzi, so crazed they emulsified each other with extreme intolerance. Then Wacky Jacks swept in to clean up and started crucifying corpses for revenge. If you can picture twenty-five thousand sabras up on stakes, you can see why 999 calls those scuzzballs Wacky Jacks.

Nobody knows for sure who to pray to over here for victory. There's Allah, Jehovah, Krishna, Lenin, Buddha, Mahavir, and good old J.C. I've got this theory that God's either an Iranian or a Pakistani because they're winning this war. The Soviets and Red Chinese haven't sent replacements to 999 in two years. They lost heart after the Ukraine got dust-bombed with anthrax and Beijing was blanketed with Sarin and GB nerve gases during the third week of the war. I like 999 the way it is, ninety-nine percent all-American. We've got the remaining force of the Israeli Saiyeret who taught us more than we want to know about desert warfare. And five Tojoe Zappers who sleep the day away in Conex body containers to build up their visual purple for night recon. Those guys could be the only living Tojoes in the world, but you know that story. They won't collect ears, but I hear that COMBANK would have to buy them prime beach property on the French Riviera if they ever let the KIA data bank tally their total confirmed kills. They never carry Chinese burpguns, only long, sharp K-bars. To tell you the truth, they scare the crap out of me.

The COMBANK directive for the En-gedi mission read as follows: Clean the caves of unfriendlies, destroy/confiscate found caches of weapons/supplies (we cop them), and assault New Jer*USA*lem to destroy the Muslim shrine on Mount Moriah, the Dome of the Rock. 999 always ignores that last directive. It crops up once a month, without fail. COMBANK says do it, it'll demoralize the enemy once and for all. 999 knows better. Touch the Dome and you'll have a suicide wave running at you, revengeful as wolves. *Pass*.

Messin' with the Dome is how this friggin' war started in the first place. Some Zealots wanted that same spot on Mount Moriah to build a new temple to replace the old one razed by the Romans in biblical times. They wanted this new temple as a house for an Englishman named Malcolm Fox-Godfrey, who he swore was the Messiah. (Daniel 8:4 thinks the guy was the Antichrist.) The Muslims wouldn't budge so some dinky-doo called the Hammer flew a Slick over the Dome and bombed it with a hundred gallons of hog blood, red-washing it good. Now Muslims feel about hogs like 999 feels about rabid palm tree rats racking up in our Quonsets. It made them real irate.

There are about one billion Muslims in this world, so you can see how they could foot an army of two hundred million Kings, Wacky Jacks, and Grunts anxious to converge on Israel and grease anything kosher. America, Japan, Russia, and Red China rushed in to help the Israelis—you may have seen the Siege of Megiddo on teevee. I was there.

That was three years ago. I hear that things are pickin' up in America. There's no chance of a UAR invasion now and there's a higher ratio of women to men, about three hundred to one. The two coasts are still hot with anthrax bugs but they've done a good job controlling those fungus spores from drifting incountry. What's left that's human lives in the Four Corners, that's Utah, Arizona, New Mexico, and Colorado. It's nice to know that the war is contained and North America is on the mend and the twelve hundred troopers of Servo-Squadron 999 are out here making things safe for the world.

December 17. Rumor has it that Bob Hope's thinking of giving a USO Christmas show down in the Gulf of Aqaba next week. Shine it boys. 999 is going to stay in En-gedi to burn Grunts.

Ta'Amire hill Grunts armed with NightSun blinders and carbon dioxide lasers hit our Ground Mobile column between a red sunset and the edge of night. The firefight lasted eight minutes—I counted. Fifteen troopers, good guys, lost their retinas, forgot to wear their quartz amber visors. They're getting court-martialed besides—I guess they forgot regulations and how to see in the same day. Ha-ha.

Before I knew it Sergeant Major Moseby sent me and those five Tojoe Zappers into the mountains near Jericho to emulsify some rabble-rousing Iranian Kings that put those Ta'Amire Grunts up to that blinding assault. By Christmas I took twenty pair of King ears and braid but them Tojoe Zappers took a hundred times my tally. Two rucksacks full. Tadashi gave them to me. Now, I'm no scuzzie and I won't take credit for another trooper's ears. It was real hard to resist because those rucksacks would've put me over the top in December for that freeze-dried pasta and hot sausage.

I figure those Tojoes felt bad about leaving me alone during the day while they meditated in their holes. So I dug a hole of my own. They liked that in me, I guess. See, they're not ear collectors. Never have been.

January 6, 1999. It took us three weeks to clean Jericho before we could get back to En-gedi for cave-cleaning duty. It's all by the numbers down here. You can diddybop up a slope to a low cave or shout down a Dragonfly Slick to LZ you on a ridge so you can rope-rappel down the headwalls to the high caves. A three-man team begins the takedown with a flashbang stun grenade to buy you time while you bust caps with your wheelgun. You always aim for the head, two shots for male Grunts and one shot each for females and their offspring. COMBANK started an ammo incentive, saying we waste brass the way we cap at Grunts. *Strakshit*. There must be a hundred thousand holes in this sector.

With luck you can go the easy route. Find an unexploded Dragontooth pod out in the desert, rewire it with a proximity fuse, and chuck it into a cave, especially one filled with fugazzi Wacky Jacks. A Dragontooth's filled with forty-eight hundred plastic and metal shards that blast through a cave the way anhydride phosphorus roots through bone marrow. I remember seeing a SHADOW drop a thousand 'tooths on a wave of Grunts working themselves into a fit near El Thamad— talk about blood rising as high as a horse's bridle! My buddy

Troggy was never the same after seeing it. Doctor Croc took Troggy out the hard way last May . . .

The desert heat greased our mascot camels last July. I don't know why I wrote that, it just popped into my mind . . .

Food fantasies are big in the 999. I'm on a corn dog, taco, and jelly bean fantasy this month. A single contraband chicken bouillon cube went for two hundred gold certificates today. Most troopers grub off the land or off the enemy. The safest stuff to eat are figs, camel (like venison), and Bam-Bam Juice.

Let me tell you about the idea I pitched to COMBANK that got me three days R&R in Sardinia. I figured that we could store water in the oversized tires of our Ground Mobile vehicles instead of those tankers that always seemed to disappear in a firefight. I even devised a way to transfer the tire water storage to spare tanks, rerimming and remounting the tire, all in five minutes flat. Not bad for a guy with a seventh-grade education.

My buddies are dearer than life to me, the best things this war has given me. There's Sex Pretzel, the Chic Concept, BRO-21X, Burnt Offerings, and Daniel 8:4. Some names. My name? Some of the troopers call me the Hump since that water-in-the-tires brainstorm. Names don't matter anymore because I'm different now. Real different.

March 1. Daniel 8:4 is going dinky-doo on a regular basis. He's got the notion that in one of those En-gedi caves he's going to find long-lost biblical scrolls written by J.C. himself. He did find some rotten reed paper but it blew to smithereens in a stiff *sharav* wind. He got worse after that but went totally fugazzi the first time we diddybopped through Bethlehem. He was frothing because he couldn't find a cave, a manger, a nativity scene . . . *nada*. It took me three hours to bliss him out. Explained to him that the place was but a wide spot on the road two thousand years ago, that they had only one motel back then, right? Daniel 8:4 will listen to logic, as long as there's a biblical slant to it.

Don't let me forget my best buddy, Sex Pretzel. He's an expert on *gorilla* war having read a bunch of three-dollar novels about a war called 'Nam. Sex Pretzel's the one who dubbed the troopers of 999 Gooks since he feels that the 'Cong really kicked American tail back then, and he likes to identify with a winner. Americans used to be called Wa-Ky Jakes by the 'Cong (we say Wacky Jacks), Grunts, and

Kings. Now we call the enemy that for good luck. 999 wants to win this war. Sure, the Pretzel's a front-runner but he's a buddy just the same. He wanted to dub us the Buddha Heads but Daniel 8:4 threw a two-day fit, so we settled on Gooks. Rumor has it that the Pretzel tipped COMBANK on the ear-collecting scheme, but he refuses to take credit for it. That's the type of guy he is, a gentleman. A real historian.

COMBANK hasn't paid up on the ear grand prize yet, but we all know they will. They're giving us goals at least, hope. Monaco, Casino de Monte Carlo, the dolls . . . *ultrareality*. I've got this theory that it's the ultrarealities that give us Gooks the desire, the hunger to survive, that makes 999 real revengeful in a firefight. The Red Chinese and the Soviets never had that in them. Commies don't like incentive programs, see? That's the great thing about a World Bank runnin' this war, because once it's over, the twelve hundred Gooks of 999 are going to each get a four-bedroom adobe equipped with NBC deterrents and a 1999 Red Chinese four-by-four diesel with plastisol paint, all courtesy of COMBANK. That's gratitude.

Daniel 8:4 says his Bible predicted this war, the Four Horsemen, the plagues, the greasing of two billion, the nuking of Japan. Calls it Armageddon. But what the hell, we've gone through all that and we've got a thousand-year Kingdom of Heaven coming to us. Paradise. COMBANK says that they'll pay for Paradise, and I believe it.

Sex Pretzel tells me that at the end of the 'Nam war all a trooper got was a plastic discharge card and some medical benefits—*no wonder they lost! No incentives*. He also told me about 'Nam troopers they called Double-Vets. (We call them scuzzies in 999.) They strangled, shot the enemy, then had sex with them. *Fugazzi*. They used a lot of drugs back then too. We had a druggie bunch in the 999 that got emulsified, *maybe fragged*, at the Siege of Revivim. Good riddance. 999 is stoked and alert, all-American in our habits, and that's the way it's going to stay.

May 9. Something happened two weeks ago that really bothers me. I'm sitting on a slope near Be'er Ora eating dried camel jerky when some Ta'Amire Grunt, musta been older than Allah, caught sight of me, started dancing, real joyous-like, holding out a honeyed locust and a handful of wheat. *Peace*. Had one tooth in his black gums but, all in all, a real squared-away bedouin. I didn't think. It was a reflex. I put three caseless 10mm slugs in his head, *tap-tappity-tap*. Easy. Like it was nothing.

In three years a guy can change. I've got this theory that something is seriously wrong with me . . .

Nobody in 999 ever talks about dying, death, even says those words. Bad luck. When a trooper describes our killing ways, he'll say emulsified, cleaned, burned, zapped, greased. When one of our guys gets burned, we'll say, "Didya hear? Doctor Croc took out the Boychild last night." Nothing more. That started during the Nubian Desert Campaign in '97 when some nasty river crocs caught some of our guys napping on the banks of the Nile near the Wadi Halfa. A croc will take you apart before you can scream. Just like Doctor Croc. You'll never see him, smell him, but he's always there.

You must be wondering why I'm penciling my memoirs, me, a seventh-grade graduate. The Sandbag Ambush is why. I'm finally out of this war. Writing is my way of doing something other than peeing blood into a bedpan, a souvenir of my tour so that someday my son can read how it was for his daddy to face down Doctor Croc and work for Doctor Croc, twenty-five hours a day. The kid may think his daddy's dinky-doo, maybe fugazzi. That's okay by me.

Yeah, the Sandbag Ambush. I remember every minute of that day, May 17. Me and my buddies are taking our daily float in the Dead Sea—talk about ultrareality! The salt is so velvety and dense that you can float on all sides of your body. *Forever*. Problem is some guys fall so deep asleep that they float out a mile and nearly drown. Or you swallow a mouthful of Sea and puke for a day afterward. Your skin gets as tough as croc hide, but it's worth a bath to get the sand out of your crotch and ears.

The Chic Concept swore that it was so relaxing his soul flew out of his body and went to Monaco without him. I told him that I'd believe it when he brings back a doll or a casino chip to me.

The Sandbag Ambush was sort of a letdown for me. I'm diddyboppin' on a recon west of the Sea and I come upon a freshwater wadi, so I have no choice but to squat on it, break UHF squelch, and have 999 bring up the column to fill the empty tires. It was dark so I set up an electronic perimeter, a people sniffer, and two acoustic trail sensors. Nothing would get within twenty meters without me hearing their steps in my earphone. Just my luck that some Wacky Jack Zapper's got herself wired into a Black Hole Sensor Suppression System. She's stalkin' me, and what am I doing? Filling sandbags to make a chair so I don't have to dip my dainty ass in the wet wadi. Dumbo. So I'm shoveling and filling and before I can scream I've got a 4.5mm tumbler in my gut. That was her first and last mistake. She's wired, but so am I. Troopers on solo recon wear a custom set of body-pressure-point collars, so if you're zapped your body can absorb the initial impact of the bullet or the knife, slowing the bleeding, saving the strength you need to react. She had one shot and I've got my collars tight and . . . *whump*! My K-bar's stickin' out of her eye. Like I said, if you want to put them in Wacky Jack heaven fast, go for the skull.

Three weeks later I wake up in a Swiss hospital in Monaco, right next door to the newest casino in the Acropolis! Doctor Croc nearly took me out, I'm seventeen pounds lighter, and . . . lordy, the war's over! It ended on George Herbert Walker Bush Memorial Day, 6:00 P.M., June 12, 1999. I swear, that Moseby must be psychic or something!

All my buddies are in town, intact, except for Burnt Offerings, who broke his ankle coming to see me, slippin' on the wet marble floor of the reception area! Wild. They tell me that Europe is the Paradise COMBANK promised us, that most of it was spared in the war while the rest of the world is Number Ten. The Worst. COMBANK moved out of Dallas and set up permanent shop in Brussels. All the guys want to settle down in Utah, since they hear that the women there passed a bunch of pro-polygamy laws. They decided to share rather than go without. Smart. I hate to break up a team, but I'm partial to Colorado, a ranch by the river, fishin', farmin', and loafin'. I hear some foreigners in this ward write off America as if it were a leper colony or something. Me, well, I like the idea of playing frontiersman as long as COMBANK's willing to pick up the tab.

It's not that I'm deserting my buddies. I never would've made it without them, never survived this war. Get this: they took a unanimous vote, saying they wouldn't step into a casino or out with a doll until the day comes when I'm able to stand and go with them as a team—three weeks, a month, no matter how long it takes for me to get my walking papers.

That's just the kind of guys they are, true-blue. Solid. Squared away. They kill me . . .

*　　*　　*

191

777 Dispensary Lane was the address of York Memorial, a hospital only six months old if you considered the two years of renovation that transformed a crumbling wreck into a glittery glass and steel complex rimmed by six 5-story surgical towers. All that remained to remind the many of the past was a solitary orange-brick power plant surrounded by construction rubble, ringed by a high link fence crowned with razor ribbon.

A perfect place. A place easily overlooked. A place inspected twice a year whose only function was to support the Department of Power and Water as it scrambled to fix a downed power line or ease an overloaded circuit.

A hiding place. In front of a mass of cables and meters a ten-by-five-by-five teakwood trapezoid Samadhi tank brimful with 185 gallons of chlorinated water held at a constant ninety-six degrees. A 25 percent saline of Epsom salt solution supported the ossified floater on a bed of endless sleep.

Rubber-clad feet shuffled in, sensible, hospital shoes. A single 200-watt blue bulb, suspended from the ceiling by a frayed extension cord, swayed and flickered at the touch of Mike Moseby's shoulder. He went to work immediately, switching on a 25-watt bulb within the tank, opening the latchless door smoothly to check his experiment. In his haste he found a moment to hang a rusty, discarded sign found on a junk pile marked HEAD SCAN/ULTRASOUND/NUCLEAR MEDICINE/ RADIOLOGY.

Mary Lou Goings was not amused. Her slate-gray eyes, as hard and intimidating as hot lead, flashed sparks at the mocking display.

"You're one hell of a paramedic, Mike," she seethed. "Can't you get it through your head that you aren't qualified?"

"Fleming, Ehrlich, and Pasteur weren't physicians either," he shot back, his gloved hands deftly replacing the prior day's programming with fresh input into the ports of the multiple sound cassette console he had built from scratch. New fantasies. War stories. Moseby called it *building the dream* . . .

Moseby looked at those ferrety, armor-piercing eyes, wondering if she could go the distance. "We're doing nothing wrong, Mary Lou. You know I care. If you're looking to label me, think of me as a subliminalist."

She nodded grudgingly, handing him the results of the morning's blood testing. "Weird. It's usually high blood

192

cortisol in the morning and low blood levels at night. Our boy reverses this pattern at will."

Moseby sighed. "He's merely resetting his cerebral clock, the day/night cycles, to stay in sync with the time frame of the fantasy programs."

Floating on top of the Dead Sea, me and my buddies, my belly's stuffed with sweet figs and Bam-Bam Juice . . . Paradise. Pretzel, keep your nose above the water! Chic! Daniel's out too far . . .

"I wish I could be in his head, building that dream," said Moseby wistfully. "Free of guilt. Dreams evolving as a real dimension. Blue lights, white lights flashing in the sybaritic cell of the mind. The final, soaring release from the superego. Ultrareality."

Soft, strong hands flexed nervously. "I'm happy that you can wax poetic about a borderliner when I'm the one who has to change his diapers every hour, no less find a way to get him back unseen to Subintensive Care by six A.M."

Moseby shook his head good-naturedly, turning his attention to the curled mounds of graph paper churned out in their absence by his crude diagnostic monitors. A combination voltmeter and oscilloscope measured brain wave trains, a polygraph measured muscle tension.

"We have Delta here at one hertz," he began to read aloud. "Then sporadic Theta at five hertz, then REM, the dream state." A pause. "REM at fourteen hertz, shifting back to an Alpha harmonic. Beta is nonexistent in him."

He could imagine those REM eyes shifting rapidly beneath those blue-veined eyelids. "Hypnagogic Theta is the state we must prolong so he can use the knowledge assimilated in the Alpha state to create his own free-flowing fantasy script." An awkward silence, then euphoria. "Look at this! A tripling of Alpha amplitudes for eighteen seconds! He's relaxed! He's attentive! He's identifying!"

"Swell," Nurse Goings droned, kneading her aching neck muscles. "I'm up for a day post in Orthopedics. I'd rather hear the slipped discs wailing then watch the borderliners waste away in Subintensive. Hearing Sonnyboy crying No! Don't pull the plug, while Momma screams, Don't let Poppa suffer any longer! Then the long faces of the doctors, the lawyers, state officials, in the middle crooning To Pull Or Not to Pull? Keep that money machine rolling along."

Moseby wasn't listening. "One morning three years ago

193

this guy's changing bus tires and in the afternoon he's a botched lobotomy. A faulty tire explodes, a two-piece rim becomes a rocket-powered guillotine that takes off a part of his head. The prefrontal lobe is mostly gone and the neocortex is hamburger, yet he still listens, he dreams! Isn't the brain a wonder, Mary Lou? As long as the motor and sensory centers are left intact, his mind will function without a measurable decrease in intelligence."

The nurse regarded him mistrustfully. "He's never been well fed. They cut his food and water this morning. They asked me to put him down, Mike. I won't do it."

"Then you'd better kiss that Orthopod job good-bye," Moseby snorted his ridicule. "Get involved, Mary Lou. Feel for this guy! No friends, family. A specter living in the same furnished room for twenty-two years. I've been to that rat hole. I've seen how this cipher lives, and you know what? He lives for war, for the screaming glory of it. He's got hundreds of books where a family should be, all about war. Especially Vietnam. The funniest thing is that he never served a day in uniform. The Board aced him. High blood pressure."

The nurse's gray eyes kindled. "Those tapes are about Vietnam?"

"A war, Mary Lou, a war that never happened but could occur in twenty years because war is inevitable, don't you agree?" he questioned vaguely. "A war of lunacy as in the *Number of the Beast*."

Point-eight volt charges were relayed from a hand-held stimulator console to the electrode package attached to the shaven scalp of the experiment. Buttons were pushed in sequence, light-emitting diodes flashed over plastic strips marked URGES, EXCITE, JUDGMENTS, EVALUATIONS.

"Emotion is the key to remembering," Moseby began. "Let's hope that his hippocampus within the limbic can convert the scripting into a long-term memory."

Mary Lou jumped, stunned. "Heartbeat's up fifty beats! There's no discernible muscle tension on the poly—he's going, Mike."

"Live, Gook! Live!" he beseeched, chattering, "I'll stim his prefrontal—that's the center of personality, oversees his goals, his limits of perseverance. Then I'll zap his hypothalamus to create a moment of sublime ecstasy, follow that with twin charges to the lower temporal lobes so he can relive these positive sensations many times. *Hang on, Hump! Run it back at Doctor Croc!"*

REM and midbrain Theta interspersed in violent convulsions on the oscilloscope's fluorescent screen. Fantasies played havoc with the near-dead mind. A sudden shift to a calming Alpha harmonic. Moseby was out of breath, but relieved.

"Why didn't I realize that before? The prefrontal is the jailer holding back the savage rat and reptile of the limbic region from escaping through the human neocortical mantle. Our boy doesn't have a properly functioning prefrontal. He may react in the fantasy I wrote for him with violent mood swings, or laugh, cry at inappropriate times in his dreams. He may be unable to understand the consequences of his actions, no matter how savage, how immoral."

Nurse Goings' face flushed the color of her pink apron. "Then he could be having a nonstop nightmare, filled with death, killing . . . *insanity*?"

"War is all those things," he replied strongly, his soft brown eyes aflame with memories of a time best forgotten. "I know about that kind of insanity, of being a gunner in 'Nam, hanging out of Huey Slick bay doors mowing down villes and dinks with my trusty twin-fifties. So I'm like a lot of guys who got a Soviet round in my back who can't move their legs but promise God that if He lets me walk again I'll save lives, not take them. So here I am, Mary Lou, Mr. Blue Tailored Jumpsuit, Rolex watch, amber aviator shades, Cabretta leather jacket, aka Mike the Paramedic. A guy with a future. Maybe. But all our boy has is a bunch of well-intentioned types deciding when and who's going to pull his plug!"

The nurse clucked her tongue rapidly. "You think that by filling this guy's head with atrocities you're helping him? You're the one who's dreaming, Mike."

Moseby shrugged sleepily. "That's what he wants, Mary Lou. Most men never make closer friends during their lifetimes than the ones they make sharing a war. Together. Closer than their wives, their kids."

"Hump, you're going to make it, bro'—can you hear me? It's Burnt Offerings and the Concept. You really burned that Wacky Jack good. No, you can't have no water for a belly wound . . . the Slick's coming, you're only six klicks from a surgeon. Hump! Start building the dream!"

It was a side glance borne of habit that brought the flat waves on the monitoring screens to her attention. She said the

195

words many times, on cue. Too many times. "He's gone, Doctor . . . Mike . . ."

Mike Moseby managed a gallows laugh. "Didya hear? Doctor Croc took down the Hump last night."

Mary Lou Goings began the tidying up, using her capable arms to lift the hundred-pound corpse out of the tank and into a small plastic wading pool filled with a cool, biodegradable wash. She brought the body to its feet, slippery dead weight, losing control of her grip, allowing the body to collapse and fall to the concrete floor with a sickening thud, impacting its already damaged head.

A bloody nose, that's all, she groaned inwardly, sprawling the body in the wading pool to scrub it clean of the telltale salt residue. Maybe I'll get that Orthopedics post now, she mused as she scrubbed. Maybe it's better to pull the plug than go through all this bullshit again . . .

"Build that dream. *Ultrareality*," he mumbled to himself. "Be a brave young man, Michael. Accept death. It's just a Gook, a Buddha Head."

Platoon Sergeant Michael D. Moseby wept.

July 23, 1999. Let me spit out the bad news first. Rumor has it that some UAR Kings are using Cyprus as a staging area to launch a final counteroffensive in the South Sinai. Must be a wave of Wacky Jacks because Kings have the sense to know when a war is over. I also hear that some fugazzi Iranian Grunts have a vendetta going against 999 and are recruiting a wave of Pakistani Wacky Jacks down in Hyderabad to hunt us down. Just an hour ago I heard that COMBANK says to ignore that talk, the war is *kaput. Finito.* Like I said before, I'm out of this war for good, but I'm not against re-upping, if you get my drift.

Somebody once told me that bad news comes in threes. That was Sergeant Major Moseby, the resident swami of 999. Seems that those five Tojoe Zappers committed suicide last week, chomped down on their tongues and bled themselves dry. BRO-21X tells me that some scuzzies in the 999 razzed them Zappers during the truce, told them that they were valuable commodities that could make a million gold certificates on an exhibit tour of Europe. I don't buy the freak show angle—sure, they were proud, but logical. I think they just wanted to go on emulsifying Kings forever. I think they never forgave the Libyans for igniting that H-bomb in the light atmosphere over Japan that cleaned that nation of every living thing. They have a nice name for it now, *dusty asphyx* . . . whatever. Man, those Tojoes loved to burn them Kings! Now peace broke out, took that pleasure away from them. They had no country to go to, no family—no future. I guess that counts more than I care to admit . . .

Now for the good news—I'm getting my walkin' papers tomorrow! And I'm getting married! In two weeks I'll be back in the Four Corners with my wife, my buddies—can you believe it? Her name is Mary Lou Goings. (As in comings-and-goings: ha-ha.) She's the nurse who's been showering, shaving, and trying to put twenty pounds on my skeleton these past two weeks. She's not exactly my dream girl but she's tough, fair, and she cares about me. I like a doll who cares. Mary Lou's got these gray, gray eyes that look right into you. Like a Tojoe Zapper K-bar. Only sharper.

Of course, my buddies think I'm dinky-doo for fallin' for the first American doll I've seen in three years. They're still building the dream of going to Utah and having harems of dolls like some UAR King. What they really need is one doll like Mary Lou, that's all. Get this: she told me today she's willing to go to Utah and share me with any number of dolls as long as I tell her every day that I love her—can you believe that? Guess I'm going to Utah after all.

Tomorrow is July 24. That's Pioneer Day in Utah. Could it be an omen for me? I should ask Moseby to look into that for me.

My buddies and me are going to set up a closed community in a place called Heber Valley. We're going to build a permanent firebase of two-story log cabins for our families and stay together like it was meant to be. *Forever.* In Paradise. I'll grow veggies, watch the polestar, and have eight kids with Mary Lou and Mary Lou alone. That polygamy stuff sounds harassing to me. It's like that Double-Vet crap that went on in 'Nam years back. Either you want to or you don't.

Let me tell you the best part of leaving this war. It's spittin' in Doctor Croc's mouth knowing that's all he got of me this time. Sure, he'll get me someday. Doctor Croc works in mysterious ways, like he did with those Tojoe Zappers. Who knows? When I get to Utah, Doctor Croc may give the Hump a little push in the shower and . . .

EDITOR'S INTRODUCTION TO:

LEARNING FROM VIET NAM
by Doan Van Toai and David Chanoff

The fog of war covers more than battlefields. If we do not know the strategies employed by our enemies, we handicap ourselves enormously.

Herewith a lesson from one who knows.

Doan Van Toai was a ranking officer with the Vietcong and worked briefly with the Hanoi government after the fall of South Vietnam. He soon learned the true nature of the cause he had supported.

He is now a research associate at Tufts University's Fletcher School of Law and Diplomacy.

David Chanoff is a Teaching Fellow at Harvard University.

LEARNING FROM VIETNAM: THE PATTERNS OF LIBERATION MOVEMENTS
Doan Van Toai and David Chanoff

There may well be a "Viet Nam" of the 1980s, and for a while it seemed that El Salvador was well on its way. All the ingredients are there: an oppressed peasantry, an entrenched landlord class, a history of corrupt government, a pseudo-colonial past, an energetic leftist guerrilla movement, and a U.S. government with the will to intervene. Domestic confrontation within the United States also appears ready to take up precisely where it was interrupted by the signing of the Paris Peace Accords.

Only nine years have passed since Viet Nam provided much of the American and European Left with the chance to define a posture *vis-à-vis* international intervention by the USA. In the process, Viet Nam developed into a moral symbol that transformed the U.S. national debate into a drama of civil disobedience and street violence that added a heavy emotional overlay to the anti-intervention position. Although there have been a few notable defections from the peace movement since then (Joan Baez, Bernard-Henri Lévy, Jean Lacouture, and now Susan Sontag), that same emotion-charged resistance seems still to be on tap. Already Noam Chomsky has warned that "there is overwhelming opposition to U.S. involvement in El Salvador; the popular response has been quite vocal. . . ." Even the offer to send a peace-keeping force of U.S. Marines to the Lebanon to "help" the evacuation of the PLO evoked nightmarish fears of a "Viet Nam syndrome."

Yet even so, reappraisal is in the air, and the once apparently clear "lessons of Viet Nam," both pragmatic and moral, are being subjected to review. Facing such a reappraisal is particularly unpleasant for those who once believed that the NLF/Vietcong was in fact "the sole genuine representative of the South Vietnamese people" (as Le Duc Tho so often expressed it), and that the eventual goal was "socialism in the North, democracy in the South" (Le Duan's phrase, the most popular revolutionary slogan of the early 1970s). But there appears to be a growing consensus that understanding American involvement in Viet Nam is a prerequisite to formulating a foreign policy for El Salvador or anywhere else in an endangered world that is different from the reflex strategy of *escalating military entanglement* or the equally reflex strategy of *withdrawal*. In Viet Nam, the former approach brought the USA 300,000 casualties and military failure; the latter, 500,000 refugees and political failure. No one wants to be doomed to repeat that particular history.

First among the lessons that Viet Nam teaches concerns the composition of liberation-war guerrilla movements. It is perhaps not widely remembered that the Viet Minh was born in 1941 as an anti-French "front" organization that included nationalists, religious groups, and non-Communist Leftists, together with a tightly disciplined Communist minority that effectively, though covertly, exercised control. After Dien Bien Phu (1954), non-Communist revolutionaries were still employed in the government to continue attracting popular support, even while all anti-Communist factions were being eliminated. It was only when Ho Chi Minh had sufficiently consolidated power that the turn of the nationalists and non-Party militants came.

Exactly the same tactic was re-employed in the 1960s when the National Liberation Front was founded to rally all those who sympathized in any way with Communist goals. Later, NLF operatives created the Alliance of National, Democratic and Peace Forces to provide a link with the nationalist intellectuals who opposed the regime and American intervention, but were sufficiently unenchanted with the Left to keep away from the Viet Cong. Both the Alliance and the NLF served as umbrella groups until 1975 when, with the establishment of the unified government, the Communists felt comfortable enough to eliminate their former allies. Even the NLF/Vietcong itself was eradicated, and its demise went unnoticed and unmarked by the same media that had formerly accorded it such lavish attention. Having used the organization, its army, its supporters, its people, the Vietnamese Communist Party simply disposed of it, along with the load of propaganda that

200

had depended on the appearance of NLF's "independence" and its inclusion of "moderates."

There are two points to be made here, both obvious but often overlooked. One is that Communist "liberation war" strategy calls for the creation of guerrilla fronts representing many shades of political feeling, within which the Communists themselves are likely to be a minority. Antagonists are thus faced with an enemy which attracts diversified support and whose leadership is difficult to identify. The foreign propaganda effect alone of such an organization is more than worth the minor risk to the Communist nucleus that it will be outmaneuvered by some temporarily allied faction. Foreign journalists, for example, can be counted on to make a cogent case for the moderate, the liberal, and the nationalist struggle for a homeland rather than for the Communist flavor of the guerrilla movement. They will note that apparently leading figures are intellectuals or religious leaders whose standpoints may be distinctly non-Communist. And over time their reportage will convey to their democratically and pluralistically inclined readers the impression of a movement that is itself "pluralistic," and to that extent representative and even democratic.

The fact is, however, that the actual layers of guerrilla control are immensely difficult to lay bare even for historians with perspective and leisure, let alone for reporters whose job requires quick insights for urgent deadlines on the basis of limited observation. Even so astute an observer as Bernard Fall could argue in his book *Vietnam in the Balance* (1966) that the Viet Cong, though aided and partly directed by North Viet Nam, was in fact a distinct entity that included substantial support from various politico-religious sects (among others) and that had its own program quite separate from Hanoi's. Yet in his May 19, 1975, Victory Day speech, Le Duan let the cat out of the bag:

> Our Party [the Vietnamese Communist Party] is the unique and single leader that organized, controlled and governed the entire struggle of the Vietnamese people from the first day of the revolution.

His remarks were later echoed by Nguyen Huu Tho, the NLF's former president, who matter-of-factly commented that the organization had always been "wholly obedient to the party line" (address on the 15th Anniversary of the NLF, December 19, 1975), while the Ho Chi Minh City party newspaper (*Saigon Giai Phong*) editorialized that "under the leadership of the Workers Party of Viet Nam [the Vietnamese Communist Party], the National Liberation Front was founded, and under the wise leadership of the Party, the Front gained victory after victory. . . ." If the Viet Nam experience has taught Liberation Movement organizers anything, it is the value of maintaining a reformist, nationalist, and non-aligned façade. There is no doubt that the Salvadoran movement (or indeed the Palestine liberation movement) will follow that same strategy, and that the façade will be virtually impenetrable to outside analysis.

There is also no doubt (and this is the second point) that the non-Communist elements in the guerrilla front will be destroyed as soon as feasible. Ton Duc Thang, president of North Viet Nam's Fatherland Front, succinctly characterized Communist strategy in this regard: "Rally all forces that can be rallied, neutralize all forces that can be neutralized, eliminate all forces that can be eliminated."

Ton was referring here to the standard Communist device of shifting coalitions in order to make use of opposition forces and eventually eliminate them piecemeal. For example, to deal with three enemies, alliances are formed with two while the primary enemy is attacked. The process is then repeated until Communist power stands unopposed.

This strategy governed the creation of the Viet Minh coalitions and the employment of non-Communist revolutionaries in the Ho Chi Minh government while resources were coordinated against the French, just as it governed the elimination of those same elements once the primary enemy was defeated. The same pattern followed suit in the South where the Cao Dai and Hoa Hao sects were initially welcomed and became a substantial part of the NLF. Since the overthrow of Saigon, however, both sects have been suppressed and their leaders imprisoned or executed. They were first rallied, then neutralized, then eliminated.

In fact, none of the former non-Communist Leftists— progressive intellectuals, religious leaders, or student militants who figured so importantly in the anti-American, anti-regime conflict—now hold any major position in the unified government. On the contrary, many of them are either jailed or dead. The former Buddhist leader, the Venerable Thich Tri Quang, whose picture appeared at one point (May 30, 1966) in *Newsweek* and in *L'Express* (Paris) with the caption "The Man Who Makes America Tremble," is now under house arrest in Ho Chi Minh City as are his two chief assistants. Another major Buddhist anti-war figure, the Venerable Thich Thien Minh, who was sentenced to fifteen years imprisonment by the Thieu government, survived the regime that condemned him only to die a Communist prisoner in the Ham Tan Gulag in 1979. The activist priest Father Tran Huu Thanh, responsible for organizing mass movements against Thieu (most prominently the People's Movement Against Corruption), is presently meditating on life's ironies in a Northern re-education camp. Professor Chau Tam Luan, formerly vice-president of the Association of Patriotic Intellectuals, has recently escaped the homeland he fought so determinedly to liberate. The list goes on: Tran Van Tuyen (nationalist opposition leader), dead in a Communist prison in 1976; Ho Huu Tuong (Sartre's classmate and Viet Nam's leading philosopher), dead in Ham Tan in 1980; Thich Man Giac (Buddhist strategist), a refugee; Phan Ba Cam (secretary-general of the opposition Democratic Socialist Party), dead in the Chi Hoa Gulag in 1979.

To Westerners who are not Viet Nam specialists these names evoke little or no recognition: no faces come to mind, no personal histories. But to those who are educated about the anti-regime, anti-American period, these people and their numerous colleagues among the refugees, the imprisoned and the deceased represented the heart of the non-Communist resistance. These are the people who created and led the organizations that elicited passionate support from the American and European peace movements. They are the ones who made Le Duc Tho believable in the Paris peace talks (1970–73) with his refrain that "we [North Viet Nam] do not want to impose Communism on South Viet Nam," and his persistent advocacy of a postwar coalition government. Today, of course, seven years after the annexation of the South, Le Duc Tho's Paris positions have long been revealed as nothing more than disingenuous rhetoric. At the time they were taken seriously, and by no one more than those who had bound their fortunes to the Communists. Truong Nhu Tang (a founder of the NLF, Minister of Justice in the Provisional Revolutionary government, now an exile in France) put it this way:

The Communists are expert in the art of seduction and will go to any length to woo you over to their side, as long as they don't control the government. But once they are in power they suddenly become harsh, ungrateful, cynical, and destroy you without hesitation.

These two lessons from the Vietnamese primer are available to those who report the Salvadoran and other liberation movements, as well as to those who are inclined actively to support the economic and political aspirations of a dispossessed peasantry. It is not that such aspirations are unworthy; quite the opposite. It is simply that alliance with or support of a Communist front in order to achieve anything other than strictly Communist goals is suicidal. Eventually they will, in Tang's words, "destroy you without hesitation." That at least is what happened in Viet Nam, and the Viet Nam experience seems applicable to any protracted liberation movement that becomes the focus of East/West confrontation. The non-Communist Left, as well as other revolutionary factions, is simply not capable of long-term survival within a Communist-led movement.

One reason for this is that in a protracted "liberation war," shipments of supplies and arms to guerrilla forces must move through foreign Communist countries; military training and direction for guerrilla forces must be carried on by foreign Communist governments; and effective worldwide propaganda must be orchestrated by foreign Communist governments. The entire support system necessary to carry a modern liberation war to a successful conclusion relies on a power base outside the host country. Such a base is only available through the Soviet Union or one of her regional proxies, so that revolutionary groups not aligned with the Soviets are inevitably submerged by their more powerful competitors.

In Viet Nam, the Communist strategy of "rallying all those who can be rallied" in order to isolate and eliminate enemies one by one was extraordinarily successful. Unfortunately, the Saigon government was incapable of emulating that strategy and found itself operating from an increasingly narrowing popular base. The same self-defeating polarization appears to be operating in El Salvador today with the recent setbacks to the Christian Democrats and the apparent dismantling of land reform measures. Here too the Vietnamese experience is worth reflecting on.

In Viet Nam, the hard-line right-wing orientation of successive Southern regimes often radicalized and alienated those who should have been made into allies. In many cases, the government's habitual brutality transformed a loyal opposition into Leftists, moderate Leftists into Communists, and reluctant Communists into zealots. Many students who at first only knew that they were "against the regime" learned through a term or two in prison to be confirmed revolutionaries. The regime, utilizing its French-trained police, was adept at torture, but hopelessly inept at any other type of persuasion. Government leaders simply had no concept of the need to differentiate among opposition groups and to split the non-Communist elements from their deadly allies. Instead they regarded as Communists virtually all on the Left (and many in the Center as well), and so played precisely into the hands of the Communists whose strategy was to "rally all who can be rallied." This appalling obtuseness gave additional credence to the NLF's claim to be a "true coalition" and vastly more representative of the South Vietnamese people than the government. In the long run, this claim, and the corresponding image that Diem, Ky, and Thieu established for themselves as self-seeking despots, played a significant role in the erosion of American domestic support for the war, and it was in the American domestic arena that the outcome was decided.[1]

Viet Nam was the West's first experience with a protracted war of liberation, and perhaps the single most important lesson it taught concerns the power of public dissent. That lesson is particularly ominous since it confirms that ideologized opinion-makers have become central to the West's ability to wage this sort of war, while Communist planners have no equivalent need to take into account the complex domestic role of a free press. At the same time they are highly attuned to the impact of the media among their adversaries. One of the authors of this article (Doan Van Toai) spent two and a half years in the Tran Hung Dao Gulag after an earlier career as a pro–Viet Cong student leader, publisher, and sometimes prisoner of the Thieu regime. While in Tran Hung Dao he was part of a group of political prisoners chosen at one point to listen to an address by Mai Chi Tho (a Central Committee member and brother of Le Duc Tho). Tho told them:

Ho Chi Minh may have been an evil man; Nixon may have been a great man. The Americans may have had the just cause; we may not have had the just cause. But we won and the Americans were defeated because we convinced the people that Ho Chi Minh is the great man, that Nixon is a murderer, and the Americans are the invaders. . . . The key factor is how to control people and their opinions. Only Marxism-Leninism can do that. . . . Between you—the bright intellectuals—and me, I tell you the truth.[2]

Tho was referring not only to the success of Communist propaganda within Viet Nam, but also to its worldwide impact.

One reason that the American antiwar movement is reluctant to look back at that period is not simply that the postwar history of Viet Nam has been so tragic; it is that people do not relish acknowledging their own gullibility. Harrison Salisbury, Staughton Lynd, Tom Hayden, David Schoenbrun, among others, all found themselves popularizing in the West Hanoi's position on such themes as the "absence" of Northern troop infiltration into the South, the "independence" of the NLF/Vietcong, and Northern innocence of plans to "annex the South." Pham Van Dong in particular developed a special adroitness in dealing with American visitors, who almost always heard remarks calculated to exploit their own predispositions.

Yet even when the full story of Communist manipulation of American opinions is known,[3] we will still need to anticipate the likely effect of media-related pressures should the United States become militarily involved in El Salvador or elsewhere. In that event we would undoubtedly witness over a period of time incidents every bit as vivid and dehumanizing as those that Viet Nam still evokes for almost all of us. Children running from napalm, murder in the street, villages burning—the whole iconography of war. In a conflict where the media have access to one side and not to the other, these incidents will regularly depict the brutality of our allies and ourselves and rarely that of our enemies.

At the same time, the mechanisms our society has evolved to achieve "open government" will ensure that much of our tactics and strategy will be public knowledge and open to criticism both emotional and rational. We will know exactly the extent of our economic and military assistance to a government many feel to be unsavory. But the truth about foreign supply and troop inflation to the guerrillas will remain conjectural. We will have detailed reports on how our soldiers feel about fighting and dying in an alien place. But we will know little that is credible about the enemy except for his courage and perseverance. The stupidity, negligence, and failures accompanying our involvement will be spotlighted each night on television. But the same kind of information about guerrilla troubles will simply not be available. Consequently, media reportage will seem to maximize our difficulties and minimize those of the other side. Over time, such things will have a corrosive effect on even hardened patriots. That at least was the experience in Viet Nam, and it is difficult to imagine anything different coming out of another overseas engagement, in Salvador or elsewhere.

Reinforcing the predictable bias of Western news coverage is the predictable bias of editorial analysis. The function of a free press in keeping a vigilantly skeptical eye on government had the long-term effect in Viet Nam of turning the majority of American commentators against the administration. David Halberstam's letters to his daughter describe the changes even the most initially supportive observers went through when confronted with the official hypocrisy and duplicity that inevitably accompany war, and especially a prolonged and confused guerrilla war. During the Viet Nam period none of the major television commentators, other than Howard K. Smith, maintained anything vaguely resembling a pro-Administration perspective. For its part, of course, the Administration displayed disappointment and hostility toward media luminaries who failed to appreciate the government's theories of geopolitical confrontation or even to maintain, in its opinion, decent objectivity.[4]

But a balanced historical perspective is not what we should expect from the media. Their traditions are those of adversarial confrontation and investigative reporting, of scoops and hot news, not scholarly objectivity. Even though they are the conduit through which current history becomes known, they are not historians. By and large they are not equipped for the role and they are not comfortable with its demands. They didn't fulfill it well in Viet Nam, and there is no reason to believe they would be more suited to it in Latin America or the Middle East.

All this suggests that what we can be sure of in El Salvador, or any other liberation war that attracts serious American attention, is a domestic antiwar movement that will trigger off at a fairly high level and intensify as the flow of news and analysis affects public thinking. Over time, the impact of continuous war coverage will inevitably erode popular support for U.S. involvement and will help generate a progressively more militant resistance. This effect can almost be taken as a given. After Viet Nam, political strategists have no choice but to include the media factor in their equations and to weight it more and more heavily over time.

Another given is the predilection of the American Left to embrace "national liberation movements" of every stripe as long as there is an element of anti-Americanism in them. Even the anti-regime movements of Pol Pot and the Ayatollah Khomeini attracted their share of initial support. Viet Nam, however, remains the textbook case. In that conflict a pattern of domestic resistance developed around radicalized intellectuals and other public figures that can be viewed as a militant model for domestic reaction in any future engagement. In terms of the American ability to commit troops over an extended period, this resistance must be considered ominous. Its obvious continued vitality brings into relief the major problems facing American foreign policy today—the enlightenment of public opinion in the United States, and especially the education of the adversarial culture that Viet Nam galvanized throughout the West.

That education has begun already with the reassessment of Viet Nam currently under way. As public understanding grows of what the North Vietnamese and Southern front objectives really were, how their military and propaganda organizations operated, and what the postwar realities in Indo-China are, it will become increasingly clear that American involvement there was supportable on both moral and geopolitical grounds.

Viet Nam, in fact, should be regarded as an object lesson for the American Left, a lesson in the manipulative strategies of Communist-led liberation war movements and the subversion of popular aspirations for independence and economic and political reform. The flow of political prisoners within Viet Nam and the flow of refugees out of Viet Nam included large numbers of former Viet Cong freedom-fighters, socialist revolutionaries, nationalist intellectuals, and religious activists who have learned in their flesh the consequences of embracing the Communists as allies. American progressives, it is fervently hoped, will never have the opportunity to learn

208

the same lessons in the same way. But if the Viet Nam scenario is not to be repeated, they must be encouraged to discard their studied ignorance of recent Vietnamese history.

The Northern burial of the Viet Cong, whose program was espoused by many in the domestic antiwar movement, should be the subject of detailed public examination, as should the fate of the various other anti-regime, anti-American factions. The single-minded Northern pursuit of annexation, the bloody suppression of the land redistribution under Ho Chi Minh, the campaign to smother religion and culture in unified Viet Nam, these should all be as well known in the United States and Europe now as the My Lai massacre, Thieu's "tiger cages," and massive South Vietnamese corruption were then. This history is alive and can be told with best effect, not by the people perceived as conservative ideologues, but by the dissident and dispossessed Vietnamese Leftists and intellectuals who lived it, people like Nguyen Cong Hoan and Truong Nhu Tang, for whose ideas the Left committed itself and who have the standing to make themselves heard by their erstwhile supporters.

It can be said, of course, that current Vietnamese history merely reteaches the lessons of other Communist revolutions. But in certain ways Viet Nam is special. Viet Nam was the crucible of the modern American Left. It was the Viet Nam war that also radicalized much of the intelligentsia in Western Europe ("*Ho-Ho-Ho-Chi-Minh*" shouted the tens of thousands of APO and SDS demonstrators in the streets of Bonn and Berlin). The theme continues to provide the Left with its reference points. Almost as significant is that Viet Nam was one of the few—with Castro's Cuba—contemporary forces in the Communist world that stirred deep ideological sympathy in the West. Russia has been bankrupt as a moral force for decades. China is rightly perceived as a nation more concerned with internal difficulties and security problems than with its role as champion of international Communism. Insurgent Viet Nam, on the other hand, is still lionized for its courage, its ability to face and overcome colonialism and imperialism, domestic right-wing dictators, and American militarism. It is thus a model for present and future East-West conflicts in Latin America and Africa, conflicts which can be expected to draw a great deal of American and West European support to the revolutionary side, fighting at once for homeland and radical social ideals.

209

But the fact is that Viet Nam is an idol with clay feet, and persistent, thorough exposure of the monumental deceit with which the war was carried on and of the cynical suppression of human rights afterward will work to split domestic opposition. During the Viet Nam period the American Left had little concept of the role it played (along with the NLF and so-called third force elements) in the Communist war game, and so allowed itself to be manipulated in embarrassing fashion. But as the old antiwar leadership achieves literacy about "liberation movement" strategy, its willingness to sponsor and organize future opposition should become less reflexive. Joan Baez two years ago and Susan Sontag recently have surely done more to provoke objectivity and self-awareness within the American Left than the most convincing conservative arguments ever could. Intensified education is in order, not to divert the Left from its social ideals, but to divorce it from its thoughtless support of Communist-led and/or Soviet-sponsored liberation movements. As trade used to follow the flag, Gulag follows "the final contest."

There is a necessary complement to education, however, and that is the creation of a Western policy for liberation war situations that is capable of drawing support within the United States. Unfortunately, though, in this era of liberation movements the Americans and the Europeans have until now failed to furnish the Third World with its type of pro-Western revolution. They simply have not developed a coherent, positive approach to resolving the social inequities that provide the framework for present-day international competition. Our failures in this area have forced us into, at best, a defensive "containment" posture which, among other misfortunes, had led to a history of American support for the status quo defended by unpopular authoritarians. Consequences have included the identification of the United States with old-time oppression rather than change, reform, and social amelioration. We ourselves have fostered the impression that, in the Third World context, to be progressive or innovative means to be pro-Communist.

This apparent truth has had tragic effects on populations involved in "liberation wars." But the more profound catastrophe is that domestic American opinion has been so alienated that any scenario which includes a prolonged U.S. military commitment is problematical. The chief effect of this is substantially to reduce American leverage and thus to encourage guerrilla movements in their reliance on the violence of military solutions. In Mai Chi Tho's words: "The key factor is how to control people and their opinions"; and that observation applies every bit as much to sophisticated Western opinion as it does to the "hearts and minds" of Vietnamese and Salvadoran farmers.

Given the opportunity, the American and European Left could find its natural home backing non-Communist factions in Nicaragua, El Salvador, and elsewhere. But for this to happen, and for the consequent neutralization of the general "antiwar" movement to materialize, the West must learn from the Communist strategy of gathering all the support available in order to confront the common enemy. That means a policy, undertaken within the context of regional alliances, of pressing conspicuously for reform in countries not yet embroiled, working to achieve coalitions rather than polarization where there is already substantial guerrilla activity, and actively supporting indigenous non-Communist "people's movements" in areas where they enjoy significant popular support (in Afghanistan, for example, in Indo-China, and now in the Lebanon).

Appropriate support along with regional allies of such movements would have several positive effects. It would throw doubt on the commonly held belief that Communist revolutions are irreversible. It would further drain Soviet resources, already badly extended. And it would spur development of a comprehensive Western "Third World strategy" different from the defeatist alternatives of reaction or isolation. The development of such a strategy, together with continuing public education about Viet Nam and its aftermath, will go a long way toward restoring viability to Western objectives in the developing nations.

NOTES

1. See the two articles which represent the first real efforts to "learn from Viet Nam": Robert Elegant, "How to Lose a War" (*Encounter*, August 1981); and H.J. Kaplan, "With the American Press in Vietnam" (*Commentary*, May 1982, pp. 42–49).

2. *New York Times Magazine*, March 30, 1981.

3. Stanley Karnow, "Viet Nam Duplicity Reconsidered," *Encounter*, August 1981.

4. See Peter Braestrup, *The Big Story* (Westview Press, in cooperation with Freedom House, 1977).

MAJOR PUGACHOV'S LAST BATTLE
by Shalamov

The story of the Soviet death camps is known to the West through Solzhenitsyn's *Gulag Archipelago*; but the story is so monstrous that we in the West either do not believe it or refuse to act as if we do.

It is even worse in the Soviet Union, where the story of the Red Terror is known but never discussed. The Terror has done its work well.

It is axiomatic that deception is a major tool of war. The Soviets have been uncommonly successful in deceiving the West, not only about Soviet intentions and capabilities but about the very nature of Soviet society. Sometimes, though, there are leaks in the iron curtain.

Robert Gleason put himself through university to a master of fine arts degree by working as a steel puddler in Gary, Indiana. He doesn't look much like an intellectual, which often fools people, sometimes to their dismay.

Bob Gleason early discovered both Larry Niven and Jerry Pournelle; he bought *Mote in God's Eye* when he was an editor at Pocket Books and *Lucifer's Hammer* after he moved to Playboy Books. He has since become a novelist in his own right, as well as Tor Books' general editor for this series. It has always been a pleasure to work with him.

When Bob Gleason sent us "Major Pugachov's Last Battle," he sent a letter that will do better to introduce the story than anything I could ever write. Here it is:

Dear Jerry

Enclosed is the Shalamov story which we discussed. It's from Shalamov's book *Kolyma Tales*. Solzhenitsyn saw Shalamov as the finest writer of his period and wanted him to co-author *The Gulag Archipelago*. As Solzhenitsyn pointed out, Shalamov witnessed and endured the absolute nadir of the Gulag. "Shalamov's experience in the camps," Solzhenitsyn writes, "was longer and more bitter than my own, and I respectfully confess that to him and not me was it given to touch those depths of bestiality and despair toward which life in the camps dragged us all." Solzhenitsyn also writes that when he first read Shalamov's poetry, he "trembled as if he were meeting a brother."

Shalamov was too ill to work on *The Gulag Archipelago* and died before its completion.

Briefly, Kolyma, where Shalamov did eighteen years, was a complex of gold mining camps above the Arctic Circle in the Kolyma River Basin. Between 1937 and 1953 we know that around 3,500,000 zeks perished there. Approximately, one life for every kilo of gold.

It is clear now that along with gold, death was the other chief product of these camps. The slaughter was grossly deliberate. Radical malnutrition, confiscation of winter clothing, unspeakable brutality, ghastly mass executions, and the endless mining accidents have all been redundantly documented. Over one hundred Kolyma memoirs appeared after the Khrushchev amnesty testifying to the genocide. These works included Eleanor Lipper's *Eleven Years in the Soviet Camps*, Eugenia Ginzburg's *Into the Whirlwind*, Michael Solomon's *Magadan*, and most recently, Robert Conquest's superb study of life in these camps, *Kolyma*.

Needless to say, after somehow getting into these camps for a visit back in 1944, Henry Wallace and Owen Latimore compared them to "the TVA and the Hudson's Bay Company."

It's also worth noting that these two may have the last word. In America, this massively important body of literature is passing almost unread.

Cordially,
Robert Gleason

P.S. By the way, the USSR is at present pretending that Shalamov's *Kolyma Tales* doesn't exist. A recent Soviet review of his work says: "Shalamov writes primarily about nature. One gets the impression that his surroundings interest him only on an impressionistic level."

MAJOR PUGACHOV'S LAST BATTLE
Shalamov

A lot of time must have passed between the beginning and end of these events, for the human experience acquired in the far north is so great that months are considered equivalent to years. Even the state recognizes this by increasing salaries and fringe benefits to workers of the north. It is a land of hopes and therefore of rumors, guesses, suppositions, and hypothesizing. In the north any event is encrusted with rumor more quickly than a local official's emergency report about it can reach the "higher spheres."

It was rumored that when a party boss on an inspection tour described the camp's cultural activities as lame on both feet, the "activities director," Major Pugachov, said to the guest:

"Don't let that bother you, sir, we're preparing a concert that all Kolyma will talk about."

We could begin the story straightaway with the report of Braude, a surgeon sent by the central hospital to the region of military activities. We could begin with the letter of Yashka Kuchen, a convict orderly who was a patient in the hospital. Kuchen wrote the letter with his left hand, since his right shoulder had been shot clean through by a rifle bullet.

Or we could begin with the story of Dr. Potalina who saw nothing, heard nothing, and was gone when all the unusual events took place. It was precisely her absence that the prosecutor classified as a "false alibi," criminal inaction, or whatever the term may be in a legal jargon.

The arrests of the thirties were arrests of random victims of the false and terrifying theory of a heightened class struggle accompanying the strengthening of socialism. The professors, union officials, soldiers, and workers who filled the prisons to overflowing at that period had nothing to defend themselves with except, perhaps, personal honesty and naïveté—precisely those qualities that lightened rather than hindered the punitive work of "justice" of the day. The absence of any unifying

215

idea undermined the moral resistance of the prisoners to an unusual degree. They were neither enemies of the government nor state criminals, and they died, not even understanding why they had to die. Their self-esteem and bitterness had no point of support. Separated, they perished in the white Kolyma desert from hunger, cold, work, beatings, and diseases. They immediately learned not to defend or support each other. This was precisely the goal of the authorities. The souls of those who remained alive were utterly corrupted, and their bodies did not possess the qualities necessary for physical labor.

After the war, ship after ship delivered their replacements— former Soviet citizens who were "repatriated" directly to the far northeast.

Among them were many people with different experiences and habits acquired during the war, courageous people who knew how to take chances and who believed only in the gun. There were officers and soldiers, fliers and scouts. . . .

Accustomed to the angelic patience and slavish submissiveness of the "Trotskyites," the camp administration was not in the least concerned and expected nothing new.

New arrivals asked the surviving "aborigines":

"Why do you eat your soup and kasha in the dining hall, but take your bread with you back to the barracks? Why can't you eat the bread with your soup the way the rest of the world does?"

Smiling with the cracks of their blue mouths and showing their gums, toothless from scurvy, the local residents would answer the naïve newcomers.

"In two weeks each of you will understand, and each of you will do the same."

How could they be told that they had never in their lives known true hunger, hunger that lasts for years and breaks the will? How could anyone explain the passionate, all-engulfing desire to prolong the process of eating, the supreme bliss of washing down one's bread ration with a mug of tasteless, but hot melted snow in the barracks?

But not all of the newcomers shook their heads in contempt and walked away.

Major Pugachov clearly realized that they had been delivered to their deaths—to replace these living corpses. They had been brought in the fall. With winter coming on, there was no place to run to, but in the summer a man could at least die free even if he couldn't hope to escape completely.

It was virtually the only conspiracy in twenty years, and its web was spun all winter.

Pugachov realized that only those who did not work in the mine's general work gang could survive the winter and still be capable of an escape attempt. After a few weeks in the work gang no one would run anywhere.

Slowly, one by one, the participants of the conspiracy became trusties. Soldatov became a cook, and Pugachov himself was appointed activities director. There were two work gang leaders, a paramedic, and Ivashenko, who had formerly been a mechanic and now repaired weapons for the guards.

But no one was permitted outside "the wire" without guards.

The blinding Kolyma spring began—without a single rain, without any movement of ice on the rivers, without the singing of any bird. Little by little, the sun melted the snow, leaving it only in those crevices where warm rays couldn't pierce. In the canyons and ravines, the snow lay like silver bullion till the next year.

And the designated day arrived.

There was a knock at the door of the guard hut next to the camp gates where one door led in and the other out of the camp. The guard on duty yawned and glanced at the clock. It was 5:00 A.M. Just five, he thought.

The guard threw back the latch and admitted the man who had knocked. It was the camp cook, the convict Gorbunov. He'd come for the keys to the food storeroom. The keys were kept in the guardhouse, and Gorbunov came for them three times a day. He returned them later.

The guard on duty was supposed to open the kitchen cupboard, but he knew it was hopeless to try to control the cook, that no locks would help if the cook wanted to steal, so he entrusted the keys to the cook—especially at five in the morning.

The guard had worked more than ten years in Kolyma, had been receiving a double salary for a long time, and had given the keys to the cook thousands of times.

"Take 'em," he muttered and reached for the ruler to write up in the morning report.

Gorbunov walked behind the guard, took the keys from the nail, put them in his pocket, and grabbed the guard from behind by the neck. At that very moment the door opened and the mechanic, Ivashenko, came through the door leading into the camp.

Ivashenko helped Gorbunov strangle the guard and drag his body behind the cabinet. Ivashenko stuck the guard's revolver into his own pocket. Through the window that faced outward they could see a second guard returning along the path. Hurriedly Ivashenko donned the coat and cap of the dead man, snapped the belt shut, and sat down at the table as if he were the guard. The second guard opened the door and strode into the dark hovel of the guardhouse. He was immediately seized, strangled, and thrown behind the cabinet.

Gorbunov put on the guard's clothing; the two conspirators now had uniforms and weapons. Everything was proceeding according to Major Pugachov's schedule. Suddenly the wife of the second guard appeared. She'd come for the keys that her husband had accidentally taken with him.

"We won't strangle the woman," said Gorbunov, and she was tied, gagged with a towel, and put in the corner.

One of the work gangs returned from work. This had been foreseen. The overseer who entered the guardhouse was immediately disarmed and bound by the two "guards." His rifle was now in the hands of the escapees. From that moment Major Pugachov took command of the operation.

The area before the gates was open to fire from two guard towers. The sentries noticed nothing unusual.

A work gang was formed somewhat earlier than usual, but in the north who can say what is early and what is late? It seemed early, but maybe it was late.

The work gang of ten men moved down the road to the mine, two by two in column. In the front and in the rear, six meters from the column of prisoners as required by the instructions, were two overcoated guards. One of them held a rifle.

From the guard tower the sentry noticed that the group turned from the road onto the path that led past the buildings where all sixty of the guards were quartered.

The sleeping quarters of the guards were located in the far end of the building. Just before the door stood the guard hut of the man on duty, and pyramids of rifles. Drowsing by the window the guard noticed, in a half sleep, that one of the other guards was leading a gang of prisoners down the path past the windows of the guard quarters.

"That must be Chernenko," the duty officer thought. "I must remember to write a report on him."

The duty officer was grand master of petty squabbles, and he never missed a legitimate opportunity to play a dirty trick on someone.

This was his last thought. The door flew open and three soldiers came running into the barracks. Two rushed to the doors of the sleeping quarters and the third shot the duty officer point-blank. The soldiers were followed by the prisoners, who rushed to the pyramid of weapons; in their hands were rifles and machine guns. Major Pugachov threw open the door to the sleeping quarters. The soldiers, barefoot and still in their underwear, rushed to the door, but two machine-gun bursts at the ceiling stopped them.

"Lie down," Pugachov ordered, and the soldiers crawled under their cots. The machine gunners remained on guard beside the door.

The "work gang" changed unhurriedly into military uniform and began gathering up food, weapons, and ammunition.

Pugachov ordered them not to take any food except biscuits and chocolate. In return they took as many weapons and as much ammunition as possible.

The paramedic hung the first-aid bag over his shoulder.

Once again the escapees felt they were soldiers.

Before them was the taiga, but was it any more terrible than the marshes of Stokhod?

They walked out onto the highway, and Pugachov raised his hand to stop a passing truck.

"Get out!" He opened the door of the driver's cab.

"But I . . ."

"Climb out, I tell you."

The driver got out, and Georgadze, lieutenant of the tank troops, got behind the wheel. Beside him was Pugachov. The escapee soldiers crawled into the back, and the truck sped off.

"There ought to be a right turn about here."

"We're out of gas!"

Pugachov cursed.

They entered the taiga as if they were diving into water, disappearing immediately in the enormous silent forest. Checking the map, they remained on the cherished path to freedom, pushing their way straight through the amazing local underbrush.

Camp was set up quickly for the night, as if they were used to doing it.

Only Ashot and Malinin couldn't manage to quiet down.

"What's the problem over there?" asked Pugachov.

"Ashot keeps trying to prove that Adam was deported from paradise to Ceylon."

"Why Ceylon?"

"That's what the Muslims say," responded Ashot.

"Are you a Tartar?"

"Not me, my wife is."

"I never heard anything of the sort," said Pugachov, smiling.

"Right, and neither did I," Malinin joined in.

"All right, knock it off. Let's get some sleep."

It was cold and Major Pugachov woke up. Soldatov was sitting up, alert, holding the machine gun on his knees. Pugachov lay on his back and located the North Star, the favorite star of all wanderers. The constellations here were arranged differently than in European Russia; the map of the firmament was slightly shifted, and the Big Dipper had slid down to the horizon. The taiga was cold and stern, and the enormous twisted pines stood far from each other. The forest was filled with the anxious silence familiar to all hunters. This time Pugachov was not the hunter, but a tracked beast, and the forest silence was thrice dangerous.

It was his first night of liberty, the first night after long months and years of torment. Lying on his back, he recalled how everything before him had begun as if it were a detective film. It was as if Pugachov were playing back a film of his twelve comrades so that the lazy everyday course of events flashed by with unbelievable speed. And now they had finished the film and were staring at the inscription, "THE END." They were free, but this was only the beginning of the struggle, the game, of life. . . .

Major Pugachov remembered the German prisoner-of-war camp from which he had escaped in 1944. The front was nearing the town, and he was working as a truck driver on cleanup details inside the enormous camp. He recalled how he had driven through the single strand of barbed wire at high speed, ripping up the wooden posts that had been hurriedly punched into the ground. He remembered the sentry shots, shouting, the mad, zigzag drive through the town, the abandoned truck, the night road to the front and the meetings with his army, the interrogation, the accusation of espionage, and the sentence—twenty-five years.

Major Pugachov remembered how Vlasov's emissaries had

come to the camp with a "manifesto" to the hungry, tormented Russian soldiers.

"Your government has long since renounced you. Any prisoner of war is a traitor in the eyes of your government," the Vlasovites said. And they showed Moscow newspapers with their orders and speeches. The prisoners of war had already heard of this earlier. It was no accident that Russian prisoners of war were the only ones not to receive packages. Frenchmen, Americans, Englishmen, and prisoners of all nations received packages, letters, had their own national clubs, and enjoyed each other's friendship. The Russians had nothing except hunger and bitterness for the entire world. It was no wonder that so many men from the German prisoner-of-war camps joined the "Russian Army of Liberation."

Major Pugachov did not believe Vlasov's officers until he made his way back to the Red Army. Everything that the Vlasovites had said was true. The government had no use for him. The government was afraid of him. Later came the cattle cars with bars on the windows and guards, the long trip to Eastern Siberia, the sea, the ship's hold, and the gold mines of the far north. And the hungry winter.

Pugachov sat up, and Soldatov gestured to him with his hand. It was Soldatov who had the honor of beginning the entire affair, although he was among the last to be accepted into the conspiracy. Soldatov had not lost his courage, panicked, or betrayed anyone. A good man!

At his feet lay Captain Khrustalyov, a flier whose fate was similar to Pugachov's: his plane shot down by the Germans, captivity, hunger, escape, and a military tribunal and the forced-labor camp. Khrustalyov had just turned over on his other side, and his cheek was red from where he had been lying on it. It was Khrustalyov whom Pugachov had first chosen several months before to reveal his plan. They agreed it was better to die than be a convict, better to die with a gun in hand than be exhausted by hunger, rifle butts, and the boots of the guards.

Both Khrustalyov and the major were men of action, and they discussed in minute detail the insignificant chance for which these twelve men were risking their lives. The plan was to hijack a plane from the airport. There were several airports in the vicinity, and the men were on their way through the taiga to the nearest one. Khrustalyov was the group leader whom the escapees sent for after attacking the guards. Pugachov didn't want to leave without his closest friend. Now Khrustalyov was sleeping quietly and soundly.

Next to him lay Ivashenko, the mechanic who repaired the guards' weapons. Ivashenko had learned everything they needed to know for a successful operation: where the weapons were kept, who was on duty, where the munitions stores were. Ivashenko had been a military intelligence officer.

Levitsky and Ignatovich, pilots and friends of Captain Khrustalyov, lay pressed against each other.

The tankman, Polyakov, had spread his hands on the backs of his neighbors, the huge Georgadze and the bald joker Ashot, whose surname the major couldn't remember at the moment. Head resting on his first-aid bag, Sasha Malinin was sound asleep. He'd started out as a paramedic—first in the army, then in the camps, then under Pugachov's command.

Pugachov smiled. Each had surely imagined the escape in his own way, but Pugachov could see that everything was going smoothly and each understood the other perfectly. Pugachov was convinced he had done the right thing. Each knew that events were developing as they should. There was a commander, there was a goal—a confident commander and a difficult goal. There were weapons and freedom. They slept a sound soldier's sleep even in this empty pale-lilac polar night with its strange but beautiful light in which the trees cast no shadows.

He had promised them freedom, and they had received freedom. He led them to their deaths, and they didn't fear death.

"No one betrayed us," thought Pugachov, "right up to the very last day." Many people in the camp had known of the planned escape. Selection of participants had taken several months, and Pugachov had spoken openly to many who refused, but no one had turned them in. This knowledge reconciled Pugachov with life.

"They're good men," he whispered and smiled.

They ate some biscuits and chocolate and went on in silence, led by the almost indistinguishable path.

"It's a bear path," said Soldatov, who had hunted in Siberia.

Pugachov and Khrustalyov climbed up to the pass to a cartographic tripod and used the telescope to look down to the gray stripes of the river and highway. The river was like any other river, but the highway was filled with trucks and people for tens of miles.

"Must be convicts," suggested Khrustalyov.

Pugachov examined them carefully.

"No, they're soldiers looking for us. We'll have to split up," said Pugachov. "Eight men can sleep in the haystacks, and the four of us will check out that ravine. We'll return by morning if everything looks all right."

They passed through a small grove of trees to the riverbed. They had to run back.

"Look, there are too many of them. We'll have to go back up the river."

Breathing heavily, they quickly climbed back up the riverbed, inadvertently dislodging loose rocks that roared down right to the feet of the attackers.

Levitsky turned, fired, and fell. A bullet had caught him square in the eye.

Georgadze stopped beside a large rock, turned, and stopped the soldiers coming after them with a machine-gun burst. But it was not for long; his machine gun jammed, and only the rifle was still functioning.

"Go on alone," said Khrustalyov to the major. "I'll cover you." He aimed methodically, shooting at anyone who showed himself. Khrustalyov caught up with them, shouting: "They're coming." He fell, and people began running out from behind the large rock.

Pugachov rushed forward, fired at the attackers, and leaped down from the pass's plateau into the narrow riverbed. The stones he knocked loose as he fell roared down the slope.

He ran through the roadless taiga until his strength failed.

Above the forest meadow the sun rose, and the people hiding in haystacks could easily make out figures of men in military uniforms on all sides of the meadow.

"I guess this is the end?" Ivashenko said, and nudged Khachaturian with his elbow.

"Why the end?" Ashot said as he aimed. The rifle shot rang out, and a soldier fell on the path.

At a command the soldiers rushed the swamp and haystacks. Shots cracked and groans were heard.

The attack was repulsed. Several wounded men lay among the clumps of marsh grass.

"Medic, crawl over there," an officer ordered. They'd shown foresight and brought along Yasha Kushen, a former resident of West Byelorussia, now a convict paramedic. Without saying a word, convict Kushen crawled over to the wounded man, waving his first-aid bag. The bullet that struck Kushen in the shoulder stopped him halfway.

The head of the guard detail that the escapees had just disarmed jumped up without any sign of fear and shouted:

"Hey, Ivashenko. Soldatov. Pugachov. Give up, you're surrounded. There's no way out!"

"Okay, come and get the weapons," shouted Ivashenko from behind the haystack.

And Bobylyov, head of the guards, ran splashing through the marsh toward the haystacks.

He had covered half the way when Ivashenko's shot cracked out. The bullet caught Bobylyov directly in the forehead.

"Good boy," Soldatov praised his comrade. "The chief was so brave because they would have either shot him for our escape or given him a sentence in the camps. Hold your ground!"

They were shooting from all directions. Machine guns began to crackle.

Soldatov felt a burning sensation in both legs, and the head of the dead Ivashenko fell on his shoulder.

Another haystack fell silent. A dozen bodies lay in the marsh.

Soldatov kept on shooting until something struck him in the head and he lost consciousness.

Nikolay Braude, chief surgeon of the main hospital, was summoned by Major General Artemyev, one of four Kolyma generals and chief of the whole Kolyma camp. Braude was sent to the village of Lichan together with "two paramedics, bandages, and surgical instruments." That was how the order read.

Braude didn't try to guess what might have happened and quickly set out as directed in a beat-up one-and-a-half-ton hospital truck. Powerful Studebakers loaded with armed soldiers streamed past the hospital truck on the highway. It was only about twenty miles, but because of frequent stops caused by heavy traffic and roadblocks to check documents, it took Braude three hours to reach the area.

Major General Artemyev was waiting for the surgeon in the apartment of the local camp head. Both Braude and Artemyev were long-term residents of Kolyma and fate had brought them together a number of times in the past.

"What's up, a war?" Braude asked the general when they met.

"I don't know if you'd call it a war, but there were twenty-eight dead on the first battle. You'll see the wounded yourself."

While Braude washed his hands in a basin hanging on the door, the general told him of the escape.

"And you called for planes, I suppose? A couple of squadrons, a few bombs here and there . . . Or maybe you opted for an atom bomb?"

"That's right, make a joke of it," said the general. "I tell you I'm not joking when I say that I'm waiting for my orders. I'll be lucky if I just lose my job. They could even try me. Things like that have happened before."

Yes, Braude knew that things like that had happened before. Several years earlier three thousand people were sent on foot in winter to one of the ports, but supplies stored on shore were destroyed by a storm while the group was under way. Of three thousand, only three hundred people remained alive. The second-in-command in the camp administration who had signed the orders to send the group was made a scapegoat and tried.

Braude and his paramedics worked until evening, removing bullets, amputating, bandaging. Only soldiers of the guard were among the wounded; there were no escapees.

The next day toward evening more wounded were brought in. Surrounded by officers of the guard, two soldiers carried in the first and only escapee whom Braude was to see. The escapee was in military uniform and differed from the soldiers only in that he was unshaven. Both shinbones and his left shoulder were broken by bullets, and there was a head wound with damage to the parietal bone. The man was unconscious.

Braude rendered him first aid and, as Artemyev had ordered, the wounded man and his guards were taken to the central hospital where there were the necessary facilities for a serious operation.

It was all over. Nearby stood an army truck covered with a tarpaulin. It contained the bodies of the dead escapees. Next to it was a second truck with the bodies of the dead soldiers.

But Major Pugachov was crawling down the edge of the ravine.

They could have sent the army home after this victory, but trucks with soldiers continued to travel along the thousand-mile highway for many days.

They couldn't find the twelfth man—Major Pugachov.

Soldatov took a long time to recover—to be shot. But then that was the only death sentence out of sixty. Such was the number of friends and acquaintances who were sent before the military tribunal. The head of the local camp was sentenced to ten years. The head of the medical section, Dr. Potalina, was acquitted, and she changed her place of employment almost as soon as the trial was over. Major General Artemyev's words were prophetic: he was removed from his position in the guard.

Pugachov dragged himself into the narrow throat of the cave. It was a bear's den, the beast's winter quarters, and the animal had long since left to wander the taiga. Bear hairs could still be seen on the cave walls and stone floor.

"How quickly it's all ended," thought Pugachov. "They'll bring dogs and find me."

Lying in the cave, he remembered his difficult male life, a life that was to end on a bear path in the taiga. He remembered people—all of whom he had respected and loved, beginning with his mother. He remembered his schoolteacher, Maria Ivanovna, and her quilted jacket of threadbare black velvet that was turning red. There were many, many others with whom fate had thrown him together.

But better than all, more noble than all, were his eleven dead comrades. None of the other people in his life had endured such disappointments, deceit, lies. And in this northern hell they had found within themselves the strength to believe in him, Pugachov, and to stretch out their hands to freedom. These men who had died in battle were the best men he had known in his life.

Pugachov picked a blueberry from a shrub that grew at the entrance to the cave. Last year's wrinkled fruit burst in his fingers, and he licked them clean. The overripe fruit was as tasteless as snow water. The skin of the berry stuck to his dry tongue.

Yes, they were the best. He remembered Ashot's surname now; it was Khachaturian.

Major Pugachov remembered each of them, one after the other, and smiled at each. Then he put the muzzle of the pistol in his mouth and for the last time in his life fired a shot.

EDITOR'S INTRODUCTION TO:

A GLORIOUS TRIUMPH FOR THE PEOPLE
by E. Michael Blake

The most important book I have read this year is *Survival Is Not Enough*, by Richard Pipes (Simon & Schuster, Touchstone Books, 1986). Pipes is Baird Professor of History at Harvard University and formerly a deputy secretary of defense; his book is about U.S. strategic requirements in the modern age.

Before we can develop strategic requirements, we need to understand the motives of our enemy, which Pipes shows very well in a book that is entertaining as well as demanding. He tells the story of the *nomenklatura*, the bureaucratic organization of thugs who own the Soviet Union in fee simple: who they are, how they got there, and what their motivation is.

The *nomenklatura* know no frontiers, and hold nothing dear but power.

Of course they may be displaced. E. Michael Blake gives us one view of how that may happen.

A GLORIOUS TRIUMPH FOR THE PEOPLE
E. Michael Blake

In a specially fitted wheelchair, the legally alive form of
T. N. Bugliev faced the tediously lapping Black Sea wavelets
on the beach at Sochi. It no longer bothered him that the sun
seemed to take sudden leaps across the sky. Electrical activity
in his brain came and went lately, and sensory awareness with
it. What bothered him were the moments when he remembered the strange business going on these days.

Why had it turned out this way? He remembered that there
had been some problem, an impending crisis, and he had
been the first one to see it and the main one to campaign for
action. The memories were there, he was sure, like books on
a shelf. He just had to find the right one—

*—and he is back in the Kremlin, walking briskly down a
narrow hallway, to—*
—the conference room of the Karelian Agricultural, Min-
eral, and Industrial Planning Board. He was fully armed with
statistics, graphs, and determination. Bugliev often stirred
things up, forced the others to face facts they hoped would
vanish. Some of the old men on the KAMIPB had begun to
hope that Bugliev, too, would vanish. Once he had even
overheard a mutter of regret that the 1935 purges in Lenin-
grad had not been thorough enough. Hearing that, Bugliev
had allowed himself only a smirk, but he had dearly wanted
to reply, "Do not blame the authorities, *tovarisch.* I was but
a child of twelve at the time."

Handing his slides to the projectionist, Bugliev looked at
all the withered heads in the room and wondered again if the
Americans still believed, as was hoped, that the KAMIPB
was just another bureaucratic backwater. In fact, the KAMIPB
was the topmost level of the Soviet government, and had little
to do with development projects in Karelia. On this committee sat string-pullers from the party rank and file, the Presid-

ium, the Central Committee, the Politburo, the Supreme Soviet, the KGB, the Red Army, and some less-renowned Kremlin nooks and crannies. What the Central Committee announced in September, the KAMIPB had formulated in August.

The secrecy was so tight that no aides or functionaries were allowed. The projectionist, this week, was the Chief of Staff of all naval forces in the Indian Ocean. One did not seek to get into the KAMIPB. The KAMIPB would eventually seek you out if it considered you a worthy addition. Of course, your chances of being sought out were fleetingly slim if you didn't happen to be the protégé of someone already on the KAMIPB.

When his item of business was called, Bugliev advanced to the lectern and without preamble asked the gathering, "Will everyone in this room younger than sixty-five please raise a hand?"

After a brief, quizzical silence, thirteen hands were elevated above the sixty-two withered heads.

"Yes. And is any one of you younger than fifty?"

All of the raised hands dropped from sight.

"You make my point for me, comrades," said Bugliev dourly. "The greatest socialist nation of all time is controlled by old men in failing health. You may think this is just the way of things. I say it is an oncoming disaster."

Bugliev thumbed a button, and the West German slide projector at the far corner of the room lit the screen to Bugliev's right. "This is the average life expectancy of the Soviet citizen. Socialist medicine has made great strides, of course, but the figures now available for 1966 show the average to be sixty-nine years. In 1986 it was sixty-eight."

He thumbed the control again, and the slide changed to show the same graph with the addition of another line—a steeply ascending diagonal approaching the level of the near-horizontal of life expectancy. "This new line," said Bugliev, "is the average number of years required by a public official to rise to the highest levels of power—that is, to this room. As the Revolution has progressed, the apparatus of the state has grown—making the career climb longer each year. Now it takes fifty-three years, on the average, to rise through the bureaucracy—assuming a stay at each level just long enough to offer the expertise of leverage needed to move to the next higher level."

Another thumb-press, another slide: the same graph extended some years into the future. Bugliev leaned over the lectern, forcing eye contact on one unwilling withered head, then another, then another. "The trend is obvious, comrades," he said with harrowing mildness. "In the year 2005 a person with an average life span can expect to reach power only if he begins his career at the age of five. Or fourteen if he has relatives with extremely good connections. And by 2020, this room would surely be empty, because no one could survive the eighty-one years of grueling advancement needed to rise to this level."

Suddenly, everything began to darken, to slow down. What—
RECALL TERMINATED. INSUFFICIENT RECEPTOR VOLTAGE.

Waves. Beach. Sochi.

Bugliev roused himself somewhat. Yes, now he remembered. The problem was life span. The bureaucracy always grew in complexity, there were always more levels to rise through, and a human body had only so much time.

"Bugliev. You fool."

Bugliev stirred. His neck muscles were in command of enough resources to let him turn his head in the direction of the voice. His West German retinal implants registered a wheelchair beside his own. Seated on it—encased in it, really— was M. Ya. Vunshin, the former premier.

"You truly believed that longer life would save our nation."

If memory served Bugliev, Vunshin had been premier from August of 2017 to January of 2018—but memory did not serve Bugliev, and it was all he could do to remember that Vunshin had been premier at some point in time. He at least recognized Vunshin's long, pouched face, and remembered how it—

—is transfixed with shock—

—as Bugliev peered over the lectern at him. Even from the third row, Vunshin seemed to recoil as if he were but inches away. "We have lately been governed, if that is an accurate term," Bugliev was saying, almost reveling in his brashness, "by compromise choices too weak to consolidate their own power, and too ill to remain in control for long. Need I point out"—Bugliev shifted his gaze again, this time to the assistant chief administrator of the Presidium—"that our current premier is not even in this room, and may not know of its existence?"

Now he chose to raise his voice. "And—let us be frank—does anyone in this room believe he still has the vigor to climb over all the rest of us and then govern forcefully, for many years?

"And it is not merely the top that suffers," Bugliev pressed on through the growing group hubbub. "Five, six echelons down, the key personnel are nearly as old and as ineffectual as we. The spread downward is certain to continue. I tell you, comrades, we are faced with anarchy!"

This time, the dark came *at once*.

RECALL TERMINATED, CARDIAC FIBRILLATION LEVEL UNAC-CEPTABLE.

Bugliev could never determine whether those words were spoken inside his ears, or shown inside his eyes.

"—never finds out," said the voice from Vunshin's wheel-chair. Bugliev no longer saw Vunshin. He saw his own chalk-stick fingers inert on his lap blanket. His head had fallen limply.

"Bugliev. You fool."

Somehow, that sounded familiar to Bugliev.

"You truly believed that longer life would save our nation."

It *was* familiar. Curiosity kindled Bugliev, forcing more nutrients from his wheelchair. This in turn raised him to greater lucidity than he had known in months.

"You told us we had only four choices: stabilize or shrink the bureaucracy, speed advancement through the ranks by purges, turn the government over to computers or robots, or lengthen the human life span to outpace the growth of bureau-cratic hierarchy. And we all agreed that the first was a flatly ridiculous notion, the second would probably upset the peo-ple, and the third would deprive the state of its essential Marxist-Leninist vision. You had us all convinced that day, Bugliev. It would have to be a major crash program in medical life extension."

And so it was. Without the need for another forced mne-monic replay, Bugliev remembered the overall plan. Of course it was too late for anyone on the KAMIPB at that time to benefit from the crash program, but each man had a protégé or two, some only in their early fifties, who might be the first freed from the ravages of further aging and enabled to *lead*. And surely each protégé had favorites at the next lower level, and so on. From patronage came privilege, from connections would come continuity.

"—pass on the torch to successors who would never age," Vunshin was saying. "But there was no reason for us to just give up ourselves, was there? Certainly not. There were some early developments, and it was only natural for the KAMIPB to review them first, because of the highly secret nature of the whole project. Didn't we all say that, Bugliev?"

Well, of course, thought Bugliev. And it would have been foolish to dispense with the experience of someone on the KAMIPB just because he happened to be about to celebrate—

—his ninety-first birthday in a new position—

—as COMECON Finance Director, playing host at his *dacha* to none other than the premier of Bulgaria himself. "I assure you, Comrade Kivra, there is nothing the London moneylenders can do for you that we cannot do better."

"But you Russians borrow in London," remarked Kivra sourly. He was a short, wiry man who seemed very impatient. *Everyone* Bugliev dealt with lately seemed to be impatient. Perhaps it was because of his breathing. This flexure adjustment in his diaphragm, it sometimes made him inhale very audibly.

"Hm? Yes," Bugliev replied at last. "It's important that we all manage these credit matters with the West as a unit. And if you could reduce your budget for fiscal year 2016 by eight percent—"

"Yes, yes!" snapped Kivra, "you said that five minutes ago!" Suddenly the Bulgarian stood and began to pace on the terrace, muttering. "Is *everyone* in Russia a senile—"

"Isn't it a beautiful day?" Bugliev said, realizing that Kivra might say something everyone would regret. "The Ministry of Atmospherics says that lasting weather control for all our nations may be only ten years away, and on a day like this I quite believe it."

Kivra slowed his pace and let himself look around at the birch grove, the rolling fields. "Yes, it is pleasant here." He inhaled deeply, his gnomish features softening. Then he looked back at Bugliev, and they began to harden again. "Comrade Bugliev, you know I want very much to work with you. Without Russia, our party would never have come to power in my country. Without Russia, my country would have no presence on the world stage. Through you, I am influential.

So you must realize that just because I want to arrange some credits in London—''

''Please, please,'' said Bugliev, holding out a motor-controlled hand. ''We must discuss this matter further, Comrade Cirnek.''

The Bulgarian halted, glared at Bugliev, and barked, ''Kivra! Cirnek is the premier of Czechoslovakia! You saw him *yesterday*—!''

Bugliev drew back, alarmed by the man's impatience. Everyone seemed so impatient these days. Perhaps it was because of the fusion reactor manufacturing delays. Well, all of that would be worked out eventually. New departments were being set up. He was adding four new administrative sections in his own office—

The dark came in wavering blotches.

RECALL TERMINATED. LACK OF CLARITY IN STORED INFORMATION.

''—couldn't trust just anyone,'' came Vunshin's voice. ''And soon every new nomination for the KAMIPB was being questioned. Can't let in one protégé without everyone else's. Besides, openings on the Board were coming up less often. Many of us stayed alive. Our protégés were not so lucky. They all died, wondering why we did not.''

Why was Vunshin saying all this? Bugliev finally convinced his much-put-upon neck that he wanted it to turn his head, again, toward Vunshin's chair.

''And we certainly couldn't give life extension to everyone. Trouble enough feeding the masses when they live sixty, seventy years.''

Bugliev faced Vunshin's chair again. Something did not seem right.

''The scientists may indeed have discovered how to keep a young man from growing old. This should have been miracle enough, but we could never agree on which young men to select for testing. And, besides, that wasn't what we *really* wanted, was it, Bugliev? No! We wanted to make old men young!''

Bugliev saw it at last. Vunshin's lips were not moving. Some mechanism in the chair was producing the voice of the former premier.

The former premier—

Suddenly jarred loose was a stunning revelation: *I too am a former premier!*—

—premier—

—premier—was it in 2032?—a blazing summer—Islam—
personal attention—willing to negotiate, but all this Asiatic
jabber—you are still Soviet citizens first—aerial photos, riot-
ing in Tashkent, or was it Baku?—rumble of armored personnel carriers—always that wailing, their call to prayer—all
their grizzled leaders, with stained teeth—more jabber, but in
Russian—calls for sterner measures—vote of no confidence—
and still summer—

—blur, dark—

RECALL NOT FULLY ESTABLISHED.

Bugliev reeled but did not pass out. The nutrient surge kept
him awake and aware. And anguished.

"This was asking far too much," Vunshin was saying.
"So we had only old men who grew older, and weaker, and
more feeble-minded, but would not die—or step down. We
had put glue on the torch, Bugliev, so that it could not be
passed."

Bitterness clamped Bugliev's jaw. They had ousted him
after only seven weeks . . . best to forget again . . .

"And from the anarchy came the highest of all ironies. Our
satellites moved in and took over the Soviet Union."

Yes! thought Bugliev, *that's the strange business going on
these days!* To him, perhaps it was only a matter of days, but
the COMECON Coordinating Committee had been firmly, secretly lodged in the Kremlin for nearly twenty years.

"Think of it, Bugliev. The Poles and Czechs and all the
rest. It would almost have been better if they had just turned
capitalist, as the Americans still dream they might. But no—
the party leaders there knew what they had to do to stay in
power. They do not have our problem, yet. Smaller countries,
smaller bureaucracies. Now *they* maintain the Warsaw Pact,
control our nuclear arsenal, and remind us of how to be
Communists!"

The lips were not the only part of Vunshin that didn't
move. He appeared to be in a coma. With all the techniques,
it was hard to tell. A body could rally without cause or
justification. At one of the last KAMIPB meetings, Bugliev
remembered dimly, one member had died, begun to stiffen,
and snapped back to debate a point settled two hours earlier.

"Imagine, Bugliev. There is a Bulgarian living in your *dacha*."

Bugliev's eyes widened in shock. This itself was a further surprise; he hadn't known that they could widen any longer.

"And they keep us around for appearances. The miraculous old men. The people, they worship us like Lenin. I tell you this, Bugliev. It is all your fault. We should have taken your second option—a rational, systematic purge of the ranks. But you insisted on the fourth, and we are all puppets now. I only hope that the average Russian worker never finds out."

There was a click, then silence. Bugliev realized that this had been a recording. He realized also that he had realized it before. He wondered if Vunshin was dead. Irrevocably.

My fault? he thought, hurt and confused. *But I was the only one who cared . . . what else was there to do? . . .*

The strain of all this activity finally caught up with Bugliev. His brain paths stilled again.

Eventually, when the sun neared the horizon, the West German wheelchairs activated their motors, turned about, and carried their occupants back to their ward.

EDITOR'S INTRODUCTION TO:

POEMS
by Peter Dillingham and Robert Frazier

In *Blood and Iron*, Volume III of this series, we presented the first part of Peter Dillingham's new saga of conquest in space. Part one was called "The War Without."

There is another conquest to be made.

Robert Frazier's first contribution to this series was in Volume II, *Men at War*.

PSI-REC: PRIEST OF ROSES, PALADIN OF SWORDS, THE WAR WITHIN
Peter Dillingham

Head bowed, chest bared, he kneels
Priest of Roses in a pool of light,
Beneath a holographic tomogram of his lungs.
Two worlds at war and he their proxy.
The flowers cast, guerre à mort,
To one the Red Rose of malignancy,
To the other the White of health and wholeness.

That deadly, radiant rose touched to his breast,
He waits.
A tumor buds,
Calls forth its vassals, angiogenesis,
That nurturing, crimson web of capillaries,
Then blossoms brilliant, virulent red,
Menacing metastasis
(And epidemic contagion) . . .
He withdraws within, deep, then deeper still,
Quieting brain and heart and breath,
Beta, Alpha, Theta . . .
Now, coup de main!

Paladin of Swords, he visions
Flamborge, Durendal and Curtana,
Flashing, phantom blades
Of searing, healing light to fight the infidel.
Back and forth the battle rages:
The tumor swelling, shrinking,
Rallying, then at last retreating
Before his psychic onslaught . . .
The victory falls to White,
As it has fallen once before—
A different war waged for other worlds—
As it may fall but once again.

ENCASED IN THE AMBER OF PROBABILITIES
Robert Frazier

i.
The sails are pitted in fine lacework,
shredded like mylar snow
trailing out behind in spinning clouds.

ii.
Hopes are as rich as vacuum,
encased in the amber of probabilities
sparse as interstellar dust.

iii.
Starwrecked I wait, the raku warrior,
sweating in the kiln of my EVA armor,
for a sun to fire my flesh and glaze my bones.

iv.
A winter field on constellations
spin about my head
in battle array; I plot rebirth.

EDITOR'S INTRODUCTION TO:

LIGDAN AND THE YOUNG PRETENDER
by Walter Jon Williams

"Britain Is Fine in '79" was the slogan of the British bid to host the 1979 World Science Fiction Convention, and indeed Britain *was* fine in '79; the Worldcon was held in Brighton, and we all much enjoyed it.

Lucifer's Hammer, by Larry Niven and Jerry Pournelle, was just coming out in Britain that year, so it made sense for Mrs. Roberta Pournelle and me to go on a book-signing tour. Part of that tour went through Scotland.

We went from London to Edinburgh by train, and on that train I was made very much aware that Scotland is not England. We had met a teacher on the train. He was very polite, and Mrs. Pournelle had a pleasant chat with him about the British school system. When we got to the Scottish border, he stood and said loudly, "Home again! I've not been home for five years!"

When I asked where he'd been, he said, "I've been in bloody England!"

England and Scotland were officially united into one nation by the Act of Union of 1704, which followed the Glorious Revolution of 1688 in which the Stuart kings of England and Scotland (then two separate kingdoms which happened to have the same man as king of both) were overthrown and replaced by the heirs of the body of the Electress Sophia of Hanover.

Many Scots have never cared much for either the Act of Union or the new royal family. We rented a car and drove into the Highlands; and in Inverary we found just how strong Scottish sentiment can be. In the Highland Museum there we saw a curious portrait. It was painted in a distorted fashion so that you saw only blobs when you looked at it directly.

The placard below it said:

"After the uprising of 1745 all portraits of members of the House of Stuart were outlawed. It became the fashion of Loyalists to keep portraits of their King and Princes in a secretive manner. When you look at the decorations with the special mirror, what appears to be a meaningless blob becomes a portrait of the man known to history as 'The Young Pretender.'

"He was no pretender. He was Charles Edward Stuart, rightful King of Scotland."

To the best of my knowledge this placard is still technically treason in the United Kingdom. That doesn't seem to bother the Highlanders much. We also heard in several shopping malls a tape of a song denouncing King William for the Massacre of Glencoe . . .

One does wonder just how strong this nostalgia for the Stuarts really is. Highlander troops have certainly fought well for the Hanoverian dynasty (now called the House of Windsor) which at present holds the British throne. Moreover, I understand there is no universally recognized Stuart heir. One gets the impression that Highlander sentiment for the restoration of the Stuarts would be a great deal weaker if there were any real chance of its happening.

Suppose, though, that one could *really* bring back the Stuarts? Walter Jon Williams tells us a lively, if wildly improbable, tale . . .

LIGDAN AND THE YOUNG PRETENDER
Walter Jon Williams

We had just spent six whole months making the Hypsipyle System safe for Standard Oil of Ohio and now the war was over, the Tandies having been forced into concessions. We had been pulled back to Nova Caledonia awaiting transport to our homes in Agaratu, where we would be demobbed, and where the *Daily Star*, no doubt, would return me to my pointless and depressing job of chasing down advertisers.

After spending many weeks playing Beau Geste in a lonesome, godforsaken wilderness, our delight was palpable when we discovered that we were sharing a barrack compound with the Highland Light Infantry. Not because they were Highlanders, mind, but because it was an all-woman battalion, from the white-haired lantern-jawed colonel to the puff-cheeked pipe sergeant.

Our delight, I suspect, was somewhat lessened by our first leave, when we were at last free to fraternize with the apple-cheeked Caledonian lassies. Apple-cheeked they proved to be—also clog-footed, hoarse-voiced, brawny-armed, and drunk as only veterans on their first three-day pass can be.

I remember watching in fascinated horror at the scene in the Braigh Mhàr pub, after the Kilties decided to dance the Highland Reel. Agaratans tend as a rule to be short, bandy-legged, wiry, and Mongolian, and to see those great-bosomed brawny red-haired women, skirts flying, all screeching like the damned as they flung our terrified lads from one pair to another, while half the battalion pipers perched on the bar to provide a heathen wailing accompaniment—well, if Dante had seen it after his journey through Hell, he would have keeled right over in shock, I assure you.

I was lucky; I was fortified behind a majestic oaken bar table, with my arm around Lance Corporal Sandy MacDonald. Sandy was petite, for this company anyway, which meant she was about my size. She was raven-haired and lovely, with a pert nose and a peaches-and-cream complexion that was set off with breathtaking beauty by her black jacket and the dab of white lace at her throat. Under her green bonnet her blue eyes sparkled with amusement and delight at the horrible scene spread before us; I therefore concluded that she was a hardened warrior, used to the dismal sight of many a battle-field, and not susceptible to my usual run of impressive war stories, all of which are lies anyway.

My arm was around this lovely prize not because I was the greatest Don Juan in my regiment, but rather because we had met twice earlier in the week standing sentry, which duty consisted of sitting in the duty hut, drinking coffee, and staring at a succession of monitors hoping to have our bore-dom relieved by the sight of a saboteur. We had talked, I of my various careers before my conscription, she of her inter-rupted university career. We discovered that we shared an interest in nineteenth-century English literature, the works of Thackeray in particular. She had also been fascinated to dis-cover that I had actually been to Scotland, several years before, having got a grant to go to Terra to write my disserta-tion. I had actually spent most of my time in London, but had got to Scotland on a holiday after I'd decided to throw my dissertation to the winds. My committee chairman was a great Bulwer-Lytton man, you see, and had more or less forced me to follow in his footsteps. The great liberation had come when I realized that I hated Bulwer-Lytton *and* my committee chairman, and I was damned if I'd spend the rest of my career with either one. So much for academics.

Sandy, it turned out, didn't like Bulwer-Lytton either—which is not an unusual response, by the way. She also wanted me to describe Scotland to her, comparing it with Nova Caledonia. I didn't want to tell her that Nova Caledonia is a ghastly awful place resembling a strip-mined ash heap, and so I'd said that, barring the heather, they looked enough alike.

"If it were spring, Dan," she said, "ye could see the heather. We imported it, o' course, but it isnae in bloom noo."

"I'd like to see that," I said. So she'd said she could show me pictures, and in the end we'd agreed to meet at the Braigh Mhàr. We had each brought a friend: on the other end of the bench was Communications Specialist Ghantemur—he was an exception to the usual run of Agaratans, being the Chingiz

242

Khan type: six feet four, red-haired, and, with the exercise he'd been getting from humping his communications pack all over the Great Hypsipyle Antediluvian Desert, a solid block of muscle. He was making shameless advances toward Lucy Macdonough, a heavy-weapons specialist, who showed every sign of inviting same. Both being brawny red-haired giants, Sandy and I had figured they would get along, and we were right—as I watched, Ghantemur began a lazy, deliberate exploration of Lucy's sporran, while she swallowed her single-malt in one gulp, waved her hand dismissively, and said, "G'wan, ye bluidy awfu' heathen, ye."

I looked up from the grinning pair as something jostled the table, sending half my beer in a brown tidal wave out of the pint glass. As I mopped myself, I saw the interrupted was Corporal Galdan, who had been flung against the table by his companion, a Q.M.C. corporal with the forearms of a blast furnace operator. I caught a glimpse of mingled terror and appeal in Galdan's eyes in the mute half-second or so before his guffawing partner seized him and whirled him back into the dance. "Poor bastard," thought I. "Well. Better him than me."

As Galdan was dragged back into the reel a G'nartan ghost appeared in the middle of the room, its three soulful eyes widened, its mouth opened in a dismal shriek—a shriek made completely inaudible by the pipers wailing away at the bar. The ghost, apparently offended, drew its shroud about itself indignantly and prepared to give vent to another banshee moan, but just at that moment the Q.M.C. corporal, who had polished her technique, no doubt, flinging the caber in the Games, hurled Corporal Galdan clean through the G'nartan and into the arms of another red-faced bawling Kiltie. The G'nartan gave the entire room a look of indignant majesty and left, walking straight through the wall behind the bar.

"Ye look, Dan," said Sandy MacDonald, "as if ye havnae seen a gheistie before."

"I've never seen one this close," I said. "I did see that one through the monitor, remember, the other night."

"Aye. Ye get used to 'em after awha'." She looked up and then quailed for a moment under my protective arm as one of my company—I think it was Private Toton, but I'm not sure—came thundering backward into the table, then was snatched back into the reel before he could so much as moan for mercy. Then she looked up at me.

243

" 'Tis a wee bit noisy here, Dan," she said, leaning close to my ear in order to be heard over the howling of the pipes. "Dinnae ye want to find a place a leetle more quiet? I've a nice place a wee drive frae here—it's closed down till I'm demobbed, but I think I could make ye some tea."

Anything seemed better than continuing to watch the decimation of my battalion at the hands of the Picts while having my eardrums blasted out by the demented godforsaken pipe band, and having a quiet, deserted house in which to enfold a willing Sandy MacDonald in my arms without having an entire battalion of her comrades on hand to defend outraged virtue seemed too good to be true. I nodded hastily and gulped the remains of my beer. Sandy reached over to bash Ghantemur on the shoulder and mime that he and Lucy were to precede us, and he gave her a nod and Lucy a coarse grin.

It was lucky Ghantemur and Lucy left first; I doubt Sandy and I could have made our way through that close-packed reeling mob without our comrades forming a battering ram before us. And then at last we were out in the cool Caledonian night, with the unspeakable moan of the pipes muted by the door. There was a light rain coming down, and so I pulled my cap out of my back pocket and put it on my head while Sandy used her bleeper to call for a cab. When it arrived, I settled down with her in the back seat, and she coded in her destination and put the bleeper back into her sporran.

"I'm so glad the traditionalists lost on this one," she said with a smile, patting the sporran again.

"On the bleeper?" I asked.

"Nay, th' sporran!" he said. "It used tae be tha' only Highland men wore the kilt an' sporran, while women wore the pleated tartan skirt. When the female battalions began tae be recruited, we were given trews tae wear—but some o' the officers wanted kilts for dress parade, and got 'em. But there wasnae a sporran, that bein' for men only, and so we had these bluidy great shoulder bags weighin' us doon. Finally there was almost a mutiny, all the women insistin' on bein' allowed tae wear the sporran and the kilt at all times—an' thank the guid Goad we won." She sniffed. "Can ye imagine us haulin' those damn' manky shoulder bags aroun' the flamin' desert? It don't bear thinkin' about."

"I'm glad you won," I said. "I think you look lovely in kilts. That dark green suits you very well."

"I thank ye, Dan," she said, smiling. "Annaway, tha's

244

how we got our nickname o' Kilties. It's also the name of a Highland spirit, sort o' like a wee elf, alwa' makin' mischief.'' She pursed her lips doubtfully. ''I dinnae ken whether I like all the implications o' that, but it's better than bein' called what the men are called. Jocks, that is.''

There was a guffaw from the front seat, where Ghantemur had apparently made a scandalous suggestion to Lucy, which she seemed all for implementing right there and then. I looked forward and saw that the taxi had taken us well outside of Glasgow, and that the terrain around us was a kind of desolate hillocky moor, with little circular outcrops like pimples. It was the kind of horribly unlovely country for which Nova Caledonia is famous, and which resulted in most of it being settled by disgruntled Scottish nationalists in the first place—all the civilized nations, you see, having already claimed all the garden spots. I half expected the Hound of the Baskervilles to jump up on top of one of the hills and slaver at the moon. Had there been a moon, of course: Nova Caledonia lacks even that.

''Where are we heading?'' I demanded. ''I didn't realize you had a place in the country.''

''I'm takin' ye tae see some gheisties,'' she said, with a sweet smile that let me know instantly I'd been had. ''Ye said ye havenae seen the like before.''

I looked at her for a moment and wondered what kind of horrific surprise she was going to hand me. We don't find the idea of spirits congenial on Agaratu, not that there are any, mind . . . but when a man expects to spend the evening snuggling in some cozy little cottage with the most lovely woman on Nova Caledonia, and then discovers she intends to spend the night stirring up the long-dead residents of the planet, it's enough to make him sit up and think.

''Ah—that won't be necessary,'' I said. ''I'll leave all that table-tapping stuff to the scientists.''

Because, you see, the phenomenon of spirit manifestation on Nova Caledonia *had* been a topic of scientific research, not that they'd ever managed to discover anything that wasn't already apparent to the layman. Call it a ghost or call it a ''self-generating plasma field, origin unknown, endowed with the sentient personality and appearance of a predeceased being,'' it's all one. I'd even read some of the reports, trying to lay the phenomenon on to a unique pattern of cosmic rays, a peculiarly unbalanced magnetic field, or miniature black holes

245

hidden somewhere at the planet's core, and great nonsense they all were. The truth is, no one understands it, and no one has a clue.

But it was undeniable that there were a *lot* of ghosts on Nova Caledonia. For whatever reason they came into existence, there were virtual swarms of them. By far the vast majority of the ghosts were G'nartans, the previous civilized inhabitants of the place. They were shaped something like squared-off refuse containers with an arm and leg at each corner, three platter eyes, a doleful mouth, and various other sensory apparatus scattered promiscuously about their anatomy. Perhaps intimidated by the inexpressible bleakness of their planet, they'd huddled in small, isolated communities. They'd developed technology but didn't, apparently, do much with it. And eventually, just after the first earth ship landed, they'd all died of chicken pox, or some other silly earth disease.

The crew of the first earth ship also died, presumably of the G'nartan equivalent of the common cold. Who would have suspected that two species so dissimilar would have been susceptible to the same bugs? At any rate, by the time the second earth ship landed, the G'nartans were gone. The explorers found a bare, arid, ugly planet, mostly grassy and with no native vegetation taller than my shoulder, a few mildly interesting aboriginal dwelling places, and no animal life whatever. Barring, of course, the ghosts.

It was lucky that the G'nartans never really existed in large numbers, because otherwise the planet would have been absolutely swarming with the things. As it was, there seemed to have been only a small chance that any given G'nartan would return from the dead, but over a couple million years of inhabitation all those numbers added up. Fortunately the G'nartan ghosts seemed to confine themselves principally to their own areas.

The odd thing was that whatever strange local conditions that led to the appearance of G'nartan ghosts led to the production of the human variety as well. It must have been a shock to the inhabitants of that second earth vessel, as they approached the still, dead hulk of their predecessor with fear, trepidation, and all the vacuum suits they could find, to discover three or four human spirits inhabiting the place, doing all the usual useless spiritlike things—moving objects, walking through solid walls, clanking chains, uttering doleful wails—nothing with any point to it, mind, just the usual asinine spirit behavior.

Everyone saw them, not just a few sensitives. Cameras took their pictures. Instruments detected their emanations. And all the mediums in the civilized galaxy failed to put a single one of them to rest. They were here to stay.

Now that the Hibernians had been inhabiting the planet for over a century, all the living inhabitants stood a reasonable chance of having their long-deceased Great-Uncle Angus appear suddenly over their breakfast table to utter a moan of Celtic drear—quite enough to put a man off his porridge, I'd imagine. Still, I suppose one gets used to these things; but even so I'd hate to visit Nova Caledonia in a few hundred years, when the spirits begin to outnumber the living.

All this aside, ghost hunting was not my intended sport of the evening. "Say, Sandy," I said. "We don't need to go bothering the spirits, you know. Let 'em rest in peace—they've lived hard lives, they probably deserve it."

"Oh, it isnae a *bother*, Dan," said Sandy, a twinkle in her eye. Oh, well, thinks I to myself, I might as well steel myself to acquaint myself with Dear Dead Papa, or whoever it is she's setting me up to meet. Ligdan has never yet quailed before man nor beast—not more than once or twice, anyway— let it not be said he shrank before the hosts of Hades.

And then, through the clear window of the taxi, I saw Sandy's home drawing near and sat up in amazement. Black-toothed battlements rearing up on a desolate crag, looming over the surrounding moor like a vast and malevolent condor . . . a sight to gladden the heart of any hunchbacked bell-ringer. "What in hell is *that*?" I gasped, or something like it.

"Ach, noo," Sandy shrugged. "It's ma family's little place, Castle Beinnean. It was brocht here frae Scotland a hundred year ago, stone by stone, and set oop on yon mount— the MacDonalds couldnae live wi'oot it, ye see. It disnae belong tae me, but the family lets me use it—I'm the only one who likes the place, see."

The place grew worse as we approached; it was the most monstrous pile of ungainly stonework I'd ever seen, all crags and towers and black foreboding, bringing thoughts of rack and wheel and thumbscrew . . . Otrante would have been right at home. Even Ghantemur, who hadn't so much as turned a hair when we discovered that the Tandies' voracious sand toads were only angered by our sonic guns instead of killed, though our weapons worked well enough on their riders—even Ghantemur sat up with a horrified gasp once the place finally caught his attention. We were right up to the gate by then, and Sandy opened the door and nonchalantly straightened her kilt.

I stepped out of the taxi and stood looking up at the appalling place while Sandy operated the lock. It was the first, and I hope the last, glimpse I've ever had of a palm-lock keyed to open a portcullis. The great iron-shod wooden fangs rose, the inner gate opened, and then as I followed Sandy inside, a great shuddering, burbling shriek rose up from the courtyard, enough to send a ripple of cold up my spine. Ghantemur's eyes were as wide as platters. "Ligdan . . ." he said softly, and then another shriek rose up from the interior of the castle. I'm sure he would have bolted had not Lucy kept a firm grip on his arm.

Well, I wasn't about to admit to being shaken by that bloodcurdling wail, so I just straightened my shoulders, frowned a bit as if I'd just heard an exhibition of bad manners, and strode on in. There in the castle courtyard was a ghost—a G'nartan, by the way—wailing away as if Torquemada had just turned the screws. It was looking right at us as we walked in, and he showed every sign of recognizing us for what we were, for he promptly sent up a series of wails that was louder than the first, as if whatever was distressing him was our fault. Which, come to that, it probably was.

Sandy just marched past him as if he weren't there, so I took my cue from her and followed, only nodding to the little transparent fellow as we passed, a little how-d'ye-do. It seemed only the polite thing.

We passed a little miniature chapel set in one corner of the courtyard, apparently as an afterthought, and then Sandy keyed the lock on the largest pile of masonry, obviously the keep, and we stepped into a short flagstoned foyer, lined with about what I'd expected, namely family portraits, old flags, weapons, suits of armor, and other complicated iron objects of uncertain purpose that must have kept the robot housekeeping staff busy with their dusting. Sandy led us through a number of passages and alcoves to a pleasant snug little room, leather chairs and couches, dark old paintings, and a huge fireplace which lit itself at her verbal command. She turned to me and grinned.

"It's got all the comforts of home, does it nae?" she

248

asked. "Make yersel' at home, an' I'll fetch ourselves some tea. Unless ye'd like somethin' a wee bit stronger?"

"I'll take tea, thanks," I said, my voice half drowned by another call from Old Yowler in the courtyard. Sobriety, I thought, might be in order; one never knew that the late Hilda MacDonald, currently a whiz at telekinetics, might decide to avenge some ancient grudge against my race and animate one of those suits of armor to my intense pain and displeasure. Lucy asked for single-malt once more, evidently being on a firm footing with the MacDonald shades, and Ghantemur, a bit white about the eyes, called for the same.

Sandy was gone for a few minutes; Lucy and Ghantemur settled onto the couch to begin again where they'd left off in the cab, and I stuck my hands in my pockets and looked out the ancient leaded windows past the chapel and into the courtyard, where the G'nartan was still serenading. Beyond him there was movement on the battlements, and I caught a brief sight of an unearthly figure all in armor, pacing along above the barbican, the starlight shining on his plume . . .

"Who's the ghost of Hamlet's father?" I asked as Sandy returned with a tray holding a teapot, cups, and a dusty bottle of malt whiskey, the latter of which Ghantemur seized with all the delight of Galahad reaching for the Grail.

"Who?" Sandy asked. She narrowed her eyes as she peered out the windows. "Och, that'll be the man in armor," she said. "We're not sure who he was. We think he may be Sir David MacDhòmhnuill, who returned frae Flodden Field only to be poisoned by his faithless wife. But we arnae sure—he keeps his visor doon, an' disnae say a word."

I turned toward Sandy. She'd taken off her bonnet, jacket, and jabot, and looked lovelier than I'd ever seen her—but the distracting sight of her only slowed my thinking for a few moments.

"But it couldn't be Sir David, could it?" I asked. "I mean, his ghost would be back on earth . . ." My words trailed off as the G'nartan let go another wail, but it wasn't the howling outside that sent a cold realization trickling up my neck. Sandy paused, tray in hand, her eyes expectant as she awaited my revelation. "Wait a minute," I said. "D'you mean to say that—that the castle ghosts—that they all came with the castle when it was moved?"

"That's a fly man, tha' Ligdan," Lucy called from the

sofa, and then turned to grin at me. "You're verra good. They usually take longer tae realize."

"Congratulations, Dan," Sandy said, beaming. "Aye, it's true. All the Beinnean gheisties came wi' us." She set the tray down, patting the teapot in its cozy. "I'll let ye steep awha'," she said to the teapot, and then turned back to me.

"They all came," she said. "But we didnae ken just how many there were. The manifestations are stronger on this planet, you know. We thought the castle had only three or four ghosts, but now we know we have *dozens*! That one on the battlements, for example—he hadnae been seen, before. And then there's Sir Thomas MacDonald. He'd just been a puir lonely legend, slammin' doors and settin' chairs tae rockin' by themselves, throwin' books down frae shelves in his temper. Now tha' he's on Nova Caledonia, ev'raone can see him, and he's a perfect gentleman."

"I thank ye, Sandy dear," said a new voice. I turned to discover a slender man in a white-powdered wig, dressed in an eighteenth-century coat and waistcoat over his kilt. Only the fact that I could see the flames through his dark red MacDonald tartan gave him away. He was middle-aged, with a shrewd face and a genteel air. He gave me a brief bow. "Sir Thomas MacDonald, at yer service," he said.

"Corporal Ligdan, at yours," I said, and bowed back— allow me to recommend a career of reading nineteenth-century historical romances to give a courtly polish to your manners, by the way. He smiled as if pleased to see me, then turned to Ghantemur, who looked as if he were wishing to be back among the sand toads.

"An' whom do I have the pleasure of addressin'?" he asked.

"This is Ghantemur, Uncle Tom," Lucy said with a grin; apparently they were old friends. "Here's to yer health?" She downed her glass of malt. Sir Thomas looked longingly at the bottle for a long moment, then glanced up with a scowl as the G'nartan uttered another yowl.

"Yon G'nartan's a-greetin' again!" he barked. "Ev'ra fortnight for fivescore year—I wish he'd give't a rest!"

"After all, it's his planet," Sandy said sympathetically, then looked at me and brightened. "I think the tea's ready. D'ye take twa lumps or just th' one?"

"None," I said. "And just a wee drop—just a little milk, thanks." The local dialect was beginning to seize control of my speech centers. I took the tea from Sandy, thanked her, and took a sip. I glanced at Sir Thomas, then looked at Sandy.

"Are you—ah, has he—have the scientists found an explanation for your Uncle Thomas yet?" I asked. "A ghost that holds conversations, I mean—that isn't in the literature, I suppose." It was growing difficult to talk about Sir Thomas as a specimen, with him looking on, and I sensed he was growing impatient. I blundered on. "I mean—perhaps they can—they can cure his condition, or something, if you see what I mean."

Sandy pursed her lips in anticipation of reply, but was cut short by a blast from Sir Thomas. "Corporal Ligdan," he snapped, "I'll ha' ye know tha' on my death I swore a michty oath tha' I wouldnae rest in peace until the glorious House o' Stuart was restort tae the throne o' Scotland! An' I have *kept* tha' oath, sir, through five centuries, like the Highland gentleman tha' I was in life!"

"Besides, Dan," Sandy said, giving an affectionate glance at her remote ancestor, "the family wouldnae have scientists pokin' and proddin' at Sir Thomas as if he were some freak o' nature. He's a proper Scottish gheistie, an' we wouldnae ha' him disturbed. He can walk our ancestral halls as long as he wishes."

"Tha's my lass, Sandy!" Sir Thomas beamed. I took another sip of tea, beginning to understand why the family MacDonald had vacated their ancestral home, leaving it to Sandy and the likes of Sir Thomas—it was one thing to look up genealogical charts of one's ancestors and wonder what they might have been like, and quite another to have to watch them demonstrate every day what a lot of contumacious, arrogant old bores they all really were. And Sir Thomas seemed tame compared with what I knew of my own ancestors, who seemed to have spent most of their time drinking, cutting one another's throats, and occasionally mounting up to ride off and have another whack at the Great Wall—no thanks, I thought, let the dead stay dead, for all I care.

"Sir Thomas, I beg your pardon," I said. "But I wonder about your oath, now—the House of Stuart, if memory serves, is extinct. And so for that matter are their enemies, the House of Hanover. I'm afraid, Sir Thomas, you're condemned to walk the halls of Castle Beinnean for a very long time."

Sir Thomas drew himself up, and I suspect the fire in his

eye was not a reflection of the blaze behind him. "Tha's as may be, Corporal Ligdan. But the word o' a Highland gentleman is intended tae stand forever! Besides, it may not be as long as a' that . . ." He softened for a moment, looked as if he were about to continue, but then he gave his head a shake. "Ye'll pardon me, ladies an' gentlemen," he said, "but maintainin' my form at its present level of materialization is a wee bit wearyin'. An' I just wanted tae welcome our Sandy back frae the wars—ye'll have tae tell me all aboot it, dear, next time we meet!" He gave a gentlemanly smile to us and dematerialized. I heard a little choking sound from Ghantemur and then the sound of malt whiskey being gulped at great speed.

Sandy looked at me with an indulgent smile. "He's a wee bit fanatic on the subject o' Charlie Stuart, but ye cannae blame him," she said. "After Culloden he had tae flee tae France, but they caught him in Scotland later, in '49, tryin' tae get back in tae collect his rents. They hanged him in front o' his tenants." She nodded toward the window. "Right oot there, in the castle courtyard. Where yon four-legged beastie was howlin' not a few minutes ago."

"Oh," I said. "Sorry."

"Tha's all right, Dan. It wasnae ye who did it," Sandy said. She frowned, still looking down at the courtyard. "We're lucky his wife isnae hauntin' the place, too. She married a Whig afterwards, an' a Campbell tae boot." She sipped her tea and looked at me doubtfully. "Still, 'twas she who reconciled us tae the House of Hanover, so her son by Sir Thomas could inherit. She did as she thought best, puir creature, but I'm glad I dinnae have t' hear her an' Uncle Tom refightin' the '45 ev'ra day in the parlor."

"Lord, yes," I said, only now becoming aware of some of the implications of having the former owners cluttering up one's castle. It would be bad enough if they didn't like one another, but what if they didn't like *you*? My mind quailed before a vision of books, furniture, weapons, and household implements tearing themselves loose and flying against me while the room echoed with barbaric Highland wails, and I vowed my manners would be at their best whenever I encountered another of Sandy's ancestors.

"Uncle Tom's made a friend, thank Goad," Sandy went on. "Margaret, Lady Macleod—who is actually his great-aunt, though they never met in life. She's verra nice, almost

252

as guid at materialization as Uncle Tom, an' with a talent for telekinesis. They're great friends, th' auld dears, an' o' course he's made a great Jacobite oot o' her, the Macleods havin' been a wee bit infirm on the subject." She smiled affectionately. "They play duets together in the music room, him an his pipes and she at the harpsichord. It's a pleasant way to spend eternity, isnae?"

I sipped my tea and said it seemed a very nice way, indeed. Sandy beamed, and took me by the hand.

"Would ye like tae see th' battlements, Dan?" she asked. "The view is verra lovely, wi' the stars an' all."

I looked at her lovely face and smiled. "Of course," I said. "I'd love it." I put down my teacup and squeezed her hand. She turned to Lucy and Ghantemur.

"Wi' ye be comin' along wi' us, then?" she asked.

Ghantemur still looked as if he'd been whanged across the skull with a skillet, but Lucy waved a hand and shouted, "Nay, we'll stay here an' enjoy the fire. Ah've seen the bluidy battlements annaway."

Sandy led me to a steep old oaken stairway that went up to the roof of the keep. She released the lock from the inside and led me up into the air.

I had been half expecting another ghostly uncle, but saw only a flagged square with a flagpole standing bare against the sky. Its halliards rattled in the brisk northern wind that tugged at Sandy's hair. The sky had cleared, with only a few low clouds skidding away on the northern horizon, and the stars were out in all their rare beauty, burning in the heavens like a river of diamonds. Sandy walked across the stones and leaned out through a crenellation, smiling into the wind.

"I love this place, truly," she said. "It isnae much tae look at, all bare an' drear, but when all's said and done, it's home." I leaned on the nearest merlon and gazed at her, knowing what she meant: a place doesn't have to be beautiful to be home, but just the cradle of one's memories, a place that one can look at when far away, say in a sand-bound post in Hypsipyle, and remember an earlier happiness. So it had been with me and Agaratu, a place of harsher contrasts than this; so, no doubt, had it been for Sandy and Castle Beinnean. She looked over her shoulder at me and smiled wistfully. "It does look like the real Scotland, hey?" she asked again.

"Like parts of it. Scotland tends to be greener."

"Och, well," she said, turning back to look over the moor. "I like it well enough as it is."

"That's what matters, then," I said. I waited a few moments while she drank her fill of the place, the darkling moor beneath the star-spattered sky, and then she sighed and turned back to me, her eyes dreamy. "Hey," I said. "I was wondering about Charlie Stuart."

"Wha' aboot him?"

"What's this fascination with the man?" I demanded. "I've read enough books about his time, and about the Jacobites, and I've seen the memorials to him all over the Highlands, but by everyone's account he was a fool and an ingrate—he didn't give the Highlanders a single word of thanks for all they did for him, after all they'd suffered."

She frowned and cocked her head to one side. "Weel, I was brocht up wi' a Jacobite tradition, so ye'll have to forgive a wee family bias," she said. "But when all's said and done, I cannae understand it, either. I think it may have tae do more wi' Charles as King than Charles as a man, if ye see wha' I'm drivin' at. Scarce enna one would fight for Charlie Stuart the man, but tae them he was King Charles, an' they owed him their loyalty for that reason, just as the tenants owed loyalty tae their lairds. An' their sufferings just confirmed them in their loyalty; with Sackville and the bluidy Campbells in power in the Highlands, it just showed the clans their enemies were villains all along." She smiled. "An' there's always a great romance in a lost cause, is there nae?"

Personally I thought that the comforts of romance were scarce compensation for burned cottages, confiscated cattle, and all those bodies lying cold on Culloden field, but I didn't say it. I just nodded and smiled and hugged Sandy as seemed called for. "Welcome home, Lance Corporal MacDonald," I said, and kissed her.

"Ye're a fly man, Ligdan," she said, and took me by the hand to lead me to the stair. We passed the crenellations overlooking the courtyard as we walked, and then Sandy looked down, hesitated, and then came to a stop.

"Look ye there, noo," she said, nodding. "What in blazes d'ye suppose is goin' on in the chapel?"

I peered through the battlements and saw ghosts below, four of them drifting toward the chapel. One was Sir Thomas, in full tartan fig, broadsword and all, walking arm in arm with a lady in early eighteenth-century dress; he carried a set of bagpipes in the crook of his free arm. There was another less distinct personality, still in the dark red MacDonald tartan, but wearing the breastplate and helmet of Mary Stuart's time, just disappearing into the chapel door; and walking from the keep below us to the chapel was a tall strapping dark-haired woman in a pleated tartan skirt with a sash and a glengarry bonnet, complete with the tails and the red and white dicing, perched on the side of her head.

"Tha's my grandmother!" Sandy gasped. "She hasnae ever materialized ootside the drawin' room before!"

I could see, glowing softly through the stained-glass windows of the chapel, a strange, subtle, shifting light, as of moving will-o'-the-wisps; it was a stirring, eerie sight, that light, and I could feel a whisper of warning crawling up my spine. Sandy, feeling it, too, looked at me, her eyes wide. "We've got tae get doon there, Dan," she said. "There's somethin' verra wrong!"

My mind urged me to let the dead walk in peace, but something in me felt an eldritch pull drawing me to the chapel, a pull with something of the same urgency a person feels when reading a good fright novel, that keeps him turning the pages even though he's scared out of his wits. Besides, it was clear that Sandy was alarmed, so I nodded swift agreement and followed her down the stair, out of the keep, and across the courtyard to the chapel. The same strange, shifting light glowed out the wide-flung iron-bound doors, and I could feel my heart beating faster as I approached. I swallowed my fear and stepped up onto the threshold.

I'll never forget the sight. The pews of the little chapel were filled with a congregation of spirits, all moving, all flickering transparencies in various degrees of substantiality, an eerie multitude dressed in every kind of clothing from a blue, scowling Pict in his breechclout to a stern leather-clad trooper in his lobster-tail burgonet. The shades were all astir, moving, flickering, as if they were in a state of high excitement—but they shifted, moved, and conversed in absolute silence, as if a sheet of thick translucent glass had been dropped between us. I could see the dim shade of a clergyman standing in the pulpit; I could see Sir Thomas' companion of a moment before stooping in the aisle to talk to a little fair-haired girl; and near a side chapel stood Sir Thomas, frowning, in grim conversation with a pair of armored pikemen. Above them ten centuries of battle flags waved solemnly in some unfelt wind, and I realized with a shiver that all here—the chapel, the flags, the castle itself, everything but Sandy and me—belonged more to these shades than to us. It was all from their time, not mine, and I wondered with what grim ferocity they would dispute its possession.

The sight was so awesome, so unearthly, that I stopped dead in my tracks and stood rooted to the spot. Sandy stopped dead, too, though I think in her case it was more from amazement. "Ah niver knew!" she gasped, looking left and right and back again. "Where'd they all come frae? There must be four dozen!"

That outburst turned their heads, and I felt in the silence all the ponderous weight of those long-dead eyes as they fell upon me, looking across the gap of centuries . . . The hairs rose on my neck. "Uncle Thomas!" Sandy snapped. "Wha's goin' on here?"

Sir Thomas MacDonald looked worried for a moment, then he gathered himself, smiled, and walked toward us, his footfalls silent. "Sandy dear," he said, " 'tis a solemn moment, a solemn moment. Our plans are fulfilled at last." He leaned close to her, his voice a breathless rush, as if a long-delayed joy was upon him. "We ha' our King, Sandy!" he said. "Our King is come a' last!"

Sandy gasped and took a step back. "Name o' Goad," she said, stunned. "What ha' ye been up tae?"

"We ha' raised the banner o' the Stuarts," Sir Thomas proclaimed. "The royal remains o' the prince lie yonder, brocht hither tha' his spirit may return tae us!"

"Name o' Goad," Sandy said again, her eyes turning to the little side chapel where Sir Thomas had been standing, and where we now saw a long, narrow packing crate, just the size to encompass a tall coffin. I received a sensation of other eyes, spirit eyes, turning as well, the dead looking on the coffin with silent, dreadful anticipation and hope. Sandy seemed struck dumb, and she raised a hand to her forehead as if to somehow clear it, but then she gathered herself together and walked toward the side chapel with slow steps. Sir Thomas, his thin face contorted with fanatic rapture, followed in her footsteps—and somehow I followed, too, moving my leaden feet in slow reluctance. Sandy stopped dead at the arched entrance to the chapel; she paused, took a breath, and reached out a wondering hand to touch the crate.

"Has he come?" she asked finally, in a tone of strange wonderment.

"Weel, noo," Sir Thomas said, and for a second there was hesitation in his manner. "Not yet. But ye cannae expect a prince o' the blood royal tae just leap right out o' a packin' crate like a joompin jack, noo, can ye? He must be welcomed among us wi' all proper ceremony."

Sandy turned to the transparent shade of her ancestor. I could see her recovering slowly from her astonishment, her intelligence returning to her eyes. Look out, I thought, here comes the storm; and sure enough she flashed clear anger.

"Ye've stolen the Prince's tomb from Rome!" she cried.

"Weel. Aye, we did," Sir Thomas said. It may have been an illusion in that ghostly light, but I thought I saw the shadow of a blush stealing across Sir Thomas' cheek. He looked at Sandy sharply, his face showing stubborn resolve. "We spirits all agreed," he said, "that we needed a King. Tae rule amongst us, an' resolve disputes betwixt us all."

"Ye could resolve disputes amongst ye," Sandy said, her eyes flashing blue fire, "by leavin' each other alone, did ye evair think o' that? And wha's yer bluidy King goin' tae think when he's asked tae judge disputes over who's goin' tae haunt the parlor at a given hour, which is all that ye fight aboot anaway, for Goad's sake? An' why Charlie Stuart? Whynae Robert the Bruce, or James the Fourth, or even bluidy Macbeth—why the hell must it be Charlie Stuart?"

Sir Thomas looked a bit uncomfortable, but he held his head high with undiminished pride. "There was a wee bit o' discussion, but once I told these others aboot Prince Charlie's virtues—" There was a smugness in his tone that, I could tell, was driving Sandy into fury. "—weel, it was almost unanimous, in the end. Yon Pict held oot for someone called Goieidh. Besides," he added, "the MacDonalds alwa' were divided on the subject o' the Bruce, and it was easier for us tae get tae the tomb in Rome than tae those others."

"For *ye* tae get tae the tomb!" Sandy shrieked, and for a moment I knew what it must be like to face an entire battalion of Kilties, with the pipes wailing away and all of them screaming for blood. No doubt Sir Thomas was somewhat fortified by the knowledge that he was already dead, but still he seemed to shrink before the force of her words. "For *ye*!" she cried. "Ye cannae leave the planet, and ye know it. Ye cannae even carry the blasted crate! Ye had tae hire it done,

257

and wha' I want tae know is *who paid for it*, ye blasphemous shilpit schemer, ye?'' She wheeled, singling out the tall woman in the glengarry cap, her grandmother. "How could ye do it?'' she demanded. "I would ha' thought ye'd have had more sense?''

The woman shrugged and glanced away. "Ah guess Ah'm just a romantic a' heart, dear,'' she said, but Sandy was not mollified.

"Romantic!" she bellowed. *"Romantic!* How much did this *romantic* excursion cost, I want tae know!''

"Calm yersel', Sandy dear,'' said a low female voice. "Wha's done is done.'' Sandy whirled to face the newcomer, her face like thunder and her fists bunched. Margaret, Lady Macleod—or so I assumed—had moved from her place to stand by Sandy. She was a willowy, gentle-seeming lady, in a gown of heavy green silk with an ermine collar, her auburn hair curled into ringlets to frame an intelligent, sympathetic face.

"I *know* wha's *done!*'' Sandy roared in a voice that Ahab might have used to carry past the royal yard in a force-ten gale. "Wha' I cannae seem tae find oot is who paid for it!''

"If ye'll calm yersel', lass, I'll explain it tae ye,'' Sir Thomas said, trying nervously to pat her on the arm—his hand went right through her, and she glared at him for trying. He pulled his hands back. "It only required a wee sum o' money frae oot o' the reserve kept frae the oopkeep o' the castle.''

"An' how did ye get yer hands on it?'' Sandy demanded, her nose only an inch from Sir Thomas' chin. He blinked and drew back.

"The same way ye would yersel', child,'' Lady Macleod said softly. "We accessed to the bank account through one of the terminals in the castle.''

"We used the bonds, none o' the ready money,'' Sir Thomas explained. "Caledonian twenty-year bonds at eighteen an' one-quarter percent redeemable at five an' one-half percent . . .''

"Ye cashed my *bonds*?'' Sandy shrieked.

"Nay, o' course not! D'ye take me for a fool?'' Sir Thomas was indignant. "I borrowed on 'em, at a verra reasonable rate o' interest, eight and three-quarters percent. The payments can be spread oot over twelve year, an' taken frae the revenues laid aside for the castle oopkeep.''

Sandy listened to this, quietly nodding, chin in hand. I could see that her initial rage had passed, to be replaced by a cold, merciless calculation. "How," she said, her voice calmer now, "could ye use the terminals wi'oot knowin' the codes?"

Sir Thomas turned away, unable to meet her eyes, his cheek twitching. "Weel . . ." he began, but could go no further. It was Lady Macleod who had to say it for him.

"Ye understan', dear, that we shades, because we can move verra quietly an' sometimes we're nae seen because we're nae fully materialized . . ."

"Ye stole 'em," Sandy said. "Ye lookt over my shoulder when I was doin' the accounts an' ye stole my access codes. An' then ye waited till I was off in the army, an' then Margaret here used her telekinetic ability to manipulate the terminal. Ye puisny leetle thieves," she said sadly, shaking her head. "Ye sorry wretched bluidy lyin' thieves!"

Sir Thomas, his head turned away, seemed to shrink into himself at the accusation, parts of him fading away altogether. He seemed too mortified to speak.

"Sandy, dear," said Lady Macleod, her sympathetic eyes looking at Sandy gently, "it's been many centuries since Sir Thomas here had a King. And it's so *important* tae him. I'm afraid the rest o' us were just carried awa' by his enthusiasm." She looked at Sandy with sorrow. "We really should ha' told ye, Sandy. I'm sorry tha' we didnae."

"Tae steal a bluidy coffin," Sandy said, shaking her head. She glared up at Sir Thomas. "D'ye realize the chance any Nova Caledonian has o' becomin' a ghost? Only twelve percent, d'ye know that?"

"I ha' read the stateestics," Sir Thomas said, his voice choked. "I felt it wa' worth . . ."

"And of the thousands o' people who lived an' died in Castle Beinnean on earth, only three or four became shades on earth, aye?" Sandy went on, remorselessly. "An' maybe twa—" She looked around the chapel, at all the flickering shadows that were watching the debate in all their utter graveyard silence. "Three or four dozen," she amended, "became apparent once the castle was moved here, is that nae true?"

"Aye," Sir Thomas conceded. But then he looked up. "But there's a better probability for the Celts. I've heard we carry a gene o' witchcraft and so on . . ."

Sandy just shook her head, and Sir Thomas' voice faded. It

259

was a pretty lame point at that, I thought; and besides, even if the Celts carried a gene for witchery, it hadn't done them much good whenever the Saxons had decided to throw their weight around.

"So tha's perhaps two or three percent at the most, correct?" Sandy asked. "An' therefore ye have decided, wi'oot consultin' any of yer livin' kin, tae put our family in debt for twelve year, hopin' that yer precious Charlie Stuart is one o' the two percent who can manifest themselves."

Sir Thomas, even considering he'd been dead for five centuries, looked thoroughly miserable. He turned away, his head hanging down, and Lady Macleod walked over to him, looking at him with concerned attention. "Bluidy hell," Sandy said, her anger fading. "Could ye nae have asked me?"

Lady Macleod looked at Sandy, her face full of concern. "We're all sorry, Sandy," she said. "But cannae ye understan' how badly he wants his King? He's been so long wi'oot him."

I can still see Sandy standing there, a small, dark form in her kilt, the shifting, eerie light of the assembled spirits flickering off her features, and standing by her the sorrowing figure of an eighteenth-century gentleman bereft of the King he worshiped, with Lady Macleod looking at him, sorry for him in his misery. "I'm verra sorry, Sandy," he said.

"No, ye're nae, ye lyin' wee boy," she said, cocking her head, her lips curled in a wry, affectionate smile; and then she stepped forward to try to hug her old Uncle Tom, and promptly won every heart in the place, mine included. She turned to me.

"Weel, Dan," she said, "we may as well see wha' we boucht oursel'. I think yon crate is beyond the ability of any o' the gheisties, here, so wha' d'ye say tae havin' a whack at it?"

"Happy to," I said. There was movement among the shades in the pews, the lights flickering as they shifted in their excitement. A claw hammer and chisel floated up into my hands from the top of the crate where they'd been sitting, and I said, "Thank you," to whoever had moved them. I set to work. It was a sturdy crate, and several sweaty minutes passed before I had the crate knocked to pieces and the pieces stowed away. What was within proved disappointing: it was a plain lead inner coffin that had obviously been ripped from the embrace of some grander memorial. I stood back, hammer and chisel still in hand, and waited. Sandy stood in the wide chapel door, looking dubiously at the dark coffin; Sir Thomas and Lady Macleod flanked her; and I could sense the shades gathering behind, waiting for the appearance of their promised King.

Minutes passed, and nothing happened. I could feel a wave of aching disappointment welling out from the congregation, and then I saw Sandy shake her head. "Maybe," I said, "it'll help if we can open the coffin and, ah, liberate the remains."

"Nay," Sandy said. "He should a' come, if he were comin'."

Sir Thomas seemed too stricken to speak; he had wilted into himself, despairing agony in his eyes. "I'm so sorry, Tommy," Lady Macleod said slowly. "I knew how much ye wanted it tae happen."

And then, with slow dignity, Prince Charles Edward Stuart, the Young Pretender, rose from the dead, first coming through the coffin lid to a sitting position, then rising awesomely to his full height. Sandy took a step back, thunderstruck. With slow astonishment, Sir Thomas went down on one knee in hushed reverence, and the rest of the spirits followed suit, their faces upturned, in blazing hope, to view Bonnie Prince Charlie as he rose.

He was a couple inches over six feet and handsome in an imperturbable way that can either reflect great strength of character or great density of mind—from what I'd heard of him, I'd suspect the latter. His eyes were blue, and he wore a white-powdered wig with side-curls. I had expected him to be dressed in the Highland tartan and homespun coats of his followers, but his clothes were of silk, and cut to a continental pattern—knee breeches in garish yellow and green, lots of gold lace around the buttonholes of his coat, lace billowing at throat and wrist. He carried a long walking stick in his hand, and his speech, when it came, was purest Saxon upper crust.

"We are pleased," he said, "to have awwived at last. We are wegwetful that this has not happened sooner."

In other words, I thought, what took you so long? And please note there was not a word of thanks, either.

Bonnie Prince Charlie looked down his long nose at Sir Thomas. "We wecognize you, Sir Thomas MacDonald," he said. "Pway pwesent us to our subjects."

Sir Thomas, that proud, stiff-necked Highland laird, was gazing up at his King with the cringing, abject adoration of a

261

basset hound for his master. Scraping like any serf, he stepped forward and said, "If it please Your Highness, may I present my living descendant, Sandrea MacDonald." Sandy, looking up at the Young Pretender as if she had half a mind to tweak him by the nose to see if he was real, stepped forward and curtsied—which is not an easy motion in a kilt, by the way. The other ghostly presences came forward to bow and back away, Sir Thomas giving their names where he knew them— some of the more obscure ones he simply referred to as "Your Highness' loyal subject"—and last of all he introduced me. I bowed civilly, but Prince Charlie took no more notice of me than he would of any laborer, which is to say none.

"Is this all?" asked Charles Edward Stuart when all had come before him. "Vewy well." He looked up at the chapel, at the dusty flags hung on high, at the brass memorial plates screwed into the walls. "Will we be staying here for the pwesent?" he asked, as if he didn't much relish the idea. "Sir Thomas, I would be obliged if you would escort us to our place of wesidence."

"O' course, Your Highness," Sir Thomas said, still bowing and scraping, and then he straightened and turned to his shades, his eyes shining with Gaelic exultation. "Let us pipe the Prince to his bower!" he proclaimed. "God save the King!"

"God save the King!" they all echoed, the first sound most of them had made; the words rang echoing from the walls of the small chapel, filling the air with wild joy—and then drums crashed out from somewhere in the mob, and the pipes began to drone the most stirring of Highland marches, "Hey, Johnnie Cope, are ye waukin' yet?" the wild and barbaric battle hymn commemorating the day the Highland broadswords chopped up General Cope's redcoats at Prestonpans, one of Charlie Stuart's better days . . . I put down my hammer and chisel and went to stand near Sandy at the chapel door as the procession surged past, all the ghostly flickering spirits from all the ages since being a Highlander had begun to mean something, all the old mountain folk with the blaze of battle in their eye as they walked behind their King. What did it matter that he was a fool or an ass? He was theirs, their old King come back to his rightful place among them, and they were mad with the joy of it. Even the old armored figure from above the gate was there, his visor up to reveal a craggy old face with a white mustache, his mouth open to cry, *"Vive le roi!"* Sandy pursed her lips.

"Ach, me," she said. "It disnae Sir David after all—he's some kind of Frenchman." She shook her head. "I'll nae ever get it sortit oot. I've nae seen half this lot before."

And then she shivered, and I took her hand, knowing how she felt. We were alone, the two of us, among the long procession of the dead, the half-seen, flickering figures who marched to the weird and savage call of the pipes, moving in their ghostly armor and twilight tartans, waving their fans and old pikes and ancient dim banners. We watched as they poured into the keep and the old tower's windows began to flash with strange, shifting light, and the courtyard echo to the sounds of ghostly revelry. We stood hand in hand and listened to the wild celebrations of the dead, and we could see those shadows marching on behind their dim piper, going on through the centuries, growing in numbers, eventually submerging the living beneath their roistering swarm, triumphing over death itself as they piped, and sang, and marched, obedient servants to their long-dead, newfound King.

EDITOR'S INTRODUCTION TO:

DECISIVE WARFARE: RETROSPECT AND PROSPECT
by Reginald Bretnor

It must have been a good year for books on strategic theory: both Reginald Bretnor's *Decisive Warfare* and my own (with Stefan Possony) *Strategy of Technology* were published in 1969. Alas, both are out of print, although I am revising *Strategy of Technology* at this moment.

In *Decisive Warfare* Bretnor reviewed the Lanchester Equations. These were derived from military history and applied to modern war: the basic theory is that other things being equal, the actual strengths in a military contest should be thought of as the ratio of the squares of the numbers engaged. Thus, if the forces are in a 3:2 ratio, one ought to think of this as 9:4, or slightly better than 2:1; while a 3:1 superiority is really overwhelming.

Bretnor went on to examine the "other things" which in practice are never equal, and came to some interesting conclusions on decisiveness in war. His book, while hard to obtain, should be read by every military theorist.

In this present essay Bretnor looks at developments since his book appeared: what he has learned, and what the world has learned.

DECISIVE WARFARE: RETROSPCT AND PROSPECT
Reginald Bretnor

> . . . Though the Art of War be a Practical one, yet the Theory is
> so needful, that without it you may be Common Souldiers good
> enough, but not good Commanders; you are to know more than
> you daily see; for it is a sign of a very mean Officer, when he tells
> you he likes not such a thing, because he never saw it before.
> —Sir James Turner, *Pallas Armata.*
> *Military Essayes of the Ancient*
> *Grecian, Roman, and Modern Art*
> *of War . . .*, London, 1683

RETROSPECT

My interest in matters military arose, originally, from my
boyhood fascination with weapons and history, and my interest in military theory developed gradually as I read more and
more about wars and their conduct, about command decisions
and their outcome, about great generals and generals who
were dunderheads—and the more I read, the less satisfied I
was with the various systems set forth by the philosophers
and theorists of war.

At their simplest, these consisted of a few aphorisms; at
their most profound, of very carefully derived and developed
systems of "principles of war." (Outstanding are those set
forth by Major General J. F. C. Fuller in *Foundations of the
Science of War*,[1] for they are based on a thorough consideration of all war's elements, physical and mental.) Yet I found
none of these satisfactory. They seemed, ultimately, to be
rules for the conduct of a war rather than statements of basic
cause and effect in warfare. None of them, to my mind,
offered frames of reference consistent and coherent enough
for accurate predictability. In part, I think, this was due to the

fact that any set of principles attempting to comprehend within itself both the physical and nonphysical factors in war, both destructive force and the minds and wills that guide it, invites confusion, for it risks the *implication* that each listed principle must be observed and that all are of approximately equal value. For that reason, it seemed to me that they should always be differentiated, and that the differentiation should be explicit, for such unintended sources of semantic confusion are responsible for many of our difficulties, civil and military.

Very well, what does one do if one is dissatisfied with someone else's map of structure and process (which is, after all, what any theory is)? One either gives up the whole business or else cudgels one's brain trying to develop one's own, and this is what I decided to do.

Here, of course, we encounter the nicely loaded question of "how well are you qualified?"—loaded because it carries the clear implication that there *are* curricula which qualify one to abstract and elaborate those relationships of cause and effect that constitute a valid and generally applicable theory of war. The answer to that was obvious: in that sense I certainly was not qualified, but to that answer there was an obvious corollary: if such curricula existed, there would be no question either of revising existing theories or of elaborating a new one. It would be unnecessary.

It took me some time to quit worrying about my lack of qualifications and set to work. I was first encouraged by the late Colonel William Fergus Kernan, USA, artillery officer and author,[2] and for that encouragement I was, and have remained, deeply grateful, especially as it came at a time of much personal distress. Colonel Kernan recommended me to his publishers, and shortly before Pearl Harbor Mrs. Blanche Knopf wrote to me, expressing interest in whatever work I might be planning. Unfortunately, my ideas were still too amorphous and too disorganized for me even to think of attempting publication, and it was not until the 1960s that I felt I had something really coherent to say.

By that time the general body of theory incorporated in the book eventually published as *Decisive Warfare* had pretty well taken shape. It is based, first, on an examination of the *physical processes* of war, those that involve the generation and exercise of destructive force. In this, I more or less followed Fuller's dictum:

> Mental force does not win a war; moral force does not win a war; physical force does not win a war; but what *does* win a war is the highest combination of these three forces acting as *one* force. Do not let us, therefore, belittle physical force, for it is an essential of this trinity, and all other forces are as nothing without it.[3]

What I could not quite accept was the concept of the three forces acting, except in a very general and symbolic way, as one force. I saw the overall military equation as one based entirely on destructive force, with absolute limits on the realization of that force's potential imposed by the nature of weapons, enabling devices, instrumentalities, and terrain. Thus, it was *not* true that "the moral is to the physical as three to one"—at least not in any sense other than the symbolic—for the highest value as multipliers nonphysical factors can attain in the military equation is exactly *1*. Thus, no matter how high your men's morale, no matter how well trained they are, they cannot force an automatic weapon to *exceed* its designed cyclic rate of fire, or an armored vehicle its built-in limitations of speed and fuel requirements. The true difference between first-line troops and slobs, then, is that a really good soldier can get the very most out of his equipment and the slob can't—and that goes also for generals and their armies. Any other assessment of the nonphysical factors in the equation is an invitation to military disaster—witness Japanese miscalculations in World War II.

The second basis for my formulation was a recognition of the fact that the emphasis in virtually all statements of military theory has been on the *positive*, rather than on the equally vital *negative*, aspects of the equation. Therefore, to escape residual connotations, I avoided such traditional military terms as *mass*, and substituted the symbol M for all aspects of destructive force, and the corresponding symbol V for the vulnerability of man and his works to destruction. Every military equation must contain both.

In 1966 I published what would become the book's first chapter, "Vulnerability and the Equations of War," as an article in the Command and General Staff College *Military Review*,[4] and this was followed in 1967 by another, "Destructive Force and the Equations of War."[5] With these as a basis, I sold the book to Stackpole Publishers, who issued it in 1969.

Essentially, it is an examination of the processes of war, primarily the physical processes, tracing the stages in the expression of both destructive force and vulnerability, and illustrating these in a rough sequence of unquantified equations—unquantified because many of the factors, especially in modern technological warfare, are much too complex to quantify practically and because any attempt at quantification, in such a study, besides being absurd, would have sacrificed the universality desired.

The main factor treated, in addition to Vulnerability (V) and Destructive Force (M), was, of course, Time (T), so that every equation contained V and $\dot{V}$ (one's own and the enemy's), M and $\dot{M}$, T and $\dot{T}$. The discussion of various phases in the expression of M gives a good general idea of how these were approached. There are five such phases: *Preparation* (industrial production, organization, training); *Logistics* (movement "out of action"); *Maneuver* (movement "in action"); *Weapons, primary radius of expression* (*i.e.*, the flight of an artillery projectile to its target); *Weapons, secondary radius of expression* (*i.e.*, bursting radius of an artillery shell). Obviously, Vulnerability also had its more or less comparable phases of realization. Where Time entered the equation M and $\dot{M}$, V and $\dot{V}$, were represented followed by an arrow, thusly: $M\rightarrow$ and $V\rightarrow$.

In view of this presentation, I discussed what I felt—and still feel—to be one of the most urgent and critical and, in spite of everything, least understood aspects of war today, the fact that destructive force at our disposal has mounted along a curve so steep as to be, in some areas, asymptotic. This was vividly illustrated by the lethality tables compiled by Colonel T. N. Dupuy in a study prepared for the United States Army by the Historical Evaluation and Research Organization (HERO) in 1964. The geometric progression of scientific and technological development is indisputable, but it is also indisputable that almost all our thinking where weaponry is concerned is still arithmetical and linear. It seems—frighteningly—as though the very concept of geometrically accelerating power is understood by almost no politicians, by few military men, and (appallingly) by only a minority of scientists. How else can one explain such idiocies as our "civil defense" plans to evacuate our major cities in event of an all-out war? Are their authors really ignorant of the brutal reality that a single freeway accident can often stop the flow of traffic for hours, or that sometimes it can take hours to evacuate a single crowded stadium?

The lesson taught by World War I—that, confronted by overwhelming firepower, you either disperse, take adequate cover, or die—had been learned by the military by World War II, but there seems to have been no general understanding of its universality. We have done little to diminish our vulnerability to superweapons. Instead of decentralizing industry, instead of attempting to disperse our population, instead of doing our utmost to avoid dependence on concentrated essential supplies—water and electricity, for example—we have actually continued to centralize. It is true that there are nations with valid civil defense programs—Switzerland and Sweden notably—but we, who stand in greater need of one, have nothing except the sound of bureaucratic whistling in the dark.

These matters were discussed at some length in *Decisive Warfare*, for while the book is basically a statement of theory, there would have been little point in leaving it at that, without any attempt to apply the theory to the problems of the moment. Consequently, considerable space was devoted to considering the inevitable proliferation of superweapons, which were bound to become more powerful, easier to manufacture, cheaper, and therefore more generally available, so that what had (then) only recently been a Two-Power problem was destined, before too long, to become an Nth-Power problem. Again, a good deal was said about the vulnerability of enormous ships, both ships of war and merchantmen, and about such vessels as concentrations of vulnerability, as well as about the vulnerability of helicopters and the eventual phasing out of manned aircraft (at least in combat roles). The vastly increased complexity of weapons, enabling devices, and instrumentalities also, of course, came in for considerable discussion, even though at the time the microelectronic revolution was hardly hatched, laser development was primitive, and the military possibilities of the space adventure had scarcely been explored except in science fiction. Finally, I emphasized the point that at the time we already had behind us almost twenty-five years of unprecedentedly tight secrecy (now stretched out into forty) so that probably *no one* really knew exactly what would happen in event of an all-out war.

PURPOSE AND REALIZATION

From the outset, the primary purpose of the book had been to derive and set forth, first a general analysis of the physical processes of war, and second the ways in which these are determined by the nonphysical processes, by the mind and the will of man. My original title was *The Processes of War*, but this, possibly because they deemed it commercially unexciting, did not please my publishers, and *Decisive Warfare*, which I myself felt placed undue emphasis on what was, after all, a less important section of the book, was the best compromise I could get. I had entitled the fourth chapter of the book "The Critical Imbalance," and summarized what it dealt with in my table of contents as follows:

> The equations of war always have two sets of values: one's own and the enemy's. When these are too nearly balanced, the attrition of force tends to be slow, and action indecisive. When, by military art or natural circumstance, they are thrown sharply out of balance, attrition can be swift and action decisive. The battles and campaigns where decisive victories are achieved are usually those in which a critical imbalance has been established— that point of no return where, inevitably, the enemy's realized vulnerability escalates and his force decays. Therefore the critical imbalance should be the goal of all military theory, of all military planning, of all commanders.

As examples of the achieved critical imbalance, I chose Lord Nelson's splendid sea victories, notably Aboukir Bay and Trafalgar, quoting Lanchester's application of his N^2 Law to Trafalgar to analyze Nelson's accomplishment in terms of the military equation's essential factors. I also chose, as examples from land warfare, Scipio Africanus' brilliant double envelopments, at Ilipa, Baecula, and Zama. I also discussed situations where a critical imbalance was, for one or more reasons, impossible to achieve—the Western Front in World War I, for instance, where destructive force had escalated to an unprecedented and never generally understood degree, and where techniques to minimize the realization of vulnerability had yet to be developed.

There was quite a bit in the first draft of the book to which my publishers took exception, and I have had something to say about this in my foreword to the new edition. Much of it, they apparently thought, was heretical. They sent the manuscript to a very well known authority who, judging by his reaction, seemed to have found it profoundly disturbing, and who denounced both book and author so extravagantly that the publishers sent it on to another expert, who found some faults and much to praise in it.

Also, we went round and round on such matters as certain of my opinions, the way I expressed them, and what I chose to criticize. The ultimate result was that I did a considerable amount of rewriting, compromising where I had to and deleting some conclusions I would rather have kept in—and ending up with a book which was not quite what I had set out to write and in some ways a disappointment to me, not where the theory set forth was concerned, but in its treatment of that theory's applications.

Decisive Warfare met with a strangely mixed reception. Brigadier General William K. Ghormley, then editor of *Ordnance*, made it the magazine's Book of the Month and gave it what was probably the best review I have ever received. The *Library Journal* slammed it down with a sneer in a couple of paragraphs. The Air Force *Friday Review of Defense Literature* and one or two other professional publications gave it good reviews, and a few others contented themselves with noncommittal statements of content. The *Michigan Quarterly Review*, where I had published, printed a long article-review airing its author's dovish views about Vietnam and hinting that I undoubtedly was a warmonger.

PROSPECT

Although *Decisive Warfare* wasn't quite the book I had wanted it to be, I saw no reason to make major revisions for the new Borgo Press edition, for to my mind the equations of war had not changed since the first printing, and it was these, and their interrelationships, that I wanted to emphasize.

The equations remain the same. It is their values that have changed, are changing, and will continue to change—all at geometrically accelerating rates.

First let us consider weapons, our own and any possible enemy's, for it is weapons which are the basic element in M and M'. Foremost in most minds, of course, are the world's nuclear stockpiles. Their individual power, as far as published data would indicate, has not increased greatly since 1969—but their numbers and accuracy and variety all have. Again, while there would appear to be no more hydrogen powers now than there were then—five—there seems to be no doubt that there are now several new conventional atomic powers: India? Pakistan? The Union of South Africa? Israel? Or perhaps Sweden, the Benelux countries, Switzerland? And it is an absolute certainty that, however many there may be now, before very long their numbers—barring effectively imposed controls—will increase dramatically and will include certain of those thoroughly irresponsible nations now supporting international terrorism.

The geometrical progression of weapons development applies also to other radiation weapons, to lasers, to particle-beam weapons, to chemical and bacteriological weapons. It operates as a direct and inevitable function of the amounts of money funding it, and here once more the prospect of quite the wrong people taking advantage of it is extremely alarming, especially as the weapons just mentioned will probably be cheaper and easier to produce than nuclear weapons have been.

So much for weapons insofar as they are involved with the terminal phase of the expression of M and M'—more or less general-purpose weapons and those mislabeled "strategic." There is another class of weapons to consider: those auxiliary weapons designed expressly to interfere with this expression—"smart" antiaircraft missiles, antimissile missiles, and all those special-purpose weapons devised to carry out specific and role-limited functions on land, at sea, in the air, and inevitably in space. (The fact that many of them can, at times, be employed as general-purpose weapons does not invalidate our thesis. It just complicates it—and if there is any single factor muddling the military picture today it is the geometrically increasing complexity in every phase of the expression of M and M', in our attempts to effect the realization of V', and in the measures we take to prevent an enemy from realizing V—that is, our own vulnerability.)

SPECIALIZATION AND COMPLEXITY

The rule that complexity follows on specialization applies to virtually every weapon and every enabling device (defined here as any device not itself a weapon without which weapons either cannot function or can function only at reduced efficiency). Thus, while we speak of, say, a battleship as a weapon, properly it is nothing of the sort—and has not been since the last ram was discarded. It is a mobile, more or less invulnerable, seagoing platform for its guns and, nowadays, missiles—in short, an enabling device. Its engines, its communications equipment, its computers, and for that matter its laundry and kitchens and sick bays—all are enabling devices, just as its purely defensive armament consists of enabling weapons.

To illustrate this complexity, it is only necessary to consider the communications equipment available to naval commanders in Nelson's day, during the Civil War, during World Wars I and II, and today, or to compare the information-gathering abilities of cavalry patrols or of observation balloons with those of radar and sonar, of stratospheric aircraft and spy satellites. Even a comparison of the instrument panels of, say, a Sopwith Camel or Nieuport, a Messerschmitt or Spitfire, with those of a Mystère or F-15 will demonstrate the point.

And the complexity is not simply on the surface. It means that every problem of supply and replacement is multiplied in direct ratio, that jury-rigging and cannibalization become largely things of the past, that military dependence on a continuity of production and supply has been critically increased. (Witness what happened to the Tehran rescue mission when one helicopter failed.)

In short—and we can argue legitimately that our specialization has been justified by military necessity—it still violates a fundamental military principle: *the principle of simplicity*.[6]

Why is this so important? Simply because every complication of an enabling device or process, anywhere along the line of the expression of M in war, implies a corresponding new and increased value, or a new focal point of concentration, of V.

Perhaps we ought to paraphrase Ben Franklin's "for want of a nail, the shoe was lost; for want of a shoe, the horse was lost; and for want of a horse . . ." by starting out with *for want of a byte . . .*

This technological complexity is giving rise to an entirely new class of devices which must be classified as weapons, those designed to disable enemy devices dependent on elec-

273

tronic circuitry, not by the direct expression of physical force, but by the use of one form or another of radiation.

The process would appear to be open-ended, something that is true of most scientific and technological progress, for when a curve of progress appears to have reached asymptote, almost invariably the curve of an analogous development catches up and passes it. A good example is what happened when the curve of artillery development appeared to have peaked—the analogous curve of rocket development appeared and left it far behind.

(This is why the arithmetic, linear thinking characteristic of so many politicians, military men, and media pundits is a deadly danger, not only to those who indulge in it but to all of us.)

The increase in the complexity and specialization of weapons and enabling devices has other unhappy consequences. Inevitably, the instrumentalities necessary to their functioning become more and more complex. Personnel procurement and training become more of a problem. And finally, perhaps most important, inevitably there is some division of the *totality* of destructive force available.

Let us take a simple example of how this functions. In the days of cavalry, it was axiomatic that cavalrymen fighting on foot could not match an equivalent infantry unit in firepower for the simple reason that, depending on the situation and the degree of mobility to be retained, from 12.5 percent to 25 percent of their strength had to stay out of a firefight as horse-holders—either one to each set of fours or one per eight-man squad.

Similarly, as infantry began to employ—and were reorganized to employ—more and more special-purpose weapons, naturally the total rifle firepower of infantry battalions would—given no improvement in the basic rifle—be reduced. Thus, while specialization in certain respects can and does multiply the relizable value of $M \rightarrow$, in certain other respects it can subtract from it, and this further complicates the military equations which the commander must evaluate and juggle. The involved orchestration of complex modern armies is a very different thing from the beautiful simplicity of armies like those of the Mongols, where every man was an expert mounted archer and swordsman, every man was equally mobile, and no man required a more involved supply system than his comrades.

As another example, we can take the very simple specialization of warships in, again, Nelson's day, and compare it with the constantly increasing specialization that followed steam and speed and the invention of the torpedo. In the days of sail, there was no question of smaller vessels protecting the main line of battle, which was quite able to protect itself. The only exception was in their reconnaissance role. Even frigates, to say nothing of their smaller cousins, had as their function the protection of merchant craft and the raiding of the enemy's, and those other duties that, sometimes as independent cruisers and sometimes as fleet auxiliaries, they were designed to perform. Compare this with the situation which has developed in the last century: torpedo boats and torpedo-boat destroyers (the second term soon to be stripped of its adjective), submarines and aircraft carriers and antiaircraft and antimissile vessels, PT boats and hovercraft and kindred small ships with big weapons, all with their individual (or class) requirements where supply and maintenance are concerned.

Here again, the present-day admiral's problems of orchestration are comparable to those confronting today's generals.

One is tempted to question whether the necessity for specialization, and a fascination with the complex technological gadgetry of specialization, may not on occasion blind one to the possibility of achieving great things with massive concentrations of simpler, cheaper weapons. I often wonder what the results might have been had either the British or the Germans, at Jutland, been able to deploy, say, three hundred destroyers—or what would have happened during the Japanese invasion of the Philippines had our own forces been able to oppose the initial landings with massed mortars. These are now vain speculations, but they might still be kept in mind to illustrate the principle, especially when cheap, simple weapons are being replaced by much more expensive, much more complex ones.

In our quite justified eagerness to develop new and superior specialized weapons and enabling devices, we seem to have quite forgotten the possibilities which may still exist in new general-purpose weapons less dependent on supply complexities and, because of their uniformity, ultimately simpler to employ on all levels of application and command decision. To my mind, the most promising area from which these may be developed would seem to be that of lasers and other beam

275

weapons. A quantum jump advance comparable to that which gave us microelectronics but in the area of power supplies could provide us with some very flexible weapons indeed.

MAD AND THE HIGH FRONTIER

The subject of laser weapons brings us immediately to the question of the Strategic Defense Initiative as urged by General Daniel Graham. As this is being written, it is being wrangled over and argued against by a wide variety of scientists and media people. A Los Angeles *Times* report,[7] for instance, quoted a study by R&D Associates, "an influential defense think tank," indicating that,

> in a matter of hours, a laser defense system powerful enough to cope with the ballistic missile threat can also destroy the enemy's major cities by fire. The attack would proceed city by city, the attack time for each city being only a matter of minutes.

Furthermore,

> "The lasers can be employed in a manner not contemplated by the SDI," cautioned Albert L. Latter and Ernest A. Martinelli, authors of the eight-page R&D Associates study and advocates of a stronger U.S. defense. ". . . After spending hundreds of billions of dollars, we would be back where we started from: deterrence by retaliation."

The L.A. *Times* report did say that "*many* advocates of SDI, often called Star Wars, say they *hope* that lasers *may one day* be part of a defensive shield against enemy missiles [italics mine]." However, the whole tenor of its argument conveys the idea that laser armament not only is a certainty but will be of prime importance; and I think we can assume that this is partly because of our sensation-oriented media's fascination with Luke Skywalker and his friends, and partly because opponents of SDI are not always too scrupulous where propaganda is concerned.

In view of all this, it may be interesting to cite another news story, from the January 25, 1986, issue of the San Francisco *Chronicle*:

> The government has awarded Lockheed Missiles & Space Co.

in Sunnyvale a $468 million Star Wars contract to develop an interceptor that can smash enemy missiles 100 miles up in space. . . .

Lockheed will build a non-nuclear, lightweight, low-cost interceptor that can destroy ballistic missile warheads by smashing into them above the atmosphere. The impact would harmlessly disintegrate nuclear warheads. . . .

The . . . program is related to the homing overlay experiment, also conducted by Lockheed. On June 10, 1984, Lockheed interceptor hit and destroyed a dummy warhead hundreds of miles up in space.

This scarcely sounds as though SDI's central thrust, at least at present, is in the direction of main reliance on lasers. However, as a supporter of SDI, I myself hope that ultimately it will be.

In my opinion, the type of laser defense contemplated would be *very* much to the advantage of the United States *whether or not in due course it became an offensive system*. The reason lies in a comparison of our vulnerabilities and those of the Soviet Union. Certainly, in its initial stages it would be an extremely useful defense. However, I do not think that its acquisition could ever render us completely secure against nuclear—or other—attack. Modern war, as we know it, is much more complex than that, and future warfare will be no simpler.

Let us hark back for a moment to the entire MAD concept and to the R&D suggestion that satellite laser systems would simply be more of the same. In effect, the people who dreamed up MAD erected a vast, static military equation which fear was supposed to keep in some sort of balance. The idea was hatched when there were only two major values of M to be considered—in other words, when only the United States and the Soviet Union really had the power to upset the balance. However, as I believe we have shown, what was a Two-Power problem has now come very close to being an Nth-Power problem. In short, the balance becomes more and more precarious as science and technology arm more and more second- and third-rate nations—and even groups of savages and semisavages—with what we have been thinking of as superweapons.

At its best, SDI will provide us with an effective defense against nuclear missile attack, and at its worst—if indeed it does become an offensive instrument and both sides get it—it

277

will at least restore something of the Two-Power balance, for the cost of lofting laser satellites in adequate numbers and defending them in space will be beyond what powers that are less than superpowers will be able to afford.

The Two-Power standoff as represented by MAD is, of course, not an ideal to be devoutly hoped for. It represents an almost incredible failure to understand how science and technology affect the military process: arithmetical and linear thinking at its most miserable. The proof of this is the naked fact that "deterrence" has deterred the communists from *nothing* except all-out nuclear war—if, indeed, they have refrained from starting such a war because of the deterrent. It has not deterred them from subverting other governments, from arming revolutionaries worldwide, from training and assisting terrorists, and from waging war against the free world in a dozen different ways and in a hundred different areas. I myself think that they are upset about SDI because they fear that once we have such a defense our technological superiority may put us in a position where we can effectively call a halt to their international subversion.

The equations of war are very cold equations. Their values change with science and technology, but the equations do not, and today they tell us that we confront a future in which M values will continue to increase geometrically, but in which all indications are that little or nothing will be done to reduce corresponding values of V, a future which holds too strong a likelihood that any major war, instead of being a matter of generalship and strategy, may be nothing more nor less than a gigantic artillery problem.

In this situation, we continue to play games: blithering about "arms control," writing new and even emptier treaties and agreements to follow those which have been written and repeatedly violated during this century. Considering that it is we of the free world who have been the prime sufferers from these violations—violations of the Kellogg-Briand Pact, Hitler's taking of the Rhineland, the violations by Japan and Germany and the Soviet Union of how many nations' neutrality and sovereignty?—one would think that common sense would dictate a different approach—for instance, the scrapping of the so-called United Nations in favor of a civilized union of free countries. A world organization of nations, like any club, has to have rules, and has the right to demand that the membership abide by them.

In short, we need very badly to revise the ancient equations of international law and diplomacy.

THE MIND, THE WILL, AND THE EQUATIONS OF WAR

Again, the equations of war are very cold equations, and we delude ourselves if we think their operative physical values, M and M', V and V', T and T', can be *directly* changed either by the mind and will of a commander or by those of his command. The role of the mind and the will is not to multiply M, but rather to force the maximum realization of its inherent potential. Similarly, they can only act to divide the maximum value of realized V by means of measures taken *before* they become necessary: by interposition of materials less vulnerable than man's body, by dispersal, by rapid movement or appropriate training. The same rules apply to the Time factor, T.

Where the mind and the will are of maximum importance is in their effect on the mind and will of the enemy: by perceiving vulnerabilities of which he is unaware, by the sort of deceptions of which Sun Tzu was so fond, by superior doctrine and training and determination so that one may realize M to the fullest while preventing a comparable realization of M'. Again, they cannot substitute *directly* for a deficiency of M. Nor can they *directly* lessen the intrinsic value of V. Paradoxically, this makes them far more important in their ultimate influence on the realized equation than if they are employed blindly in attempting to accomplish that which, physically, is an impossibility. (No, there are no exceptions. All those incidents in military history that appear to contradict the rule actually, given deeper analysis, confirm it. If the enemy's guns suddenly fall silent as a tiny band of heroes launches its hopeless charge, we can be sure that a psychological impact, unplanned and unpredictable, has caused the momentary paralysis of the gunners—the event has not proven that raw courage can triumph over disciplined firepower. This does *not* mean that courage can never snatch victory out of the jaws of grim defeat, nor that such attempts should never be made. But it does mean that any general planning in these terms is less than sane.)[8]

I discussed the vulnerability of our cities, industrial complexes, and other concentrations of V at some length in *Decisive Warfare*, and nothing that has transpired since its publication has led me to change the assessment except perhaps to point out that we have continued to concentrate where we should have been dispersing.

Quite as foolish, in my opinion, has been our policy with regard to preparations for war at sea. In the first place, we have not only continued to build giant carriers but have also resurrected battleships at considerable expense. I have read quite a number of justifications of this policy, many of them professional, others by media apologists, and every one that has come to my attention has been based on the implied, even if not explicitly stated, assumption that these vessels will encounter only conventional weapons. The harsh lessons of Eniwetok and Bikini seem to have been forgotten. Yet if there is any area in which tactical nuclear weapons could be employed without necessarily touching off an all-out holocaust, it is at sea, for the psychological impact of the killing of a battleship by such a weapon would be far less traumatic—at least to a general population and a government—than the killing of a city or several cities.

The necessary weapons exist. They are only too readily available to the enemy. There is *no* good reason to trust that they will not be used. Then why not prepare for the contingency—especially if, by doing so realistically, we would not in any way diminish our potential power? Here we come to the nub of the argument: is it better to have a great number of cheap, fast platforms mounting weapons as powerful as possible, or to have a few gigantic, expensive platforms mounting greater concentrations of the same weapons? (I am not considering heavy naval guns, which are weapons of rather limited utility.)

Or the question can be phrased in slightly different terms: is it better to have a relatively few high concentrations of vulnerability, trusting that they will be able to defend themselves, than to distribute the same values of M among many lower V concentrations?

This very important problem of the size of ships does not concern ships of war alone. It is also critical to the design of those auxiliary vessels on which they will have to depend, and here we find that big-ship advocates are securely in the saddle. Tankers, which were already giants in 1969, have become supergiants. Giant container ships have replaced great numbers of smaller vessels. All are becoming more and more automated, so that where it once required thirty or forty or fifty men to manage, say, twenty thousand tons, now often several hundred thousand tons can be crewed by a baker's dozen.

The reason for this is very simple. Politely, we can call it "efficiency." Analytically, we can say it is economic determinism. Less politely, we can express it as, "If it makes a buck, it's *good*," or, "What's good for General Motors is good for the country."

Maybe so, in the piping times of peace. It is *not* so in war—witness the application of Mr. McNamara's "cost-efficiency" concepts in Vietnam. Each huge merchant vessel is a concentration of V which does not even have the naval giant's ability to defend itself. Finally, a merchant marine consisting largely of such vessels—many of them flying foreign "flags of convenience"—cannot provide adequate training facilities for the rapid expansion of a merchant fleet in an emergency.

Let us grant that, under existing circumstances, smaller vessels are more expensive to operate, and consequently less profitable to operate, than huge ones. The remedy, then, might be for the government to phase out such indefensible subsidies as that to the tobacco industry at home and those to more or less hostile nations abroad in favor of a strong merchant marine subsidy to restore and maintain our strength at sea in both peace and war.

No profit imperative should be allowed to influence the design and acquisition of weapons and enabling devices adversely in either peace or war, and this rule, if we are determined to survive, should be carried a step further: no profit imperative should be permitted to dictate national policy against the national interest.

LESSONS FROM LIMITED WARS

Every war fought since 1945 has been a limited war in one way or another, either because the combatants have lacked the ultimate in armament and equipment, because they have been restrained by political considerations, or because their high commands have not deemed it expedient to reveal the full extent of their power. We have learned much from the several Arab-Israeli wars. We learned something about aluminum warships and guided missiles in the Falklands dust-up. We are still learning from the Russian terror in Afghanistan. Whether we did indeed learn much from our experience in Vietnam remains to be seen. (Somehow I doubt that we should take Mr. Rambo's exploits very seriously.)

The main point here is—to repeat what I said earlier—that we are living on the sharp edge of more than forty years of what amounts to wartime secrecy, and if any of us in this world has weapons or devices that hold the promise of being able to effect a critical imbalance—weapons or devices capable of a decisive technological surprise—it is highly unlikely that they have been allowed to surface. As we know from World War II, secrets *can* be kept, even major secrets. I do not say, of course, that this is indeed the case, but the possibility certainly must be taken into consideration and, if possible, prepared against.

THE CRITICAL IMBALANCE: POSSIBLE OR IMPOSSIBLE?

In the past, the achievement of the critical imbalance has occasionally made it possible for battles, campaigns, and even wars to be won in a minimum of time at a minimum cost in lives and resources. The Mongols, because their way of achieving it was actually part of their way of life, left behind almost endless examples. More recently, the German use of armor in their initial offensives against Poland and France provides one more clear instance: if France and Poland had been their only opponents, the war would have ended there, and a very cheap victory it would have been.

The question now is whether, given what we know of modern weaponry, any critical imbalance on the grand scale can possibly be achieved. My own opinion would be that in any unlimited war it very probably cannot—not if the combatant powers possess any degree of parity in their ability to express M and are equally vulnerable. I can see no way in which, under these circumstances, the grand military equation could be thrown out of balance to the necessary degree.

The only exception would be a technological surprise capable of effecting a maximum realization of the enemy's vulnerability or one which could destroy or drastically curtail his ability to express $M' \rightarrow$.

Of course, I am speaking here of the physical factors in the military equation. God alone knows what might happen given some cataclysmic failure of will—something similar to the state of mind into which the Allies fell during the Chamberlain years—either in response to a threat or as a reaction to an outright attack.

THE EQUATIONS OF WAR AND PEACE

Of the five phases in the expression of M and M' probably none is now more important than the first, the preparatory phase, which includes the invention and development of new weapons and enabling devices, new instrumentalities and techniques. Semantically, we still draw a hard line between *peace* and *war*: if war has not been formally declared, we consider ourselves to be at peace (at least until somebody pulls a Pearl Harbor on us or sends armor across our borders to support a puppet government). And while this idyllic state of affairs persists, we ship scrap iron to Japan or—as at present—enough wheat to the Soviet Union to save them from the agricultural disaster their clumsy system has been inviting for many years. It is true that once upon a time the line between war and peace was considerably more definite than it is today, but that was when the governments of "civilized" powers played more or less by the same rules, and when the preparatory phase in the expression of M and M' was not as critical as it is today.

Let us consider the specious "peace" that exists between the Soviet Union and ourselves. We go through the motions of normal, peaceful international intercourse, and perhaps because of this (and also because of unremitting Soviet and fellow-traveler propaganda) many of us forget that the communist world declared war on us many years ago, and officially and ideologically has been at war with us ever since. (Perhaps it is inaccurate to say "the communist world," for there are many peoples in that world—the Poles, the Hungarians, the Latvians and Esthonians and the Czechs—who want no part of their Russian masters, and it is also possible that recent Chinese departures from Marxist dogma are genuine. However, for practical purposes we can still speak of the communist world centering on the Kremlin and obeying its dictates.)

How has the Soviet Union managed to build up the tremendous destructive force now only too obviously at its disposal? First, by giving military preparations first priority, even to the extent of imposing scarcity and poverty on its populations. Second, by relying on Western nations and Western business organizations to sell it materials, technologies, and factories which it either could not produce itself or could have produced only at the sacrifice of military production. (The recent building, by Fiat, of an enormous automobile production plant in Russian is a case in point. How many Russian engineers and other high-tech personnel were freed to work in, for example, tank production?) It is no exaggeration to say that the Russians have lifted themselves by our bootstraps, and when I say *our* I am referring primarily to us, here in the United States (though the same thing is true of all major free world powers). Where would the Russian Communists be today had it not been for the help they received even in the 1920s and '30s from our banks and industries, to say nothing of our charitable organizations and our government in times of famine, and the constant assistance they derive from our relatively wide-open publication of patent and other scientific and technological data?

Today, we continue along this foolish course while the Comintern gobbles up nations once friendly to us, especially those upon whose strategic minerals we depend, and we—God help us!—more often than not give them a helping hand, as our media and our intellectualoids have been doing with regard to South Africa. (Granted, there is injustice in South Africa, but why has it suddenly eclipsed in importance far greater, far more sadistic injustices being perpetrated in Afghanistan, Ethiopia, and any number of independent African nations recently emerged from colonial rule into the savagery of leftist military dictatorship? Why do we hear so little of the barbarities of privacy reborn around the perimeter of Southeast Asia, the Arabian seas, even the Mediterranean? Why almost nothing of the persecution by the Ayatollah's fanatics of the harmless Bahais? The reason is cruelly simple: if South Africa can be thrown into chaos first, and then follow so much of the dark continent into the leftist jungle, we would lose a prime source of strategic minerals, and the Comintern would profit. The black population of South Africa might very well gain the "one man, one vote" that Bishop Tutu is demanding—but would it be worth any more than the "one man, one vote" now enjoyed by the slave populations behind the Iron Curtain?)

The Comintern does not consider itself at peace with us. It believes itself and all its subject populations to be fighting a holy war against all those nations with free enterprise economies. Under these circumstances, we should follow Solzhenitsyn's advice and cut off our massive aid to our declared enemies.

Again, where we are confronted—as we were in Iran—by the necessity for supporting governments of which we may not wholly approve, we should always, in the face of a highly probable communist or communist-influenced takeover, support them wholeheartedly, at the same time doing our very best to urge necessary, peaceful, democratic reforms.

Let us realize that we are at peace with the Comintern and the Soviet Union only in the sense that formal war has not been declared between us, and therefore we should not continue the absurd charade of negotiating treaties and agreements, of arguing back and forth about arms control and "disarmament," of solemnly participating in such frauds as the Helsinki Pacts, and of holding still while the only real empire in the world continues to accuse us of imperialism even after we and our allies have divested ourselves of all our once-imperial holdings.

What we need from our Russian opponents is an unequivocal renunciation of their declaration of war against us, of their entire Marxist doctrine of violent world revolution. In other words, we need a Declaration of Peace—and not one confined to empty words. To be valid, it would have to be accompanied by internal reforms in the Soviet Union and its spheres of influence: freedom of the press, freedom of speech and of dissent, free elections, and freedom from the tyranny of a police state. It would have to be demonstrated by frontiers at least as open as they were when the Tsars ruled.

Yes, it's damned unlikely—and because it is, we should, in our dealings with these, our declared enemies, never forget the equations of war and how cold they are.

NOTES

1. Major General J. F. C. Fuller, *The Foundations of the Science of War* (London: Hutchinson & Co., Ltd., 1926).
2. *Defense Will Not Win the War* (Boston: Little, Brown & Co., 1942).
3. Fuller, *op. cit.*
4. Published as "Vulnerability and the Military Equation," Vol. XLVI, No. 9 (September 1966).
5. Published as "Destructive Force and the Military Equation," Vol. XLVII, No. 5 (May 1967).
6. General Fuller did not list the principle of simplicity among those he set forth in the worked cited. It appears in those taught at the United States Army Command and General Staff College, which derive in part from his work.
7. Reprinted in the San Francisco *Chronicle*, January 11, 1986.
8. Suggested reading: Martin Middlebrook, *The First Day on the Somme, 1 July 1916* (New York: W. W. Norton & Co., 1972).

EDITOR'S INTRODUCTION TO:

CROWN OF THORNS
by Edward P. Hughes

Throughout this series we have told the story of what happened to the Irish town of Barley Cross after World War III when an ecological crisis destroyed most of civilization and rendered sterile most of the males in the world.

Barley Cross is an odd place. It fell under the domination of Patrick O'Meara, onetime sergeant major in the British Army, who brought his tank to the gates and proceeded to become the O'Meara, Master of the Fist, and supreme dictator of the village.

In due course the O'Meara died, and Liam McGrath became Master of the Fist. Liam hadn't really wanted the job in the first place.

Now someone else claims it.

CROWN OF THORNS
Edward P. Hughes

Angry voices outside his dining room window disturbed the
peace of Liam McGrath's breakfast. The Fist was usually
quiet at this hour, apart from the racket the birds made. He
got up to peer out of the casement.

Four young men stood on his doorstep, disputing with
Eamon Toomey, who was guard for the day. Liam recognised
the men as the Achill Island Irregulars now enlisted in the
troop which guarded the Fist. Eamon Toomey faced them, his
rifle at the high port.

Liam hesitated. Sometimes poor Eamon took his duties too
seriously. Should the Lord of Barley Cross intervene? Eamon's
rifle held only one bullet, but one bullet could do serious
damage if the gun went off.

He heard Eamon's stolid tones. "You know you lads ain't
supposed to be up here when you're off duty."

Dominic Nunan, always leader to the Achill immigrants,
shouted loud enough to be heard indoors, "We want a word
with the Master."

Eamon stood unmoved. "I told you. The Master don't see
no one without an appointment."

"Ah, come on, Eamon!" Nunan's voice was persuasive.
"He will see me. It won't take but a minute. It's important."

Eamon's tone was stubborn. "The Master is having
breakfast."

"I don't mind waiting."

Liam heard a rifle being cocked. "This is your last
warning—"

It was time to intervene. He leaned out of the window.
"What's the trouble, Dominic?"

Nunan tugged off his cap. "Can I have a word with you,
me lord?"

Liam didn't quite trust the young Islander. The immigrants
had proved to be a wild bunch, and Dominic Nunan the

wildest. Nunan had jeered at Liam's request for a conspiracy of silence regarding Bishop Zbigniev of Achill, neither promising nor refusing to keep silent. Liam was still unhappy about the incident. For, if Zbigniev's episcopacy was a fraud, so also was his ordination of young Adrian Walsh. And, if young Adrian's orders were invalid, Barley Cross would be priestless when Father Con went. Liam refused to contemplate the prospect. The village needed someone to marry its brides, comfort its sick, and bury its dead. And, if a handful of citizens, Nunan among them, could be persuaded to keep their mouths shut, there would be no danger of the secret leaking out. Liam sighed. He pitied Kathleen Mulroon, the girl Nunan had married. Several unmarried girls remained in the village, but no more recruits had been sought from Achill. In some ways Liam was not sorry. He said, "Speak up then, Dominic. I'm listening."

Nunan twisted his cap like a bashful gossoon. Liam was not deceived. Dominic Nunan was as bashful as a gin trap.

The Islander said, "It's kind of private, me lord. If I could come inside for a minute?"

Liam caught Eamon Toomey's eye. "Let him in, Eamon. Put him in the parlour. I'll be along in a tic."

The Achill Islander got up out of Celia Larkin's chair when Liam entered the room. Nunan's eyes gleamed like those of a wild animal venturing onto cultivated ground. "I wanted to be first to tell you the news, me lord." Nunan cocked his head to leer at the Lord of Barley Cross. "Doctor Denny says my Kathleen is pregnant!"

Liam stood stiff with shock. Kathleen Nunan was one of the few young wives in the village on whom he had not exercised his droit du seigneur. She had married Nunan on Achill in a ceremony presided over by Bishop Zbigniev, and Liam had not been sure if his droit extended as far as the island. Well, now it didn't matter. Kathleen Nunan pregnant meant there was another male in Barley Cross who could father children, and Liam McGrath need no longer carry his burden alone.

Liam's smile was genuine. "That's great news. Congratulations, Dominic."

Nunan smirked. "I guessed you'd be pleased, me lord, seeing as childer are kind of hard to come by. But it sets us a problem."

Liam raised his eyebrows. "What sort of problem?"

Nunan fiddled with his cap. "I know it's meant to be a secret about how kids are conceived in Barley Cross. But if you want me to spread my new genes around—how am I going to manage it?"

Liam's heart missed a beat. For almost a year, since the expedition to Achill, he and his councillors had prayed that one of Islander Rory MacCormick's bastards might prove fertile. But they hadn't considered how to spread those new genes, should their hopes be fulfilled. Now this youth was dropping the problem right in his lap!

"Well, I can't go about raping the village wives like you can," Nunan pointed out. "I'd get shot, or Kathleen would divorce me. But, if you was to abdicate in my favour—"

The words echoed in Liam's mind, like a highwayman's challenge from the bad days. *Abdicate in his*—! Liam held his face expressionless. This Achill youth had thought it through, and come up with a novel, but logical, solution.

He temporised. "Do you think you could manage the Master's job?"

Nunan shrugged. "I could try."

"Do you fancy being Master?"

Nunan stroked the plush back of a settee. "Reckon I might get used to it."

"What does Kathleen—your wife think about it?"

"Oh—we haven't discussed it yet. But she knows about this droyt lark of yours. I reckon she'd get used to me having it off around the village, like you do."

Liam compressed his lips. Nunan's blunt vernacular left him feeling prosy and old-fashioned. What to do? He dared not ignore the youth's suggestion. Denny Mallon was forever harping on about the need for new genes. If Nunan could provide them, the doctor was going to grab him with both hands. But the Achill youth couldn't be let go at it like a cock in a farmyard. There were conventions. Could Barley Cross support two Masters? Liam cursed inwardly. This sort of thinking should have been done months ago. He would have to talk to Doctor Denny.

He said, "Give me a couple of days, Dominic. We'll work something out."

Dominic Nunan put on his cap. His humility had vanished. He grinned. "Okay, me lord. I can spare you a couple of days."

Liam let it pass. The fellow held the cards. No point in betting yet.

Barley Cross' ruling caucus assembled in Liam's parlour that afternoon. Liam told them of the morning's visitor, and of Nunan's ambitions.

Denny Mallon, M.D., shifted uneasily in his chair. "Young Dominic's telling the truth. I examined his wife this morning. She's pregnant all right."

Four pairs of eyes turned towards Liam McGrath. He flushed. "Don't ask me what to do about it. I got you here so we could talk things over."

Denny Mallon sucked an empty pipe. "Dominic's suggestion has merit. We do need his genes. But he can't donate them like Liam does unless he has Liam's authority."

General Andy McGrath coughed to catch the meeting's attention. "The village wouldn't like that. Liam was chosen by the O'Meara himself to succeed him as Master. Who's going to choose this fellow?"

Kevin Murphy at the other end of the settee to the general studied a bottle of poteen on the floor by his foot. Voice gently mocking, he said, "Andy, let me explain. The council chose Liam. And we chose him because he was the only male in the village who could do for us what the O'Meara had been doing for years. Do I have to spell it out further for you?"

Andy McGrath coloured. "Ah, no, Kevin. I appreciate what you are getting at. But there are a lot of folk in the village what aren't so sophisticated as us council members. We've got to bear them in mind."

"I wonder!" Celia Larkin lowered her knitting. "Still, it would be safer to proceed on Andy's premise. Could we appoint this young man to be deputy to the Master?"

Kevin Murphy choked on a cough.

The schoolmistress eyed the vet acidly. "There is nothing humorous in my proposal, Kevin. Most rulers have deputies."

The vet got his face straight. "No offence, Celia. I appreciate your point. But no lord that I ever read about would have delegated our Liam's particular droit."

Denny Mallon waved a pipe stem. "How about us having two Masters? A sort of duumvirate? There are Roman precedents."

The vet's voice had an edge like a scythe. "Denny, as Andy has pointed out, we are not dealing with sophisticated Romans. The village wouldn't stand for nonsense like that."

The doctor opened a grubby, plastic pouch. He pushed dried grasses into his pipe bowl. "Nonsense or not, Kevin, we need the fellow's blood. Half our genetic pool has been contributed by Liam or Patrick O'Meara, and it ain't healthy. You know the fruits of inbreeding. We are building up a load of trouble for ourselves. We need what Dominic can provide. And he's already told us on what terms he'd be willing to provide it." He turned his head. "No offence, Liam. But this is something I've prayed for since the world went sterile. We can't afford to turn Nunan down."

The Lord of Barley Cross straightened up in his battered armchair. You couldn't dispute the facts of biology. Dominic Nunan had to have the Master's position, if he were to do the Master's job.

Liam made his sacrifice. "I'll resign if you wish, Denny."

Denny Mallon puffed on his pipe, the smoke screen hiding his rueful grimace. "That's an idea, Liam. If the village will accept it. An abdication in favour of young Dominic on health grounds."

Kevin Murphy nodded gravely. "Until the Achill felly has done his duty a few times—then we bring Liam back."

Liam shook his head. Doctor and vet were fools. "You won't get away with that. Dominic Nunan's not the sort of fellow you can push about. Once he's Master, he'll stay Master."

The vet reached down for the bottle. "No need to let him into our plans. Let him worry about what hits him when it happens."

Celia Larkin's needles flashed in a sunbeam. "What health grounds? Liam is as fit as a fiddle."

Much as he disliked the discussion, Liam felt obliged to show some enthusiasm. "I'll catch anything you like," he volunteered. "Measles? Mumps?" He swallowed his irritation. Sometimes, listening to the four of them, you could believe he wasn't even present.

"It would need to be something that got him off Barra Hill," the vet reasoned. "Altitude sickness?"

Denny Mallon lowered his pipe. "That supposed to be a joke? I'll think up something suitable. A nervous breakdown might do. We only want him *hors de combat* until a few of our brides have picked up a different set of chromosomes."

Celia Larkin peered over her spectacles. "And who will promulgate the news to the populace?"

292

The doctor waved his pipe. "Sure, that'll have to be Liam himself. The Master must announce his own abdication, *and* name his successor."

Celia Larkin put down her knitting. "And who's going to persuade the people that Dominic Nunan is fit to be our Lord and Master?"

Denny Mallon shifted uncomfortably. "Sure, they'll accept Liam's word on that matter."

Celia Larkin kept her gaze fixed on the doctor. "Why? The fellow doesn't belong to the village. He's an immigrant from Achill. Why should they accept him?"

Kevin Murphy put down his glass carefully. "Jasus, Celia— hasn't Dinny just said? The Master will choose him, and they'll accept the Master's decision."

The schoolteacher's needles began clicking again. "I doubt it. I very much doubt it. But, if that's the best you men can think up, we'll have to try it."

Liam felt his gorge rising. This cold-hearted crew were planning his removal far too slickly. He said, "Do I announce the abdication from my sickbed? Swathed in bandages? Or waving a crutch? And, incidentally, where do I live after this abdication? The Dooleys have our old cottage."

The vet stooped to top up his glass. "You could move into Nunan's place. Surely the felly won't need *two* homes?"

Andy McGrath coughed. "We'll take you in, Liam. Your ma would be pleased to have you back."

Liam scowled at his stepfather. No doubt Andy McGrath was thinking of the fun he'd have with his grandchildren. Four to a room they'd be sleeping! He got up, anger choking him. He glared at them. "Just a bloody stud bull for you, that's all I've ever been! And now you've no further use for me. Well, thank you for nothing! Just decide what you want me to do, and let me know. I'll try not to disappoint you." He ran from the room.

The vet stared at the doctor and the schoolmistress. "Seems the Master is a wee bit touchy today."

Celia Larkin rolled her knitting round the needles. "Wouldn't you be touchy—being rejected in favour of a hooligan from Achill? We didn't even give him a vote of thanks!"

Denny Mallon seemed to shrivel, sinking even deeper into his plush armchair. He puffed hard on a dying pipe. "Let it be! We've a couple of marriages scheduled for this summer. He should be glad of a vacation."

Liam sat alone at the breakfast table. Michael, stained waistcoat concealed by a green baize apron, hovered, steaming teapot in hand. The servant said, "I am sorry to hear your news, me lord."

Liam kept his face down, concentrating on eggs and rashers. "Does everyone know about it, Michael?"

His man poured tea, then placed the pot on a silver trivet, and pulled a cosy over it. "Your letter of resignation is posted at the gate, sir. And there's a copy on Seamus Murray's wall, and another on the church board."

Liam gulped. It had all happened so quickly. One day he was Master, the next he had notice to quit. Celia must have duplicated his instrument of abdication; Denny Mallon's and the vet's scribbles were illegible. How had he ever fooled himself into thinking he could dominate those three!

"May I say, me lord," Michael added. "The parlour, kitchen, and garden staffs have all asked me to convey their sympathy with your illness, and their regrets at your departure."

"Thank you, Michael." Liam put down his fork. The servant didn't deserve the lie the councillors had manufactured for him. "Doctor Denny says it may cure itself in time, but I've got to rest. If I carry on as Master, he guarantees me a nervous breakdown."

"That would be a pity, sir."

"Dominic Nunan will make a good Master." Liam forced out the words. "He is young. He'll have no favourites, since he is new to the village. And I'm sure he has our welfare at heart. Didn't he choose to become a citizen? Hasn't he volunteered for Fist duty?"

"I'm sure you're right, sir." Michael brushed crumbs from the tablecloth. "Will me lady be down soon?"

Liam met the man's troubled eyes. "She has gone to my mam's already, with the children. She won't be coming back."

"I see, sir. And her things? Shall I be after packing them?"

"She has taken all she wants. The Nunans can have what's left."

"Very good, me lord . . . sir?" Michael hovered, like a butterfly over a flowerbed. "Would it be possible for me to come with ye? I could serve ye down below, just like I've done up here."

Liam swallowed a lump which hadn't come with the breakfast. "There's no room at my mam's, Michael. She can scarcely fit in the four of us."

"I understand, sir." Michael's lip trembled. "May I add a personal comment, sir? You have been a good master to me. It's been like serving the late O'Meara over again. I shall miss you."

Liam pushed away his plate. Food had lost its appeal. He got up. "I'll start putting my things together, Michael, then I'll get off. No use hanging on until the new man arrives." He held out a hand. "You won't see me up here again. Look after my successor."

Michael took his fingers, solemn-faced. "I'll try, me lord."

Liam found a smile. "It's 'Liam' now—not 'my lord,' Michael."

"Yes, sir, Liam. Thank you, me lord."

Liam fled, before control went.

Shirt-sleeved and sweaty, plain Liam McGrath pushed the potato fork into the soil to unearth another clutch of early Arrans. It was his job to lift the praties while his stepfather stayed up at the Fist supervising modifications the new Master required.

A shadow fell across the tines of the fork. He looked up. A man sat a horse on the path bordering the field. Liam shaded his eyes, and recognised the new Lord of Barley Cross. He stuck the fork upright, and went towards the path. "Were you looking for me, Dominic?"

The man on the horse scowled down at him. "I was. And the title is 'Lord' or 'Master.' Take your pick."

Liam wiped earthy hands on his overalls, disguising the hurt. "I see, my lord. Point taken. What can I do for you?"

Dominic Nunan gestured with his thumb. "You can get up to that bloody Fist and warn those servants of mine that there'll be trouble if they don't mend their ways."

Liam hid his surprise. What villainy was Michael up to? He said, "What are they doing, my lord?"

Dominic flicked at the flies with his riding crop, lips twisted in a sneer. "Damned hot down here in the fields. Don't know how you put up with it, man."

Liam ignored the barb. "The servants?" he prompted. "What are they getting up to?"

The horse moved restlessly, and the Lord of Barley Cross jerked hard on the bridle. "It's not what they're doing. It's what they are *not* doing. Cold food. Beds not made. Towels

295

not changed. Can't hear the bell when I ring. No cleaning done. Sudden shortage of decent drink. Chatting with the guards when they should be working. I could go on for hours.''

Liam kept his face straight. "Why not get a new lot of servants?"

"Tried. No one will come."

Liam shrugged. "I don't know what I can do about it, my lord. I have no authority up at the Fist now. They'd take no notice of me."

Dominic Nunan's face reddened. "You mean you refuse to go up there? You know they'd do anything you ask."

Liam grimaced. "Since I abdicated, I have no power over them."

"If I order you up to the Fist will you talk to them?"

Liam shook his head. "No, my lord. Your authority don't cover me that far. If you want me up there, you'd better send your soldiers for me."

The new Lord of Barley Cross jerked his horse's head round, and flicked its rump. "Right—we'll see about that!"

General Andy McGrath came home with a frown. He found his stepson bagging potatoes in the barn. "What have you been saying to the new Master? He came back in a rare old state."

Liam tied the neck of a sack. "He came down here seeking help, but he got none from me. He's the fellow with the power now. Seems that Michael and the staff are giving him the runaround, and he can't stop them. Well, if he can't control his own household, he's not fit to run the village."

Andy McGrath sighed. "Michael's lot are giving him a rough ride."

Liam shovelled potatoes into another sack. "Then let him sort them out himself. We all have problems. But we don't go shouting for help without first trying to sort them out for ourselves."

Andy McGrath picked up a potato, rubbed the dirt from it, and sniffed the skin. "Dominic's been having trouble for a fortnight. He's not had a warm meal nor a good night's sleep in that time. Kathleen is threatening to go home to mam. A cat yowled outside their window most of last night. There was no hot water this morning because the gardener forgot to stoke the furnace before he went home."

Liam grinned. "Jasus, da—they're murdering him!"

296

Andy McGrath didn't smile. He tossed the potato back into Liam's sack. "They'll push him too far. He ordered me to come down here for you, today—with an escort."

Liam stopped shovelling spuds. "What did you say to him?"

"I told him he couldn't order that sort of thing unless you had committed an offence. He said you *had* committed an offence by refusing to help him. I talked him out of it, but he wasn't happy."

Liam leaned the shovel against the barn wall. "Maybe you didn't pick a winner this time, Andy."

His stepfather scratched his head. "Lord love us, son—I didn't pick him in the first place. 'Twas Dinny and Kevin thought it up between them, they being so obsessed with the idea of getting new blood into the village. They never considered what kind of a fellow they were getting it from. For meself, I never trusted that Achill ruffian. But Dinny and Kevin were keen, so I went along with them."

Liam's grin was lopsided. "They caught Celia that way, too." He pulled off his shirt, and headed for the pump. "But she went a bit further to help them." He stuck his head under the pump. His stepfather worked the handle while he soused head and arms. "Writing out those copies of my resignation!" Liam dried himself on an empty sack. Then he clapped his stepfather on the back. "Come on in to supper, da. Let Dominic look for solutions without us."

Andy McGrath was an hour gone on duty the following morning when four horsemen galloped up the lane to Killoo Farm. Liam, in the potato field, recognised the ex-Achill Islanders, led by the new Master.

He shouldered the fork, and trudged along the furrow to meet Dominic Nunan.

The new Master scarcely gave him time to get within earshot.

"Liam McGrath," he shouted, "I have decided that you are an unsettling influence in Barley Cross. While you are around, reminding people of the old days, I can get nothing done. I hereby proclaim you *persona non grata*, and I give you an hour to quit Barley Cross."

Liam almost dropped the fork in his astonishment. "You're joking, Dominic!"

Nunan's face twisted in anger. "I've told you how to address me. And I don't joke."

297

Liam weighed the odds. One man with a potato fork against four horsemen carrying FN rifles. Not that it would come to shooting, but he would have liked a go at their loud-mouth boss if he could have banked on the other three not interfering.

From the side of his eye, Liam saw Eileen come to the farmhouse door with the children. He drew closer to Nunan, and lowered his voice. "Where am I supposed to go?"

The new Master towered over him, face white. "To hell, if you like. I don't care, so long as you get out of Barley Cross."

"An hour doesn't give me much time."

"It's all you're getting. I could walk through your bloody village in five minutes."

"And if I refuse to go?"

"We'll burn your house down—and any house you go to for shelter."

"I have a wife and two children."

"Take them with you. You'll be glad of their company."

Nunan's face loomed before Liam, like a hateful gargoyle. He choked. "Dominic, you're a pure bastard. Just give me the chance, and I'll—"

Dominic Nunan jeered. "Go on! It's a crime to threaten the Master. Say it, and I'll clap you in jail until people forget you ever lived!"

Liam waited until he could see the man clearly. "Can I take anything with me?"

The new Master's eyes roved the farmyard, lighting on a handcart employed to transport light loads to market. "You can take all you can fit on that cart, and no more."

"But I'll need food, clothes . . . a tent . . . two beds at least . . ."

Nunan laughed. "Your problem, man. I've just solved mine. I'll leave Paedar here to keep an eye on you. I've other matters to see to. But I'll be along in an hour to see the back of you."

Liam watched three horsemen gallop down the track to the main road. The new Master had soon started throwing his weight about. Liam contemplated disobedience. But it was Andy McGrath's home that Nunan had threatened to burn. How would Andy react to the threat? It wasn't fair to put his stepfather to the test. Andy McGrath had always respected authority. Dominic Nunan had been legally proclaimed Lord of Barley Cross, and Liam McGrath was a nobody. Liam sighed. He would leave the village sooner than embarrass his stepfather.

He trudged back to the farmhouse. Eileen waited at the door. He said, "I'm sorry, alanna, I seem to have mucked things up. I've got to leave the village. We'd better start packing my things."

Eileen picked up the younger child. "*Your* things?"

Liam ran his hands through the curls of the elder. "You can stay here. Nunan's not banishing you."

Eileen's mouth set in the stubborn O'Connor line. "Where you go, lad, I go, too. And the children."

Liam knew better than to argue. He took her arm. "So be it. Let's pack."

He became aware of a figure at his side. Paedar Fahey, the Islander who had married Nora Kelly, said, "I ain't happy with this, Liam. I think Dominic's gone power crazy. But he'll have me blood if I don't see you off the premises. Can I give ye a lift in any way?"

Liam was about to reject the olive branch, when Eileen thrust past him. She held the child out. "If you'd just mind the kids, Paedar—?"

The ex-Lord of Barley Cross trundled his loaded handcart towards the main road. His wife walked beside him. His two children perched precariously atop a pile of blankets, clothes, pots and pans, folding chairs and a picnic table, towels and nappies, and a basket of food. Astonished faces were pressed to windows as they reached the village.

At the smithy, where a copy of Liam's abdication notice decorated the wall, Seamus Murray came to the door of the forge. Eyes crinkling with the light, he wiped his hands on a leather apron, then waved. "Where are you off to, lad, with your bits and pieces all piled on a barrow?"

Liam put the cart legs down onto the road. He waited to get his breath. "I have to leave the village, Seamus. The new Master has banished me."

The blacksmith leaned against his door frame, and got a clay pipe from his pocket. "And what have ye been up to, to upset the new chap?"

Liam shrugged. "I guess he don't care to have his predecessor hanging around reminding folk of other times."

Seamus Murray found a pouch, and thumbed dried grass

into the bowl of his pipe. "Didn't think you'd knuckle under to that sort of nonsense."

Liam got a fresh grip on the cart handles. "He threatened to burn down my da's house if I didn't leave—and any place else I go to in the village. He gave me an hour to get out."

Seamus Murray stuffed the pipe, unlit, back into his pocket. He gripped the ear of an urchin lingering by the smithy door. "Run and tell Mrs. Murray that I want her here quick. Tell her to put on a coat, and to bring mine too."

The child fled on his errand.

The blacksmith advanced into the roadway. He laid a fist on the shaft of the cart. With a sweep of the other hand, he removed Liam from between the shafts. "Out of the way, me lord." Then he took Liam's place, and stood waiting.

Liam gasped. "Seamus—you can't! I have to go . . ."

Mary Murray came hurrying down the path from the house adjoining the smithy. She wore her best black gabardine, and carried a jacket for her husband. The smith took the jacket, donned it, then picked up the shafts.

"Which way, me lord?"

Liam couldn't find words. He pointed down the street.

Seamus Murray began to push the cart. His wife linked an arm through Eileen McGrath's, and fell in beside her. The urchin who had run the smith's errand was off like a hare.

Sally Corcoran stood in the doorway nursing the child born the day of General Desmond's funeral. Her husband gaped over her shoulder. He called, "What's going on then, Seamus?"

The blacksmith put up a hand to steady one of Liam's children. "Sure, aren't I just giving an old friend a lift to quit the village?"

Charlie Corcoran's eyes bulged. "Quit the village—*Liam*?"

The smith nodded. "Aye. On the new fellow's orders."

"And who's minding the forge?"

Seamus Murray spat. "Sod the forge. I may not be coming back either."

Charlie Corcoran grabbed two coats from behind his front door. He pushed his wife and child into the path, and pulled the door to behind him. "Would ye mind if we came along with ye?"

Seamus Murray heaved the cart into motion. "Sure, and ye'd be welcome, lad."

Charlie Corcoran, his wife and child, formed up behind Eileen McGrath and Mary Murray.

Tom and Biddy O'Connor were waiting at the gate with

Liam's mother. Tom shouted, "Hi, Liam! Weren't we just thinking of a stroll ourselves!" He fell in beside his daughter. Brigit O'Connor pushed an arm through Liam's, and said, "Ye didn't think, now, ye could walk out on yer old ma-in-law?"

Liam's mother said, "If I'd been there, I'd have given that fellow a piece of my mind."

Liam grimaced through moisture that unaccountably glistened in his eyes. At least he wasn't going alone into exile.

The new curate, his too large collar chafing his ears, waited at the church gate. Father Con sat patiently in the wheelchair Tom O'Connor had built for him. As the blacksmith rumbled abreast of them with Liam's handcart, the apprentice priest piped, "Not too fast now, Mr. Murray. Father Con will only grumble if I shake him up."

Villagers were emerging from every door. Liam acknowledged the salutes of the Kennedys, the O'Malleys, the Flanagans, Franky Finegan with his fiddle . . . suddenly, it seemed, the entire population of Barley Cross had decided to follow its ex-Master into exile.

At the end of the street, where the road forked for Barra Hill and the Fist, Seamus lowered the legs of the cart. Down from the Fist came a gentleman wearing a hard hat, and a green baize apron showing under his shiny black topcoat. A crowd of women and a couple of soldiers trooped behind. Eamon Toomey and Sean O'Rourke had their rifles slung, muzzle down.

Michael halted before Liam. He raised his billycock. "Me lord, Liam, with your permission, I will take my place among these friends of yours?"

Before Liam could speak, Eamon Toomey presented himself, and came to a quivering salute. "Beg to report, sir," he began, using the formula drilled into him years back by Sergeant McGrath, "I have relinquished me post up there. I don't find it palatable no longer. Would ye care to reassign me to something a whit more pleasant?"

Liam began to feel dazed. He said, "I don't have any place to reassign you to, Eamon. The new Master has banished me from Barley Cross completely."

Eamon Toomey remained at attention. "Sure we all know that, sir. Could I not act as yer personal bodyguard?"

Liam sighed. Eamon Toomey's loyalty shone like a jewel among brilliants. He said, "If you want to, Eamon. Go ahead. You are my bodyguard."

By now, several of the more mature citizens had seized the

opportunity to rest on the stone wall flanking the Fist road.

Liam said, "Can we spare a few minutes, here, Seamus?"

The blacksmith put his bottom over a shaft, and hoisted a small McGrath onto his shoulders. "Ah—it's as good a spot as any to settle the future of Barley Cross, me lord. Let's wait here 'til the new fellow comes down to see what all the shindig is about."

"That's not what I meant—" Liam began. But it was too late.

Franky Finegan struck up a jig. A space was cleared in the centre of the road for two of Celia Larkin's pupils to exhibit their skill at covering the buckle. On the far verge, several men got down in a circle while one of them dealt hands for poker.

Liam gave up. Barley Cross had its own way of handling emergencies.

The councillors were next out of the Fist. The crowd fell silent at the sight of them. Led by wizened Denny Mallon, they descended Barra Hill like prisoners released after a long sentence. The doctor paused by the tank guarding the Fist approach, and, in a gesture of irritation, struck one of his few remaining sulphur matches on its rusty flank.

Liam could hear his comments.

"Damn the fellow!" The doctor puffed out smoke that smelled like a grass fire. "The impertinence of sacking us!"

Kevin Murphy got to windward. "Buggers as bright as him don't need our advice. I'd have sacked him one meself, had I been twenty years younger!"

Celia Larkin flourished her knitting, her spectacles awry. "So much for your new Master. Goddammit—I wouldn't give him house room!"

Liam grinned. The councillors seemed to have fallen out with Dominic Nunan.

Kevin Murphy made a rude gesture up the hill. "Banishing our Liam and threatening to bring an army from Achill! By God, Andy McGrath will show him, when he learns what's happened."

Dominic Nunan snarled. "I didn't order you to take the whole village with you!"

Liam spread his hands. "I didn't tell anyone to come with me."

Nunan raised his quirt. "Well, you can bloody well tell someone to go back!"

Liam stood, arms down by his sides, fists clenched, a red weal on his cheek. "I can't tell anyone to do anything. I'm not the Master."

Dominic Nunan grinned evilly. "By Christ—if you don't, *I'll* tell them something to upset you and your gang of religious hypocrites. I bet that will move you fast enough!"

Liam knew he referred to Adrian Walsh's lack of genuine orders. He said, "I have your promise on the matter, my lord."

Nunan laughed. "By Christ—you have nothing atall!" He stood on his stirrups. "Listen to me, citizens of Barley Cross. I'll tell you how Liam McGrath has been fooling you. That lad of—"

Liam hurtled at the horseman, grabbed a leg, and heaved. Dominic Nunan toppled sideways off his beast, clutching at Liam, and bringing him to the ground. They rolled in the dust.

"Damn you, let me speak!" The new Master's words expired in a gurgle as Liam squeezed his throat.

"Keep quiet!" Liam panted. "Or you die!"

The crowd formed a ring about the combatants, watching fascinated as their old and new ruler threshed on the road.

Liam released the pressure on Nunan's throat a fraction. "Are you going to keep quiet?"

Dominic Nunan dropped an arm down to his fisherman's boot, and came up with a seal-skinner's knife in his fist.

He grunted, "You asked for this, McGrath!"

The knife took Liam in the thigh. He spasmed, losing his grip on the Achill man's throat. Nunan raised his arm for another stab. Liam grabbed his wrist. They rolled over and over, leaving a trail of blood on the road.

Then Nunan was on top, each man clutching the other's wrist. The knife point quivered an inch above Liam's throat.

Liam couldn't hold the blade back much longer. His leg had gone numb. His shoulder ached from the bruise he had got when Nunan knocked him down.

The new Master of Barley Cross forced the knife lower. "Die, you bastard!" he screamed.

In extremis, Liam shouted, "Eamon!"

From somewhere came the crack of a shot. A cavity opened in the side of Dominic Nunan's head. Blood sprayed over Liam. Nunan's body went limp. The knife clattered onto the tarmac.

Liam pushed the corpse away. He staggered to his feet. Gripping the bleeding leg with one hand, he wiped bits of Dominic Nunan from his face with the sleeve of his other arm. The world was spinning.

"Holy Mother of God! This disgraceful exhibition would never have been allowed in the O'Meara's day!"

The voice was Father Con's. Liam peered through a mist of sweat. The old priest was so blind and deaf, he couldn't possibly appreciate what had happened. But the words rang like an accusation. Liam croaked, "Nor will it be allowed in McGrath's day from now on, Father!"

They buried the mortal remains of Dominic Nunan that afternoon. Most of the villagers stayed away. Father Adrian Walsh officiated, his piping treble faltering over the tremendous words of the burial service.

Then Liam went back to the Fist.

On the morrow the weather turned cool. A mist hid Leckavrea and Loch Corrib. Liam settled a turf on the parlour fire with the sole of the boot on his good leg. A typical Connemara day. Would the villagers have turned out so cheerfully in today's drizzle?

Michael set bottle and glasses on the floor by Kevin Murphy, and withdrew.

Liam turned to face his councillors. Time, now, it was, to come to terms with them. The days of their bullying the Master were over and done. "Well?" he challenged.

Dr. Denny Mallon steepled his fingers, not quite avoiding Liam's eye. "Seems we are back at square one, more's the pity."

Celia Larkin's needles clicked like castanets. "In my opinion, we are well rid of the fellow."

Kevin Murphy grunted as he reached for the bottle. "I don't agree. We mishandled the whole business, and we ought to be ashamed. We have lost the only other stud that ever came our way."

General McGrath coughed. "It ain't so bad as that. There's Katy Nunan's child to be. And, from what I hear, Dominic had his way with a couple of the kitchen staff. There may be hope for us there, too."

Liam could hardly believe his ears. Andy McGrath was beginning to sound like the other three. He said, voice loaded with sarcasm, "Don't any of you want to know what *I* think?"

Kevin Murphy spilled poteen onto the carpet. Denny Mallon lost his pouch down the side of the cushion, and had to search for it. Celia Larkin dropped a stitch, and hoped it was the only one she'd missed.

General McGrath was the first to find his voice. He coughed. "Sure, Liam, me lord, we'd all be glad to hear your opinion."

Liam eased his bandaged leg out in front of him, feeling a savage glee in exhibiting his wound. He raised his stick. "This is no opinion. This is my firm decision. So listen. We lost Dominic Nunan through your incompetence and my foolishness in putting up with it. From now on, I listen to you, and if I don't like what I hear, I ignore it. And, if you don't care for that, you can get yourselves another Master."

Kevin Murphy took a gulp from his glass. "There's no need to go on like that . . . me lord. We all know we made a mistake."

Liam hung on to his temper. "It's the last mistake you'll make with my help."

Doctor Denny found his pouch, and his courage. "I think you are overreacting, Liam. Sure—anyone can slip up."

Liam felt like striking the man. "Slip up? The biggest boob anyone will ever make in the whole wide world, and you call it a slip-up? Why didn't you let the fellow have his harem? Instead of disagreeing, and getting sacked? It was one way of solving our problem. The Master of the Fist is supposed to be a tyrant. We could have put up with a genuine despot for a year or two. I was prepared to go into exile, wasn't I?"

"The village would never have let you go alone."

Liam sighed. "How long do you think they would have stayed with me once it started raining? They wanted a confrontation with Dominic, and you stirred him up to provide one."

Kevin Murphy spread his hands. "Okay, me lord. We were stupid. On behalf of Dinny, Cee, and meself, I apologise. Andy was out back at the time, supervising Dominic's modifications, so he's just an ordinary fool, not a super-bloody fool like the rest of us."

Liam lowered his stick. He felt tired. The leg had begun to ache. "Okay," he admitted. "We were all fools. I shouldn't have shouted for Eamon. But I never dreamt he would shoot to kill."

The vet looked up. " 'Twasn't Eamon that shot him. That fool was still fiddling with his gun when the Nunan felly was dead."

"Not Eamon?" Liam searched their faces. "Then who—?"

" 'Twas Paedar Fahey. Him that married Nora Kelly."

"And I made him sergeant, for saving your life," added Andy McGrath.

Liam choked. Promoting a fool for an act of idiocy! "By

God, if I was his general, I'd sooner have had him shot!"

Celia Larkin said placidly, "Don't let on about that to Paedar. He thinks you're wonderful. As far as that lad is concerned, you've inherited all the old O'Meara charm."

"Though there's little evidence of it today," added the vet.

Liam blinked. One apology, and their short-lived penitence was over. There was no way he was ever going to reform this crafty gang. For good or ill, they, along with Larry Desmond and Patrick O'Meara, had supervised the fortunes of Barley Cross for the last thirty years, and now regarded it as their God-given right. Could Liam McGrath manage without them? Perhaps his stepfather had summed things up accurately. There was Katy Nunan's child to look forward to, and cherish. And maybe one or two more out of the kitchen staff, if rumours were to be believed. He could organise another expedition. Not to Achill. Perhaps out Sligo way. See if any other villages had their Nunan, or McGrath, or O'Meara. Barley Cross might be luckier, next time.

He shook his head. "What baffles me is—no one asked after my health while I was deposed. And me supposed to be heading for a nervous breakdown."

Dr. Denny Mallon sniffed. "Ye've still a thing or two to learn, Liam. On serious matters, such as the Master's health, we have to take the village into our confidence—in a roundabout way, like."

Liam frowned at the doctor. Denny Mallon sounded far too cocky. They were already beginning to manipulate him again. "What do you mean—in a roundabout way?"

Denny Mallon scooped up a pipeful of dried grasses. "Sure, Michael doesn't miss a thing that goes on in here—and we wouldn't have it otherwise."

Liam gaped at the doctor. Michael? His quiet, man-for-all-seasons in collusion with this cunning crew? Did his servant crouch, ear-to-door, during their discussions? With Denny Mallon's tacit approval? And then retail it to confidants in the village?

Liam clutched the arms of his shabby armchair, seeking the feel of something solid. Was there anything in this community of Barley Cross that was as simple as it appeared on the surface?

Faintly, he heard the doctor's voice. "Don't worry about it, Liam. Remember—we all play for the same team!"

Against his will, Liam began to grin.

EDITOR'S INTRODUCTION TO:

THE EYES OF ARGOS
by Harry Turtledove

After the fall of the Roman Empire, Byzantium—the second Roman Empire, based on Constantinople—endured for nearly a thousand years. Much of its strength was built around a navy that won all its battles: it was so successful that it has almost no history. The armies of Byzantium were skilled in military science. Their officers studied textbooks on tactics. One of their writers said, "No commander who has the favor of God and a few regiments of our heavy cavalry need fear much on this earth," and he was nearly right. Byzantium held the remnants of Classical civilization.

Mohammed was born in A.D. 570. By the time he died in 632 he had changed the world. He united the pagan Arab tribes into a formidable army that swept across the Levant and Near East and eventually brought Persia, North Africa, Spain below the line of the olive, and the entire Middle East under the sign of the crescent.

From then on Christian Constantinople was more or less constantly at war with Islam. If that weren't enough, the Western Christians kept sending armies to liberate the Holy Land from the Moslems—but those Crusaders were often as much threat to Constantinople as to their Saracen enemies. Meanwhile the Jurchen tribes—ancestors of modern Turks—kept sweeping in from north and east. Originally pagan, they too embraced Islam, and became the leaders of the Moslems.

The combination of enemies proved to be too much, and mighty Byzantium fell.

Harry Turtledove has a doctorate in Byzantine history. There aren't too many openings for teachers in that field; but he uses his skills by writing of a world in which Mohammed, on one of his frequent trips to Syria, was converted to Christianity and thus never had the revelation of Islam. Here is a story from that world.

There are many ways to dispel the fog of war. Some are more difficult than others.

THE EYES OF ARGOS
Harry Turtledove

The steppe country north of the Danube made Basil Argyros think of the sea. Broad, green, and rolling, it ran eastward seemingly forever, all the way to the land of Serinda, from which, almost eight hundred years before, the great Roman Emperor Justinian had stolen the secret of silk.

The steppe was like the sea in another way. It offered an ideal highway for invaders. Over the centuries, wave after wave of nomads had dashed against the frontiers of the Roman Empire: Huns and Avars, Bulgars and Magyars, Pechenegs and Cumans, and now the Jurchen. Sometimes the frontier defense would not hold, and the barbarians would wash over it, even threatening to storm into Constantinople, the imperial capital.

With a deliberate effort of will, Argyros drew back from the extended nautical metaphor into which he had fallen. What with the motion of his horse beneath him, it was threatening to make the scout commander seasick.

He turned to his companion, a blond youngster from Thessalonike named Demetrios after the city's patron saint. "Nothing so far. Let's ride on a little farther."

Demetrios made a face. "Only if you say so, sir. I don't think the devils are anywhere around. Couldn't we just head back to camp? I could use a skin of wine." Demetrios fit three of the military author Maurice's four criteria for a scout: he was handsome, healthy, and alert. He was not, however, markedly sober.

Argyros, for his part, did not quite pass the first part of Maurice's test. For one thing, his eyebrows grew in a single black bar across his forehead. For another, his eyes were strangely mournful, the eyes of a sorrowing saint in an icon or of a man who has seen too much too soon. Yet he was only in his middle twenties, hardly older than Demetrios.

He said, "We'll go on another half mile. Then if we still haven't found anything, we'll call it a day and turn around."

"Yes, sir," Demetrios said resignedly.

They rode on, the tall grass brushing at their ankles and sometimes rising to tickle their horses' bellies. Argyros felt naked in his long goat's-hair tunic. He wished he had not had to leave his mailshirt behind; the Jurchen were ferociously good archers. But the jingle of the links might have given him away, and in any case the weight of the iron would have slowed his mount.

He and Demetrios splashed across a small stream. There were hoofprints in the mud on the far bank: not the tracks of the iron-shod horses the Romans rode, but those made by the shoeless hooves of steppe ponies.

"Looks like about half a dozen stopped here," Demetrios said. His head swiveled as though he expected all the Jurchen in creation to burst out from behind a bush and ride straight for him.

"Probably their own scouting party," Argyros judged. "The main body of them can't be far behind."

"Let's go back," Demetrios said nervously. He took his bow out of its case, reached over his shoulder for an arrow to set to the string.

"Now I won't argue with you," Argyros said. "We've found what we came for." The two Roman scouts wheeled their mounts and trotted back the way they had come.

The army's hypostrategos—lieutenant general—was a small, hawk-faced man named Andreas Hermoniakos. He grunted as he listened to Argyros' report. He looked sour, but then he always did; his stomach pained him. "Fair enough," he said when the scout commander was through. "A good trouncing should teach these chicken thieves to keep to their own side of the river. Dismissed."

Argyros saluted and left the lieutenant general's tent. A few minutes later, a series of trumpet calls rang out, summoning the army to alert. As smoothly as if it were a drill, men donned mailshirts and plumed helmets; saw to bows and lances, swords and daggers; and took their places for their general's address and for prayer before going into battle.

As was true of so many soldiers, and especially officers, in the Roman army, John Tekmanios was Armenian by blood, though he spoke the Latin-flavored Greek of the army without eastern accent. From long experience, he knew the proper tone to take when speaking to his troops:

309

"Well, lads," he said, "we've beaten these buggers before, on our side of the Danube. Now all that's left is finishing the job over here, to give the barbarians a lesson they'll remember awhile. And we can do it, too, sure as there's hair on my chin." That drew a laugh and a cheer. His magnificent curly whiskers reached halfway down the front of his gilded coat of mail.

He went on, "The Emperor's counting on us to drive these damned nomads away from the frontier. Once we've done it, I know we'll get the reward we deserve for it; Nikephoros, God bless him, is no niggard. He came up from the ranks, you know; he remembers what the soldier's life is like."

Having made that point, Tekmanios used it to lead to another: "Once the battle's won, like I said, you'll get what's coming to you. Don't stop to strip the Jurchen corpses or plunder their camp. You might get yourself and your mates killed, and miss out on spending your bonus money."

Again, he got the tension-relieving laugh he was looking for. He finished, "Don't forget—fight hard and obey your officers. Now join me in prayer that God will watch over us today."

A black-robed priest, his hair drawn back in a bun, joined the general on the portable rostrum. He crossed himself, a gesture Tekmanios and the whole army followed. "*Kyrie eleison*," the priest cried, and the soldiers echoed him: "Lord, have mercy!"

They chanted the prayer over and over. It led naturally to the hymn of the Trisagion—the thrice holy—sung each morning on arising and each evening after dinner: "Holy God, holy mighty one, holy undying one, have mercy on us!"

After the Trisagion usually came the Latin cry of "*Nobiscum Deus!*"—God with us. Tekmanios' priest, though, had imagination. Instead of ending the prayer service so abruptly, he led the army in a hymn composed by that great author of religious poetry St. Mouamet.

"There is no God but the Lord, and Christ is His son," Argyros sang with the rest. St. Mouamet was a favorite of his, and after Paul probably the most zealous convert the church had ever known. Born a pagan in an Arabian desert town, he came to Christianity while trading in Syria, and never went home again. He dedicated his life to Christ, producing hymn after impassioned hymn, and rose rapidly in the church hierarchy. He ended his days as archbishop of New Carthage in distant Ispania. Canonized not long after his death, he was, not surprisingly, venerated as the patron saint of changes.

Once the service was done, the army formed up, each of the three divisions behind the large, bright banner of its merarch. The moirarchs, or regimental commanders, had smaller flags, while the banners of the tagmata—companies— were mere streamers. The tagmata were of varying size, from two hundred to four hundred men, to keep the enemy from getting an accurate estimate of the army's size by simply counting banners. A small reserve force stayed behind to protect the camp and the baggage train.

The horses kicked up clods of earth and a thick cloud of dust. Argyros was glad to be a scout, well away from the choking stuff. The men in the second battle line would hardly be able to breathe after an hour on the move.

The scouts rode ahead, looking for the dust-plume that would betray the Jurchen army, just as their own was being revealed to the enemy. Argyros chewed a handful of boiled barley meal, ate a strip of tough smoked beef. He swigged water from his canteen. From the way Demetrios grinned and smacked his lips when he drank in turn, Argyros suspected that his flask, contrary to orders, held wine. He scowled. Combat was too important a business to undertake drunk.

To give credit where due, the wine did not affect Demetrios' alertness. He was the first to spot the gray-brown smudge against the sky in the northeast. "There!" he shouted, pointing. When several of his comrades were sure they saw it too, a scout raced back to give the word to Tekmanios.

The rest of the party advanced for a closer look at the Jurchen. All the nomad tribes were past masters at spreading out their troops to seem more numerous than they really were. Given over to disorder, they did not fight by divisions and regiments as did civilized folk like the Romans or Persians, but mustered by tribes and clans, only forming their battle lines at the last minute. They also loved to set ambushes, which made careful scouting even more important.

The terrain sloped very gently upward. Squinting ahead to lengthen his sight as much as he could, Argyros spied a group of plainsmen at the top of a low rise: undoubtedly the Roman scouts' opposite numbers. "Let's take them out," he said. "The high ground there will let us see their forces instead of them being able to watch us."

Nocking arrows, the scouts kicked their horses into a trot. The

Jurchen saw them coming and rode out to defend their position, leaving behind a few men to keep observing the Roman army.

The nomads rode smaller horses than their foes. Most of them wore armor of boiled leather instead of the heavier chainmail the Romans favored. Curved swords swung at their sides, but they had more confidence in their horn-reinforced bows.

A Jurchen rose in his stirrups (which were short, plainsman-style) and shot at the Roman scouts. The arrow fell short, vanishing into the tall steppe grass. "Hold up!" Argyros called to his men. "Their bows outrange ours, so we can't possibly hit them from this far away."

"I'm stronger than any damned scrawny Jurchen!" Demetrios shouted back as he let fly. All he accomplished was to waste an arrow.

A horse screamed as a shaft pierced its flank. The beast ran wild, carrying the scout who rode it out of the fight. A moment later a Jurchen clutched at his throat and pitched from the saddle. The Romans raised a cheer at the lucky shot.

An arrow flashed past Argyros' ear with a malignant, wasplike buzz. He heard someone grunt in pain close by. From the inspired cursing that followed, he did not think the wound serious. Along with the rest of the scouts, he shot as fast as he could. Forty arrows made a heavy quiver, but they were spent so fast in combat.

The Jurchen also filled the air with hissing death. Men and horses fell on both sides. The Romans bored in, knowing their mounts and armor would give them the edge in a hand-to-hand fight. Argyros expected the plainsmen to break and run like a lump of quicksilver smashed with the fist. Instead they drew their sabers, standing fast to protect the little group that still stood on the rise.

One of those nomads—an older man, his hair almost white—was holding a long tube to his face; its other end pointed toward the main Roman force. Argyros would have crossed himself had he not held his sword in his right hand. It looked as though some Jurchen wizard had invented a spell for projecting the evil eye.

Then he had no attention to spare for the wizard, if that was what he was. A nomad in a sheepskin coat and fox-fur hat was slashing at his face. He turned the stroke awkwardly, cut down at the Jurchen. The plainsman leaned away. He grinned at his narrow escape, teeth white in a swarthy face made darker still by grease and dirt.

They traded blows for a minute or so, neither able to hurt the other. Then out of the corner of his eye Argyros saw a tall lance bearing seven oxtails coming over the rise: the standard of the Jurchen army. "Break off!" he shouted to the rest of the scouts. "Break off, before they're all on top of us!"

Unlike the Franco-Saxons of northern Gallia and Germany, the Romans did not make war for the sake of glory. They felt no shame in pulling back in the face of superior force. Their opponents, who had been hard-pressed, were glad enough to let them go.

Argyros looked round to make sure all his surviving men had succeeded in disengaging. "Demetrios, you fool, come back!" he screamed. The scout from Thessalonike had succeeded in breaking through the picket line of Jurchen and, perhaps buoyed by the grape into thinking himself invincible, was charging single-handed at the little group of nomads that included the man with the tube.

His folly got what folly usually gets. He never came within fifty yards of the Jurchen; their arrows killed him and his mount in quick succession.

There was nothing whatever Argyros could do to avenge him, not with the whole nomad army coming up. He led the scouts off to another small rise, though not one with as good a view of the upcoming battlefield as the one the Jurchen held. He sent one of his men to report the situation to Tekmanios, and another to bring back more arrows. He hoped the fellow would return before the plainsmen took too great an interest in his little band.

Whenever he got the chance, he kept an eye on the Jurchen scouting party, which was now a good mile away. Riders went back and forth in a steady stream. Squint though he would, he could not quite make out the nomad with the tube. He frowned. He had never seen anything like that before, which automatically made it an object of suspicion.

The scouts cheered. Argyros' head whipped around. The Roman army was coming into sight. Seen from the side, as the scouts did, Tekmanios' plan was plain. He had a couple of tagmata on the right wing riding slightly ahead of the rest, concealing a strong force behind them that would dart out to outflank the Jurchen once the two armies were engaged. From the nomads' angle of view, the outflankers should have been invisible.

But they were not. Maneuvering without the neat evolutions of the Roman cavalry, but with great rapidity, the

Jurchen shifted horsemen to the left side of their line. "They've spotted the screen!" Argyros exclaimed in dismay. "Gregory, off to Tekmanios, fast as your horse will take you!"

The scout galloped away, but battle was joined before he reached the general. The Roman outflankers never got a chance to deploy; they came under such heavy attack that both they and a detachment of troops from the second line had all they could do to keep the Jurchen from flanking them.

Nothing if not resourceful, Tekmanios tried to extend the left end of his line to overlap the nomads' right. The Jurchen khan, though, might have been reading his mind. The attempt was countered before it had fairly begun. It was not that the nomads outnumbered the Roman forces; they did not. But they seemed to be spotting every move as fast as Tekmanios made it.

The scout returned with the arrows. "I'm just as glad to be here," he said, tossing bundles of shafts from his saddlebags. "They're too fornicating smart for us today."

A horn call sounded over the din of battle: the order to retreat. Withdrawal was also risky; it turned with such ease to panic and rout. Against the nomads it was doubly dangerous. Unlike the Romans and Persians, the plainsmen, more mobile than their foes, liked to press pursuit to the limit in the hope of breaking the opposing army.

Even if he had been beaten, though, Tekmanios knew his business. In a retreat it mattered less for the Jurchen to be able to anticipate his movements; they were obvious anyway. His goal was simply to keep his forces in some kind of order as they fell back to their camp. And they, recognizing holding together as their best hope, obeyed his orders more closely than they would have in victory.

With the Jurchen between them and their countrymen, the Roman scouts swung wide of the running fight. Away from landmarks familiar to him, Argyros steered by the sun. He was surprised to notice how low in the west it had sunk. At last he spotted a line of willows growing along a riverbank. They were also visible from camp. "Upstream," he said, pointing.

The scouts were the first troops to reach the camp: not surprising, for they did not have to fight their way back. The men of the tagmata guarding the baggage train crowded round them, firing anxious questions. They cried out in alarm when Argyros and his comrades gave them the bad news. Then, as they were trained to do, they hitched their oxen to the wagons and moved the wains into place behind the camp ditch to serve as a barricade against arrows.

That work, in which the scouts lent a hand, was not finished when the Roman army, still harassed by the Jurchen, drew near. Several oxen were shot and had to be killed with axes before their rampaging upset the wagons to which they were yoked.

Tagma by tagma, the Roman cavalry entered the campsite by way of the four gaps in the ditch. The companies that held off the nomads while their comrades reached safety scattered caltrops behind them to discourage pursuit to the gates. Then they too went inside, just as the sun finally set.

That night and the next three days were among the most unpleasant times Argyros ever spent. The moans of the wounded and the howls and shouts of the Jurchen made sleep impossible, and little showers of randomly aimed arrows kept falling into the camp until dawn.

As soon as it was light, the nomads tried to rush the Roman position. Concentrated archery drove them back. They drew out of range and settled down to besiege the encampment.

Andreas Hermoniakos helped lift the Romans' spirits. He went from one tagma to the next, saying, "Good luck to them. We're camped by water and we have a week's worth of food in the wagons. What will the Jurchen be eating before long?"

The question was rhetorical, but someone shouted, "Lice." The filthiness of the nomads was proverbial.

The lieutenant general chuckled grimly. "Their bugs won't feed even the Jurchen more than a couple of days. Eventually they'll have to go back to their flocks." So it proved, though the plainsmen persisted a day longer than Hermoniakos had guessed.

After scouting parties confirmed that the nomads really had withdrawn, Tekmanios convened an officers' council in his tent to discuss the Romans' next move. "It galls me to think of going back to the Danube with my tail between my legs, but the Jurchen—may Constantinople's patron St. Andreas cover their khan with carbuncles—might have been standing with their ears to my mouth as I gave my orders. One more battle like that and we won't have an army left *to* take back to the Danube."

"They shouldn't have been able to read our plan that well," Constantine Doukas grumbled. He had commanded the right meros, the one whose screening force and flankers the nomads had discovered. "They would have had to be right on top of us to see anything amiss. The devil must have been telling the khan what we were up to."

Hermoniakos looked down his long, straight nose at the grousing merarch. "Some people blame the devil to keep from owning up to their own shortcomings."

Doukas reddened with anger. Argyros normally would have sided with the lieutenant general. Now, though, he stuck up his hand and waited to be recognized; he was very junior in this gathering. Eventually Tekmanios' attention wandered down to the far end of the table. "What is it, Basil?"

"The devil is more often spoke of than seen, but this once I think His Excellency Lord Doukas may be right," Argyros said. That earned a hard look from Hermoniakos, who had been well disposed toward him until now. Sighing, he plunged ahead with the story of the tube he had seen in the hands of the white-haired Jurchen. "I thought at the time it had to do with the evil eye," he finished.

"That's nonsense," one of the regimental commanders said. "After our prayers before the battle and the blessing of the priest, how could any foul heathen charm harm us? God would not permit it."

"God ordains what He wills, not what we will," Tekmanios reproved. "We are all of us sinners; perhaps our prayers and purifications were not enough to atone for our wickedness." He crossed himself, his officers imitating the gesture.

"Still, this is a potent spell," Doukas said. The commanders around him nodded. Trained in Aristotelean reasoning, he reached a logical conclusion: "If we do not find what it is and how it works, the barbarians will use it against the Roman Empire again."

"And once we do," Tekmanios said, "we can bring it to the priest for exorcism. Once he knows the nature of the magic, he will be better able to counteract it."

The general, all the officers, looked expectantly toward Argyros. He realized what they wanted of him, and wished he had had the sense to keep his mouth shut. If Tekmanios had it in mind for him to kill himself, why not just hand him a knife?

"Cowardly wretch!" Andreas Hermoniakos exploded when Argyros came to him the next morning. "If you disobey your general's orders, it will be the worse for you."

"No, sir," the scout commander said, speaking steadily in spite of the heads that turned to listen. "It will be the worse for me to follow them. To do so would be no less than suicide, which is a mortal sin. Better to suffer my lord Tekmanios' anger awhile in this world than the pangs of hell for eternity in the next."

"You think so, eh? We'll see about that." Argyros had never realized what a nasty sneer the lieutenant general had. "If you won't do your duty, by the saints, you don't deserve your rank. We'll find another leader for that troop of yours, and let you find out how you like serving him as his lowest-ranking private soldier."

Argyros saluted with wooden precision. Hermoniakos glared at him for close to a minute, his hands curling into fists. "Get out of my sight," he said at last. "It's only because I remember you were once a good soldier that I don't put stripes on your worthless back."

Argyros saluted again, walked away. Soldiers stepped aside as he went past. Some stared after him, others looked away. One spat in his footprint.

The line of horses was only a couple of minutes away from the lieutenant general's tent, but somehow, in the mysterious way news has of traveling through armies, word of Argyros' fall got there before him. The horseboys gaped at him as they might have at the corpse of a man blasted by lightning. Ignoring that, he mounted his horse without a word and rode to the tent of Justin of Tarsos, until a few minutes ago his aide and now, presumably, his commander.

Justin turned red when he saw Argyros coming, and redder still to receive his salute. "What are your orders for me, sir?" Argyros asked tonelessly.

"Well, sir, uh, Basil, uh, soldier, why don't you take Tribonian's place in the eastern three-man patrol? His wound still pains him too much for him to sit a horse."

"Yes, sir," Argyros said, his voice still dead. He wheeled his horse and rode out to the eastern gate of the camp, where the other two scouts would be waiting for him.

Having made up the patrol roster, he knew who they would be: Bardanes Philippikos and Alexander the Arab. Justin had been kind to him; both were steady, competent men, though Alexander did have a ferocious temper when he thought himself wronged.

It was plain Argyros' presence made them nervous. Bardanes'

317

hand twitched in the beginning of a salute before he jerked it down to his side. And Alexander asked, "Where to, sir?"

"You don't call me 'sir'; I call you 'sir.' And you tell me where to go."

"I've wanted to do that for weeks," Bardanes said. But he spoke without malice, using the feeble joke to try to get rid of the tension he felt. To meet him halfway, Argyros managed the first smile since his demotion.

Still, it was the quietest patrol on which he had ever gone, at least at first. Bardanes and Alexander were too wary of him to direct many words his way, and his being there kept them from talking between themselves about what they most wanted to: his fall.

Bardanes, the more forward of the two, finally grasped the nettle. The camp had long vanished behind them; there was no evidence of the Jurchen. The three horsemen could not have been more alone. And so Argyros was not surprised when Bardanes asked, "Begging your pardon, but what was it you fell out with the lieutenant general over?"

"I made a mistake at the officers' meeting," Argyros replied. He tried to leave it at that, but Bardanes and Alexander were waiting expectantly, so he went on, "I showed Hermoniakos to be in the wrong for taking Constantine Doukas to task. After that, I suppose all I would have had to do was blink at the wrong time and Hermoniakos would have come down on me."

"That is the way of things when you mix in the quarrel of men above your station," Alexander said with Arab fatalism. "Whether the bear beats the lion or the lion the bear, the rabbit always loses."

"Lions and bears," Bardanes snorted. "A damn shame, if you ask me."

"No one did," Argyros said.

"I know," Bardanes said cheerfully. "Another damn shame they didn't break some other officers I could name instead of you. There's more than one I owe plenty to, and I'd enjoy getting some of my own back. You, though—well, shit, you're a hard-nosed bastard, aye, but I can't deny you're fair."

"Thank you for that much, anyhow."

"Don't mention it. It's as much as we can hope for from an officer, and more than we usually get. You'll find out."

They gradually drew near another treelined creek, a good spot for a band of Jurchen to be lying in ambush. Bardanes and Alexander both unconsciously looked in Argyros' direction; old habits died hard.

"Let's split up," he said, accepting that in their eyes he still held rank. It warmed him for what he was about to do, but only a little. He went on, "You two head down to the south end of the stand. Remember to stay out of arrow range. I'll go north. We'll all ford the stream and meet on the other side."

The other two scouts nodded and took their horses downstream. Neither looked back at Argyros; their attention was on the trees and whatever might be lurking among them. As he had told them he would, he rode north. He splashed over to the eastern side of the stream. But he did not turn back to meet the other Romans. Instead he kept heading northeast at a fast trot.

He could imagine the consternation Alexander and Bardanes would feel when they came to the rendezvous point and found he was not there. The first thing they would do, no doubt, would be to race back to the western bank of the creek, to see if he had been waylaid there.

When they discovered he had not, they would follow his tracks. They would have to. He wondered what they would do when they saw the direction he was taking. He did not think they would follow him. He was riding straight toward the Jurchen.

Even if they did, it would not matter. By then he would have a lead of half an hour and several miles: plenty of time and distance to confuse his trail. In the end, his erstwhile companions would have only one choice—to go back to John Tekmanios and report he had deserted.

Which was only fair, because that was exactly what he intended to do.

The biggest worry, of course, was that the first Jurchen he met would shoot him on sight. But when he came riding up openly, one hand on the reins and the other high in the air, the nomad horseman was bemused enough to decide that taking him into camp would be more interesting than using him for target practice. He was not, however, bemused enough to keep from relieving Argyros of his bow, sword, and dagger. The Roman had expected that, and did not resist.

The tents of the plainsmen sprawled in disorderly fashion over three times the ground the Roman camp occupied, although Argyros thought the Jurchen fewer in number. The black tents themselves were familiar: large, round, and made of felt. The Romans had borrowed the design from the plains-men centuries ago.

Men walked here and there, clumping about in their heavy boots. The nomads spent so much time on horseback that they were awkward on the ground, almost like so many birds. They stopped to eye Argyros as the scout brought him in. He was getting tired of people staring at him.

The khan's tent was bigger than the rest. The oxtail stan-dard was stuck in the ground in front of it. Argyros' captor shouted something in the musical Jurchen tongue, of which the Roman knew nothing except a couple of foul phrases. The tent flap drew back and two men came out.

One was plainly the khan; he carried the same aura of authority Tekmanios bore. He was a small, stocky man in his mid-forties, narrow-eyed and broad-faced like most of the nomads, but with a nose with surprising arch to it. A scar seamed his right cheek. His beard was sparse; he let the few hairs on his upper lip grow long and straggle down over his mouth, which was thin and straight as a sword cut.

He listened to the Jurchen who had first encountered Argyros, then turned to the Roman. "I am Tossuc. You will tell me the truth." His Greek was harsh but understandable.

Argyros dipped his head. "I will tell you the truth, O mighty khan."

Tossuc made an impatient gesture over the front of his tunic. The garment was of maroon velvet, but of the same cut as the furs and leathers the rest of the Jurchen wore: open from top to bottom, fastened with three ties on the right and one on the left. The khan said, "I need to hear no Roman flattery. Speak to me as to any man, but if you lie I will kill you."

"Then he will not speak to you as to any other man," chuckled the Jurchen who had accompanied the khan out of his tent. His Greek was better than Tossuc's. He was white-haired and, rare among the nomads, plump. His face some-how lacked the hardness that marked most of his people. The Roman thought he was the man who had had the tube that caused his present predicament, but had not come close enough during the fighting to be sure.

Seeing Argyros' gaze shift to him, the plainsman chuckled again and said, "Do not place your hope in me, Roman. Only you can save yourself here; I cannot do it for you. I am but the shaman of the clan, not the khan."

"You also talk too much, Orda," Tossuc broke in, which seemed to amuse Orda mightily. The khan gave his attention back to Argyros. "Why should I not tie you between horses and rip you apart for a spy?"

Ice walked up Argyros' back. Tossuc was not joking; unlike his shaman, the Roman did not think he could joke. The ex-commander of scouts said, "I am no spy. Would a spy be fool enough to ride straight to your camp and offer himself up to you?"

"Who knows what a Roman spy would be fool enough to do? If you are no spy, why are you here? Quick, now; waste no time making up falsehoods."

"I have no falsehoods to make up," Argyros replied. "I am—I was—an officer of scouts; some of your men will have seen me, and can tell you it is so. I told the Roman lieutenant general he was wrong in a council, and showed him it was true. As reward, he took away my rank. What was I to do?"

"Kill him," Tossuc said at once.

"No, because then the other Romans would kill me too. But how can I serve the Empire after that? If I join you, I can gain revenge for the slight many times, not just once."

The khan rubbed his chin, considering. Orda touched his sleeve, spoke in the nomad tongue. He nodded, short and sharp. The shaman said, "Will you swear by your Christian God that you speak the truth?"

"Yes," Argyros said. He crossed himself. "In the name of the Father, the Son, and the Holy Spirit, by the Virgin and all the saints, I swear I have left the Romans after my quarrel with Andreas Hermoniakos, the lieutenant general."

Orda heard him out, then said to Tossuc, "His truth is not certain, Khan, but it is likely. Most of these Christians are too afraid of this hell of theirs to swear such an oath wantonly."

"Fools," Tossuc grunted. "Me, I fear nothing, in this world or the next." It was not meant as a boast; had it been, Argyros would have paid no attention to it. Spoken as a simple statement of fact, though, it commanded belief—and the Roman knew only too well he was not without fear himself, for the khan inspired it in him.

"Maybe it is as you say," Tossuc said at last. "If it is, you will not mind telling all you know of the Roman army." He bowed with a mocking irony more sophisticated than anything Argyros had thought to find in a nomad, waved for the Roman to precede him into his tent.

321

"Do not step on the threshold," Orda warned. "If you do, you will be put to death for the sin. Also, as long as you are among us, do not piss inside a tent, or touch a fire with a knife, or break a bone with another bone, or pour milk or any other food out on the ground. All these things offend the spirits, and only your blood will wash away the offense."

"I understand," Argyros said. He had heard of some of the Jurchen customs, just as the plainsmen knew something of Christianity. A couple, though, were new to him. He wondered nervously if Orda had left anything out.

The Roman had never been in the tent of a nomad chief; its richness surprised him. He recognized some of the displayed wealth as booty from the raid across the Danube: church vessels of gold and silver, hangings of cloth-of-gold and rich purple, bags of pepper and cinnamon and scarlet dye.

But some of the riches the Jurchen had produced for themselves. The thick wool carpets, embroidered with stylized animals or geometric shapes, would have sold for many nomismata in the markets at Constantinople. So would Tossuc's gold-inlaid helmet and his gem-encrusted sword, scabbard, and bow case. And the cushions, stuffed with wool and straw, were covered in silk.

Except for a looted chair, there was no wooden furniture. The life of the Jurchen was too mobile for them to burden themselves with large, bulky possessions.

Tossuc and Orda sat cross-legged with a limberness that Argyros, years younger than either, could not match. The khan began firing questions at him: How big was the Roman army? How many horses did it have? How many men were in the first meros? In the second? The third? What supplies did the baggage wagons carry?

On and on the interrogation went. After each of Argyros' replies, Tossuc would glance toward Orda. The Roman could not read the shaman's flat, impassive face. He knew he was not lying; he hoped Orda did too.

Apparently he did, for at last Tossuc fell silent. The khan reached over his shoulder for a jar of wine, another bit of plunder from the Empire. He drank, belched, and passed the jar to Orda. The shaman took a pull, then belched even louder than Tossuc had. He offered Argyros the wine. The Roman drank in turn, saw both nomads intently watching him. The belch he managed was paltry next to theirs, but enough to satisfy them. They smiled and slapped his back. Tentatively, at least, he was accepted.

After riding with the Jurchen for a couple of weeks, Argyros found himself coming to admire the nomads he had fought. It was no wonder, he thought, that they raided the Roman frontier districts whenever they saw the chance. Living as they did on the yield of their herds alone, never stopping to plant a crop or settle down, they provided themselves with food and shelter, but no more. Luxuries had to come from their sedentary neighbors, whether through trade or by force.

The Roman came to see why the plainsmen judged wasting food a capital crime. The Jurchen ate anything they came across: horsemeat, wolves, wildcats, rats—all went into the stewpot. Along with other imperial troopers, he had called them louse-eaters, but he did not think it as anything but a vile name until he saw it happen. It sickened him, but also made him understand the harsh life that made the nomads the soldiers they were.

For, man for man, they were the finest warriors Argyros had ever met. He had known that for years; now he saw why it was so. They took to the bow at the age of two or three, and began riding at the same time. And herding and hunting and struggling to get enough to eat merely to stay alive hardened them in a way no civilized man could match.

He was glad he was a good enough archer and horseman not to disgrace himself among them, though he knew he was not equal to their best. And his skill at wrestling and with the dagger won him genuine respect from the Jurchen, who had less occasion than the Romans to need the tricks of fighting at close quarters. After he had thrown a couple of plainsmen who challenged him to find out what he was made of, the rest treated him pretty much as one of themselves. Even so, he never lost the feeling of being a dog among wolves.

That alienation was only strengthened by the fact that he could only speak with the few nomads who knew Greek. The Jurchen speech was nothing like the tongues he had already learned: along with his native language, he could also speak a couple of Latin dialects and a smattering of Persian. He tried to pick it up, but the going was slow.

To make matters worse, Tossuc had little time for him. Planning each day's journey and keeping peace among his people—who quickly turned quarrelsome when they drank—

kept the khan as busy as any Roman provincial governor. And so Argyros found himself seeking out the company of Orda the shaman more and more often. Not only did he speak better Greek than any of the other plainsmen, his mind also ranged further than theirs from the flocks and the chase.

Constantinople, the great capital from which Roman emperors had ruled for almost a thousand years, was endlessly fascinating to the shaman. "Is it really true," he would ask, "that the city is almost a day's ride across, with walls that reach the clouds and buildings with golden ceilings? I've heard tribesmen who visited the city as envoys to the imperial court speak of these and many other wonders."

"No city could be that big," Argyros replied, sounding more certain than he was. He was from Serrhes, a town in the province of Strymon in the Balkans, and had never seen Constantinople. He went on, "And why would anyone build walls so high the defenders could not see their foes down on the ground?"

"Ah, now that makes sense." Orda nodded in satisfaction. "You have on your shoulders a head. Now what of the golden ceilings?"

"It could be so," Argyros admitted. Who knew what riches could accumulate in a town unsacked for a millennium?

"Well, I will not tell Tossuc," Orda laughed. "It would only inflame his greed. Here, have some kumiss and tell me more of the city." All through the Empire, even here on the plains beyond its border, Constantinople was *the* city.

Argyros took the skin of fermented mare's milk from the shaman. Drinking it, he could understand why Tossuc so relished wine. But it did make a man's middle glow pleasantly. The nomads loved to drink, perhaps because they had so few other amusements. Even the Roman, whose habits were more moderate, found himself waking up with a headache as often as not.

One evening he drank enough to poke a finger at Orda and declare, "You are a good man in your way, but eternal hellfire will be your fate unless you accept God and the true faith."

To his surprise, the shaman laughed until he had to hold his belly. "Forgive me," he said when he could speak again. "You are not the first to come to us from the Romans; sooner or later, every one speaks as you just did. I believe in God."

"You worship idols!" Argyros exclaimed. He pointed toward the felt images of a man on either side of the doorway into Orda's tent, and to the felt udders hanging below them. "You offer these lifeless, useless things the first meat and milk from every meal you take."

"Of course I do," Orda said. "The men protect the men of the clan; the udders are the guardians of our cattle."

"Only the one God—Father, Son, and Holy Spirit, united in the Trinity—gives true protection."

"I believe in one god," the shaman said imperturbably.

"How can you say that?" Argyros cried. "I have seen you invoke spirits and take omens in all manner of ways."

"There are spirits in everything," Orda declared. When Argyros shook his head, the shaman chuckled. "Wait until morning, and I will show you."

"Why wait? Show me now, if you can."

"Patience, patience. The spirit I am thinking of is a spirit of fire, and sleeps through the night. The sun will wake it."

"We will see," Argyros said. He went back to his own tent and spent much of the night in prayer. If God had cast demons from men into the Gadarene swine, surely He would have no trouble banishing a heathen shaman's fire-spirit.

After breakfasting on goat's milk, cheese, and sun-dried meat, the Roman tracked down Orda. "Ah, yes," Orda said. He pulled up some dried grass, set it in the middle of a patch of barren ground. The nomads were always careful of fire, which could spread over the plains with devastating speed. More than Orda's talk of the night before, that caution made Argyros thoughtful. The shaman thought he could do what he had claimed.

Nevertheless, Argyros kept up his bold front. "I see no spirits. Perhaps they are still sleeping," he said, echoing Elijah's gibe to the false priests of Baal.

Orda did not rise to the bait. "The spirit dwells in here," he said. From one of his many pockets he drew out a disk of clear crystal—no, it was not quite a disk, being much thinner at the edges than in the center. It was about half as wide as the callused palm of the shaman's hand.

The Roman expected an invocation, but all Orda did was to stoop and hold the piece of crystal a few digits in front of the dry grass, in a line between it and the sun. "If it is supposed to be a fire-spirit, aren't you going to touch the crystal to the tinder?" Argyros asked.

"I don't need to," the shaman answered. Blinking, the Roman came round for a better look; this was like no sorcery he had ever heard of. When his shadow fell on the crystal, Orda said sharply, "Stand aside! I told you last night, the spirit needs the sun to live."

Argyros moved over a pace. He saw a brilliant point of light at the base of a yellow, withered blade of grass. "Is that what you call your spirit? It seems a trifling thing to—"

He never finished his sentence. A thin thread of smoke was rising from the grass, which had begun to char where the point of light rested. A moment later, the clump burst into flames. The Roman sprang away in alarm. "By the Virgin and her Son!" he gasped. Triumph on his face, Orda methodically stamped out the little fire.

Argyros felt about to burst with questions. Before he could ask any of them, a shouted order drew him away from the shaman. A nomad used many gestures and a few words of Greek to set him repairing bird nets made of rawhide strips. By the time the plainsman was finished telling him what to do, Orda had gone off to talk with someone else.

As he worked, the Roman tried to puzzle out why his prayers had failed. The only answer he could find was that he was too great a sinner for God to listen to him. That gave him very cold comfort indeed.

It was evening before he finally got another chance to talk with the shaman. Even after most of a day, he was shaken by what he had seen, and gulped down great swigs of kumiss before he nerved himself to ask Orda, "How did you find that that spirit lived in the crystal?"

"I was grinding it into a pendant for one of Tossuc's wives," Orda answered. Argyros had not met any Jurchen women; the khan's raiding party had left them behind with a few men and most of their herds, for the sake of moving faster. The shaman went on, "I saw the little spot of light the fire-spirit makes. Then I did not know its habits. I put the bright spot on my finger, and burned it. The spirit was merciful, though; it did not consume me altogether."

"And you still claim to believe in one god?" Argyros shook his head in disbelief.

"There are spirits in all things," Orda said, adding pointedly, "as you have seen. But the one god is above them. He gives good and evil to the world. That is enough; he does not need prayers or ceremonies. What do words matter? He sees into a man's heart."

The Roman's eyes widened. That was a subtler argument than he had expected from a nomad. He took another long pull at the skin of kumiss—the more one had, the better the stuff tasted—and decided to change the subject. "I know why you use that fig—figure of speech," he said accusingly, punctuating his words with a hiccup.

"And why is that?" The shaman was smiling again, in faint contempt. He had matched Argyros drink for drink, and was no more than pleasantly drunk, while the Roman was acting more and more fuddled.

"Because you are like Argos Panoptes in the legend." After a moment, Argyros realized he was going to have to explain who Argos Panoptes was; Orda, after all, had not enjoyed the benefits of a classical education.

"Argos had eyes all over his body, so he could see every which way at the same time. You must have learned some of the magic that made him as he was." He told how he had led the Roman forces who had tried to attack Orda and the Jurchen scouting party on their little rise during the battle. "Wherever you pointed that tube, you seemed to know just what the Romans were going to do. It must have been a spell for reading the officers' minds."

The shaman grinned, in high good humor now. "Your first guess was better. I do have these eyes of Argos you were talking about." His sibilant accent made the name end with a menacing hiss.

Argyros started to cross himself, checked the gesture before it was well begun. Even without Orda's remarks, the church vessels Tossuc had stolen showed how little use the Jurchen had for Christianity. And no wonder—the Empire used religious submission as a tool for gaining political control. Now that he was living with the nomads, the Roman did not want to antagonize them. But he felt a chill of fear all the same. He had always thought of Argos as a character from pagan legend, and from ancient legend at that. To conceive of him as real, and as still existing thirteen centuries after the Incarnation, rocked the foundations of Argyros' world.

Shivering, the Roman said, "Let me have the kumiss again, Orda." But when the Jurchen shaman passed him the skin, he almost dropped it.

"Aiee! Careful! Don't spill it," the shaman exclaimed as Argyros fumbled. "Here, give it back to me. I won't waste it, I promise."

327

"Sorry." The Roman still seemed to be having trouble getting control of the leather sack. Finally, shaking his head in embarrassment, he handed it to Orda. The shaman tilted it up and emptied it, noisily smacking his lips.

"Tastes odd," he remarked, a slight frown appearing on his face.

"I didn't notice anything," Argyros said.

"What do you know about kumiss?" Orda snorted.

They talked on for a little while. The shaman started to yawn, checked himself, then did throw his mouth open till his jaw creaked. Even in the flickering lamplight, his pupils shrank almost to pinholes. He yawned again. As his eyelids fluttered, he glared at Argyros in drowsy suspicion. "Did you—?" His chin fell forward onto his chest. He let out a soft snore as he slumped to the carpet.

The Roman sat motionless for several minutes, until he was certain Orda would not rouse. He rather liked the shaman, and hoped he had not given him enough poppy juice to stop his breathing. No—Orda's chest continued to rise and fall, though slowly.

When Argyros saw the nomad was deeply drugged, he got to his feet. He moved with much more sureness than he had shown a few minutes before. He knew he had to hurry. As shaman, Orda gave the Jurchen—and their horses—such doctoring as they had. A plainsman might come to his tent at any hour of the night.

Several wicker chests against the far wall of the tent held the shaman's possessions. Argyros began pawing through them. He appropriated a dagger, which he tucked under his tunic, and a bow case and a couple of extra bowstrings. As soon as he was done with a chest, he stuffed Orda's belongings back into it; that way a visitor might, with the Virgin's aid, merely reckon the shaman too drunk asleep to be wakened.

Half of Orda's gear was for sorcery of one kind or another. Argyros wanted to take much of it with him to examine when he had the chance, but he was too pressed for time and too leery of magic he did not understand.

There! That was the tube he had seen Orda wielding against the Romans. He had thought it made of metal, but it turned out to be black-painted leather over a framework of sticks. Sure enough, there were two Argos eyes, one at either end, glassily reflecting the light of the lamps back at him. Shuddering, he stuck the tube next to the knife, draped his tunic to hide the bulge as best he could, and sauntered out of the shaman's tent.

His heart was pounding as he approached the long line of tethered horses. "Who goes?" a sentry called, holding up a torch to see.

Argyros walked toward him, a grin on his face. He held up the bow case. "Buka on the southern patrol forgot this. Kaidu rode in to sleep and told me to fetch it." He spoke in a mixture of Greek and the few words of the plains speech that he had.

After several repetitions and a good deal of pantomime, the sentry understood. Argyros was ready to go for his knife if the Jurchen disbelieved him. But the nomads had used him for such menial tasks before, and Buka was not renowned for brains. The watchman laughed nastily. "That stupid son of a goat would forget his head if it weren't stuck on tight. All right, get moving."

The Roman did not catch all of that, but he knew he had gained permission. He rode south, as he had said he would. As soon as he was away from the light of the campfires and out of earshot, though, he swung round in a wide circle, riding fast as he dared through the darkness. Away from the camp stench, the plain smelled sweet and green and growing. Somewhere in the distance, a nightjar gave its sorrowful call.

The waning crescent moon rose after a while, spilling pale light over the steppe. That made it easier for Argyros to travel, but also left him more vulnerable to pursuit. So much depended, he thought as he urged on his rough-coated little mount, on when the Jurchen discovered Orda in his drugged sleep. Every yard of lead he gained would make him harder to catch.

He used every trick he knew to make his trail hard to follow. He splashed along in the shallows of streams, doubled back on his own main track. Once he was lucky enough to come across a stretch of ground where the herds of the Jurchen had passed. He rode through it for a couple of miles: let the nomads enjoy picking out his horse's hoofprints from thousands of others.

Dawn was painting the eastern sky with pink and gold when Argyros began looking for a place of refuge. His horse still seemed fresh enough—the nomads bred tougher beasts than the Romans—but he did not want to break down the only mount he had. Moreover, he was so exhausted himself that he knew he could not stay in the saddle much longer.

He felt like shouting when he saw a line of trees off to his left. That meant a stream—fresh water; with a little luck, fish or crayfish; maybe even fruits and nuts. And, if worse came to worst, he would be able to fight from cover.

He let his horse drink, then tethered it close to the water, where, he hoped, no chance observer would spy it. After setting aside the dagger and tube he had stolen, he lay down close by the animal, intending to get up in a few minutes to forage. His belly was growling like an angry bear.

The sun in his eyes woke him. He looked about in confusion; the light was coming from the wrong direction. Then he realized he had slept half the day away. He breathed a prayer of thanks that the nomads had not come upon him unawares.

There were freshwater mussels attached to several stones near the edge of the stream. He smashed them open with a flat rock and gobbled down the sweet orange flesh. That helped his hunger, a little. He tried to scoop a fish out of the water with his hands, but he did not have the knack. Some of the trees bore plums—hard, green plums. He sighed. He would have to hunt soon. Now, though, he was more interested in the tube.

He thought for a moment that he had broken it; surely it had been longer than this when he took it from Orda's tent. Then he saw it was not one tube, but two, the end of the smaller cleverly fitted into the larger. He extended it out to its full length again.

He looked at the eyes of Argos again. In daylight, with time to examine them, they did not so much resemble real eyes. They looked more like the crystal in which Orda had trapped the fire-spirit. Argyros had been about to break the tube open to see what was inside, but that thought stopped him. Who knew what sort of demon he might release?

Maybe he could see what the demon was like. Slowly, ready to throw the tube down in an instant, he held the larger end to his face, at the same time murmuring, "Mother of God, have mercy on me!"

The horned, leering face he had feared did not leer out at him. What he saw was even stranger; he had, after all, known about demons since he was a child. But what was he to make of a tiny circle of light, far smaller than the diameter of the tube could have accounted for, appearing in the middle of a field of blackness?

And in the circle—! He snatched the tube away, rubbed at his eye in disbelief. Repeating his earlier prayer, he cautiously brought the tube up once more. Sure enough, there were the trees on the far bank, but minute, as if seen from an immense distance instead of a couple of hundred feet. And they were—by the Virgin, they *were*!—upside down, their crowns where their roots should be and the stream above them, where the sky belonged.

He lowered the tube, sat tugging at his beard in perplexity. For the life of him, he could not see how looking at the world as if it were minuscule and head over heels would help the Jurchen beat the Romans. On the other hand, maybe he did not yet fully understand Orda's magic.

Well, what could he do that he had not done? At first he could not think of anything. Then it occurred to him that he had looked through the big end of the tube both times. What would happen if he tried the small one?

He held it to one eye, closed the other so as not to confuse himself any more than he already was. This time the circle of light in the midst of the blackness was larger. But where before the image in that circle had been perfectly sharp—albeit tiny and topsy-turvy—now it was a confusing, fuzzy jumble of colors and indistinct shapes. Argyros thought of St. Paul seeing through a glass, darkly, although blurrily would have been a better word here.

He took the tube away from his face, rubbed his eyes. Orda had known how to make the accursed thing work; was he too stupid even to follow in a barbarian's footsteps? Maybe so, but he was not ready to admit it.

He pointed the tube at the very top of a tall oak across the stream, paid careful attention to what he saw through it. Sure enough, the bottom of the vague image was sky-blue, the top green. No matter which end one looked through, then, the tube inverted its picture of the world.

How to make that picture clearer? Perhaps, Argyros thought, Orda had a spell for his own eyeballs. In that case he was beaten, so there was no point worrying about it. He asked the same question he had before: what could he try that was new?

He remembered that the tube was really two tubes. The Jurchen shaman had obviously done that on purpose; it would have been easier to build as one. With a growl of decision, Argyros pushed the apparatus as far closed as it would go.

He looked through it again. The image was even worse

than it had been before, which Argyros had not thought possible. He refused to let himself grow disheartened. He had changed things, after all. Maybe he had been too forceful with his push. He drew the smaller tube out halfway.

"By the Virgin!" he breathed. The picture was still blurred, but it had cleared enough for him to see branches and leaves on the trees on the far side of the creek—and they looked close enough to reach out and touch. He pushed the tube in a bit, and the image grew less distinct. He drew it out again, to the point where he had had it before, and then a trifle beyond.

Even when the distant leaves were knife-edge sharp, the image was less than perfect. It was still slightly distorted, and everything was edged with blue on one side and red on the other. But Argyros could count individual feathers on a linnet so far away his unaided eye could barely make it out against the leafy background.

He set the tube down, awed. Aristophanes and Seneca had written of using a round glass jar full of water as a magnifying device, but only for things close by it. No ancient sage had ever envisioned so enlarging objects at a distance.

Remembering the classic authors, though, made him think of something else. That water-filled jar would have been thin at the edges and thick in the center, just as were Orda's crystals. And if that was so, then doing peculiar things to light was a property of such transparent objects, and could take place without having a fire-spirit trapped at all.

Argyros breathed a long sigh of relief. He had been horrified when his prayers did not stop Orda from making fire with the crystal. But if he had been praying for the overthrow of a natural law, even one he did not understand, his failure became perfectly understandable. God only worked miracles at the entreaty of a saint, which the Roman knew he was not. He had been in the field so long that even the Jurchen women, skin-clad, greasy-haired, and stinking of rancid butter, would have looked good to him.

He closed the tube and stowed it in a saddlebag. Now all that remained was to take it back to the Roman army. Roman artisans would surely be able to duplicate what the nomad shaman had stumbled across.

"Christ, the Virgin, and all the saints, but I'm an idiot!" Argyros burst out two days later.

His horse's ears twitched at the unexpected noise. He paid

no attention, but went on, loudly as before, "If the eyes of Argos will help Tekmanios see his foes at a distance, they'll do the same for me. And with only the one of me and heaven knows how many plainsmen looking for my trail, I need to see more than Tekmanios ever will."

He took the tube out of the saddlebag, where it had rested undisturbed since he put it away there by the stream. After a bit, he stopped berating himself for stupidity. The eyes of Argos were something new; how was he to grasp all at once everything they were good for? Old familiar things were much more comfortable to be around. At the moment, though, this new device was more useful than any old one would have been.

He tied his horse to a bush at the base of a low rise, ascended it on foot. At the very top, he went down to his belly to crawl through the grass. Even without an Argos eye, a man silhouetted against the sky was visible a long way.

By now, he was no longer startled when the world turned upside down as he put the tube to his eye. He scanned in a full circle, pausing wherever he spied motion. Without the tube, he would have fled from a small cloud of dust he spotted to the south. With it, he was able to see it was only cattle, not horsemen, kicking up the dust. He could continue on his present course, riding round the nomads to reach the Roman army before Tekmanios took it back to the settled lands south of the Danube.

Tossuc and Orda would guess what he was aiming at, of course. But the steppe was so wide that he did not think the Jurchen could catch him by posting pickets in his path. They would have to stumble across his trail, and that, *theou thelontos*—God willing—would not happen. It certainly would not, if his prayers had anything to do with it.

Once another four days had gone by, he was confident God had granted his petition. He was farther south than any line the nomads would have set to waylay him. Better still, he had just come upon tracks he recognized as Roman—the horses that had made them were shod.

"Won't do to get careless now," he said aloud; he noticed he was talking to himself a good deal, to counteract the silent emptiness of the plains. He quoted Solon's famous warning to King Kroisos of Lydia: "Count no man happy before he is dead." And so, to be safe, he used the eyes of Argos again, looking back the way he had come.

The magnifying effect of the tube seemed to send the Jurchen horsemen leaping toward him. Even seen head over heels, the grim intensity with which they rode was terrifying. They had not yet spied him; they were leaning over their horses' necks to study the ground and stay on his trail. But if they had gained so much ground on him, they would catch sight of him soon—and the last phase of the hunt would begin.

He dug his heels into his horse's flanks, but the most he could extract from it was a tired, slow trot. Only a beast from the plains could have done as much as this one had; a Roman horse would long since have foundered. Even the nomad animals had their limit, though, and his had reached it.

He looked back again. This time he could see his pursuers without the tube. And they could see him. Their horses, fresh because they had not ridden the same beast days on end, came galloping forward. It would not be long before they were in arrow range. He might pick off one or two of them, but there were far more than that in their band.

All hope died when he saw another party of horsemen ahead. If the Jurchen were in front of him as well as behind, not even the miracle he did not deserve would let him escape. Those other riders had also spotted him, and were rushing his way as quickly as the plainsmen behind: racing to see who would kill him first, he thought as he set an arrow in his stolen bow and got ready to make what fight he could.

Because they were approaching instead of pursuing, the riders from ahead drew near first. He drew his bow to shoot at the closest one, but the winking of the sun off chainmail made it hard to reckon the range.

Chainmail . . . For a second, his mind did not grasp the meaning of that. Then he lowered the bow and shouted as loudly as he could, "To me, Romans, to me! A rescue!"

The oncoming horsemen drew up in surprise, then pounded past Argyros toward the Jurchen. He wheeled his weary horse to help them. The two parties exchanged arrows at long range. The nomads, as always, were better archers than the Romans, but they were also outnumbered. They could not press the attack home; a pair of charges were beaten back.

Argyros whooped exultantly as the Jurchen sullenly rode away, shooting Parthian shots over their shoulders in their withdrawal. Then his mount gave a strangled scream and toppled, an arrow through its throat. He had no chance to jump away. The beast fell on him, pinning him with its weight. His head thumped against the ground. The world turned red, then black.

His head ached abominably when he came back to his senses; the rest of him was one great bruise. Most of all, though, he felt relief that he was no longer crushed beneath the dead flesh and bone of his horse. He tried his limbs, one after the other. They all answered to his will. Gritting his teeth, he sat up.

Half a dozen Roman scouts were standing round him in a tight circle. He craned his neck back to look up at them—that hurt too. Among the soldiers scowling down were Bardas, Alexander, and Justin of Tarsos.

"So you find you do not love the barbarians after all," Alexander said when Argyros' eyes met his. He smiled. It was a singularly unpleasant smile, the expression a falcon might wear when about to swoop on a field mouse.

"I am afraid, Basil, you cannot undesert," Justin said. He sounded sorrowful; for a soldier, he was not a cruel man. But there was no yielding in him, either. He went on, "Going over to the enemy has only one penalty."

Bardanes, who was standing by Argyros' right side, did not say anything. He kicked the returned Roman in the ribs. One of the men behind him—he did not see who—kicked him in the back.

Alexander laughed. "You get what you deserve now, for running out on us." His foot lashed out too.

Argyros realized they were going to kick him to death, right there. He rolled into a ball, his arms drawn up to protect his face and head. "Take me to Hermoniakos!" he shouted— actually, the words came out more like a shriek.

"Why should we bother the lieutenant general when we can deal with you ourselves?" Alexander said. Argyros yelped as a boot slammed into his thigh.

"Wait," Justin said.

"What for?" Bardanes spoke for the first time, though his foot had been more than eloquent. Neither he nor Alexander could forget that Argyros had ridden away from their patrol, putting them at risk of being thought accessories to his desertion.

"Because I am your commander, and I order it!" Justin snapped. That was not enough; he could read the mutiny building on their faces. He added, "If Argyros wants to see the lieutenant general so badly, we should let him. Hermoniakos has more ways to make death interesting than boots, and the temper to use them."

The scouts considered that. Finally Alexander chuckled. "Aye, that's so. The hypostrategos is a regular little hornet when he's angry. All right, we'll let him do this bastard in. I wonder what he'll come up with."

Argyros heard it all as though from very far away. None of it seemed to have any meaning; the only reality was his pain. The additional discomfort of being dragged to his feet and then lashed over a horse's back like a corpse hardly registered. Mercifully, he never remembered most of the journey back to the Roman camp.

He did recall waking in horror as he jounced along, and exclaiming, "My saddlebags!"

"Shut up," Alexander growled. "Nothing is yours anymore. We've got 'em along to share out amongst ourselves, if you stole anything from the Jurchen worth the having." Argyros passed out again; Alexander took his sigh of relief for an anguished grunt.

The next time he roused was when they cut the bonds from his wrists and ankles and he slid to the ground like a sack of barley. Someone threw a pail of water in his face. He groaned and opened his eyes. The world spun more dizzily than it had when he looked through the tube.

"So you asked to come before me, eh?" He picked out Andreas Hermoniakos' voice before his vision would focus on the lieutenant general.

"Answer His Excellency," Justin of Tarsos said. Alexander stepped forward to kick him again, but Hermoniakos halted him with a gesture. Another bucket of water drenched Argyros.

He managed a sloppy salute, wondering whether his right wrist was broken. "I beg to report—success," he said thickly. He had a cut lip, but he did not think any of his teeth were missing—his arm had taken the kick intended for his mouth.

To the amazement of the scouts, the lieutenant general stooped beside him. "Where is it? What is it?" he demanded. In his urgency, his hand clamped on Argyros' shoulder. Argyros winced. Hermoniakos jerked his hand away. "Your pardon, I pray."

Argyros ignored that; he was still working his way through the two earlier questions. "The tube—in the saddlebag," he got out at last.

336

"Thank you, Basil."

As Hermoniakos rose, Alexander put into words what his comrades were feeling: "Sir, this is a deserter!"

"So you obviously thought," the lieutenant general snapped. "Now fetch a physician at once. Yes, soldier, you!" Alexander fled in something close to terror. Hermoniakos turned on the other men. "The desertion was staged, of course—you had to think it real, so you would say as much if the Jurchen captured you. I never imagined you would be more dangerous to Argyros than the nomads."

When the lieutenant general stooped by the saddlebag, a couple of scouts seized the opportunity to sidle away. The rest looked at each other, at the ground, or into the sky— anywhere but at the man who had been first their commander and then their victim.

Several of them exclaimed as Hermoniakos took out the tube: they had seen Orda with it too, in the scouts' skirmish before the battle against the Jurchen. Justin of Tarsos solved the puzzle fastest. "You sent him out to steal the magic from the plainsmen!"

"Yes," Hermoniakos said coldly. He turned back to Argyros. "How do I make the spell work?"

"I don't think it is a spell, sir. Give it to me." He took the tube with his left hand, set it in the crook of his right elbow— yes, that wrist was broken, no doubt of it. Awkwardly, he drew out the smaller tube what he thought was the proper distance. Bardanes Philippikos made a sign against the evil eye as he raised it to his face.

He made a last small adjustment, offered the tube to Hermoniakos. "Hold it to your eye and point it at that sentry over there, sir."

The lieutenant general did as Argyros suggested. "Mother of God!" he said softly. Argyros was not really listening to him. The approaching footsteps of the army physician were a much more welcome sound.

"Well done, well done," John Tekmanios said a few days later, when Argyros was up to making a formal report to the general.

"Thank you, Your Illustriousness," the scout commander said. He sank gratefully into the folding chair to which Tekmanios waved him; he was still a long way from being steady on his feet. He accepted wine, although he was not used to having a general pour for him.

"I wish there had been two of those tubes for you to take," Tekmanios said. "One to keep, and one to send back to Constantinople for the craftsmen to use as a model to make more." He paused awhile in thought. Finally he said, "Constantinople it is. I'm pulling back to our side of the river before long. If I got by without your eyes of Argos all these years, I'll last another month."

Argyros nodded. He would have decided the same way.

The general was still in that musing, abstracted mood. "I wonder how that barbarian happened to stumble onto the device when no civilized man ever did."

Argyros shrugged. "He found that one crystal, ground properly, would start a fire. He must have wondered what two together would do, and looked through them when they were in line."

"I suppose so," Tekmanios said indifferently. "It's of no consequence now. We have the tube; it's up to us to find out all the different things we can do with it. I don't suppose the first men who got fire from Prometheus—if you believe the myth—knew everything it was good for, either."

"No, sir," Argyros agreed. That sort of speculation fascinated him. Christianity looked ahead to a more perfect time, which had to imply that times past had been less so. The concept was hard to grasp. Things had been the same for as long as he could remember, and in his father's and grandfather's time as well, from their tales.

Tekmanios had been thinking along a different line. "There also remains the problem of what to do with you."

"Sir?" Argyros said in surprise.

"Well, I can't keep you here in the army any longer, that's plain," the general said, raising an eyebrow at having to explain the obvious. "Or don't you think it would be awkward to go back to command men who've beaten you half to death?"

"Put that way, yes, sir." The scouts would be terrified of him. They would also fear his revenge, and might even arrange an accident for him to beat him to the punch. "What then?"

"As I said, you did a fine job of ferreting out the Jurchen secret. It just so happens that George Lakhanodrakon is a cousin of my wife's."

338

"The Master of Offices, sir?" The Master of Offices was one of the most powerful officials in the Roman Empire, one of the few with the right to report directly to the Emperor himself.

"Yes. Among his other duties, he commands the corps of magistrianoi. How would you like to be the one to take your precious tube down to Constantinople, along with a letter urging your admission to their ranks?"

For a moment, all Argyros heard was "Constantinople." That was enough. Along with every other citizen of the Empire, he had heard stories of its wonders and riches for his entire life. Now to see them for himself!

Then the rest of what Tekmanios had said sank in. Magistrianoi were elite imperial agents, investigators, sometimes spies. They served under the personal supervision of the Master of Offices, the only man between them and the Emperor, the vice-regent of God on earth. Argyros had dreamed of such a post for himself, but only dreamed.

"Yes, sir! Thank you, sir!" he said.

"I thought that might please you," Tekmanios said with a smile. "It's your doing more than mine, you know; you've earned the chance. Now it's up to you to make the most of it."

"Yes, sir," Argyros said again, slightly deflated.

The general's smile grew wider. "Take a couple of more days to get your strength back. Then I'll send you and your tube back to the Danube, with a good strong resupply party along to keep you in one piece. You can get a riverboat there and sail down to Tomi on the Euxine Sea, then take a real ship on to the city. That will be faster and safer than going overland."

The grin looked out of place on Argyros' usually somber features, but he could not help wearing it as he bowed his way out of Tekmanios' tent. Once outside, he looked up into the heavens to give thanks to God for his good fortune.

The pale, mottled moon, near first quarter, caught his eye. He wondered what it might look like through the eyes of Argos. Tonight, if he remembered, he would have to find out. Who could say? It might be interesting.

EDITOR'S INTRODUCTION TO:

THE HIGHEST TREASON
by Randall Garrett

Writing this is a sad task. As I write this introduction, Randall Garrett lives, but suffers from a progressive disorder which has kept him hospitalized and unable to write for several years. It's a damned shame. I prefer to remember him as I knew him: a robust man, full of life, and much larger than life.

I suppose I had previously met Randall Garrett at one or another science fiction convention, but I first got to know him when we were both guests at Poul Anderson's home. Randall and Poul are fascinating conversationalists, full of both profound and trivial knowledge; the two together could be devastating. I was not then a member of the SF writers' community, being still an aerospace engineer.

In those days we were all three active in the Society for Creative Anachronism, that odd bunch of fanatics who dress up in medieval clothing and bash each other with swords. In those days we were much concerned with how things really were in the Middle Ages; nowadays there is perhaps more creativity, and a great deal more anachronism, mostly in the name of equality of the sexes. In any event, Randall was then quite high in the Society's heraldic structure, and many of the traditions he started endure to this day.

He also constructed a helmet. Most of the SCA people do have helmets. Randall's, however, was built from a military steel pot, with considerable refinements and additions. It weighed almost twenty pounds, and rendered the wearer's head well-nigh invulnerable (although it was certain to produce a stiff neck). Naturally Randall gave it a name: *nolle me*. Those who don't understand should seek out some amontillado.

Garrett was, in a word, one of that low species: the inveterate punster. Indeed, it's hard to imagine anyone being better (worse) at the game.

In the Golden Age when John W. Campbell, Jr., was editor of *Astounding Science Fiction* (which he converted to *Analog*), Randall Garrett was almost certainly the most often printed contributor. Some issues were written almost entirely by Randall, Poul Anderson, and Robert Silverberg. Randall could take an idea from Mr. Campbell and turn it into a story within a day, sometimes quicker if the rent was due.

He was also one of the field's best satirists. Nearly every major author in the field was zapped by Randall at one or another time. In my case, Randall and William Tuning wrote a story called "A Time Machine for the Queen," which they brought out not long after my "Spaceship for the King" . . .

For all that, he could be a serious writer, and his social criticisms could bite deeply. A former Marine, he understood full well both the strengths and weaknesses of military organizations.

Randall Garrett had nothing but contempt for those who seek equality at the price of freedom. At the same time, he knew how to be loyal. I have long thought *The Highest Treason* to be one of his best stories. Query: precisely who is the traitor here?

THE HIGHEST TREASON
Randall Garrett

THE PRISONER

The two rooms were not luxurious, but MacMaine hadn't expected that they would be. The walls were a flat metallic gray, unadorned and windowless. The ceilings and floors were simply continuations of the walls, except for the glow plates overhead. One room held a small cabinet for his personal possessions, a wide, reasonably soft bed, a small but adequate desk, and, in one corner, a cubicle that contained the necessary sanitary plumbing facilities.

The other room held a couch, two big easy-chairs, a low table, some bookshelves, a squat refrigerator containing food and drink for his occasional snacks—his regular meals were brought in hot from the main kitchen—and a closet that contained his clothing—the insignialess uniforms of a Kerothi officer.

No, thought Sebastian MacMaine, it was not luxurious, but neither did it look like the prison cell it was.

There was comfort here, and even the illusion of privacy, although there were TV pickups in the walls, placed so that no movement in either room would go unnoticed. The switch which cut off the soft white light from the glow plates did not cut off the infrared radiation which enabled his hosts to watch him while he slept. Every sound was heard and recorded.

But none of that bothered MacMaine. On the contrary, he was glad of it. He wanted the Kerothi to know that he had no intention of escaping or hatching any plot against them.

He had long since decided that, if things continued as they had, Earth would lose the war with Keroth, and Sebastian MacMaine had no desire whatever to be on the losing side of the greatest war ever fought. The problem now was to convince the Kerothi that he fully intended to fight for them, to give them the full benefit of his ability as a military strategist, and to do his best to win every battle for Keroth.

And that was going to be the most difficult task of all.

A telltale glow of red blinked rapidly over the door, and a soft chime pinged in time with it.

MacMaine smiled inwardly, although not a trace of it showed on his broad-jawed, blocky face. To give him the illusion that he was a guest rather than a prisoner, the Kerothi had installed an announcer at the door and invariably used it. Not once had any one of them ever simply walked in on him.

"Come in," MacMaine said.

He was seated in one of the easy-chairs in his "living room," smoking a cigarette and reading a book on the history of Keroth, but he put the book down on the low table as a tall Kerothi came in through the doorway.

MacMaine allowed himself a smile of honest pleasure. To most Earthmen, "all the Carrot-skins look alike," and, MacMaine admitted honestly to himself, he hadn't yet trained himself completely to look beyond the strangeness that made the Kerothi different from Earthmen and see the details that made them different from each other. But this was one Kerothi that MacMaine would never mistake for any other.

"Tallis!" He stood up and extended both hands in the Kerothi fashion. The other did the same, and they clasped hands for a moment. "How are your guts?" he added in Kerothic.

"They function smoothly, my sibling-by-choice," answered Space General Polan Tallis. "And your own?"

"Smoothly, indeed. It's been far too long a time since we have touched."

The Kerothi stepped back a pace and looked the Earthman up and down. "You look healthy enough—for a prisoner. You're treated well, then?"

"Well enough. Sit down, my sibling-by-choice." MacMaine waved toward the couch nearby. The general sat down and looked around the apartment.

"Well, well. You're getting preferential treatment, all right. This is as good as you could expect as a battleship commander. Maybe you're being trained for the job."

MacMaine laughed, allowing the touch of sardonicism that he felt to be heard in the laughter. "I might have hoped so once, Tallis. But I'm afraid I have simply come out even. I have traded nothing for nothing."

General Tallis reached into the pocket of his uniform jacket and took out the thin aluminum case that held the Kerothi equivalent of cigarettes. He took one out, put it between his lips, and lit it with the hotpoint that was built into the case.

343

MacMaine took an Earth cigarette out of the package on the table and allowed Tallis to light it for him. The pause and the silence, MacMaine knew, were for a purpose. He waited. Tallis had something to say, but he was allowing the Earthman to "adjust to surprise." It was one of the fine points of Kerothi etiquette.

A sudden silence on the part of one participant in a conversation, under these particular circumstances, meant that something unusual was coming up, and the other person was supposed to take the opportunity to brace himself for shock.

It could mean anything. In the Kerothi Space Forces, a superior informed a junior officer of the junior's forthcoming promotion by just such tactics. But the same tactics were used when informing a person of the death of a loved one.

In fact, MacMaine was well aware that such a period of silence was *de rigueur* in a Kerothi court, just before sentence was pronounced, as well as a preliminary to a proposal of marriage by a Kerothi male to the light of his love.

MacMaine could do nothing but wait. It would be indelicate to speak until Tallis felt that he was ready for the surprise.

It was not, however, indelicate to watch Tallis' face closely; it was expected. Theoretically, one was supposed to be able to discern, at least, whether the news was good or bad.

With Tallis, it was impossible to tell, and MacMaine knew it would be useless to read the man's expression. But he watched, nonetheless.

In one way, Tallis' face was typically Kerothi. The orange-pigmented skin and the bright grass-green eyes were common to all Kerothi. The planet Keroth, like Earth, had evolved several different "races" of humanoid, but, unlike Earth, the distinction was not one of color.

MacMaine took a drag off his cigarette and forced himself to keep his mind off whatever it was that Tallis might be about to say. He was already prepared for a death sentence—even a death sentence by torture. Now, he felt, he could not be shocked. And, rather than build up the tension within himself to an unbearable degree, he thought about Tallis rather than about himself.

Tallis, like the rest of the Kerothi, was unbelievably humanoid. There were internal differences in the placement of organs, and differences in the functions of those organs. For instance, it took two separate organs to perform the same function that the liver performed in Earthmen, and the kidneys were completely absent, that function being performed by special tissues in the lower colon, which meant that the Kerothi were more efficient with water-saving than Earthmen, since the waste products were excreted as relatively dry solids through an all-purpose cloaca.

But, externally, a Kerothi would need only a touch of plastic surgery and some makeup to pass as an Earthman in a stage play. Close up, of course, the job would be much more difficult—as difficult as a Negro trying to disguise himself as a Swede or *vice versa*.

But Tallis was—

"I would have a word," Tallis said, shattering MacMaine's carefully neutral train of thought. It was a standard opening for breaking the pause of adjustment, but it presaged good news rather than bad.

"I await your word," MacMaine said. Even after all this time, he still felt vaguely proud of his ability to handle the subtle idioms of Kerothic.

"I think," Tallis said carefully, "that you may be offered a commission in the Kerothi Space Forces."

Sebastian MacMaine let out his breath slowly, and only then realized that he had been holding it. "I am grateful, my sibling-by-choice," he said.

General Tallis tapped his cigarette ash into a large blue ceramic ashtray. MacMaine could smell the acrid smoke from the alien plant matter that burned in the Kerothi cigarette—a chopped-up inner bark from a Kerothi tree. MacMaine could no more smoke a Kerothi cigarette than Tallis could smoke tobacco, but the two were remarkably similar in their effects.

The "surprise" had been delivered. Now, as was proper, Tallis would move adroitly all around the subject until he was ready to return to it again.

"You have been with us . . . how long, Sepastian?" he asked.

"Two and a third *Kronet*."

Tallis nodded. "Nearly a year of your time."

MacMaine smiled. Tallis was as proud of his knowledge of Earth terminology as MacMaine was proud of his mastery of Kerothic.

"Lacking three weeks," MacMaine said.

"What? Three . . . oh, yes. Well. A long time," said Tallis.

Damn it! MacMaine thought, in a sudden surge of impatience, *get to the point!* His face showed only calm.

"The Board of Strategy asked me to tell you," Tallis continued. "After all, my recommendation was partially responsible for the decision." He paused for a moment, but it was merely a conversational hesitation, not a formal hiatus.

"It was a hard decision, Sepastian—you must realize that. We have been at war with your race for ten years now. We have taken thousands of Earthmen as prisoners, and many of them have agreed to cooperate with us. But, with one single exception, these prisoners have been the moral dregs of your civilization. They have been men who had no pride of race, no pride of society, no pride of self. They have been weak, self-centered, small-minded, cowards who had no thought for Earth and Earthmen, but only for themselves.

"Not," he said hurriedly, "that all of them are that way—or even the majority. Most of them have the minds of warriors, although, I must say, not *strong* warriors."

That last, MacMaine knew, was a polite concession. The Kerothi had no respect for Earthmen. And MacMaine could hardly blame them. For three long centuries, the people of Earth had had nothing to do but indulge themselves in the pleasures of material wealth. It was a wonder that any of them had any moral fiber left.

"But none of those who had any strength agreed to work with us," Tallis went on. "With one exception. You."

"Am I weak, then?" MacMaine asked.

General Tallis shook his head in a peculiarly humanlike gesture. "No. No, you are not. And that is what has made us pause for three years." His grass-green eyes looked candidly into MacMaine's own. "You aren't the type of person who betrays his own kind. It looks like a trap. After a whole year, the Board of Strategy still isn't sure that there is no trap."

Tallis stopped, leaned forward, and ground out the stub of his cigarette in the blue ashtray. Then his eyes again sought MacMaine's.

"If it were not for what I, personally, know about you, the Board of Strategy would not even consider your proposition."

"I take it, then, that they have considered it?" MacMaine asked with a grin.

"As I said, Sepastian," Tallis said, "you have won your case. After almost a year of your time, your decision has been justified."

MacMaine lost his grin. "I am grateful, Tallis," he said gravely. "I think you must realize that it was a difficult decision to make."

His thoughts went back, across long months of time and longer light-years of space, to the day when that decision had been made.

THE DECISION

Colonel Sebastian MacMaine didn't feel, that morning, as though this day were different from any other. The sun, faintly veiled by a few wisps of cloud, shone as it always had; the guards at the doors of the Space Force Administration Building saluted him as usual; his brother officers nodded politely, as they always did; his aide greeted him with the usual "Good morning, sir."

The duty list lay on his desk, as it had every morning for years. Sebastian MacMaine felt tense and a little irritated with himself, but he felt nothing that could be called a premonition.

When he read the first item on the duty list, his irritation became a little stronger.

"Interrogate Kerothi general."

The interrogation duty had swung round to him again. He didn't want to talk to General Tallis. There was something about the alien that bothered him, and he couldn't place exactly what it was.

Earth had been lucky to capture the alien officer. In a space war, there's usually very little left to capture after a battle—especially if your side lost the battle.

On the other hand, the Kerothi general wasn't so lucky. The food that had been captured with him would run out in less than six months, and it was doubtful that he would survive on Earth food. It was equally doubtful that any more Kerothi food would be captured.

For two years, Earth had been fighting the Kerothi, and for two years Earth had been winning a few minor skirmishes and losing the major battles. The Kerothi hadn't hit any of the major colonies yet, but they had swallowed up outpost after outpost, and Earth's space fleet was losing ships faster than her factories could turn them out. The hell of it was that nobody on Earth seemed to be very much concerned about it at all.

MacMaine wondered why he let it concern him. If no one

else was worried, why did he let it bother him? He pushed the thought from his mind and picked up the questionnaire form that had been made out for that morning's session with the Kerothi general. Might as well get it over with.

He glanced down the list of further duties for the day. It looked as though the routine interrogation of the Kerothi general was likely to provide most of the interest in the day's work at that.

He took the drop chute down to the basement of the building, to the small prison section where the alien officer was being held. The guards saluted nonchalantly as he went in. The routine questioning sessions were nothing new to them.

MacMaine turned the lock on the prisoner's cell door and went in. Then he came to attention and saluted the Kerothi general. He was probably the only officer in the place who did that, he knew; the others treated the alien general as though he were a criminal. Worse, they treated him as though he were a petty thief or a common pickpocket—criminal, yes, but of a definitely inferior type.

General Tallis, as always, stood and returned the salute. "Cut mawnik, Cunnel MacMaine," he said. The Kerothi language lacked many of the voiced consonants of English and Russian, and, as a result, Tallis' use of *B*, *D*, *G*, *J*, *V*, and *Z* made them come out as *P*, *T*, *K*, *CH*, *F*, and *S*. The English *R*, as it is pronounced in *run* or *rat*, eluded him entirely, and he pronounced it only when he could give it the guttural pronunciation of the German *R*. The terminal *NG* always came out as *NK*. The nasal *M* and *N* were a little more drawn out than in English, but they were easily understandable.

"Good morning, General Tallis," MacMaine said. "Sit down. How do you feel this morning?"

The general sat again on the hard bunk that, aside from the single chair, was the only furniture in the small cell. "Ass well ass coot pe expectet. I ket ferry little exercisse. I . . . how iss it set? . . . I pecome soft? Soft? Iss correct?"

"Correct. You've learned our language very well for so short a time."

The general shrugged off the compliment. "Wen it iss a matteh of learrn in orrter to surfife, one learrnss."

"You think, then, that your survival has depended on your learning our language?"

The general's orange face contrived a wry smile. "Opfiously. Your people fill not learn Kerothic. If I cannot answerr

348

questionss, I am uff no use. Ass lonk ass I am uff use, I will liff. Not?''

MacMaine decided he might as well spring his bomb on the Kerothi officer now as later. ''I am not so certain but that you might have stretched out your time longer if you had forced us to learn Kerothic, General,'' he said in Kerothic. He knew his Kerothic was bad, since it had been learned from the Kerothi spaceman who had been captured with the general, and the man had been badly wounded and had survived only two weeks. But that little bit of basic instruction, plus the work he had done on the books and tapes from the ruined Kerothi ship, had helped him.

''Ah?'' The general blinked in surprise. Then he smiled. ''Your accent,'' he said in Kerothic, ''is atrocious, but certainly no worse than mine when I speak your *Inklitch*. I suppose you intend to question me in Kerothic now, eh? In the hope that I may reveal more in my own tongue?''

''Possibly you may,'' MacMaine said with a grin, ''but I learned it for my own information.''

''For your own what? Oh, I see. Interesting. I know no others of your race who would do such a thing. Anything which is difficult is beneath them.''

''Not so, General. I'm not unique. There are many of us who don't think that way.''

The general shrugged. ''I do not deny it. I merely say that I have met none. Certainly they do not tend to go into military service. Possibly that is because you are not a race of fighters. It takes a fighter to tackle the difficult just because it is difficult.''

MacMaine gave him a short, hard laugh. ''Don't you think getting information out of *you* is difficult? And yet, we tackle that.''

''Not the same thing at all. Routine. You have used no pressure. No threats, no promises, no torture, no stress.''

MacMaine wasn't quite sure of his translation of the last two negative phrases. ''You mean the application of physical pain? That's barbaric.''

''I won't pursue the subject,'' the general said with sudden irony.

''I can understand that. But you can rest assured that we would never do such a thing. It isn't civilized. Our civil police do use certain drugs to obtain information, but we have so little knowledge of Kerothi body chemistry that we hesitate to use drugs on you."

"The application of stress, you say, is not civilized. Not, perhaps, according to your definition of"—he used the English word—"*cifiliced*. No. Not *cifiliced*—but it works." Again he smiled. "I said that I have become soft since I have been here, but I fear that your civilization is even softer."

"A man can lie, even if his arms are pulled off or his feet crushed," MacMaine said stiffly.

The Kerothi looked startled. When he spoke again, it was in English. "I will say no morr. If you haff questionss to ask, ko ahet. I will not take up time with furtherr talkink."

A little angry with himself and with the general, MacMaine spent the rest of the hour asking routine questions and getting nowhere, filling up the tape in his minicorder with the same old answers that others had gotten.

He left, giving the general a brisk salute and turning before the general had time to return it.

Back in his office, he filed the tape dutifully and started on Item Two of the duty list: *Strategy Analysis of Battle Reports*.

Strategy analysis always irritated and upset him. He knew that if he'd just go about it in the approved way, there would be no irritation—only boredom. But he was constitutionally incapable of working that way. In spite of himself, he always played a little game with himself and with the General Strategy Computer.

The only battle of significance in the past week had been the defense of an Earth outpost called Bennington IV. Theoretically, MacMaine was supposed to check over the entire report, find out where the losing side had erred, and feed correctional information into the computer. But he couldn't resist stopping after he had read the first section: *Information Known to Earth Commander at Moment of Initial Contact*.

Then he would stop and consider how he, personally, would have handled the situation if he had been the Earth commander. So many ships in such-and-such places. Enemy fleet approaching at such-and-such velocities. Battle array of enemy thus-and-so.

Now what?

MacMaine thought over the information on the defense of Bennington IV and devised a battle plan. There was a weak point in the enemy's attack, but it was rather obvious. MacMaine searched until he found another weak point, much less obvious than the first. He knew it would be there. It was.

350

Then he proceeded to ignore both weak points and concentrate on what he would do if he were the enemy commander. The weak points were traps; the computer could see them and avoid them. Which was just exactly what was wrong with the computer's logic. In avoiding the traps, it also avoided the best way to hit the enemy. A weak point *is* weak, no matter how well it may be booby-trapped. In baiting a rat trap, you have to use real cheese because an imitation won't work.

Of course, MacMaine thought to himself, *you can always poison the cheese, but let's not carry the analogy too far.*

All right, then. How to hit the traps?

It took him half an hour to devise a completely wacky and unorthodox way of hitting the holes in the enemy advance. He checked the time carefully, because there's no point in devising a strategy if the battle is too far gone to use it by the time you've figured it out.

Then he went ahead and read the rest of the report. Earth had lost the outpost. And, worse, MacMaine's strategy would have won the battle if it had been used. He fed it through his small office computer to make sure. The odds were good.

And that was the thing that made MacMaine hate strategy analysis. Too often, he won; too often, Earth lost. A computer was fine for working out the logical outcome of a battle if it was given the proper strategy, but it couldn't devise anything new.

Colonel MacMaine had tried to get himself transferred to space duty, but without success. The Commanding Staff didn't want him out there.

The trouble was that they didn't believe MacMaine actually devised his strategy before he read the complete report. How could anyone outthink a computer?

He'd offered to prove it. "Give me a problem," he'd told his immediate superior, General Matsukuo. "Give me the initial contact information of a battle I haven't seen before, and I'll show you."

And Matsukuo had said, testily: "Colonel, I will not permit a member of my staff to make a fool of himself in front of the Commanding Staff. Setting yourself up as someone superior to the Strategy Board is the most antisocial type of egocentrism imaginable. You were given the same education at the Academy as every other officer; what makes you think you are better than they? As time goes on, your automatic promotions will put you in a position to vote on such matters—provided you don't prejudice the Promotion Board against you by antisocial behavior. I hold you in the highest regard, Colonel, and I will say nothing to the Promotion Board about this, but if you persist I will have to do my duty. Now, I don't want to hear any more about it. Is that clear?"

It was.

All MacMaine had to do was wait, and he'd automatically be promoted to the Commanding Staff, where he would have an equal vote with the others of his rank. One unit vote to begin with and an additional unit for every year thereafter.

It's a great system for running a peacetime social club, maybe, MacMaine thought, *but it's no way to run a fighting force.*

Maybe the Kerothi general was right. Maybe *Homo sapiens* just wasn't a race of fighters.

They had been once. Mankind had fought its way to domination of Earth by battling every other form of life on the planet, from the smallest virus to the biggest carnivore. The fight against disease was still going on, as a matter of fact, and Man was still fighting the elemental fury of Earth's climate.

But Man no longer fought with Man. Was that a bad thing? The discovery of atomic energy, two centuries before, had literally made war impossible, if the race was to survive. Small struggles bred bigger struggles—or so the reasoning went. Therefore, the society had unconsciously sought to eliminate the reasons for struggle.

What bred the hatreds and jealousies among men? What caused one group to fight another?

Society had decided that intolerance and hatred were caused by inequality. The jealousy of the inferior toward his superior; the scorn of the superior toward his inferior. The Have-not envies the Have, and the Have looks down upon the Have-not.

Then let us eliminate the Have-not. Let us make sure that everyone is a Have.

Raise the standard of living. Make sure that every human being has the necessities of life—food, clothing, shelter, proper medical care, and proper education. More, give them the luxuries, too—let no man be without anything that is poorer in quality or less in quantity than the possessions of any other. There was no longer any middle class simply because there were no other classes for it to be in the middle of.

"The poor you will have always with you," Jesus of

Nazareth had said. But, in a material sense, that was no longer true. The poor were gone—and so were the rich.

But the poor in mind and the poor in spirit were still there—in ever-increasing numbers.

Material wealth could be evenly distributed, but it could not remain that way unless society made sure that the man who was more clever than the rest could not increase his wealth at the expense of his less fortunate brethren.

Make it a social stigma to show more ability than the average. Be kind to your fellow man; don't show him up as a stupid clod, no matter how cloddish he may be.

All men are created equal, and let's make sure they stay *that way!*

There could be no such thing as a classless society, of course. That was easily seen. No human being could do everything, learn everything, be everything. There had to be doctors and lawyers and policemen and bartenders and soldiers and machinists and laborers and actors and writers and criminals and bums.

But let's make sure that the differentiation between classes is horizontal, not vertical. As long as a person does his job the best he can, he's as good as anybody else. A doctor is as good as a lawyer, isn't he? Then a garbage collector is just as good as a nuclear physicist, and an astronomer is no better than a street sweeper.

And what of the loafer, the bum, the man who's too lazy or weak-willed to put out any more effort than is absolutely necessary to stay alive? Well, my goodness, the poor chap can't *help* it, can he? It isn't *his* fault, is it? He has to be helped. There is always *something* he is both capable of doing and willing to do. Does he like to sit around all day and do nothing but watch television? Then give him a sheet of paper with all the programs on it and two little boxes marked *Yes* and *No*, and he can put an X in one or the other to indicate whether he likes the program or not. Useful? Certainly. All these sheets can be tallied up in order to find out what sort of program the public likes to see. After all, his vote is just as good as anyone else's, isn't it?

And a program analyst is just as good, just as important, and just as well cared for as anyone else.

And what about the criminal? Well, what *is* a criminal? A person who thinks he's superior to others. A thief steals because he thinks he has more right to something than its real owner. A man kills because he has an idea that he has a better right to live than someone else. In short, a man breaks the law because he feels superior, because he thinks he can outsmart society and the law. Or, simply, because he thinks he can outsmart the policeman on the beat.

Obviously, that sort of antisocial behavior can't be allowed. The poor fellow who thinks he's better than anyone else has to be segregated from normal society and treated for his aberrations. But not punished! Heavens no! His erratic behavior isn't *his* fault, is it?

It was axiomatic that there had to be some sort of vertical structure to society, naturally. A child can't do the work of an adult, and a beginner can't be as good as an old hand. Aside from the fact that it was actually impossible to force everyone into a common mold, it was recognized that there had to be some incentive for staying with a job. What to do?

The labor unions had solved that problem two hundred years before. Promotion by seniority. Stick with a job long enough, and you'll automatically rise to the top. That way, everyone had as good a chance as everyone else.

Promotion tables for individual jobs were worked out on the basis of longevity tables, so that by the time a man reached the automatic retirement age he was automatically at the highest position he could hold. No fuss, no bother, no trouble. Just keep your nose clean and live as long as possible.

It eliminated struggle. It eliminated the petty jockeying for position that undermined efficiency in an organization. Everybody deserves an equal chance in life, so make sure everybody gets it.

Colonel Sebastian MacMaine had been born and reared in that society. He could see many of its faults, but he didn't have the orientation to see all of them. As he'd grown older, he'd seen that, regardless of the position a man held according to seniority, a smart man could exercise more power than those above him if he did it carefully.

A man is a slave if he is held rigidly in a pattern and not permitted to step out of that pattern. In ancient times, a slave was born at the bottom of the social ladder, and he remained there all his life. Only rarely did a slave of exceptional merit manage to rise above his assigned position.

But a man who is forced to remain on the bottom step of a stationary stairway is no more a slave than a man who is forced to remain on a given step of an escalator, and no less so.

Slavery, however, has two advantages—one for the individual, and one which, in the long run, can be good for the race. For the individual, it offers security, and that is the goal which by far the greater majority of mankind seeks.

The second advantage is more difficult to see. It operates only in favor of the exceptional individual. There are always individuals who aspire to greater heights than the one they occupy at any given moment, but in a slave society, they are slapped back into place if they act hastily. Just as the one-eyed man in the kingdom of the blind can be king if he taps the ground with a cane, so the gifted individual can gain his ends in a slave society—provided he thinks out the consequences of any act in advance.

The Law of Gravity is a universal edict which enslaves, in a sense, every particle of matter in the cosmos. The man who attempts to defy the "injustice" of that law by ignoring the consequences of its enforcement will find himself punished rather severely. It may be unjust that a bird can fly under its own muscle power, but a man who tries to correct that injustice by leaping out of a skyscraper window and flapping his arms vigorously will find that overt defiance of the Law of Gravity brings very serious penalties indeed. The wise man seeks the loopholes in the law, and loopholes are caused by other laws which counteract—*not defy!*—the given law. A balloon full of hydrogen "falls up" in obedience to the Law of Gravity. A contradiction? A paradox? No. It is the Law of Gravity which causes the density and pressure of a planet's atmosphere to decrease with altitude, and that decrease in pressure forces the balloon upward until the balance point between atmospheric density and the internal density of the balloon is reached.

The illustration may seem obvious and elementary to the modern man, but it seems so only because he understands, at least to some extent, the laws involved. It was not obvious to even the most learned man of, say, the thirteenth century.

Slavery, too, has its laws, and it is as dangerous to defy the laws of a society as it is to defy those of nature, and the only way to escape the punishment resulting from those laws is to find the loopholes. One of the most basic laws of any society is so basic that it is never, *ever* written down.

And that law, like all basic laws, is so simple in expression and so obvious in application that any man above the moron level has an intuitive grasp of it. It is the first law one learns as a child.

Thou shalt not suffer thyself to be caught.

The unthinking man believes that this basic law can be applied by breaking the laws of his society in secret. What he fails to see is that such lawbreaking requires such a fantastic network of lies, subterfuges, evasions, and chicanery that the structure itself eventually breaks down and his guilt is obvious to all. The very steps he has taken to keep from getting caught eventually become signposts that point unerringly at the lawbreaker himself.

Like the loopholes in the law of gravity, the loopholes in the laws of society cannot entail a *defiance* of the law. Only compliance with those laws will be ultimately successful.

The wise man works within the framework of the law—not only the written, but the unwritten law—of his society. In a slave society, any slave who openly rebels will find that he gets squashed pretty quickly. But many a slave-owner has danced willingly to the tune of a slave who was wiser and cleverer than he, without ever knowing that the tune played was not his own.

And that is the second advantage of slavery. It teaches the exceptional individual to think.

When a wise, intelligent individual openly and violently breaks the laws of his society, there are two things which are almost certain: One: he knows that there is no other way to do the thing he feels must be done, and—

Two: he knows that he will pay the penalty for his crime in one way or another.

Sebastian MacMaine knew the operations of those laws. As a member of a self-enslaved society, he knew that to betray any sign of intelligence was dangerous. A slight slip could bring the scorn of the slaves around him; a major offense could mean death. The war with Keroth had thrown him slightly off balance, but after his one experience with General Matsukuo, he had quickly regained his equilibrium.

At the end of his work day, MacMaine closed his desk and left his office precisely on time, as usual. Working overtime, except in the gravest emergencies, was looked upon as antisocialism. The offender was suspected of having Ambition—obviously a Bad Thing.

It was during his meal at the officers' mess that Colonel Sebastian MacMaine heard the statement that triggered the decision in his mind.

There were three other officers seated with MacMaine around one of the four-place tables in the big room. MacMaine only paid enough attention to the table conversation to be able to make the appropriate noises at the proper times. He had long since learned to do his thinking under cover of general banalities.

Colonel VanDeusen was a man who would never have made private first class in an army that operated on a strict merit system. His thinking was muddy, and his conversation betrayed it. All he felt comfortable in talking about was just exactly what he had been taught. Slogans, banalities, and bromides. He knew his catechism, and he knew it was safe.

"What I mean is, we got nothing to worry about. We all stick together, and we can do anything. As long as we don't rock the boat, we'll come through O.K."

"Sure," said Major Brock, looking up from his plate in blank-faced surprise. "I mean, who says different?"

"Guy on my research team," said VanDeusen, plying his fork industriously. "A wise-guy second looie. One of them."

"Oh," said the major knowingly. "One of them." He went back to his meal.

"What'd he say?" MacMaine asked, just to keep his oar in.

"Ahhh, nothing serious, I guess," said VanDeusen, around a mouthful of steak. "Said we were all clogged up with paper work, makin' reports on tests, things like that. Said, why don't we figure out something to pop those Carrot-skins outa the sky. So I said to him, 'Look, Lootenant,' I said, 'you got your job to do, I got mine. If the paper work's pilin' up,' I said, 'it's because somebody isn't pulling his share. And it better not be you,' I said." He chuckled and speared another cube of steak with his fork. "That settled him down. He's all right, though. Young yet, you know. Soon's he gets the hang of how the Space Force operates, he'll be O.K."

Since VanDeusen was the senior officer at the table, the others listened respectfully as he talked, only inserting a word now and then to show that they were listening.

MacMaine was thinking deeply about something else entirely, but VanDeusen's influence intruded a little. MacMaine was wondering what it was that bothered him about General Tallis, the Kerothi prisoner.

The alien was pleasant enough, in spite of his position. He seemed to accept his imprisonment as one of the fortunes of war. He didn't threaten or bluster, although he tended to maintain an air of superiority that would have been unbearable in an Earthman.

Was that the reason for his uneasiness in the general's presence? No. MacMaine could accept the reason for that attitude; the general's background was different from that of an Earthman, and therefore he could not be judged by Terrestrial standards. Besides, MacMaine could acknowledge to himself that Tallis *was* superior to the norm—not only the norm of Keroth, but that of Earth. MacMaine wasn't sure he could have acknowledged superiority in another Earthman, in spite of the fact that he knew that there must be men who were his superiors in one way or another.

Because of his social background, he knew that he would probably form an intense and instant dislike for any Earthman who talked the way Tallis did, but he found that he actually *liked* the alien officer.

It came as a slight shock when the realization hit MacMaine that his liking for the general was exactly why he was uncomfortable around him. Dammit, a man isn't supposed to like his enemy—and most especially when that enemy does and says things that one would despise in a friend.

Come to think of it, though, did he, MacMaine, actually have any friends? He looked around him, suddenly clearly conscious of the other men in the room. He searched through his memory, thinking of all his acquaintances and relatives.

It was an even greater shock to realize that he would not be more than faintly touched emotionally if any or all of them were to die at that instant. Even his parents, both of whom were now dead, were only dim figures in his memory. He had mourned them when an aircraft accident had taken both of them when he was only eleven, but he found himself wondering if it had been the loss of loved ones that had caused his emotional upset or simply the abrupt vanishing of a kind of security he had taken for granted.

And yet, he felt that the death of General Polan Tallis would leave an empty place in his life.

Colonel VanDeusen was still holding forth.

"... So I told him. I said, 'Look, Lootenant,' I said, 'don't rock the boat. You're a kid yet, you know,' I said. 'You got equal rights with everybody else,' I said, 'but if you rock the boat, you aren't gonna get along so well.'

" 'You just behave yourself,' I said, 'and pull your share

of the load and do your job right and keep your nose clean, and you'll come out all right.

"'Time I get to be on the General Staff,' I told him, 'why, you'll be takin' over my job, maybe. That's the way it works,' I said.

"He's a good kid. I mean, he's a fresh young punk, that's all. He'll learn, O.K. He'll climb right up, once he's got the right attitude. Why, when I was—"

But MacMaine was no longer listening. It was astonishing to realize that what VanDeusen had said was perfectly true. A blockhead like VanDeusen would simply be lifted to a position of higher authority, only to be replaced by another blockhead. There would be no essential change in the *status quo*.

The Kerothi were winning steadily, and the people of Earth and her colonies were making no changes whatever in their way of living. The majority of people were too blind to be able to see what was happening, and the rest were afraid to admit the danger, even to themselves. It required no great understanding of strategy to see what the inevitable outcome must be.

At some point in the last few centuries, human civilization had taken the wrong path—a path that led only to oblivion.

It was at that moment that Colonel Sebastian MacMaine made his decision.

THE ESCAPE

"Are you sure you understand, Tallis?" MacMaine asked in Kerothic.

The alien general nodded emphatically. "Perfectly. Your Kerothic is not so bad that I could misunderstand your instructions. I still don't understand why you are doing this. Oh, I know the reasons you've given me, but I don't completely believe them. However, I'll go along with you. The worst that could happen would be for me to be killed, and I would sooner face death in trying to escape than in waiting for your executioners. If this is some sort of trap, some sort of weird way your race's twisted idea of kindness has evolved to dispose of me, then I'll accept your sentence. It's better than starving to death or facing a firing squad."

"Not a firing squad," MacMaine said. "That wouldn't be kind. An odorless, but quite deadly gas would be pumped into this cell while you slept."

"That's worse. When death comes, I want to face it and fight it off as long as possible, not have it sneaking up on me in my sleep. I think I'd rather starve."

"You would," said MacMaine. "The food that was captured with you has nearly run out, and we haven't been able to capture any more. But rather than let you suffer, they would have killed you painlessly." He glanced at the watch on his instrument cuff. "Almost time."

MacMaine looked the alien over once more. Tallis was dressed in the uniform of Earth's Space Force, and the insignia of a full general gleamed on his collar. His face and hands had been sprayed with an opaque, pink-tan film, and his hairless head was covered with a black wig. He wouldn't pass a close inspection, but MacMaine fervently hoped that he wouldn't need to.

Think it out, be sure you're right, then go ahead. Sebastian MacMaine had done just that. For three months, he had worked over the details of his plan, making sure that they were as perfect as he was capable of making them. Even so, there was a great deal of risk involved, and there were too many details that required luck for MacMaine to be perfectly happy about the plan.

But time was running out. As the general's food supply dwindled, his execution date neared, and now it was only two days away. There was no point in waiting until the last minute; it was now or never.

There were no spying TV cameras in the general's cell, no hidden microphones to report and record what went on. No one had ever escaped from the Space Force's prison, therefore, no one ever would.

MacMaine glanced again at his watch. It was time. He reached inside his blouse and took out a fully loaded handgun.

For an instant, the alien officer's eyes widened, and he stiffened as if he were ready to die in an attempt to disarm the Earthman. Then he saw that MacMaine wasn't holding it by the butt; his hand was clasped around the middle of the weapon.

"This is a chance I have to take," MacMaine said evenly. "With this gun, you can shoot me down right here and try to escape alone. I've told you every detail of our course of action, and, with luck, you might make it alone." He held out his hand, with the weapon resting on his open palm.

General Tallis eyed the Earthman for a long second. Then,

without haste, he took the gun and inspected it with a professional eye.

"Do you know how to operate it?" MacMaine asked, forcing calmness into his voice.

"Yes. We've captured plenty of them." Tallis thumbed the stud that allowed the magazine to slide out of the butt and into his hand. Then he checked the mechanism and the power cartridges. Finally, he replaced the magazine and put the weapon into the empty sleeve holster that MacMaine had given him.

MacMaine let his breath out slowly. "All right," he said. "Let's go."

He opened the door of the cell, and both men stepped out into the corridor. At the far end of the corridor, some thirty yards away, stood the two armed guards who kept watch over the prisoner. At that distance, it was impossible to tell that Tallis was not what he appeared to be.

The guard had been changed while MacMaine was in the prisoner's cell, and he was relying on the lax discipline of the soldiers to get him and Tallis out of the cell block. With luck, the guards would have failed to listen too closely to what they had been told by the men they replaced; with even greater luck, the previous guardsmen would have failed to be too explicit about who was in the prisoner's cell. With no luck at all, MacMaine would be forced to shoot to kill.

MacMaine walked casually up to the two men, who came to an easy attention.

"I want you two men to come with me. Something odd has happened, and General Quinby and I want two witnesses as to what went on."

"What happened, sir?" one of them asked.

"Don't know for sure," MacMaine said in a puzzled voice. "The general and I were talking to the prisoner, when all of a sudden he fell over. I think he's dead. I couldn't find a heartbeat. I want you to take a look at him so that you can testify that we didn't shoot him or anything."

Obediently, the two guards headed for the cell, and MacMaine fell in behind them. "You couldn't of shot him, sir," said the second guard confidently. "We would of heard the shot."

"Besides," said the other, "it don't matter much. He was going to be gassed day after tomorrow."

As the trio approached the cell, Tallis pulled the door open a little wider and, in doing so, contrived to put himself behind it so that his face couldn't be seen. The young guards weren't too awed by a full general; after all, they'd be generals themselves someday. They were much more interested in seeing the dead alien.

As the guards reached the cell door, MacMaine unholstered his pistol from his sleeve and brought it down hard on the head of the nearest youth. At the same time, Tallis stepped from behind the door and clouted the other.

Quickly, MacMaine disarmed the fallen men and dragged them into the open cell. He came out again and locked the door securely. Their guns were tossed into an empty cell nearby.

"They won't be missed until the next change of watch, in four hours," MacMaine said. "By then, it won't matter, one way or another."

Getting out of the huge building that housed the administrative offices of the Space Force was relatively easy. A lift chute brought the pair to the main floor, and, this late in the evening, there weren't many people on that floor. No one appeared to notice anything out of the ordinary.

As they walked out boldly through the main door, fifteen minutes later, the guards merely came to attention and relaxed as a tall colonel and a somewhat shorter general strode out. The general appeared to be having a fit of sneezing, and the colonel was heard to say: "That's quite a cold you've picked up, sir. Better get over to the dispensary and take an anti-coryza shot."

"Mmmf," said the general. *"Ha-CHOO!"*

Getting to the spaceport was no problem at all. MacMaine had an official car waiting, and the two sergeants in the front seat didn't pay any attention to the general getting in the back seat because Colonel MacMaine was talking to them. "We're ready to roll, Sergeant," he said to the driver. "General Quinby wants to go straight to the *Manila,* so let's get there as fast as possible. Take-off is scheduled in ten minutes." Then he got into the back seat himself.

Seven minutes later, the staff car was rolling unquestioned through the main gate of Waikiki Spaceport.

It was all so incredibly easy, MacMaine thought. Nobody questioned an official car. Nobody checked anything too closely. Nobody wanted to risk his lifelong security by doing or saying something that might be considered antisocial by a busy general. Besides, it never entered anyone's mind that

362

there could be anything wrong. If there was a war on, apparently no one had been told about it yet.

MacMaine thought, *Was I ever that stubbornly blind? Not quite, I guess, or I'd never have seen what is happening.* But he knew he hadn't been too much more perceptive than those around him. Even to an intelligent man, the mask of stupidity can become a barrier to the outside world as well as a concealment from it.

The Interstellar Ship *Manila* was a small, fast, ten-man blaster-boat, designed to get into the thick of a battle quickly, strike hard, and get away. Unlike the bigger, more powerful battle cruisers, she could be landed directly on any planet with less than a two-gee pull at the surface. The really big babies had to be parked in an orbit and loaded by shuttle; they'd break up of their own weight if they tried to set down on anything bigger than a good-sized planetoid. As long as their antiacceleration fields were on, they could take unimaginable thrusts along their axes, but the A-A fields were the cause of those thrusts as well as the protection against them. The ships couldn't stand still while they were operating, so they were no protection at all against a planet's gravity. But a blaster-boat was small enough and compact enough to take the strain.

It had taken careful preparation to get the *Manila* ready to go just exactly when MacMaine needed it. Papers had to be forged and put into the chain of command communication at precisely the right times; others had had to be taken out and replaced with harmless near-duplicates so that the Commanding Staff wouldn't discover the deception. He had had to build up the fictional identity of a "General Lucius Quinby" in such a way that it would take a thorough check to discover that the officer who had been put in command of the *Manila* was nonexistent.

It was two minutes until take-off time when the staff car pulled up at the foot of the ramp that led up to the main air lock of the ISS *Manila*. A young-looking captain was standing nervously at the foot of it, obviously afraid that his new commander might be late for the take-off and wondering what sort of decision he would have to make if the general wasn't there at take-off time. MacMaine could imagine his feelings.

"General Quinby" developed another sneezing fit as he stepped out of the car. This was the touchiest part of MacMaine's plan, the weakest link in the whole chain of action. For a space of perhaps a minute, the disguised Kerothi general would have to stand so close to the young captain that the crudity of his makeup job would be detectable. He had to keep that handkerchief over his face, and yet do it in such a way that it would seem natural.

As Tallis climbed out of the car, chuffing windily into the kerchief, MacMaine snapped an order to the sergeant behind the wheel. "That's all. We're taking off almost immediately, so get that car out of here."

Then he walked rapidly over to the captain, who had snapped to attention. There was a definite look of relief on his face, now that he knew his commander was on time.

"All ready for take-off, Captain? Everything checked out? Ammunition? Energy packs all filled to capacity? All the crew aboard? Full rations and stores stowed away?"

The captain kept his eyes on MacMaine's face as he answered "Yes, sir; yes, sir; yes, sir," to the rapid fire of questions. He had no time to shift his gaze to the face of his new C.O., who was snuffling his way toward the foot of the landing ramp. MacMaine kept firing questions until Tallis was halfway up the ramp.

Then he said: "Oh, by the way, Captain—was the large package containing General Quinby's personal gear brought aboard?"

"The big package? Yes, sir. About fifteen minutes ago."

"Good," said MacMaine. He looked up the ramp. "Are there any special orders at this time, sir?" he asked.

"No," said Tallis, without turning. "Carry on, Colonel." He went on up to the air lock. It had taken Tallis hours of practice to say that phrase properly, but the training had been worth it.

After Tallis was well inside the air lock, MacMaine whispered to the young captain, "As you can see, the general has got a rather bad cold. He'll want to remain in his cabin until he's over it. See that anti-coryza shots are sent up from the dispensary as soon as we are out of the Solar System. Now, let's go; we have less than a minute till take-off."

MacMaine went up the ramp with the captain scrambling up behind him.

Tallis was just stepping into the commander's cabin as the two men entered the air lock. MacMaine didn't see him again until the ship was twelve minutes on her way—nearly five billion miles from Earth and still accelerating.

He identified himself at the door and Tallis opened it cautiously.

"I brought your anti-coryza shot, sir," he said. In a small ship like the *Manila,* the captain and the seven crew members could hear any conversation in the companionways. He stepped inside and closed the door. Then he practically collapsed on the nearest chair and had a good case of the shakes.

"So-so f-f-far, s-so good," he said.

General Tallis grasped his shoulder with a firm hand. "Brace up, Sepastian," he said gently in Kerothic. "You've done a beautiful job. I still can't believe it, but I'll have to admit that if this is an act it's a beautiful one." He gestured toward the small desk in one corner of the room and the big package that was sitting on it. "The food is all there. I'll have to eat sparingly, but I can make it. Now, what's the rest of the plan?"

MacMaine took a deep breath, held it, and let it out slowly. His shakes subsided to a faint, almost imperceptible quiver. "The captain doesn't know our destination. He was told that he would receive secret instructions from you." His voice, he noticed thankfully, was almost normal. He reached into his uniform jacket and took out an official-looking sealed envelope. "These are the orders. We are going out to arrange a special truce with the Kerothi."

"What?"

"That's what it says here. You'll have to get on the subradio and do some plain and fancy talking. Fortunately, not a man jack aboard this ship knows a word of your language, so they'll think you're arranging truce terms.

"They'll be sitting ducks when your warship pulls up alongside and sends in a boarding party. By the time they realize what has happened, it will be too late."

"You're giving us the ship, too?" Tallis looked at him wonderingly. "And eight prisoners?"

"Nine," said MacMaine. "I'll hand over my sidearm to you just before your men come through the air lock."

General Tallis sat down in the other small chair, his eyes still on the Earthman. "I can't help but feel that this is some sort of trick, but if it is, I can't see through it. Why are you doing this, Sepastian?"

"You may not understand this, Tallis," MacMaine said evenly, "but I am fighting for freedom. The freedom to think."

THE TRAITOR

Convincing the Kerothi that he was in earnest was more difficult than MacMaine had at first supposed. He had done his best, and now, after nearly a year of captivity, Tallis had come to tell him that his offer had been accepted.

General Tallis sat across from Colonel MacMaine, smoking his cigarette absently.

"Just why are they accepting my proposition?" MacMaine asked bluntly.

"Because they can afford to," Tallis said with a smile. "You will be watched, my sibling-by-choice. Watched every moment, for any sign of treason. Your flagship will be a small ten-man blaster-boat—one of our own. You gave us one; we'll give you one. At the worst, we will come out even. At the best, your admittedly brilliant grasp of tactics and strategy will enable us to save thousands of Kerothi lives, to say nothing of the immense savings in time and money."

"All I ask is a chance to prove my ability and my loyalty."

"You've already proven your ability. All of the strategy problems that you have been given over the past year were actual battles that had already been fought. In eighty-seven percent of the cases, your strategy proved to be superior to our own. In most of the others, it was just as good. In only three cases was the estimate of your losses higher than the actual losses. Actually, we'd be fools to turn you down. We have everything to gain and nothing to lose."

"I felt the same way a year ago," said MacMaine. "Even being watched all the time will allow me more freedom than I had on Earth—if the Board of Strategy is willing to meet my terms."

Tallis chuckled. "They are. You'll be the best-paid officer in the entire fleet; none of the rest of us gets a tenth of what you'll be getting, as far as personal value is concerned. And yet, it costs us practically nothing. You drive an attractive bargain, Sepastian."

"Is that the kind of pay you'd like to get, Tallis?" MacMaine asked with a smile.

"Why not? You'll get your terms: full pay as a Kerothi general, with retirement on full pay after the war is over. The pick of the most beautiful—by your standards—of the Earth-women we capture. A home on Keroth, built to your specifications, and full citizenship, including the freedom to enter into any business relationships you wish. If you keep your promises, we can keep ours and still come out ahead."

"Good. When do we start?"

"Now," said Tallis rising from his chair. "Put on your dress uniform, and we'll go down to see the High Commander. We've got to give you a set of general's insignia, my sibling-by-choice."

Tallis waited while MacMaine donned the blue trousers and gold-trimmed red uniform of a Kerothi officer. When he was through, MacMaine looked at himself in the mirror. "There's one more thing, Tallis," he said thoughtfully.

"What's that?"

"This hair. I think you'd better arrange to have it permanently removed, according to your custom. I can't do anything about the color of my skin, but there's no point in my looking like one of your wild hillmen."

"You're very gracious," Tallis said. "And very wise. Our officers will certainly come closer to feeling that you are one of us."

"I am one of you from this moment," MacMaine said. "I never intend to see Earth again, except, perhaps, from space— when we fight the final battle of the war."

"That may be a hard battle," Tallis said.

"Maybe," MacMaine said thoughtfully. "On the other hand, if my overall strategy comes out the way I think it will, that battle may never be fought at all. I think that complete and total surrender will end the war before we ever get that close to Earth."

"I hope you're right," Tallis said firmly. "This war is costing far more than we had anticipated, in spite of the weakness of your—that is, of Earth."

"Well," MacMaine said with a slight grin, "at least you've been able to capture enough Earth food to keep me eating well all this time."

Tallis' grin was broad. "You're right. We're not doing too badly at that. Now, let's go; the High Commander is waiting."

MacMaine didn't realize until he walked into the big room that what he was facing was not just a discussion with a high officer, but what amounted to a Court of Inquiry.

The High Commander, a dome-headed, wrinkled, yellow-skinned, hard-eyed old Kerothi, was seated in the center of a long, high desk, flanked on either side by two lower-ranking generals who had the same deadly, hard look. Off to one side, almost like a jury in a jury box, sat twenty or so lesser officers, none of them ranking below the Kerothi equivalent of lieutenant colonel.

As far as MacMaine could tell, none of the officers wore the insignia of fleet officers, the spaceship-and-comet that showed that the wearer was a fighting man. These were the men of the Permanent Headquarters Staff—the military group that controlled not only the armed forces of Keroth but the civil government as well.

"What's this?" MacMaine hissed in a whispered aside, in English.

"Pearr up, my prrotherr," Tallis answered softly, in the same tongue, "all is well."

MacMaine had known, long before he had ever heard of General Polan Tallis, that the Hegemony of Keroth was governed by a military junta, and that all Kerothi were regarded as members of the armed forces. Technically, there were no civilians; they were legally members of the "unorganized reserve," and were under military law. He had known that Kerothi society was, in its own way, as much a slave society as that of Earth, but it had the advantage over Earth that the system did allow for advance by merit. If a man had the determination to get ahead, and the ability to cut the throat—either literally or figuratively—of the man above him in rank, he could take his place.

On a more strictly legal basis, it was possible for a common trooper to become an officer by going through the schools set up for that purpose, but, in practice, it took both pull and pressure to get into those schools.

In theory, any citizen of the Hegemony could become an officer, and any officer could become a member of the Permanent Headquarters Staff. Actually, a much greater preference was given to the children of officers. Examinations were given periodically for the purpose of recruiting new members for the elite officers' corps, and any citizen could take the examination—once.

But the tests were heavily weighted in favor of those who were already well versed in matters military, including what might be called the "inside jokes" of the officers' corps. A common trooper had some chance of passing the examination; a civilian had a very minute chance. A noncommissioned

368

officer had the best chance of passing the examination, but there were age limits which usually kept NCOs from getting a commission. By the time a man became a noncommissioned officer, he was too old to be admitted to the officers' training schools. There were allowances made for "extraordinary merit," which allowed common troopers or upper-grade NCOs to be commissioned in spite of the general rules, and an astute man could take advantage of those allowances.

Ability could get a man up the ladder, but it had to be a particular kind of ability.

During his sojourn as a "guest" of the Kerothi, MacMaine had made a point of exploring the history of the race. He knew perfectly well that the histories he had read were doctored, twisted, and, in general, totally unreliable insofar as presenting anything that would be called a history by an unbiased investigator.

But, knowing this, MacMaine had been able to learn a great deal about the present society. Even if the "history" was worthless as such, it did tell something about the attitudes of a society that would make up such a history. And, too, he felt that, in general, the main events which had been catalogued actually occurred; the details had been blurred, and the attitudes of the people had been misrepresented, but the skeleton was essentially factual.

MacMaine felt that he knew what kind of philosophy had produced the mental attitudes of the Court he now faced, and he felt he knew how to handle himself before them.

Half a dozen paces in front of the great desk, the color of the floor tiling was different from that of the rest of the floor. Instead of a solid blue, it was a dead black. Tallis, who was slightly ahead of MacMaine, came to a halt as his toes touched the edge of the black area.

Uh-oh! a balk line, MacMaine thought. He stopped sharply at the same point. Both of them just stood there for a full minute while they were carefully inspected by the members of the Court.

Then the High Commander gestured with one hand, and the officer to his left leaned forward and said: "Why is this one brought before us in the uniform of an officer, bare of any insignia of rank?"

It could only be a ritual question, MacMaine decided; they must know why he was there.

"I bring him as a candidate for admission to our Ingroup,"

Tallis replied formally, "and ask the indulgence of Your Superiorities therefor."

"And who are you who ask our indulgence?"

Tallis identified himself at length—name, rank, serial number, military record, et cetera, et cetera, et cetera.

By the time he had finished, MacMaine was beginning to think that the recitation would go on forever. The High Commander had closed his eyes, and he looked as if he had gone to sleep.

There was more formality. Through it all, MacMaine stood at rigid attention, flexing his calf muscles occasionally to keep the blood flowing in his legs. He had no desire to disgrace himself by passing out in front of the Court.

Finally the Kerothi officer stopped asking Tallis questions and looked at the High Commander. MacMaine got the feeling that there was about to be a departure from the usual procedure.

Without opening his eyes, the High Commander said, in a brittle, rather harsh voice, "These circumstances are unprecedented." Then he opened his eyes and looked directly at MacMaine. "Never has an animal been proposed for such an honor. In times past, such a proposal would have been mockery of this Court and this Ingroup, and a crime of such monstrous proportions as to merit excommunication."

MacMaine knew what that meant. The word was used literally; the condemned one was cut off from all communication by having his sensory nerves surgically severed. Madness followed quickly; psychosomatic death followed eventually, as the brain, cut off from any outside stimuli except those which could not be eliminated without death following instantly, finally became incapable of keeping the body alive. Without feedback, control was impossible, and the organism as a whole slowly deteriorated until death was inevitable.

At first, the victim screamed and thrashed his limbs as the brain sent out message after message to the rest of the body, but since the brain had no way of knowing whether the messages had been received or acted upon, the victim soon went into a state comparable to that of catatonia and finally died.

If it was not the ultimate in punishment, it was a damned close approach, MacMaine thought. And he felt that the word "damned" could be used in that sense without fear of exaggeration.

"However," the High Commander went on, gazing at the ceiling, "circumstances change. It would once have been thought vile that a machine should be allowed to do the work of a skilled man, and the thought that a machine might do the work with more precision and greater rapidity would have been almost blasphemous.

"This case must be viewed in the same light. As we are replacing certain of our workers on our outer planets with Earth animals simply because they are capable of doing the work more cheaply, so we must recognize that the same interests of economy govern in this case.

"A computing animal, in that sense, is in the same class as a computing machine. It would be folly to waste their abilities simply because they are not human.

"There also arises the question of command. It has been represented to this court, by certain officers who have been active in investigating the candidate animal, that it would be as degrading to ask a human officer to take orders from an animal as it would be to ask him to take orders from a commoner of the Unorganized Reserve, if not more so. And, I must admit, there is, on the surface of it, some basis for this reasoning.

"But, again, we must not let ourselves be misled. Does not a spaceship pilot, in a sense, take orders from the computer that gives him his orbits and courses? In fact, do not all computers give orders, in one way or another, to those who use them?

"Why, then, should we refuse to take orders from a computing animal?"

He paused and appeared to listen to the silence in the room before going on.

"Stand at ease until the High Commander looks at you again," Tallis said in a low aside.

This was definitely the pause for adjusting to surprise.

It seemed interminable, though it couldn't have been longer than a minute later that the High Commander dropped his gaze from the ceiling to MacMaine. When MacMaine snapped to attention again, the others in the room became suddenly silent.

"We feel," the hard-faced old Kerothi continued, as if there had been no break, "that, in this case, we are justified in employing the animal in question.

"However, we must make certain exceptions to our normal procedure. The candidate is not a machine, and therefore cannot be treated as a machine. Neither is it human, and therefore cannot be treated as human.

"Therefore, this is the judgment of the Court of the Ingroup:

"The animal, having shown itself to be capable of behaving, in some degree, as befits an officer—including, as we have been informed, voluntarily conforming to our custom as regards superfluous hair—it shall henceforth be considered as having the same status as an untaught child or a barbarian, insofar as social conventions are concerned, and shall be entitled to the use of the human pronoun *he*.

"Further, he shall be entitled to wear the uniform he now wears, and the insignia of a General of the Fleet. He shall be entitled, as far as personal contact goes, to the privileges of that rank, and shall be addressed as such.

"He will be accorded the right of punishment of an officer of that rank, insofar as disciplining his inferiors is concerned, except that he must first secure the concurrence of his Guardian Officer, as hereinafter provided.

"He shall also be subject to punishment in the same way and for the same offenses as humans of his rank, taking into account physiological differences, except as hereinafter provided.

"His reward for proper service"—the High Commander listed the demands MacMaine had made—"are deemed fitting, and shall be paid, provided his duties in service are carried out as proposed.

"Obviously, however, certain restrictions must be made. General MacMaine, as he is entitled to be called, is employed solely as a Strategy Computer. His ability as such and his knowledge of the psychology of the Earth animals are, as far as we are concerned at this moment, his only useful attributes. Therefore, his command is restricted to that function. He is empowered to act only through the other officers of the Fleet as this Court may appoint; he is not to command directly.

"Further, it is ordered that he shall have a Guardian Officer, who shall accompany him at all times and shall be directly responsible for his actions.

"That officer shall be punished for any deliberate crime committed by the aforesaid General MacMaine as if he had himself committed the crime.

"Until such time as this Court may appoint another officer for the purpose, General Polan Tallis, previously identified in these proceedings, is appointed as Guardian Officer."

The High Commander paused for a moment, then he said: "Proceed with the investment of the insignia."

THE STRATEGY

General Sebastian MacMaine, sometime Colonel of Earth's Space Force, and at present a General of the Kerothi Fleet, looked at the array of stars that appeared to drift by the main viewplate of his flagship, the blaster-boat *Shudos*.

Behind him, General Tallis was saying, "You've done well, Sepastian. Better than anyone could have really expected. Three battles so far, and every one of them won by a margin far greater than anticipated. Any ideas that anyone may have had that you were not wholly working for the Kerothi cause has certainly been dispelled."

"Thanks, Tallis." MacMaine turned to look at the Kerothi officer. "I only hope that I can keep it up. Now that we're ready for the big push, I can't help but wonder what would happen if I were to lose a battle."

"Frankly," Tallis said, "that would depend on several things, the main one being whether or not it appeared that you had deliberately thrown the advantage to the enemy. But nobody expects you, or anyone else, to win every time. Even the most brilliant commander can make an honest mistake, and if it can be shown that it *was* an honest mistake, and one, furthermore, that he could not have been expected to avoid, he wouldn't be punished for it. In your case, I'll admit that the investigation would be a great deal more thorough than normal, and that you wouldn't get as much of the benefit of the doubt as another officer might, but unless there is a deliberate error I doubt that anything serious would happen."

"Do you really believe that, Tallis, or is it just wishful thinking on your part, knowing as you do that your punishment will be the same as mine if I fail?" MacMaine asked flatly.

Tallis didn't hesitate. "If I didn't believe it, I would ask to be relieved as your Guardian. And the moment I did that, you would be removed from command. The moment I feel that you are not acting for the best interests of Keroth, I will act—not only to protect myself, but to protect my people."

"That's fair enough," MacMaine said. "But how about the others?"

"I cannot speak for my fellow officers—only for myself." Then Tallis' voice became cold. "Just keep your hands clean, Sepastian, and all will be well. You will not be punished for mistakes—only for crimes. If you are planning no crimes, this worry of yours is needless.''

"I ceased to worry about myself long ago," MacMaine said coolly. "I do not fear personal death, not even by excommunication. My sole worry is about the ultimate outcome of the war if I should fail. That, and nothing more.''

"I believe you," Tallis said. "Let us say no more about it. Your actions are difficult for us to understand, in some ways, that's all. No Kerothi would ever change his allegiance as you have. Nor has any Earth officer that we have captured shown any desire to do so. Oh, some of them have agreed to do almost anything we wanted them to, but these were not the intelligent ones, and even they were only doing it to save their own miserable hides.

"Still, you are an exceptional man, Sepastian, unlike any other of your race, as far as we know. Perhaps it is simply that you are the only one with enough wisdom to seek your intellectual equals rather than remain loyal to a mass of stupid animals who are fit only to be slaves.''

"It was because I foresaw their eventual enslavement that I acted as I did," MacMaine admitted. "As I saw it, I had only two choices—to remain as I was and become a slave to the Kerothi or to put myself in your hands willingly and hope for the best. As you—''

He was interrupted by a harsh voice from a nearby speaker.

"Battle stations! Battle stations! Enemy fleet in detector range! Contact in twelve minutes!"

Tallis and MacMaine headed for the Command Room at a fast trot. The three other Kerothi who made up the Strategy Staff came in at almost the same time. There was a flurry of activity as the computers and viewers were readied for action, then the Kerothi looked expectantly at the Earthman.

MacMaine looked at the detector screens. The deployment of the approaching Earth fleet was almost as he had expected it would be. There were slight differences, but they would require only minor changes in the strategy he had mapped out from the information brought in by the Kerothi scout ships.

Undoubtedly, the Kerothi position had been relayed to the Earth commander by their own advance scouts buzzing about in tiny, one-man shells just small enough to be undetectable at normal range.

Watching the positions on the screens carefully, MacMaine called out a series of numbers in an unhurried voice and watched as the orders, relayed by the Kerothi staff, changed the position of parts of the Kerothi fleet. Then, as the computer-led Earth fleet jockeyed to compensate for the change in the Kerothi deployment, MacMaine called out more orders.

The High Commander of Keroth had called MacMaine a "computing animal," but the term was far from accurate. MacMaine couldn't possibly have computed all the variables in that battle, and he didn't try. It was a matter of human intuition against mechanical logic. The advantage lay with MacMaine, for, while the computer could not logically fathom the intuitive processes of its human opponent, MacMaine could and did have an intuitive grasp of the machine's logic. MacMaine didn't need to know every variable in the pattern; he only needed to know the pattern as a whole.

The *Shudos* was well in the rear of the main body of the Kerothi fleet. There was every necessity for keeping MacMaine's flagship out of as much of the fighting as possible.

When the first contact was made, MacMaine was certain of the outcome. His voice became a steady drone as he called out instructions to the staff officers; his mind was so fully occupied with the moving pattern before him that he noticed nothing else in the room around him.

Spaceship against spaceship, the two fleets locked in battle. The warheads of ultralight torpedoes flared their eye-searing explosions soundlessly into the void; ships exploded like overcharged beer bottles as blaster energy caught them and smashed through their screens; men and machines flamed and died, scattering the stripped nuclei of their component atoms through the screaming silence of space.

And through it all, Sebastian MacMaine watched dispassionately, calling out his orders as ten Earthmen died for every Kerothi death.

This was a crucial battle. The big push toward the center of Earth's cluster of worlds had begun. Until now, the Kerothi had been fighting the outposts, the planets on the fringes of Earth's sphere of influence which were only lightly colonized, and therefore relatively easy to take. Earth's strongest fleets were out there, to protect planets that could not protect themselves.

Inside that periphery were the more densely populated planets, the self-sufficient colonies which were more or less able to defend themselves without too much reliance on space fleets as such. But now that the backbone of Earth's

375

Space Force had been all but broken, it would be a relatively easy matter to mop up planet after planet, since each one could be surrounded separately, pounded into surrender, and secured before going on to the next.

That, at least, had been the original Kerothi intention. But MacMaine had told them that there was another way—a way which, if it succeeded, would save time, lives, and money for the Kerothi. And, if it failed, MacMaine said, they would be no worse off, they would simply have to resume the original plan.

Now the first of the big colony planets was to be taken. When the protecting Earth fleet was reduced to tatters, the Kerothi would go on to Houston's World as the first step in the big push toward Earth itself.

But MacMaine wasn't thinking of that phase of the war. That was still in the future, while the hellish space battle was still at hand.

He lost track of time as he watched the Kerothi fleet take advantage of their superior tactical position and tear the Earth fleet to bits. Not until he saw the remains of the Earth fleet turn tail and run did he realize that the battle had been won.

The Kerothi fleet consolidated itself. There was no point in pursuing the fleeting Earth ships; that would only break up the solidity of the Kerothi deployment. The losers could afford to scatter; the winners could not. Early in the war, the Kerothi had used that trick against Earth; the Kerothi had broken and fled, and the Earth fleet had split up to chase them down. The scattered Earth ships had suddenly found that they had been led into traps composed of hidden clusters of Kerothi ships. Naturally, the trick had never worked again for either side.

"All right," MacMaine said when it was all over, "let's get on to Houston's World."

The staff men, including Tallis, were already on their feet, congratulating MacMaine and shaking his hand. Even General Hokotan, the Headquarters Staff man, who had been transferred temporarily to the Fleet Force to keep an eye on both MacMaine and Tallis, was enthusiastically pounding MacMaine's shoulder.

No one aboard was supposed to know that Hokotan was a Headquarters officer, but MacMaine had spotted the spy rather easily. There was a difference between the fighters of the Fleet and the politicos of Headquarters. The politicos were no harder, perhaps, nor more ruthless, than the fighters, but they were of a different breed. Theirs was the ruthlessness of the bully who steps on those who are weaker rather than the ruthlessness of the man who kills only to win a battle. MacMaine had the feeling that the Headquarters Staff preferred to spend their time browbeating their underlings rather than risk their necks with someone who could fight back, however weakly.

General Hokotan seemed to have more of the fighting quality than most HQ men, but he wasn't a fleet officer at heart. He couldn't be compared to Tallis without looking small and mean.

As a matter of cold fact, very few of the officers were in any way comparable to Tallis—not even the fleet men. The more MacMaine learned of the Kerothi, the more he realized just how lucky he had been that it had been Tallis, and not some other Kerothi general, who had been captured by the Earth forces. He was not at all sure that his plan would have worked at all with any of the other officers he had met.

Tallis, like MacMaine, was an unusual specimen of his race.

MacMaine took the congratulations of the Kerothi officers with a look of pleasure on his face, and when they had subsided somewhat, he grinned and said:

"Let's get a little work done around here, shall we? We have a planet to reduce yet."

They laughed. Reducing a planet didn't require strategy—only firepower. The planet-based defenses couldn't maneuver, but the energy reserve of a planet is greater than that of any fleet, no matter how large. Each defense point would have to be cut down individually by the massed power of the fleet, cut down one by one until the planet was helpless. The planet as a whole might have more energy reserve than the fleet, but no individual defense point did. The problem was to avoid being hit by the rest of the defense points while one single point was bearing the brunt of the fleet's attack. It wasn't without danger, but it could be done.

And for a job like that, MacMaine's special abilities weren't needed. He could only watch and wait until it was over.

So he watched and waited. Unlike the short-time fury of a space battle, the reduction of a planet took days of steady pounding. When it was over, the blaster-boats of the Kerothi fleet and the shuttles from the great battle cruisers landed on Houston's World and took possession of the planet.

* * *

MacMaine was waiting in his cabin when General Hokotan brought the news that the planet was secured.

"They are ours," the HQ spy said with a superior smile. "The sniveling animals didn't even seem to want to defend themselves. They don't even know how to fight a hand-to-hand battle. How could such things have ever evolved intelligence enough to conquer space?" Hokotan enjoyed making such remarks to MacMaine's face, knowing that since MacMaine was technically a Kerothi he couldn't show any emotion when the enemy was insulted.

MacMaine showed none. "Got them all, eh?" he said.

"All but a few who scattered into the hills and forests. But not many of them had the guts to leave the security of their cities, even though we were occupying them."

"How many are left alive?"

"An estimated hundred and fifty million, more or less."

"Good. That should be enough to set an example. I picked Houston's World because we can withdraw from it without weakening our position; its position in space is such that it would constitute no menace to us even if we never reduced it. That way, we can be sure that our little message is received on Earth."

Hokotan's grin was wolfish. "And the whole weak-hearted race will shake with fear, eh?"

"Exactly. Tallis can speak English well enough to be understood. Have him make the announcement to them. He can word it however he likes, but the essence is to be this: Houston's World resisted the occupation by Kerothi troops; an example must be made of them to show them what happens to Earthmen who resist."

"That's all?"

"That's enough. Oh, by the way, make sure that there are plenty of their cargo spaceships in good working order; I doubt that we've ruined them all, but if we have, repair some of them.

"And, too, you'd better make sure that you allow some of the merchant spacemen to 'escape,' just in case there are no space pilots among those who took to the hills. We want to make sure that someone can use those ships to take the news back to Earth."

"And the rest?" Hokotan asked, with an expectant look. He knew what was to be done, but he wanted to hear MacMaine say it again.

MacMaine obliged.

"Hang them. Every man, every woman, every child. I want them to be decorating every lamppost and roof beam on the planet, dangling like overripe fruit when the Earth forces return."

THE RESULTS

"I don't understand it," said General Polan Tallis worriedly. "Where are they coming from? How are they doing it? What's happened?"

MacMaine and the four Kerothi officers were sitting in the small dining room that doubled as a recreation room between meals. The nervous strain of the past few months was beginning to tell on all of them.

"Six months ago," Tallis continued jerkily, "we had them beaten. One planet after another was reduced in turn. Then, out of nowhere, comes a fleet of ships we didn't even know existed, and they've smashed us at every turn."

"If they *are* ships," said Loopat, the youngest officer of the *Shudos* staff. "Whoever heard of a battleship that was undetectable at a distance of less than half a million miles? It's impossible!"

"Then we're being torn to pieces by the impossible!" Hokotan snapped. "Before we even know they are anywhere around, they are blasting us with everything they've got! Not even the strategic genius of General MacMaine can help us if we have no time to plot strategy!"

The Kerothi had been avoiding MacMaine's eyes, but now, at the mention of his name, they all looked at him as if their collective gaze had been drawn to him by some unknown attractive force.

"It's like fighting ghosts," MacMaine said in a hushed voice. For the first time, he felt a feeling of awe that was almost akin to fear. What had he done?

In another sense, that same question was in the mind of the Kerothi.

"Have you any notion at all what they are doing or how they are doing it?" asked Tallis gently.

"None," MacMaine answered truthfully. "None at all, I swear to you."

"They don't even behave like Earthmen," said the fourth Kerothi, a thick-necked officer named Ossif. "They not only outfight us, they outthink us at every turn. Is it possible,

General MacMaine, that the Earthmen have allies of another race, a race of intelligent beings that we don't know of?'' He left unsaid the added implication: *"And that you have neglected to tell us about?"*

"Again," said MacMaine, "I swear to you that I know nothing of any third intelligent race in the galaxy."

"If there were such allies," Tallis said, "isn't it odd that they should wait so long to aid their friends?"

"No odder than that the Earthmen should suddenly develop superweapons that we cannot understand, much less fight against," Hokotan said, with a touch of anger.

"Not 'superweapons,' " MacMaine corrected almost absently. "All they have is a method of making their biggest ships undetectable until they're so close that it doesn't matter. When they do register on our detectors, it's too late. But the weapons they strike with are the same type as they've always used, I believe."

"All right, then," Hokotan said, his voice showing more anger. "One weapon or whatever you want to call it. Practical invisibility. But that's enough. An invisible man with a knife is more deadly than a dozen ordinary men with modern armament. Are you sure you know nothing of this, General MacMaine?"

Before MacMaine could answer, Tallis said, "Don't be ridiculous, Hokotan! If he had known that such a weapon existed, would he have been fool enough to leave his people? With that secret, they stand a good chance of beating us in less than half the time it took us to wipe out their fleet—or, rather, to wipe out as much of it as we did."

"They got a new fleet somewhere," said young Loopat, almost to himself.

Tallis ignored him. "If MacMaine deserted his former allegiance, knowing that they had a method of rendering the action of a space drive indetectable, then he was and is a blithering idiot. And we know he isn't."

"All right, all right! I concede that," snapped Hokotan. "He knows nothing. I don't say that I fully trust him, even now, but I'll admit that I cannot see how he is to blame for the reversals of the past few months.

"If the Earthmen had somehow been informed of our activities, or if we had invented a superweapon and they found out about it, I would be inclined to put the blame squarely on MacMaine. But—''

"How would he get such information out?" Tallis cut in sharply. "He has been watched every minute of every day. We know he couldn't send any information to Earth. How could he?"

"Telepathy, for all I know!" Hokotan retorted. "But that's beside the point! I don't trust him any farther than I can see him, and not completely, even then. But I concede that there is no possible connection between this new menace and anything MacMaine might have done.

"This is no time to worry about that sort of thing; we've got to find some way of getting our hands on one of those ghost ships!"

"I do suggest," put in the thick-necked Ossif, "that we keep a closer watch on General MacMaine. Now that the Earth animals are making a comeback, he might decide to turn his coat now, even if he has been innocent of any acts against Keroth so far."

Hokotan's laugh was a short, hard bark. "Oh, we'll watch him, all right, Ossif. But, as Tallis has pointed out, MacMaine is not a fool, and he would certainly be a fool to return to Earth if his leaving it was a genuine act of desertion. The last planet we captured, before this invisibility thing came up to stop us, was plastered all over with notices that the Earth fleet was concentrating on the capture of the arch-traitor MacMaine.

"The price on his head, as a corpse, is enough to allow an Earthman to retire in luxury for life. The man who brings him back alive gets ten times that amount.

"Of course, it's possible that the whole thing is a put-up job—a smoke screen for our benefit. That's why we must and will keep a closer watch. But only a few of Earth's higher-ups would know that it was a smoke screen; the rest believe it, whether it is true or not. MacMaine would have to be very careful not to let the wrong people get their hands on him if he returned."

"It's no smoke screen," MacMaine said in a matter-of-fact tone. "I assure you that I have no intention of returning to Earth. If Keroth loses this war, then I will die—either fighting for the Kerothi or by execution at the hands of Earthmen if I am captured. Or," he added musingly, "perhaps even at the hands of the Kerothi, if someone decides that a scapegoat is needed to atone for the loss of the war."

"If you are guilty of treason," Hokotan barked, "you will

381

die as a traitor! If you are not, there is no need for your death. The Kerothi do not need scapegoats!"

"Talk, talk, talk!" Tallis said with a sudden bellow. "We have agreed that MacMaine has done nothing that could even remotely be regarded as suspicious! He has fought hard and loyally; he has been more ruthless than any of us in destroying the enemy. Very well, we will guard him more closely. We can put him in irons if that's necessary.

"But let's quit yapping and start thinking! We've been acting like frightened children, not knowing what it is we fear, and venting our fear-caused anger on the most handy target!

"Let's act like men—not like children!"

After a moment, Hokotan said: "I agree." His voice was firm, but calm. "Our job will be to get our hands on one of those new Earth ships. Anyone have any suggestions?"

They had all kinds of suggestions, one after another. The detectors, however, worked because they detected the distortion of space which was as necessary for the drive of a ship as the distortion of air was necessary for the movement of a propellor-driven aircraft. None of them could see how a ship could avoid making that distortion, and none of them could figure out how to go about capturing a ship that no one could even detect until it was too late to set a trap.

The discussion went on for days. And it was continued the next day and the next. And the days dragged out into weeks.

Communications with Keroth broke down. The Fleet-to-Headquarters courier ships, small in size, without armament, and practically solidly packed with drive mechanism, could presumably outrun anything but another unarmed courier. An armed ship of the same size would have to use some of the space for her weapons, which meant that the drive would have to be smaller; if the drive remained the same size, then the armament would make the ship larger. In either case, the speed would be cut down. A smaller ship might outrun a standard courier, but if they got much smaller, there wouldn't be room inside for the pilot.

Nonetheless, courier after courier never arrived at its destination.

And the Kerothi Fleet was being decimated by the hit-and-run tactics of Earth's ghost ships. And Earth never lost a ship; by the time the Kerothi ships knew their enemy was in the vicinity, the enemy had hit and vanished again. The Kerothi never had a chance to ready their weapons.

In the long run, they never had a chance at all.

MacMaine waited with almost fatalistic complacence for the inevitable to happen. When it did happen, he was ready for it.

The *Shudos*, tiny flagship of what had once been a mighty armada and was now only a tattered remnant, was floating in orbit, along with the other remaining ships of the fleet, around a bloated red-giant sun. With their drives off, there was no way of detecting them at any distance, and the chance of their being found by accident was microscopically small. But they could not wait forever. Water could be recirculated, and energy could be tapped from the nearby sun, but food was gone once it was eaten.

Hokotan's decision was inevitable, and, under the circumstances, the only possible one. He simply told them what they had already known—that he was a Headquarters Staff officer.

"We haven't heard from Headquarters in weeks," he said at last. "The Earth fleet may already be well inside our periphery. We'll have to go home." He produced a document which he had obviously been holding in reserve for another purpose and handed it to Tallis. "Headquarters Staff Orders, Tallis. It empowers me to take command of the Fleet in the event of an emergency, and the decision as to what constitutes an emergency was left up to my discretion. I must admit that this is not the emergency any of us at Headquarters anticipated."

Tallis read through the document. "I see that it isn't," he said dryly. "According to this, MacMaine and I are to be placed under immediate arrest as soon as you find it necessary to act."

"Yes," said Hokotan bitterly. "So you can both consider yourselves under arrest. Don't bother to lock yourselves up—there's no point in it. General MacMaine, I see no reason to inform the rest of the Fleet of this, so we will go on as usual. The orders I have to give are simple: the Fleet will head for home by the most direct possible geodesic. Since we cannot fight, we will simply ignore attacks and keep going as long as we last. We can do nothing else." He paused thoughtfully.

"And, General MacMaine, in case we do not live through this, I would like to extend my apologies. I do not like you; I don't think I could ever learn to like an anim—to like a non-Kerothi. But I know when to admit an error in judgment. You have fought bravely and well—better, I know, than I could have done myself. You have shown yourself to be loyal to your adopted planet; you are a Kerothi in every sense of the word except the physical. My apologies for having wronged you."

He extended his hands and MacMaine took them. A choking sensation constricted the Earthman's throat for a moment, then he got the words out—the words he had to say. "Believe me, General Hokotan, there is no need for an apology. No need whatever."

"Thank you," said Hokotan. Then he turned and left the room.

"All right, Tallis," MacMaine said hurriedly, "let's get moving."

The orders were given to the remnants of the Fleet, and they cut in their drives to head homeward. And the instant they did, there was chaos. Earth's fleet of "ghost ships" had been patrolling the area for weeks, knowing that the Kerothi Fleet had last been detected somewhere in the vicinity. As soon as the spatial distortions of the Kerothi drives flashed on the Earth ships' detectors, the Earth Fleet, widely scattered over the whole circumambient volume of space, coalesced toward the center of the spatial disturbance like a cloud of bees all heading for the same flower.

Where there had been only the dull red light of the giant star, there suddenly appeared the blinding, blue-white brilliance of disintegrating matter, blossoming like cruel, deadly, beautiful flowers in the midst of the Kerothi ships, then fading slowly as each expanding cloud of plasma cooled.

Sebastian MacMaine might have died with the others except that the *Shudos*, as the flagship, was to trail behind the Fleet, so her drive had not yet been activated. The *Shudos* was still in orbit, moving at only a few miles per second, when the Earth Fleet struck.

Her drive never did go on. A bomb, only a short distance away as the distance from atomic disintegration is measured, sent the *Shudos* spinning away, end over end, like a discarded cigar butt flipped toward a gutter, one side caved in near the rear, as if it had been kicked in by a giant foot.

There was still air in the ship, MacMaine realized groggily as he awoke from the unconsciousness that had been thrust upon him. He tried to stand up, but he found himself staggering toward one crazily slanted wall. The stagger was partly due to his grogginess, and partly due to the Coriolis forces acting within the spinning ship. The artificial gravity was gone, which meant that the interstellar drive engines had been smashed. He wondered if the emergency rocket drive was still working—not that it would take him anywhere worth going to in less than a few centuries. But, then, Sebastian MacMaine had nowhere to go, anyhow.

Tallis lay against one wall, looking very limp. MacMaine half staggered over to him and knelt down. Tallis was still alive.

The centrifugal force caused by the spinning ship gave an effective pull of less than one Earth gravity, but the weird twists caused by the Coriolis forces made motion and orientation difficult. Besides, the ship was spinning slightly on her long axis as well as turning end for end.

MacMaine stood there for a moment, trying to think. He had expected to die. Death was something he had known was inevitable from the moment he made his decision to leave Earth. He had not known how or when it would come, but he had known that it would come soon. He had known that he would never live to collect the reward he had demanded of the Kerothi for "faithful service." Traitor he might be, but he was still honest enough with himself to know that he would never take payment for services he had not rendered.

Now death was very near, and Sebastian MacMaine almost welcomed it. He had no desire to fight it. Tallis might want to stand and fight death to the end, but Tallis was not carrying the monstrous weight of guilt that would stay with Sebastian MacMaine until his death, no matter how much he tried to justify his actions.

On the other hand, if he had to go, he might as well do a good job of it. Since he still had a short time left, he might as well wrap the whole thing up in a neat package. How?

Again, his intuitive ability to see pattern gave him the answer long before he could have reasoned it out.

They will know, he thought, *but they will never be sure they know. I will be immortal. And my name will live forever, although no Earthman will ever again use the surname MacMaine or the given name Sebastian.*

He shook his head to clear it. No use thinking like that now. There were things to be done.

Tallis first. MacMaine made his way over to one of the emergency medical kits that he knew were kept in every compartment of every ship. One of the doors of a wall locker hung open, and the blue-green medical symbol used by the Kerothi showed darkly in the dim light that came from the three unshattered glow plates in the ceiling. He opened the kit, hoping that it contained something equivalent to adhesive tape. He had never inspected a Kerothi medical kit before. Fortunately, he could read Kerothi. If a military government was good for nothing else, at least it was capable of enforcing a simplified phonetic orthography so that words were pronounced as they were spelled. And—

He forced his wandering mind back to his work. The blow on the head, plus the crazy effect the spinning was having on his inner ears, plus the cockeyed gravitational orientation that made his eyes feel as though they were seeing things at two different angles, all combined to make for more than a little mental confusion.

There was adhesive tape, all right. Wound on its little spool, it looked almost homey. He spent several minutes winding the sticky plastic ribbon around Tallis' wrists and ankles.

Then he took the gun from the Kerothi general's sleeve holster—he had never been allowed one of his own—and, holding it firmly in his right hand, he went on a tour of the ship.

It was hard to move around. The centrifugal force varied from point to point throughout the ship, and the corridors were cluttered with debris that seemed to move with a life of its own as each piece shifted slowly under the effects of the various forces working on it. And, as the various masses moved about, the rate of spin of the ship changed as the law of conservation of angular momentum operated. The ship was full of sliding, clattering, jangling noises as the stuff tried to find a final resting place and bring the ship to equilibrium.

He found the door to Ossif's cabin open and the room empty. He found Ossif in Loopat's cabin, trying to get the younger officer to his feet.

Ossif saw MacMaine at the door and said: "You're alive! Good! Help me—" Then he saw the gun in MacMaine's hand and stopped. It was the last thing he saw before MacMaine shot him neatly between the eyes.

Loopat, only half conscious, never even knew he was in danger, and the blast that drilled through his brain prevented him from ever knowing anything again in this life.

Like a man in a dream, MacMaine went on to Hokotan's cabin, his weapon at the ready. He was rather pleased to find that the HQ general was already quite dead, his neck broken as cleanly as if it had been done by a hangman. Hardly an hour before, MacMaine would cheerfully have shot Hokotan where it would hurt the most and watch him die slowly. But the memory of Hokotan's honest apology made the Earthman very glad that he did not have to shoot the general at all.

There remained only the five-man crew, the NCO technician and his gang, who actually ran the ship. They would be at the tail of the ship, in the engine compartment. To get there, he had to cross the center of spin of the ship, and the change of gravity from one direction to another, decreasing toward zero, passing the null point, and rising again on the other side, made him nauseous. He felt better after his stomach had emptied itself.

Cautiously, he opened the door to the drive compartment and then slammed it hard in sudden fear when he saw what had happened. The shielding had been torn away from one of the energy converters and exposed the room to high-energy radiation. The crewmen were quite dead.

The fear went away as quickly as it had come. So maybe he'd dosed himself with a few hundred roentgens—so what? A little radiation never hurt a dead man.

But he knew now that there was no possibility of escape. The drive was wrecked, and the only other means of escape, the one-man courier boat that every blaster-boat carried, had been sent out weeks ago and had never returned.

If only the courier boat were still in its cradle—

MacMaine shook his head. No. It was better this way. Much better.

He turned and went back to the dining cabin where Tallis was trussed up. This time, passing the null-gee point didn't bother him much at all.

Tallis was moaning a little and his eyelids were fluttering by the time MacMaine got back. The Earthman opened the medical kit again and looked for some kind of stimulant. He had no knowledge of medical or chemical terms in Kerothic, but there was a box of glass ampoules bearing instructions to "crush and allow patient to inhale fumes." That sounded right.

The stuff smelled like a mixture of spirits of ammonia and butyl mercaptan, but it did the job. Tallis coughed convulsively, turned his head away, coughed again, and opened his eyes. MacMaine tossed the stinking ampoule out into the corridor as Tallis tried to focus his eyes.

"How do you feel?" MacMaine asked. His voice sounded oddly thick in his own ears.

"All right. I'm all right. What happened?" He looked wonderingly around. "Near miss? Must be. Anyone hurt?"

"They're all dead but you and me," MacMaine said.

"Dead? Then we'd better—" He tried to move and then realized that he was bound hand and foot. The sudden realization of his position seemed to clear his brain completely. "Sepastian, what's going on here? Why am I tied up?"

"I had to tie you," MacMaine explained carefully, as though to a child. "There are some things I have to do yet, and I wouldn't want you to stop me. Maybe I should have just shot you while you were unconscious. That would have been kinder to both of us, I think. But . . . but, Tallis, I had to tell somebody. Someone else has to know. Someone else has to judge. Or maybe I just want to unload it on someone else, someone who will carry the burden with me for just a little while. I don't know."

"Sepastian, what are you talking about?" The Kerothi's face shone dully orange in the dim light, his bright green eyes looked steadily at the Earthman, and his voice was oddly gentle.

"I'm talking about treason," said MacMaine. "Do you want to listen?"

"I don't have much choice, do I?" Tallis said. "Tell me one thing first: are we going to die?"

"You are, Tallis. But I won't. I'm going to be immortal."

Tallis looked at him for a long moment. Then, "All right, Sepastian. I'm no psych man, but I know you're not well. I'll listen to whatever you have to say. But first, untie my hands and feet."

"I can't do that, Tallis. Sorry. But if our positions were reversed, I know what I would do to you when I heard the story. And I can't let you kill me, because there's something more that has to be done."

Tallis knew at that moment that he was looking at the face of Death. And he also knew that there was nothing whatever he could do about it. Except talk. And listen.

"Very well, Sepastian," he said levelly. "Go ahead. Treason, you say? How? Against whom?"

"I'm not quite sure," said Sebastian MacMaine. "I thought maybe you could tell me."

THE REASON

"Let me ask you one thing, Tallis," MacMaine said. "Would you do anything in your power to save Keroth from destruction? Anything, no matter how drastic, if you knew that it would save Keroth in the long run?"

"A foolish question. Of course I would. I would give my life."

"Your life? A mere nothing. A pittance. Any man could give his life. Would you consent to live forever for Keroth?"

Tallis shook his head as though he were puzzled. "Live forever? That's twice or three times you've said something about that. I *don't* understand you."

"Would you consent to live forever as a filthy curse on the lips of every Kerothi old enough to speak? Would you consent to be a vile, inhuman monster whose undead spirit would hang over your homeland like an evil miasma for centuries to come, whose very name would touch a flame of hatred in the minds of all who heard it?"

"That's a very melodramatic way of putting it," the Kerothi said, "but I believe I understand what you mean. Yes, I would consent to that if it would be the only salvation of Keroth."

"Would you slaughter helpless millions of your own people so that other billions might survive? Would you ruthlessly smash your system of government and your whole way of life if it were the only way to save the people themselves?"

"I'm beginning to see what you're driving at," Tallis said slowly. "And if it is what I think it is, I think I would like to kill you—very slowly."

"I know, I know. But you haven't answered my question. Would you do those things to save your people?"

"I would," said Tallis coldly. "Don't misunderstand me. I do not loathe you for what you have done to your own people; I hate you for what you have done to mine."

"That's as it should be," said MacMaine. His head was clearing up more now. He realized that he had been talking a little wildly at first. Or was he really insane? Had he been insane from the beginning? No. He knew with absolute clarity that every step he had made had been cold, calculating, and ruthless, but utterly and absolutely sane.

He suddenly wished that he had shot Tallis without wakening him. If his mind hadn't been in such a state of shock, he would have. There was no need to torture the man like this.

"Go on," said Tallis, in a voice that had suddenly become devoid of all emotion. "Tell it all."

"Earth was stagnating," MacMaine said, surprised at the sound of his own voice. He hadn't intended to go on. But he couldn't stop now. "You saw how it was. Every standard had become meaningless because no standard was held to be better than any other standard. There was no beauty because beauty was superior to ugliness and we couldn't allow superiority or inferiority. There was no love because in order to love someone or something you must feel that it is in some way superior to that which is not loved. I'm not even sure I know what those terms mean, because I'm not sure I ever thought anything was beautiful, I'm not sure I ever loved anything. I only read about such things in books. But I know I felt the emptiness inside me where those things should have been.

"There was no morality, either. People did not refrain from stealing because it was wrong, but simply because it was pointless to steal what would be given to you if you asked for it. There was no right or wrong.

"We had a form of social contract that we called 'marriage,' but it wasn't the same thing as marriage was in the old days. There was no love. There used to be a crime called 'adultery,' but even the word had gone out of use on the Earth I knew. Instead, it was considered antisocial for a woman to refuse to give herself to other men; to do so might indicate that she thought herself superior or thought her husband to be superior to other men. The same thing applied to men in their relationships with women other than their wives. Marriage was a social contract that could be made or broken at the whim of the individual. It served no purpose because it meant nothing; neither party gained anything by the contract that they couldn't have had without it. But a wedding was an excuse for a gala party at which the couple were the center of attention. So the contract was entered into lightly for the sake of a gay time for a while, then broken again so that the game could be played with someone else—the game of Musical Bedrooms."

He stopped and looked down at the helpless Kerothi. "That doesn't mean much to you, does it? In your society, women are chattel, to be owned, bought, and sold. If you see a woman you want, you offer a price to her father or brother or husband—whoever the owner might be. Then she's yours until you sell her to another. Adultery is a very serious crime on Kerothi, but only because it's an infringement of property rights. There's not much love lost there, either, is there?

"I wonder if either of us knows what love is, Tallis?"

"I love my people," Tallis said grimly.

MacMaine was startled for a moment. He'd never thought about it that way. "You're right, Tallis," he said at last. "You're right. We *do* know. And because I loved the human race, in spite of its stagnation and its spirit of total mediocrity, I did what I had to do."

"You will pardon me," Tallis said, with only the faintest bit of acid in his voice, "if I do not understand exactly what it is that you did." Then his voice grew softer. "Wait. Perhaps I do understand. Yes, of course."

"You think you understand?" MacMaine looked at him narrowly.

"Yes. I said that I am not a psychomedic, and my getting angry with you proves it. You fought hard and well for Keroth, Sepastian, and, in doing so, you had to kill many of your own race. It is not easy for a man to do, no matter how much your reason tells you it *must* be done. And now, in the face of death, remorse has come. I do not completely understand the workings of the Earthman's mind, but I—"

"That's just it; you don't," MacMaine interrupted. "Thanks for trying to find an excuse for me, Tallis, but I'm afraid it isn't so. Listen.

"I had to find out what Earth was up against. I had a pretty good idea already that the Kerothi would win—would wipe us out or enslave us to the last man. And, after I had seen Keroth, I was certain of it. So I sent a message back to Earth, telling them what they were up against, because up 'til then they hadn't known. As soon as they knew, they reacted as they have always done when they are certain that they face danger. They fought. They unleashed the chained-down intelligence of the few extraordinary Earthmen, and they released the fighting spirit of even the ordinary Earthmen. And they won!"

Tallis shook his head. "You sent no message, Sepastian. You were watched. You know that. You could not have sent a message."

"You saw me send it," MacMaine said. "So did everyone else in the Fleet. Hokotan helped me send it—made all the arrangements at my orders. But because you do not understand the workings of the Earthman's mind, you didn't even recognize it as a message.

"Tallis, what would your people have done if an invading force, which had already proven that it could whip Keroth easily, did to one of your planets what we did on Houston's World?"

"If the enemy showed us that they could easily beat us and then hanged the whole population of a planet for resisting? Why, we would be fools to resist. Unless, of course, we had a secret weapon in a hidden pocket, the way Earth had."

"No, Tallis; no. That's where you're making your mistake. Earth didn't have that weapon until *after* the massacre on Houston's World. Let me ask you another thing: would any Kerothi have ordered that massacre?"

"I doubt it," Tallis said slowly. "Killing that many potential slaves would be wasteful and expensive. We are fighters, not butchers. We kill only when it is necessary to win; the remainder of the enemy is taken care of as the rightful property of the conqueror."

"Exactly. Prisoners were part of the loot, and it's foolish to destroy loot. I noticed that in your history books. I noticed, too, that in such cases, the captives recognized the right of the conqueror to enslave them, and made no trouble. So, after Earth's forces get to Keroth, I don't think we'll have any trouble with you."

"Not if they set us an example like Houston's World," Tallis said, "and can prove that resistance is futile. But I don't understand the message. What was the message and how did you send it?"

"The massacre on Houston's World was the message, Tallis. I even told the Staff, when I suggested it. I said that such an act would strike terror into the minds of Earthmen.

"And it did, Tallis; it did. But that terror was just the goad they needed to make them fight. They had to sit up and take notice. If the Kerothi had gone on the way they were going, taking one planet after another, as they planned, the Kerothi would have won. The people of each planet would think, 'It can't happen here.' And, since they felt that nothing could be superior to anything else, they were complacently certain that they couldn't be beat. Of course, maybe Earth couldn't beat you, either, but that was all right; it just proved that there was no such thing as superiority.

"But Houston's World jarred them—badly. It had to. 'Hell

does more than Heaven can to wake the fear of God in man.'
They didn't recognize beauty, but I shoved ugliness down
their throats; they didn't know love and friendship, so I gave
them hatred and fear.

"The committing of atrocities has been the mistake of
aggressors throughout Earth's history. The battle cries of
countless wars have called upon the people to remember an
atrocity. Nothing else hits an Earthman as hard as a vicious,
brutal, unnecessary murder.

"So I gave them the incentive to fight, Tallis. That was my
message."

Tallis was staring at him wide-eyed. "You *are* insane."

"No. It worked. In six months, they found something that
would enable them to blast the devil Kerothi from the skies. I
don't know what the society of Earth is like now—and I never
will. But at least I know that men are allowed to think again.
And I know they'll survive."

He suddenly realized how much time had passed. Had it
been too long? No. There would still be Earth ships prowling
the vicinity, waiting for any sign of a Kerothi ship that had
hidden in the vastness of space by not using its engines.

"I have some things I must do, Tallis," he said, standing
up slowly. "Is there anything else you want to know?"

Tallis frowned a little, as though he were trying to think of
something, but then he closed his eyes and relaxed. "No,
Sepastian. Nothing. Do whatever it is you have to do."

"Tallis," MacMaine said. Tallis didn't open his eyes, and
MacMaine was very glad of that. "Tallis, I want you to know
that, in all my life, you were the only friend I ever had."

The bright green eyes remained closed. "That may be so.
Yes, Sepastian, I honestly think you believe that."

"I do," said MacMaine, and shot him carefully through
the head.

THE END

—and Epilogue.

"Hold it!" The voice bellowed thunderingly from the loud-
speakers of the six Earth ships that had boxed in the derelict.
"Hold it! *Don't bomb that ship!* I'll personally have the head
of any man who damages that ship!"

In five of the ships, the commanders simply held off the

bombardment that would have vaporized the derelict. In the sixth, Major Thornton, the Group Commander, snapped off the microphone. His voice was shaky as he said: "That was close! Another second, and we'd have lost that ship forever."

Captain Verenski's Oriental features had a half-startled, half-puzzled look. "I don't get it. You grabbed that mike control as if you'd been bitten. I know that she's only a derelict. After that burst of fifty-gee acceleration for fifteen minutes, there couldn't be anyone left alive on her. But there must have been a reason for using atomic rockets instead of their antiacceleration fields. What makes you think she's not dangerous?"

"I didn't say she wasn't dangerous," the major snapped. "She may be. Probably is. But we're going to capture her if we can. Look!" He pointed at the image of the ship in the screen.

She wasn't spinning now, or looping end over end. After fifteen minutes of high acceleration, her atomic rockets had cut out, and now she moved serenely at constant velocity, looking as dead as a battered tin can.

"I don't see anything," Captain Verenski said.

"The Kerothic symbols on the side. Palatal unvoiced sibilant, rounded—"

"I don't read Kerothic, Major," said the captain. "I—" Then he blinked and said, *"Shudos!"*

"That's it. The *Shudos* of Keroth. The flagship of the Kerothi Fleet."

The look in the major's eyes was the same look of hatred that had come into the captain's.

"Even if its armament is still functioning, we have to take the chance," Major Thornton said. "Even if they're all dead, we have to try to get the Butcher's body." He picked up the microphone again.

"Attention, group. Listen carefully and don't get itchy trigger fingers. That ship is the *Shudos*. The Butcher's ship. It's a ten-man ship, and the most she could have aboard would be thirty, even if they jammed her full to the hull. I don't know of any way that anyone could be alive on her after fifteen minutes at fifty gees of atomic drive, but remember that they don't have any idea of how our counteraction generators damp out spatial distortion either. Remember what Dr. Pendric said: 'No man is superior to any other in *all* ways. Every man is superior to every other in *some* way.' We may

394

have the counteraction generator, but they may have something else that we don't know about. So stay alert.

"I am going to take a landing party aboard. There's a reward out for the Butcher, and that reward will be split proportionately among us. It's big enough for us all to enjoy it, and we'll probably get citations if we bring him in.

"I want ten men from each ship. I'm not asking for volunteers; I want each ship commander to pick the ten men he thinks will be least likely to lose their heads in an emergency. I don't want anyone to panic and shoot when he should be thinking. I don't want anyone who had any relatives on Houston's World. Sorry, but I can't allow vengeance yet.

"We're a thousand miles from the *Shudos* now; close in slowly until we're within a hundred yards. The boarding parties will don armor and prepare to board while we're closing in. At a hundred yards, we stop and the boarding parties will land on the hull. I'll give further orders then.

"One more thing. I don't think her A-A generators could possibly be functioning, judging from that dent in her hull, but we can't be sure. If she tries to go into A-A drive, she is to be bombed—no matter who is aboard. It is better that sixty men die than that the Butcher escape.

"All right, let's go. Move in."

Half an hour later, Major Thornton stood on the hull of the *Shudos*, surrounded by the sixty men of the boarding party. "Anybody see anything through those windows?" he asked.

Several of the men had peered through the direct-vision ports, playing spotlight beams through them.

"Nothing alive," said a sergeant, a remark which was followed by a chorus of agreement.

"Pretty much of a mess in there," said another sergeant. "That fifty gees mashed everything to the floor. Why'd anyone want to use acceleration like that?"

"Let's go in and find out," said Major Thornton.

The outer door to the air lock was closed, but not locked. It swung open easily to disclose the room between the outer and inner doors. Ten men went in with the major, the others stayed outside with orders to cut through the hull if anything went wrong.

"If he's still alive," the major said, "we don't want to kill him by blowing the air. Sergeant, start the air-lock cycle."

There was barely room for ten men in the air lock. It had

395

been built big enough for the full crew to use it at one time, but it was only just big enough.

When the inner door opened, they went in cautiously. They spread out and searched cautiously. The caution was unnecessary, as it turned out. There wasn't a living thing aboard.

"Three officers shot through the head, sir," said the sergeant. "One of 'em looks like he died of a broken neck, but it's hard to tell after that fifty gees mashed 'em. Crewmen in the engine room—five of 'em. Mashed up, but I'd say they died of radiation, since the shielding on one of the generators was ruptured by the blast that made that dent in the hull."

"Nine bodies," the major said musingly. "All Kerothi. And all of them probably dead *before* the fifty-gee acceleration. Keep looking, Sergeant. We've got to find the tenth man."

Another twenty-minute search gave them all the information they were ever to get.

"No Earth food aboard," said the major. "One spacesuit missing. Handweapons missing. Two emergency survival kits and two medical kits missing. *And*—most important of all—the courier boat is missing." He bit at his lower lip for a moment, then went on. "Outer air lock door left unlocked. Three Kerothi shot—*after* the explosion that ruined the A-A drive, and *before* the fifty-gee acceleration." He looked at the sergeant. "What do you think happened?"

"He got away," the tough-looking noncom said grimly. "Took the courier boat and scooted away from here."

"Why did he set the timer on the drive, then? What was the purpose of that fifty-gee blast?"

"To distract us, I'd say, sir. While we were chasing this thing, he hightailed it out."

"He might have, at that," the major said musingly. "A one-man courier *could* have gotten away. Our new detection equipment isn't perfect yet. But—"

At that moment, one of the troopers pushed himself down the corridor toward them. "Look, sir! I found this in the pocket of the Carrot-skin who was taped up in there!" He was holding a piece of paper.

The major took it, read it, then read it aloud. "Greetings, fellow Earthmen: When you read this, I will be safe from any power you may think you have to arrest or punish me. But don't think *you* are safe from *me*. There are other intelligent races in the galaxy, and I'll be around for a long time to come. You haven't heard the last of me. With love—Sebastian MacMaine."

The silence that followed was almost deadly.

"He *did* get away!" snarled the sergeant at last.

"Maybe," said the major. "But it doesn't make sense." He sounded agitated. "Look. In the first place, how do we know the courier boat was even aboard? They've been trying frantically to get word back to Keroth; does it make sense that they'd save this boat? And why all the fanfare? Suppose he did have a boat? Why would he attract our attention with that fifty-gee flare? Just so he could leave us a note?"

"What do you think happened, sir?" the sergeant asked.

"I don't think he had a boat. If he did, he'd want us to think he was dead, not the other way around. I think he set the drive timer on this ship, went outside with his supplies, crawled up a drive tube and waited until that automatic rocket blast blew him into plasma. He was probably badly wounded and didn't want us to know that we'd won. That way, we'd never find him."

There was no belief on the faces of the men around him.

"Why'd he want to do that, sir?" asked the sergeant.

"Because as long as we don't *know*, he'll haunt us. He'll be like Hitler or Jack the Ripper. He'll be an immortal menace instead of a dead villain who could be forgotten."

"Maybe so, sir," said the sergeant, but there was an utter lack of conviction in his voice. "But we'd still better comb this area and keep our detectors hot. We'll know what he was up to when we catch him."

"But if we *don't* find him," the major said softly, "we'll *never* know. That's the beauty of it, Sergeant. If we don't find him, then he's won. In his own fiendish, twisted way, he's won."

"If we don't find him," said the sergeant stolidly, "I think we better keep a sharp eye out for the next intelligent race we meet. He might find 'em first."

"Maybe," said the major very softly, "that's just what he wanted. I wish I knew why."

EDITOR'S INTRODUCTION TO:

FRICTION IN WAR
by Karl von Clausewitz

One of the firmest principles of U.S. government is civilian control of the military. The United States neither wants nor needs a military establishment independent of the civil and political authorities, a military capable of setting its own budgets and raising its own taxes. England had such a military establishment during the Commonwealth period after the execution of the King in 1648: maintenance of an army which did little but collect taxes for its own pay was written into many drafts of the Commonwealth constitution. The Founding Fathers of the United States remembered that very well.

Having said that, we should also recall that the principle has never been in doubt. With the possible exception of the Aaron Burr conspiracy there has never been a serious move by U.S. military people to take over and become the government. The most powerful U.S. generals and admirals have always meekly submitted to the authority of the elected President and his Cabinet.

The danger, in fact, has generally been civilian *overcontrol*.

It is easy for scholars to believe themselves military geniuses. One of the best examples in U.S. history was Henry Carrington. An Ohio lawyer, during the Civil War he raised the 18th Infantry regiment; but he was so skillful as an administrator that he never fought with the regiment he nominally commanded. When the 18th was tested in battle, Carrington was somewhere else.

At the end of the war he chose to remain a colonel and command the 18th. He believed himself a new Xenophon, the scholarly amateur who would show the rough and rudely educated soldiers what scholarly brilliance could accomplish. In 1866 Carrington, in command of the 18th, was sent to Wyoming: the Mountain District of the Department of the Platte was ordered to hold open the Bozeman Trail through traditional Sioux hunting grounds. Red Cloud, one of the best of the Indian commanders, had sworn to close it. Carrington set out to build Fort Phil Kearney as a bastion to defend the trail.

Carrington's major accomplishment was the Fetterman Massacre, in which a detachment of Carrington's soldiers, led by the headstrong Captain William Fetterman, was killed to a man. Two years later the Sioux burned Fort Phil Kearney to the ground. The railroad was routed far to the south.

In more modern times, Secretary of Defense Robert S. McNamara and his Pentagon "whiz kids" sought to control the Vietnam War from Washington. To make matters worse, the United States adopted a policy of rotation under which we sent a new army to Vietnam every year. By the time the officers and men learned what they were doing, they were brought home.

The truth is that scholarly analysis and theory can contribute to military success, but it is rare for theorists successfully to command military operations. Certainly the military must remain under civilian control at the top, but equally certainly the actual operations must be under the control of professionals.

Clausewitz tells us why in an essay as true today as when it was written.

FRICTION IN WAR
Karl von Clausewitz

Without personal knowledge of war, we cannot perceive where its difficulties lie, nor what genius and the extraordinary mental and moral qualities required in a general really have to do. Everything seems so simple, all the kinds of knowledge required seem so plain, all the combinations so insignificant, that in comparison with them the simplest problem in higher mathematics impresses us with a certain scientific dignity. If we have seen war, all becomes intelligible, yet it is extremely difficult to describe what brings about this change, to name this invisible and universally operative factor.

Everything is very simple in war, but the simplest thing is difficult. These difficulties accumulate and produce a friction beyond the imagination of those who have not seen war. . . . The influence of innumerable trifling circumstances, which cannot be properly described on paper, depresses us, and we fall short of the mark. A powerful iron will overcomes this friction; it crushes the obstacles, but at the same time the machine along with them. Like an obelisk toward which the principal streets of a town converge, the strong will of a proud spirit stands prominent and commanding in the middle of the art of war.

Friction is the only conception which, in a fairly general way, corresponds to the distinction between real war and war on paper. The military machine, the army and all belonging to it, is fundamentally simple, and thus appears easy to manage. But let it be borne in mind that no part of it consists of one piece, that it is composed entirely of individuals, each of whom maintains his friction in all directions. Theoretically it all sounds very well: the commander of a battalion is responsible for the execution of the order given; and as the battalion by its discipline is cemented into one piece, and the chief must be a man of recognized zeal, the wheel turns on an iron bearing with little friction. In reality, however, it is not so, and all that is exaggerated and false in this conception manifests itself at once in war. The battalion is always composed of a number of men, of whom, if chance so wills, even the most insignificant is able to cause delay or some irregularity. The danger that accompanies war, the physical effort it demands, intensify the evil so greatly that they must be regarded as its most significant causes.

This enormous friction is not concentrated, as in mechanics, in a few points; it is, therefore, everywhere brought into contact with chance, and thus produces incidents which are impossible to foresee, simply because it is largely to chance that they belong. . . .

Action in war is movement in a resistant medium. Just as a man immersed in water is unable to perform with ease and regularity the simplest and most natural of movements, that of walking, so in war, with ordinary powers one cannot keep even the line of mediocrity. This is why the correct theorist is like a swimming master, who teaches on dry land movements which are required in water, which must appear ludicrous to those who forget about the water. This is also why theorists who have never plunged in themselves, or who cannot deduce any generalizations from their experience, are unpractical and even absurd, because they teach only what everyone knows—how to walk.

Further, every war is rich in individual phenomena. It is therefore an unexplored sea, full of rocks which the general may suspect but which he has never seen and round which he must steer in the night. If a contrary wind also springs up—if some great chance event declares against him—then the most consummate skill, presence of mind and effort are required, while to the distant observer everything seems to be running like clockwork. The knowledge of this friction is a major part of that often boasted experience which is required in a good general. Certainly the best general is not one who gives the largest place to this knowledge and who is most overawed by it; this constitutes the class of over-anxious generals, of whom there are many among the experienced. Nevertheless, a general must be aware of it in order to overcome it, where this is possible, and to avoid expecting in his operations a degree of precision which this friction precludes. Besides, knowledge of war's friction can never be learned theoretically. Even if it could, there would still be lacking that practiced judgment which we call instinctive, and which is always more necessary in a field full of innumerable small and diversified objects than in great and decisive cases in which our judgment may be aided by consultation with others. Just as a man of the world, in whom judgment has become ingrained as a habit, speaks and acts and moves only as befits the occasion, so only the officer experienced in war will always, in matters great and small, at every pulsation of the war, decide and determine suitably to the occasion. Through this experience and practice the thought comes into his mind of itself: this is the right decision and that is not. He will, therefore, not easily place himself in a weak or exposed position, a thing which, if it occurs often in war, shakes all the foundations of confidence and becomes extremely dangerous.

It is, therefore, what we have here called friction that makes that which appears easy actually difficult. As we proceed, we shall often meet with this subject again, and it will become plain that, in addition to experience and a strong will, there are still many other rare qualities of mind required to make a distinguished general.

UNCERTAINTY AND DEFENSE
Jerry Pournelle

The United States seeks global stability; the Soviet Union is a self-proclaimed revolutionary power. Thus our strategic objectives are not symmetrical; it would therefore be surprising if both the United States and the Soviet Union require the same mix of strategic forces.

The U.S. objective is achieved if the Soviets do nothing: which is to say that properly applied the fog of war can act in our favor.

BACKGROUND

On March 23, 1983, President Reagan challenged the U.S. scientific community to devise a means to make the ICBM "impotent and obsolete."

There are two ways to accomplish this. One is to build defenses so perfect that no missile can get through them. The other is to use defenses to eliminate the fear of ballistic missiles through enhanced deterrence: to make using ICBMs an irrational act, because the Soviets will not be able to achieve their strategic objectives.

Perfect defenses are probably impossible. They are certainly very difficult to achieve. No matter how many layers of missile defenses we construct, and no matter how effective each layer may be made, the defense umbrella will be less than perfect. This fact is recognized by every advocate of the President's Strategic Defense Initiative (called by its enemies "Star Wars"); only SDI's enemies say that the goal should be to construct perfect or "leakproof" defenses.

IMPERFECT DEFENSES

The fact is that less than perfect defenses can defeat Soviet objectives; can protect our counterattack forces; and can limit damage to our nation and casualties to our population. More, by denying the Soviets the possibility of achieving their strategic objectives by using ICBMs, we achieve the *effect* of perfect defense: the best way to limit damage from nuclear war is not to have one.

The goal, then, is to create uncertainty in the minds of Soviet planners about the final outcome of the war which would result from their attack. Defenses against ballistic missiles can reduce the missile effectiveness to the point where they lose their utility: defenses thereby "eliminate the threat of ballistic missiles."

Naturally any strategic defense system must also guard against attacks from the air, from space, and from the sea. Such defenses are not only possible, they are easier than defending against the ICBM. On the other hand, it makes no sense to ring the nation with air defenses if the enemy can simply avoid them by lobbing a missile over them. Before it makes sense to deal with airplanes, bombs smuggled into harbor in cargo ships, and all the other secondary threats the enemies of SDI conjure up daily, we must know how to deal with the ICBM.

This can be done with less than perfect defenses: an imperfect defense, even one through which a sizable force can penetrate, reduces the military effectiveness of the original ICBM attack, causes great uncertainty in the outcome of the attack, and thus dissuades the attacker from launching his contemplated strike.

ELIMINATING DEBRIS

The strategic defense debate is littered, in John Dewey's phrase, with "the debris of man's past experience." In particular, we have a popularly supposed model of a nuclear exchange in which each side simply launches everything at the other's cities, industrial base, and population. This is the extreme "countervalue" attack; the deterrence mode is, "if you kill me, I'll kill you back."

In fact, this is a highly irrational form of attack. It makes no sense for the Soviets to target a first strike against U.S. cities and populations: what they want to take out is our weapons.

At the same time, it makes no sense for the United States to then unleash a countervalue-only attack on the Soviets. What we will do is counterattack to take out their command

and control structures (police stations, KGB headquarters, etc.) as well as traditional military targets; and to eliminate the Soviet capability to do further harm to the United States by destroying their remaining ICBM forces. This, incidentally, is why the Peacekeeper MX force is vitally needed: we require the accuracy of new-generation missiles to threaten the residual Soviet ICBM force after their first wave has struck.

We would also take out Soviet reconnaissance satellites to prevent their knowing what success their first strike had; and their navigational satellites to reduce the accuracy of their sub-launched missiles.

We do not intend to target people. There's no point in it. Eliminate the *nomenklatura*'s control of the Soviet Union, and the Soviet military's ability to wage overseas war, and the Soviet Union ceases to be a threat to anyone in the West.

DISSUASION

The goal of strategic defense is to dissuade the Soviets from attacking in the first place.

Before they can attack defended targets, the defenses must be countered: penetrated, overwhelmed, used up, drawn out; by whatever means, they must be negated before attacks against military targets can be made. Thus even marginally effective defenses add uncertainties.

The timing of attacks against defended targets is made complex: the attacker must break holes in the defense to enable his offensive forces to get through. This means at the very least that the defender gets increased *warning*. Since defeating defenses takes *time*, the defender is given an opportunity to use his *offensive* forces to negate all or part of the original attacker's force.

Since the aggressor knows this, as his victim's defensive powers grow, there is less and less incentive to attack in the first place.

The result is a drawn-out and complex series of battles: not an overwhelming strike out of the blue, because the all-out first strike is the easiest one for the defender's strategic defenses to work against. Boost-phase interceptors, both laser and "smart rocks"; midrange interception; and the final layer of terminal defenses can intercept increasing numbers of the attacking missiles; the result is that the attacker does not know what will get through, or what it will accomplish.

Space-based defenses can be quite effective in boost phase. Thus a few space-based strategic defense systems can negate the massive Soviet SS-18 missiles with their ten or more warheads. Boost-phase interception would negate the tremendous investment the Soviets have made in those weapons, and may drive them away from multiple-warhead systems.

Of course the Soviets will try to restore the effectiveness of the SS-18 through improvements in the systems design, and deployment of penetration aids. This means their future investment in strategic offensive weapons does not increase their capability to harm the United States. Moreover, for each counter deployed by the Soviets, there are corresponding possible improvements in the defense systems. An arms race develops, but it is not one of increasing destructiveness.

Most important, it is an arms race that moves the world away from the out-of-the-blue first strike with ICBMs and nuclear weapons.

SUMMARY

Active defenses change the time dimension of strategic planning. The coordination in time and space of ASATs, strategic defenses, air defense, bombers, cruise missiles, SLBMs, ICBMs, brings an almost unmanageable complexity to strategic force operations.

Attacks on the warning system provide unambiguous alert warning.

Attacks which try to overwhelm the defense by saturation create uncertainties themselves, because of the mass of offensive weapons involved. More selective attacks give the defender the opportunity to counterattack.

Thus introduction of imperfect defenses creates uncertainty in the mind of the offensive planner. He cannot predict the outcome of his attack. This uncertainty stems from the interaction of force effectiveness, management, and timing.

Defenses need not be perfect to make these principles a reality. The fog of war acts to prevent war.